Yoram Kaniuk, born in Tel Aviv, is today one of Israel's foremost authors. He has been widely translated, and his previous works include *Himmo King of Jerusalem*, *Adam Resurrected*, *The Last Jew* and *Confessions of a Good Arab*.

By the same author

Himmo King of Jerusalem
Adam Resurrected
The Last Jew
Confessions of a Good Arab

YORAM KANIUK

His Daughter

Translated by Seymour Simckes

PALADIN
GRAFTON BOOKS
A Division of the Collins Publishing Group

LONDON GLASGOW
TORONTO SYDNEY AUCKLAND

Paladin
Grafton Books
A Division of the Collins Publishing Group
8 Grafton Street, London W1X 3LA

Published in Paladin Books 1990

First published in Great Britain by
Peter Halban Publishers Ltd 1988

ISBN 0-586-08920-9

Printed and bound in Great Britain by
Collins, Glasgow

Set in Times

HIS DAUGHTER

1

I last saw my daughter on 21 January at seven-thirty in the morning, at the number 4 bus stop. She pressed against me for a moment, her eyes brimming with a sudden warmth, she even called me "Daddy", I wasn't used to the word *Daddy*. I wanted to say, "Baby, take a day off, let's go to the Olympus, have something good to eat, go to a matinée," but as usual I was scared. She waited; a mischievous crinkle of understanding played in the corner of her eye – or was it pity, or perhaps contempt? "You've lost your chance, Joseph," she said with a sort of stilted anger. "Run to the pool, go and show them you're still their Tarzan and their war hero. Go and tilt at windmills for them!"

I was wearing my grey tracksuit over my bathing trunks. Miriam, in military uniform, pulled away from me. The old lady, who scrutinized us every morning with a nasty expression on her face, was busy fighting the wind, wrapped in her many scarves. The bus arrived with a clatter, Miriam got on, and I said nothing. The lady managed to laugh at us, while swallowing wind and rain from the storm that had lasted now for three days and nights. The trees lunged menacingly, and the bus sucked shut its dilapidated doors. My daughter sat close to the window which momentarily cleared to reveal her face before fogging up again. As the bus halted for the red light at the corner of Keren Kayemet Street, I thought I saw her wave at me through the blurred window, something stirred there anyway, but the bus soon moved on, disappearing into the downpour.

That morning I had shot out of bed a minute or two

ahead of my alarm clock, which I always set even though my biological clock was never out by more than a few minutes. Always quick on the draw, as my daughter would say, like a disciplined soldier rousing to the call of the bugle, as if my life were a Zionist Western.

The cold room invigorated me, but I couldn't escape my profound disquiet any more than I could avoid the sour smell of my solitary, sweat-drenched bed. As I peeked in the mirror I caught the final terrifying scene of my usual nightmare – riding in a sealed train to a field court-martial, then being torn apart naked, limb from limb. Only in that dream, never in actual life, did I experience such fear.

While shaving I worried about Miriam's travelling to her base in the torrential rain, and thought even then of insisting that she take a day off. But, knowing myself, I didn't really expect to have the guts to ask her to alter her routine for my sake. After I left the water running in the shower to heat up for her, I went to the kitchen, put on the kettle for her coffee, squeezed a few oranges into a glass and drank the juice standing, then came back down the corridor to knock at her bedroom door.

She asked of course, "How can it already be morning?", but I saw no reason to answer her. She emerged from her room draped in a blanket up to her half-closed eyes. For us, the morning was always a time to keep our distance.

Although her face was as innocent as mine, the product of our sea and sand, those sad eyes of hers, barely visible behind the blanket's fringe, had somehow trapped two thousand years of grief. As she groped her way to the bathroom, her fumbling hands scratching the wall, that ancient gloom, which came with her territory, separated her from the rest of the world and declared her irrevocable terror at the prospect of a new day.

I stepped out on to the kitchen balcony where Madame Frau Birnbaum was waiting for me with her sweet smile and her hair dyed a new colour. The horrendous rain kept us apart, but she fluttered her eyelashes at me as wildly and mournfully as ever. For over forty years she had waited every morning for my father, and now for me, in order to recite her piece about her own father who had

2

hunted lions in Africa for German zoos, to his "everlasting glory". According to her, the lions had always shown her father "respect", and the blacks had almost swallowed their hats "in sheer wonder" as her father, lying in a massive flower-bedecked hammock, would shoot without looking. But since her arrival here in 1939, fearing that the lions would avenge themselves on her ("your humble servant", as she called herself), she lived behind custom-made fortifications, extra partitions, screens, locks, all of which cost her a bundle, she proudly admitted, even during the days of the Mandate.

"How come, Mr Krieger, you haven't yet insulted me today?" she asked. "Hasn't a lion landed in Haifa? Usually you say it's already circumcised, and must be admitted into the country like any Jew. Then taken to the Elite Coffee Factory to be turned into instant powder. But once it goes down the toilet, it'll drink the water and grow and come into my – Joseph, why haven't you shamed me this morning? That's the way it's been since you were a child," she said, looking betrayed. "All of you did it, you, your father, your mother – is she still dead?" I reassured her that she was.

After all, I'd found out only a few years ago that Madame Frau and my father, who used to meet her on the balcony wearing a black hairnet and goad her in that calm monotone of his, calling her a "lying Cassandra", had been in love with one another for over forty years – quietly, hopelessly, desperately. Sometimes he would bring her a book from the German bookshop or the nearby library he was so proud of.

"Injustice is preferable to disorder," said Madame Frau, quoting from Goethe, my father's favourite. Again, as always, she went back to the story of her parents, how her mother ran off with the "Insect Inspector", as she put it, Mr Johannes Glantz, who was nobody's fool; how her father waited for the Nazis dressed in his best suit, only to meet his wife and the entomologist in Therezienstadt, where he accepted his wife back "like an idiot" and went off together with her to the camp; and how some eunuch from the Turkish consulate took her to Sweden, afterwards she

3

thought to Africa, where she got scared, and finally she reached Palestine where there were no sunsets. "How sad," she said, "and I scare at night, see, I hear tigers and lions scratching; there's vengeance in the world, no?"

Then those other Jews arrived. Mr Haim the cigar wrapper who was still looking for his wife in the fuse box; Mr Feigel, who mocked his customers in their fancy suits for buying loaves of bread every morning to hide in their armchairs so they wouldn't die of starvation, but everyone knew that he pored over German phone directories checking for names of people who might actually be his missing sons and wife. In his shop, he sold me schnitzels and shamed Madame Frau in front of those aristocrats dressed up like the dead, who bought their loaves of bread each morning with such haggard eyes – after all, they'd been searching all night long for something they'd never find.

Suddenly Madame Frau asked me, "If your wonderful father had not died on a scorching day, how many people would have come to his funeral anyway? Is that an insult, or not? Huh?" She gazed at me, her eyelashes flickering madly, one ear cocked towards the sound of the shower which was audible in spite of the storm. "What a nuthouse," she said. "Only a lunatic expects life in this world. Remember the Arab who shrieked that time he saw Mr Haim going around in a white sheet looking for his wife? Mr Klaupfer still buys a loaf of bread each morning no matter how much money he has in his Swiss bank account. Meanwhile his Bauhaus home is crumbling to bits – and what a beauty that house once was! All of us have the Mediterranean Sea, yet we all cry at night, and how many of us are left now? What about you? You stare at the sea? Your wife has run off. All you have is Miriam and me. That's it!"

Still I had no insult for her, so I said, "See you tomorrow, Fräulein," and she hurried back inside to what Miriam called another day's death.

Miriam was waiting for me in the kitchen, wearing her uniform, the coffee cup in her hand. She paced around, cup in hand, until finally, at the end of the corridor, she

4

set the empty cup down on the coffin-shaped bureau that Madame Frau had given me for my barmitzvah, then took an umbrella from the rack, and together we descended the sixty-four steps. Outside, a cloud burst. People pressed up against the closed shop fronts and waited. Miriam, with open umbrella, hooked her arm in mine.

After her departure on the bus, I ran in the rain to the pool. Eighty-six-year-old Sokolowicz was already there, the former corporal in the Jewish Brigade, who under nobody's orders had sat on this very spot during the Yom Kippur War, doing solitary guard duty with an old carbine to defend the pool against the wily enemy. His rain-struck eyes glistened. On the nearby concrete area the old men were exercising to the garbled sound of the rusty loudspeaker which screeched, as if in the throes of despair, "Hup, two three!" They looked like rare animals, flogged by the rain, mighty, noble, awesome, but Sokolowicz with his skinny legs and his tanned parchment skin seemed restless, apparently contemplating again his daring plans for routing the foe. I couldn't respond to him, even though he was whistling the enlistment song of the Jewish Brigade, "Rise and volunteer", his traditional warning for troubled times ahead.

I took off my tracksuit and jumped into the freezing water which seemed to drain away all my blood, and I swam in slow motion until I was sure that my blood had once more spread through all my limbs, while the rain made a host of ripples around me like magnetic fields. As I swam I felt that my fifty-year-old body hadn't yet let me down. After twenty laps, I got out of the pool and dried myself under the awning. Sokolowicz approached, trying to interest me in some trick he had played on his cronies, then advising me of the necessity of enlisting Japanese in the Israeli army or, better yet, installing gigantic mirrors along the border to inflict heatstroke on all our foes.

The oldtimers came over to catch some of our conversation. As usual, I had no luck explaining to them that I wasn't in the army any more, because Sokolowicz and his cronies were always conveniently deaf and simply wouldn't hear what they didn't want to hear. "My sons,"

Sokolowicz once told me, "think I'm listening to them when they keep telling me that my property, including my lovely house, is worth a million dollars, and that it's a shame to let all those greenbacks just stand there. But let them drown in their own damn materialism, let them plant the whole area with greenbacks till there's no room left. They pester me to death, but I don't hear a word." All the oldtimers had the same look in their eyes, as if they had all drunk from the fountain of spite as well as of youth, but perhaps they owed their panic to Sokolowicz. Rebecca did, to whom I now went for my sandwich and my hot coffee, though her eyes always caressed me with the sly wink of a veteran lover. Married three times to Sokolowicz, without ever bearing any of his four children, she still expected more love from him. In fact, she worked on Sokolowicz through me. "What passion," said Miriam when she came with me once to the pool. "She's for the books, I've never seen that look on anybody. How old is she?" "At least seventy-five," I told her.

All that morning I had felt anxious about Miriam. I don't get scared for myself, only for others. But what did I understand of women? Miriam used to call me a monk, an antiquated Puritan. My wife Nina was the only woman I'd ever really known. Miriam loved to taunt me with tales of her mother's adulteries, informing me about the Talmud teacher, the officers, the rich guy from Herzliya. But I never responded. What difference would it make? So Miriam always ended up screaming through her clenched teeth.

I rushed home. Something was making me hurry. Sokolowicz probably wondered what I was up to, likewise the other old men; they must have figured I had something big cooking. The rain was still pouring down. I stopped at Feigel's for a schnitzel, which was never quite as good as he claimed.

They all wondered what I was doing in a crumbling house on a street that had had its day. They often asked why I hadn't moved, like most people, to the suburbs or to America, or why I paid a monthly sum to the neighbour who had built his home on the ruins of the little house that once stood between our house and the sea. I did it so he wouldn't uproot his lemon tree. As for our view of the sea from our rounded L-shaped balcony, it had long since been lost behind new houses, except for a tiny sliver between two buildings. Perhaps Sokolowicz was the inspiration for my staying there, since he wanted to die in the very house he had built with his own hands, and in which he'd lived for over sixty years. At least that was why I let him play the expert on strategy and advise me on matters of national security. My dream had been to arrange a match between Madame Frau and Sokolowicz, but at their first fateful meeting the old man had broken down in sobs at the sight of the Diaspora Jewess in hiding from lions and tigers.

I stood in the kitchen preparing a salad for Miriam, keeping the dressing separate. I made some tomato soup, which I intended to let cool before she came. Through the windows I could see the grey, rain-battered houses. Then I began sweeping the house as I did every day. In Miriam's room I came across an unfamiliar photograph of her dog Delilah, lying with its eyes shut, taken apparently only minutes after its death. That photograph, which Miriam must have hung on her wall the previous night, somehow articulated a certain feeling in me that had been throbbing since early morning, the dull but painful sense of an accident about to happen. Then, once I started sweeping the living-room, I discovered to my surprise that Miriam had left her army skirt carelessly folded and unironed on the chair she usually sat in; and under the chair lay a pair of her army work shoes facing each other. Instead of side by side, they were toe to toe, as if challenging one another rather than co-operating like hands joined in prayer. That made me mad. Miriam knew that I couldn't bear untidiness. She had taunted me for having become what she called "Commander in Chief of Mop-Up Operations". Yoni, Mr Haim's maid, would get upset, too, whenever she met me in our common hallway, each of us with our buckets. Her son had told her a thousand and one war stories about me. "Hero or housemaker?" I asked her, but she didn't think it was funny, it pained her too much.

When Sokolowicz offered Yoni bonds from the days of the Mandate if she would reveal what her son had reported to her about my role in the Beirut operation, he was up against a tough lady who made no deals. "It's not for me to tell somebody like you what kind of a hero he was," she said. "But it's for you to tell him what kind of a fool he makes of himself. Aren't the two of you war heroes?" According to Sokolowicz, her eyes were full of tears.

After ironing the skirt, I hung it up in the bathroom. Then I transferred the shoes to Miriam's room where the dog Delilah again fixed me with her gaze, her eyes shut. That filled me with a profound sadness which made no sense. I read a bit, ate, went for a walk in the rain. At a small café, blasted by the storm, a young waitress served me a cup of coffee and sat down, bored by the sight of wet tatters of newspaper flying in the wind.

The apartment was cold when I got back. I put on the Mexican sweater Nina had sent me from America. Miriam would have laid into me for that. "You don't answer her letters," was her usual complaint, "yet you wear the clothes she buys with her harlot's pay." I would always keep quiet; I had seen Miriam burning her mother's letters to her with an intense fury and delight, as if she had to fight my fight, too. I lit the kerosene heater, which warmed the room quite nicely. The phone rang. Miriam said, "I'll be home about nine. Ciao," and hung up.

I waited, drank some brandy, then turned on the television to catch the nightly news. They were screening a government documentary called "Remedial Education in the Military". Suddenly I saw my daughter standing tall and pretty, without a trace of the wise guy in her, in front of a class of ten scowling soldiers who were scraping away with their pencils as Miriam wrote on the blackboard, *He loves, she loves, we love, they love.* Miriam had been chosen for the programme when she was still doing her regular army service. At that time my quarrel with the Chief of Staff was well under way. I was insisting there was no need to conscript delinquents, since that would only play right into the hands of those who were demoralizing the army through sheer volume. "We don't need an army of tens of thousands of cannon fodder," I argued. "All we need is a clenched fist, a small, efficient, sophisticated, crushing force that can use computers, rockets, motivation, and tactics. Forget huge divisions of grunts, forget pen-pushing officers, they're turning the army into an omelet. We want an army led by generals who can not only plan a battle but fight in it." I was condemned as an élitist, considered *passé*. The outcome of this bitter conflict was that after thirty-one years of military service I resigned with the rank of Brigadier, having received commendations from and having been decorated with medals by the Chief of Staff (not the present chief), who was like a brother to me if not a friend. After all, it was the Chief of Staff himself who had selected Miriam for the documentary.

She'd had a bad cold then, and pleaded to be let off, but she'd played her part and played it well. When the show was first shown, she and I watched it together, laughing nervously throughout. Later I told the Chief of Staff, "You're teaching them to read and write so they'll be able to identify the word *Bank*, but all those lessons on the verb *to love* will only make them want to put a bullet in your mother's head." Whenever I saw teenagers patrolling the streets with their M16s, I thought of those ten soldiers in the film and was furious that my daughter had helped to enlist them. For a short while, she had to work at their base. She taught them, then came home and wouldn't say a word. Since I was no longer an army man, she couldn't divulge details. When she started to enjoy being photographed among them, I regretted she had ever been involved in that assignment, but she denied having access to any secrets, so I simply went back to my own routine.

Once the news ended, the announcer began an almost ecstatic update on what he called the storm's "extinction". Even as he spoke, the winds were waning, and clouds sailed freely through the black sky.

My apartment on Ben Yehuda Street was my refuge. Apart from the three years we – Nina, Miriam, and I – had lived in Herzliya, this had been my home since I was six. After my father's death, my mother moved out to a small flat in Maoz-Aviv, between the Clinic where she spent most of her mornings, and the Magen David Adom* station, which had installed a private line connecting her directly to them, in recognition of her considerable donations and in hopes of forestalling what she termed "a sudden untoward event". I then bought my parents' apartment, renovated it, and have been home ever since.

The wind stopped whistling, the moon was clear in the window, an aeroplane approached Dov Airfield, and some programme I no longer remember came on. The dresser by the television set caught my eye. Above it hung an old photograph of a fallen soldier, which I'd framed back in '54. On top of the dresser stood the first-century tear vial I'd once found in the Galilee during a military exercise, after the burial cave of a Jewish nobleman was uncovered – his family and friends had placed this tear vial in the cave to accompany him on his final journey. I once asked Miriam, "How many tears will you shed for me?" She became angry and said, "Don't push me, Joseph." I answered back, just as angry, "I'm making a request, not a demand!" That startled her. She let me hold her then, but she seemed preoccupied, as if she were trying to determine the intensity of the anger inside her. "You can always add water to your tear drops," I said. Then Nina got angry, too. For a long time she had wanted to take down that photograph. For years she'd said, "When so many of your close friends have been killed, why must you hang only that photograph of a soldier whose name you don't even remember? And what's a tear vial doing in the house? Death isn't for decoration, Joseph!"

Nina knew what she was talking about. When Miriam was fifteen, after her dog Delilah died, Nina told me that Miriam would sit for hours looking at the photograph of the soldier, talking to him, even writing him letters. I still wasn't convinced. "Miriam's a logical girl," I told my wife. "She has a good head, so what are you talking about?" Nina screamed at me practically choking on her words, which sounded as if they were coming from deep down inside her, while her gorgeous face was almost beyond recog-

*The Israeli equivalent of the Red Cross.

nition. "You can't even see the disaster you've brought on your own daughter," she said. But even that didn't persuade me. The photograph remained where it was, together with the vial of tears.

It was already close to midnight but Miriam wasn't back yet. She had never been late before, and I was worried. Maybe that was why I'd begun to think about the dead soldier, whom I always considered my own casualty. Miriam had never broken our long-standing agreement. When she was a child, she had asked me to set limits for her. She wanted to be restricted like all the other children, to be told what was allowed and what was forbidden, where she could go and how long she could stay there. Even Nina advised me to give in to our daughter's request. But I told Miriam, "Absolutely not! You must learn from childhood the terrible cruelty of freedom. Soon enough you'll have your fill of rules and regulations to last you a lifetime. It isn't necessary to tell me what you do and with whom you spend your time. Only one thing is important to me, that if you say you'll be home by a certain hour, stick to it!" She pleaded with me to place other restrictions on her, but I was adamant – in keeping with what she derisively called my "military personality". I told her, "Children in ancient Persia were taught three things, for which they were thankful when they grew up; to ride a horse, to shoot a straight arrow, and to speak the truth." She rebelled, enlisted her mother, but I didn't surrender. In the end she was always punctual to the second, as if she enjoyed being her own drill sergeant – I'd almost say her own taskmaster.

I must have fallen asleep for a bit, because the television had finished for the night and bluish smoke was rising now from the heater, which meant that the kerosene was used up. I hazily remembered how some years ago Miriam had telephoned in the middle of the night and said, "Joseph, I'm calling from the Galilee. We're not coming back tomorrow, but in two days. You can expect me at five in the afternoon." Somehow I knew immediately that she had walked alone along the wadi between Eilon and Admit to phone me, and that her friends had been afraid to accompany her in that dangerous unsecured zone – an area I was well acquainted with from the days of the ambushes on the Lebanese border. She had wanted me to understand not only that she was okay, but that I was a bastard. It was our game, the only way we could come together as father and daughter.

I dozed again, to wake in a sweat as cold as the room. I went to my bedroom to check the exact time, since my biological clock had suddenly stopped working. It was one-fifteen in the morning. Miriam wasn't home.

I found myself putting the soup and salad into the refrigerator, and feeling the same sense of foreboding that had plagued me from the moment I looked in the mirror the previous day. I was familiar with it. My speciality was anticipating trouble, not my own, but other people's. Fear was something I never felt in my gut; I learned about it only through conversation, books, research, the army. Death didn't frighten me. Nor the fears that gripped my mother, morning after morning, at the Clinic in her constant attempts to prevent her sudden heart failure. I could always catch a quick nap in the midst of the fiercest battles. Only the subsequent looks my comrades gave me made it clear to me what an anomaly my knack was. Once, on a bridge over the Suez Canal, during the Yom Kippur War, at the height of a battle, I was ordered by headquarters back to my company at Suez. I was so exhausted I fell asleep in the command car. Hundreds of people were dying all around us, shells fell like rain, but the big news for everybody was how I'd slept like a baby throughout our nightmarish journey.

Even if death were just a game to me, I was periodically shaken by premonitions of doom for others. Perhaps that harked back to that part of me I knew only in dreams, or to the child I had once been and had now forgotten. When I returned to duty after an officers' course in the early fifties, I was sent to a paratroop unit. I stood before a platoon of soldiers reading a sheaf of orders, when suddenly my eye fell on a certain soldier, nobody I knew, and I told myself, "This soldier won't come back alive." I ordered him to fall out. He protested, but finally obeyed, and stayed

12

behind. The other officers were furious. They said it couldn't work like that; if every officer was to pick one soldier for safe-keeping, who would fight our wars? I did the same thing a few more times, then stopped, even though my premonitions continued. What calmed me down a little was that some of those I'd feared for returned safely.

Then, in an orchard outside Bet-Lid near the old border, on a dark night, I met some young soldiers just out of basic training. "Fresh meat," my lieutenant said to me. Among them was one conspicuous for his extraordinary beauty and height, as well as a brooding arrogance which burned in his eyes. I couldn't help but stare at him, he looked so spoiled and dolled up, so coquettishly hostile.

We officers were battle veterans by then, I think I was already a captain, and all of us were eager to penetrate enemy territory and teach them a lesson. Our lust for battle was perhaps shameless, but necessary. The enemy had almost made inroads into our major cities and we had incurred many casualties. Scores had been butchered in cold blood. Vengeance, never mind retaliation, was called for. Also, our army, which had lost a few battles on the borders, was in the throes of reorganization after the War of Independence, whose glory our generation had missed by some three years.

When the young soldier gave me a challenging look of scorn, I said nothing. I feared for him and he sensed it; he understood that I had compassion for him, and he hated my compassion. He recognized that I had seen right through him to his fear, to his unspoken plea for rescue, but I couldn't submit to it. His mockery was like salt on an open wound. I gave the order to move out, and he walked behind me whispering quietly as though to himself, but his malice was as audible as his words, "What's the good of killing some more Arabs? You'll have to kill a hundred million of them to have any peace around here, and you don't have a hundred million bullets for that."

We entered the target village in total silence. Nobody knew we were there. Since the wind was blowing towards us, not even a dog barked. Everybody went about his task. We were searching for terrorists, called fedayeen* then. One of them had poked out the eyes of an old man near Kfar Saba. When we came to the last house, we were discovered. A brief battle erupted. Suddenly, a toothless old woman climbed up on to the roof with astonishing speed, shouting that she would rather be blown up together with her house. Time was running out. Jordanian reinforcements were on the way. We tried to get the old woman down but she was immovable. Sometimes children and old people can be as strong as iron. There was no alternative. The dynamite was already in place. I gave the order to light the fuse. The beautiful soldier was in charge of detonation. I'm no longer sure whether I chose him out of anger or pity; after all, he didn't have to break into the houses and endanger himself. But the fear in his face and the mockery in his voice was as intense now as before. When he refused, I smacked him. He didn't look in the least offended, which added to my anger and helplessness. He looked contemptuous, as though I were too insignificant to insult him. I never saw such a look before or since.

When I'd knocked him down, the exhausted soldiers seemed unconcerned; they just wanted to get back to our base. Shots were coming from all directions. We were practically trapped. I rushed over to the explosives and lit the fuse, ordering everyone to get back. For a moment the soldier froze in terror, like a fox caught in a brush fire, not knowing which way to turn. Then instead of running towards us, he ran towards the house.

"Get out of there!" I yelled. He shouted, "No, I can't! Cut the fuse!" "It's too late, run!" I screamed, but he froze again as bullets criss-crossed the area between us. The Jordanians were getting closer and my soldiers were wetting their pants. As I started to run towards him, I heard the old woman's laughter and I stumbled over an empty cartridge. Just then the house began to buckle, folding in upon itself like a flower closing in the evening. The smell

*An Arab commando group operating mainly against Israel.

of shrubs was in the air, cactus, oleander, combined with the aroma of sweet basil and the stench of goat droppings. At exactly the moment the house began to fall, the soldier had gone inside. It all lasted no more than a minute, and not one of us moved. Then we took him back on a stretcher – he was totally crushed. That was when the rumours started about my ordering my soldiers to return from the front with the enemy's blood in their canteens. Pure slander. Somebody had probably seen the tear vial I kept on display at home.

What had cost that soldier his life was my brand of rashness, what Miriam calls my instinct of pride, labelling me a mix of mediaeval fanatic and modern square, capable of extraordinary stubbornness and unconditional loyalty to a secret Order. From now on, I would probably carry his soul around with me like a tatoo, together with his venom. When I visited his home in Ramat Gan, his mother, an English teacher, looked at me with hollow eyes, which then filled with the same quiet scorn I had seen on her son's face. She didn't want to waste any emotion on me. I attempted to comfort her. "Your son leaped into death," I said, "it was so sudden, after he refused to obey my order. Look, maybe he pitied the Arab woman and decided to die with her. Perhaps he was the real hero of the battle."

She studied me with contempt and grief, then said softly, "You ruined them with your stories of heroism and the right stuff. Couldn't you see he wasn't a fighter? That he became a paratrooper only because of peer pressure?" She sounded as though she herself were looking for a fight but, amazingly enough, didn't care about the outcome. The mixture of hatred and indifference in her voice reminded me of her son's lovely bright eyes which could turn poisonous and blank.

"He died embracing the old woman," I said. "Perhaps trying to protect her." Again she peered at me for a long while, her tears falling from what looked like a death's head.

"You're wasting your words on us," she said calmly. "He wasn't rescuing any Arab woman, he was too spoiled and whimsical for that. You took a delicate, lovely boy, a baby

15

actually, and murdered him. Now you're already making a legend of him to trap other boys like my son. We Jews used to give the world Yasha Heifetzes and Gustav Mahlers, now we produce dirty killers like you. My son wasn't protecting any old woman, he was protecting himself. A frightened, finicky, mischievous kid? Yes! But he had a charm and a beauty you wouldn't understand."

I told her that before the battle I knew something bad was going to happen to him, but I couldn't take pity on him. If I did, what about all the others?

She laughed. I've never heard anybody laugh the way she did, with anger and indifference, as if she was hurt to the quick but couldn't care less. Her husband, who had been sitting quietly until now, flipping through a pile of photographs, a good-looking but submissive man, handed me an old photo of his son and some friends on a school outing to Caesarea. The boy glowed in his innocently decadent beauty. The father, who already then probably wanted a hero for a son, said, "Just look!" I asked if I could keep the photograph. He said, "Take it, take it, we have others." The mother said, "What for? Another scalp under your belt? Hang it on your wall and in a few years you'll understand what I'm talking about." The father got up and, practically supporting himself by leaning against the walls, saw me out. The mother neither got up nor said goodbye, but sat quietly staring at some point on the wall.

As soon as I hung up the photograph, Nina asked me to take it down. I couldn't. When my daughter would sit for hours examining the photograph, I thought she was trying to get to the bottom of my pain. I must admit, of all the hundreds I saw killed in battle, some of whom were childhood friends, my deepest longing was for this soldier whose name I could not even remember after a few years.

I rose from the armchair, put out the light, drank half a bottle of brandy, got into bed in my clothes, and fell asleep. Every hour or so I'd wake up and look around for Miriam. When I opened the window in spite of the bitter cold, the smell of the sea filled the room, mixed with the fragrance of the lemon tree downstairs and the sweet basil that grew in pots on the balcony. In the end, I slept in fits and starts, and awoke at six-thirty in the morning drenched in sweat, scruffy as an alley cat.

To freshen up I showered and drank some juice but, at the sight of the kettle which I normally put on to boil for Miriam, my heart sank. I got into my swimming trunks and tracksuit, then went out to the balcony. Madame Frau was waiting for me, looking radiant, as though she had been to a health and beauty spa the day before. With her new hair-do and elegant posture, she seemed reconciled to growing old and frail, a virgin to the end. "Has something happened?" she said. "Skip the insults, then, this morning. I didn't hear Miriam showering yet, and she's off-duty today." The sadness in her face touched me. She looked like the mother she had wanted to be to me all these years.

I left her and ran to the pool. Under the bright sun, the concrete was crowded with thirty- and forty-year-olds. Sokolowicz was furious. He couldn't bear "these youngsters", as he called them, who came only when the sun was out. "Look at their pot-bellies," he said, "they can barely swim. Look at those women with their heavy bosoms, lying there like the Cows of Bashan, thinking if they catch a few rays, they'll turn into high class call-girls!" His words were always amusing, if harsh. The men knew him well, and sniggered. He was like a character out of a cartoon. But while I was swimming, he looked grief-stricken. Here at the pool, the oldtimers were still dreaming about establishing the model State of Israel, while the country was turning ugly before their unseeing eyes. I didn't want to have a conversation with anybody. Rebecca spread butter on a roll and tried to pump some gossip from me about her lover's sons, but I wouldn't respond to any of her cues. I quickly dried myself and ran home.

Ordinarily I would have gone into Feigel's shop – and I still wanted to – but there was no reason for it now. He stood outside his shop basking in the pleasant winter sun. Waving at me, he shouted, "A new telephone directory came from Munich!" I answered, "Maybe I'll need your help yet, Mr Feigel, to find my relatives." He looked astonished, almost put down. When I went upstairs, the note I'd left on the front door was still there.

Inside, I heard something fluttering in the kitchen. But only after the muffled sound stopped and I was entering the bathroom did I realize that it must have been the telephone. Why hadn't there been a true ring? I urinated sitting down, probably so I could see the faded stain on the bathroom wall – a memento of an argument I'd had with Miriam two years ago. She'd thrown a bottle of after-shave at me, I'd ducked, and somehow she herself got cut, which made me laugh. I hadn't realized how much she was suffering, and the thought that she might have cut herself on purpose almost disgusted me. She had been counting up Nina's lovers, and I'd told her again that it didn't interest me. "Love isn't just loyalty, Joseph!" my daughter had shouted. "Betrayal can also be a sign of love. Loyalty isn't even love, it's shackles!" I disinfected her wound with brandy, then licked the blood off her hand. She sat quiet, subdued, aloof, as if after an epileptic fit, and her ridicule no longer bothered me. All of a sudden she said, "You deserve whatever you get, Joseph, you do, just like any dog!" And she wept.

Remembering now how crushed she looked, I felt as though I'd been hit by a sudden fever and couldn't breathe. Who was that phone call from? Why hadn't the phone rung normally? Last night, when I was half-asleep, half-drunk, I must have accidentally hit the volume control button on the phone. I was furious at myself. I should have been as clear-headed as always, and should have lived up to my self-image of somebody who never loses his sense of direction. I hurried to her room. The photograph of dead Delilah again aroused a mute fear in me.

I drank coffee facing the break between the buildings through which the sea showed. By now the storm was dead and buried in the calm waters. The sea wasn't as smooth as silk yet, but by tomorrow or the day after it would surely be as crystal-clear as it knew how to be in winter. I dialled Miriam's army base, searching in my throat for a voice that for a fraction of a second wouldn't come.

2

THE soldier who answered was a nervous wreck. Before I'd managed to get a word out, she scolded me for cutting in on her line – or maybe she said I was holding up the line. I tried to be courteous. "Everybody wants me to connect them but all the lines are busy," she said, suggesting that I try calling later. I could almost see her startled eyes, her smooth transparent skin, and – what I so loathed in the army – the swarm of middle-ranking officers who called their wives and mistresses all day long but who were unable to shoot a toy gun, who prettified the dark and gloriously dangerous business of the professional soldier, including the single, absolutely crucial task of facing danger alone. I hated their picnic of khaki and matching cars, and I almost felt sorry for the poor soldier having to filter our conversation through the barrage of chitchat from these fighters in silk underwear. But today I had my own troubles to deal with and couldn't allow myself to get trapped in my pet grievance against the army and its commanders who cherished their own authority and image at everybody's expense, including their own.

"Listen, miss," I said, "this is Brigadier Krieger speaking, Captain Miriam Krieger's father, and I want to speak with Captain Krieger right away." That made her even more disconcerted. "I didn't know you were . . . I mean, that Miriam had a Brig for a father." I cut her short, but the tone I adopted was really directed at her officers rather than at her. "*Captain* Krieger," I said, and she repeated after me, "Captain Krieger, Sir," duly rebuked, "I didn't know that." Then she put me through to Captain Gideon,

19

who came across as pleasant, level-headed and strong, if somewhat fake in his effort to be intimate. He claimed he knew who I was, but Miriam wasn't around. When I asked him when she'd left, he answered, "One moment, Sir, stay on the line."

After a minute in which I smoked a cigarette that for some reason had decided to singe my shirt a little by way of a loose thread at a seam, he returned with the message that as far as he knew, she hadn't shown up this morning. And that he hadn't phoned her at home yet because he seemed to recall her informing him that she would be coming in late today. "Maybe I misunderstood her," he added. "She left the base yesterday in the middle of a meeting, so we didn't discuss details." But details were exactly what I wanted from him. After I continued to cross-examine him for a while, he began to sound hesitant, as though he was no longer sure of himself. As far as he could remember, Miriam had left the meeting around six-thirty in the evening. Through the window he'd seen her heading for the car park, which meant she must have had a ride, otherwise she would have gone to the hitching station or waited for her usual ride with Major Mishka. As I questioned him further, I could smell his apprehension, his unease, his remoteness, but I liked the way he kept his head, the way he understood that I was worried even though I didn't sound it. I had adopted a curt, military tone. After thirty-one years in the army, I knew the game. He said, "Look, Sir, I'm sure there's some explanation. I'll check it out and call you back later," but his voice lacked the earlier assertiveness.

I went to the police station and was referred to a ser-geant named Rose, who was in charge of Missing Persons (just the words gave me goose pimples). Rose, a bony girl with a sweet puffy face, full lips, dark skin, and bold lipstick, explained that Miriam wasn't a missing person yet. "Not for another twelve hours," she said. She had the same voice and look, bureaucratic and melancholic, that one sometimes finds in old machines or secretaries who've become glued to their seats over the years. She was merely a cog in the wheel, soon to be forgotten, abandoned on the threshold of events. This was her moment. As she drank her coffee, she regarded me with almost enthusiastic sadness, explaining that lately quite a few parents – she almost said "bereaved parents" but stopped herself – had filled out forms. I couldn't even smile to myself. A weeping grief, which had perhaps lain buried in an old shroud inside me, now turned in my gut. I held back my impatience, as though every word I exchanged with Rose was a piece of the puzzle, and the time I was wasting in her Northern District police station would somehow reduce the danger of Miriam's disappearance, a daughter who was never late without a reason and who had never given me occasion to worry about lateness. Suddenly I thought Rose looked like a lonely homeless dog, abandoned in a village after a battle. That ridiculous lipstick of hers had made me feel so guilty that I wanted to kiss her (maybe strangle her too), but I kiss only my legal wife, and she left me two years ago.

After filling in all the blanks – name, telephone number, father's name, address – I went home. I hadn't explained to Rose all the real signs of danger, the photograph of the dog Delilah, the skirt, the shoes, the agreement with Miriam which she had never broken before. I tried to come up with an answer on my own, but could think of nothing but the worst possibility. Maybe Delilah had the answer. Looking at that photo, I remembered the period when Miriam usurped my camera and would always photograph her mother and me, and then the night I returned late from an army exercise to find Miriam weeping on the floor alongside her dying dog. Nina sat exhausted in the armchair, her eyes blank, while Miriam shed tears, face to face with her dog. Delilah gasped, her body moving slightly as Miriam administered mouth-to-mouth resuscitation. Nina said with drained hysteria, "Tell her to stop, she'll die with the dog, she's kept that up for five hours, she hasn't any air left, look how pale she is!" Finally the dog flopped sideways, cast a veiled glance at my daughter, rattled loudly, tried to get up, couldn't, exhaled her last breath, and that was it. At once, my daughter stopped crying and got the camera to photograph her dog. Then she went over to Haviv, the neighbourhood lunatic who lived on Keren

Kayemet Street in a hut behind the synagogue, who occasionally brought me old newspapers, saying that he fixed stoves, washing machines and restored domestic peace. He made a little coffin, because Miriam said she wouldn't let her dog be buried in a shroud like some impoverished Jew. I remember the way her face froze with sorrow as she gazed in disbelief at her dog, as though its death were a sort of betrayal. That night she dug a grave in the yard, in the hardened summer earth, not allowing any of us to assist her. I still remember how she stood facing the coffin under a full moon. Four Arabs who worked in the area stood holding candles, paid by Nina at Miriam's request, and they were all trembling.

The neighbours, thinking that the Nazis had reappeared, emerged with brooms and kitchen knives, Madame Frau with a toy gun my father had once bought for her as a joke, while other neighbours peered out of their windows. Miriam prayed for her dog's soul, but refrained from mentioning God, with whom she now had an account to settle. Instead, she prayed to mighty nature, to some forsaken glory out in space where wondrous things still occurred. The candles shuddered in the night breeze. After burying Delilah under a marker, Miriam was covered with loose earth.

But studying the photograph only increased my pain, not my understanding. Then the telephone, which rang right beside me, sounded as though it was ringing in another room.

A young woman asked, "Is Miriam at home? This is Didi speaking." I felt under attack. Maybe it was the way she put the question, first asking for Miriam and then introducing herself, instead of the other way around. Or maybe it was just her voice, which sounded staged, vaguely derisive, instilling in me a kind of panic. Her very name, Didi, unnerved me, but I couldn't unravel the hidden associations, I just felt that I was conversing with someone already dead. I sat down in front of the electric stove, which I'd turned on for heat. "I must buy some kerosene," I reminded myself, trying to feel less vulnerable. From where I was, I could look into Miriam's room and see reflected in her mirror the photograph of the dead dog pinned to the wall. I knew there was some link between the photograph and Didi, but I couldn't put my finger on it. "Miriam isn't home," I told her, "can I give her a message?" Didi said, "That's odd, she should have been home by now, maybe she's at her base?" "She's not there either," I said and asked, "What's so strange?" I was getting more mixed up and needed to think slowly, but Didi wouldn't let me, she answered immediately in rapid speech, "Miriam said she would be home this morning." "Which morning? At what time?" Now she let me wait and stew for a bit. She obviously realised how confused I was. "Miriam's Dad," she said, "we didn't bother to specify the time or give it a moment's thought. The morning was too lovely for that."

"What more do you know?" I asked and waited for her reply, which didn't come right away. I wondered how many more Didis I'd have to deal with, or rely on, all of them capable of turning the screws on me. Her sensual voice was drenched in malice. I could easily have despised her, but I needed to understand whatever she could tell me. Again I asked, "What happened this morning?" Didi said, "Look, Daddio, you must know she came to me yesterday. She told you by phone from the base, that she was visiting me first, and afterwards –"

"She never said she was going to you, I don't even know who you are!"

"Weird, that Miriam of yours is weird," said Didi, her voice still playfully derisive. "Look," I said to her, "I'm worried, very worried. Last night Miriam phoned to say she was on her way, but she didn't come home. Kindly be decent enough to explain to me exactly what you know."

Again, the link between her name and the photograph of the dog was at the tip of my tongue, but I still couldn't say what it was. My head throbbed while I waited for her explanation wondering who she was and why she sounded so familiar to me, why she gave me the feeling that I was conversing with a corpse, when suddenly I realized why the documentary last night had taken me by surprise. It wasn't scheduled to be aired then! I wasn't sure how I knew that. Obviously it was crucial for me to figure it out, but Didi broke into my train of thought before I'd got anywhere.

"Hey," she said, then paused, "Miriam was exhausted. She phoned me last night at seven-thirty, said she was on Dizengoff Street and would come by soon, that you knew she was with me and might phone here. 'Tell him I'm on my way to you,' she instructed me. About an hour later she arrived in a tizzy. She seemed confused, said she'd been walking along Dizengoff as the storm let up, there were still a few scattered showers but the sky had begun to clear. 'You could even see the moon,' she reported, as if my own window hadn't shown me everything she was talking about, moon, idling clouds, and a sea that no longer tossed in its sleep. Miriam said she'd met a silver balloon vendor who told her he hadn't sold a single balloon all day because of the rain, and she'd felt sorry for him and bought all his balloons for two thousand shekels. That left her with no money for the bus. So she walked along the seashore, met the old men with their dogs, said she had a great time, got thoroughly soaked traipsing into the water like a queen of the sea, with about fifty balloons in her hand, and the waves almost over her head. I offered her some tea, then a joint, which she declined, saying, 'Didi, I've got to fly those balloons on the open sea.' I told her, 'Sweetie, that's dangerous. The storm hasn't let up at sea yet, the waves are still rough.' But when Miriam feels like doing something, who can stop her? I gave her a raincoat to put over her coat, and she left. Then I heard her downstairs talking to two junkies I know, who hang around the piers –"

"Who are you talking about, Didi?" I was boiling. "I don't follow you. Are you sure you're talking about Miriam Krieger?"

She didn't bother to answer me. After a long silence, she continued from where she'd left off, like a record, as though she was scared of a confrontation, or any change in the sequence of her story. "I heard her and those junkies asking a fisherman to take them out to sea, but that's all I heard, because I just crashed in front of the television, like I was flying pretty high myself."

24

"Did you see the documentary?"

"I saw nothing, Brig," she said fiercely, "don't mix one thing with another. If you want to know about your daughter, just don't start up about documentaries!" She sounded not merely angry, but vicious, as if she would bite me if she could. But she was my only lead to my daughter and I couldn't afford to challenge her.

"Please go on," I said, "and thanks for what you've told me so far." As she spoke, I could see her smiling over our petty quarrel, until I was suddenly swamped by the vision of my daughter on a boat at night lost on a stormy sea, and I felt as if I would soon need a strait-jacket to restrain my panic. And Didi said, "She came back early in the morning. Her eyes looked empty and disappointed, but she acted satisfied, as though she'd enjoyed the storm. To me, though, she seemed like an abused kid. She asked me in a flat voice if I remembered where she'd put her two thousand shekels. 'Sweetie,' I said, 'I may have wasted myself getting stoned last night, but I remember that you wasted all your money on balloons.' When she asked me 'What balloons?', I began laughing, which isn't easy after you've been stoned all night long. But all of a sudden she said, 'Didi, you've no idea what cosmic loneliness is until you've faced a vast empty sea under a moon, with balloons taking off one by one towards a freedom neither you nor I will ever have. What's happened to me? Am I dead? If I were home, my Dad would take me to a restaurant, tell me to forget the army for a day, take me to his favourite matinée, an action film, he's crazy about them but he only goes in the afternoons – which he did even when he was a kid!' " Then Didi added, "Brig, you can take your army and stuff it."

I shuddered like an old engine after the motor has been turned off. Suddenly the name Didi came back to me from where it lay buried – and the photograph of the dog wasn't so far off – the whole memory closed in on me and helped me make some sense of this terrible day. It went back to when I was a junior officer and Miriam was a young child. We'd just moved from Herzliya to Ben Yehuda Street where Miriam made a new friend. They became like sisters, never out of each other's sight for a moment. The girl's name was Nina. Because that was my wife's name, we called her Little Nina. She was the one who gave the dog Delilah to Miriam, after her mother began having nightmares and couldn't live with a dog in the house. The dog was a "reminder of something bad", as Miriam explained it to me at the time. She and Little Nina always used to speak as one. Little Nina's mother was a widow who lived on Lasalle Street in a small house with a fig tree in the yard, its shutters painted blue and the roof covered with old-fashioned tiles bleached almost white with the years, dust, and sun. Then Little Nina contracted leukaemia, and was dying for almost a year. Miriam visited her every day, brought Delilah to her, even inside the hospital, getting a special permit. It was astonishing to see how Little Nina awaited her end with such wise clarity. She wasn't afraid, her short laugh had no bitterness in it. Maybe she was too young to blame anyone. She lost weight, she lost her sight. She would feel her way with her hands, or Miriam would see for her. At night Miriam would sit up in bed crying, her mother beside her. I didn't know what to do, although I understood her pain. Having no words to comfort her, I tried to amuse her, but she merely looked at me wide-eyed and said, "Comforting isn't your speciality, Joseph, you're good at eulogies. When Little Nina dies, you'll find the necessary words."

Little Nina was Miriam's first death. My wife Nina and Little Nina's mother, who had emigrated to Palestine in the same illegal boat, now stood together at the cemetery, their arms around each other. Miriam spoke over the grave like an adult: "Your mother and mine brought along with them the smell of fire, fear and urine." People were surprised, even the cantor who arrived just to do his job and was waiting for it all to be over so as to collect his fee, shed tears. With calm bitterness she said, "When two are separated, God weeps. But any God who takes Didi from me cannot remain God any more." That was the first time Miriam called Little Nina by the name Didi. "He's not my God," she said, "he's on the side of the wicked." As Little Nina's mother broke away from our Nina and hugged Miriam, Miriam said, "Didi hasn't died, Little Nina has, she's someone else now, call her Didi, that's how I'll remember her!"

On the way home my wife Nina told Miriam, "Fill Daddy's tear vial," and Miriam looked at me with eyes of wrath and love, saying, "Didi doesn't need Father's theatrical tears. He's good for eulogies or decorating walls with two thousand-year-old tear bottles. He's a soldier. They need him in all our wars, even the ones in the movies." Nina burst out laughing, then crying, while Miriam hugged me and said, "It's okay, Joseph. At least you're not the cause of Didi's death." It took me a long time to understand what she meant, but even when I realized that she was referring to the dead soldier in the photograph, I didn't say anything. Afterwards Miriam practically never mentioned Didi's name again. She switched to another school in the neighbourhood. Her new friends had never known Didi. Miriam was no chatterbox, she kept her nightmares to herself, though she never forgot Didi nor her dog Delilah. Who else could have known the story? And who was this Didi on the other end of the phone? How had she found out that I'd wanted to take Miriam to a matinée yesterday? Why was her voice so familiar?

Keeping my voice down, I asked Didi where she lived and where she was calling from. For a disturbing instant, last night's documentary flashed across my mind, as Didi said, "But you know where. In the custom-house at the port of Jaffa. You brought Miriam here once yourself. Near the entrance to Shabtai's fish restaurant," and she hung up.

Then I remembered when I'd actually taken Miriam there, before she'd rejoined the armed forces permanently. Miriam was still studying at art school and had an appointment to meet some model she knew, who also played jazz. I'd driven her there, she ran off, I left, and hadn't had any cause to think of the place since.

I ran outside to my Mustang, which was waiting in my private parking space at the entrance to the house. I tore up Ben Yehuda Street against the one-way traffic, with drivers cursing me, then down to the promenade. The sea still surged but without foam or fury. What a pity. I have always worshipped storms, heat waves, torrential rains, sometimes taking long solitary hikes in the desert, obeying the old rules for conserving one's drinking water through control over thirst, stretching out a single canteen for as long as possible, walking right through exhaustion, testing my endurance against the forces of heat, wind, desert, thirst, hunger, proving my discipline and my ability not to surrender even as an army of one. A soldier alone in the cruel glare of the August desert. Several times Miriam wanted to join me, but I refused. When I would return looking like a skeleton, frostbitten or sunburnt (which was exactly what I wanted), Nina would greet me with silent scorn. It was Miriam who understood me.

I reached the port in a jiffy, parked my Mustang at the gate, and started running – through the crumbling concrete entrances of the old disintegrating custom-house and up stinking broken staircases shut off from the light. I saw a few fishermen warming themselves in the sun around a campfire where they were heating coffee. Finally I noticed somebody's washing hanging out to dry, a faded sign of life. I climbed the stairs, stumbling on two steps, and came to a blue door on which I banged. But I couldn't outdo the deafening music inside. Not waiting any more, I barged in.

Some youngsters were sitting on old mattresses and armchairs opposite windows overlooking the sea. A few of them jumped up in panic and began throwing cigarette butts into the sea. The music and the smell in the room almost overwhelmed me. Then a tall blue-eyed boy, who looked familiar, tried to stop me, but he was hardly a match for me. No matter how tough he acted, he was just a skinny delicate kid whose beauty I couldn't help but admire. I shoved him away and hollered, "What's going on here?" The tall one kept looking at me until he burst out laughing and said, "He's not a cop, he's Miriam's father," and his voice rose to a screech which he knew how to intensify. I was dumbfounded. Suddenly I saw the image of an Arab holding a candle at the dog Delilah's funeral, it emerged from some hidden recess in me like everything else since Miriam's disappearance. I was so confused that I could very well have imagined there was a conspiracy against me, as pathetic as that may sound. But nothing was further from my mind. I simply stood there speechless before the music, the view, the vision of a fishing boat rocked by the sea.

The boys gave me angry looks, grieving already over the few joints they'd flung into the sea. Again, the tall kid approached me, but all I noticed, I admit, was what an easy target he made. That, after all, was my one true skill. I hit him hard; he buckled, collapsing into an armchair, then smiled at me as though he'd expected me to act like a brute. As though he'd planned it this way, knowing all along how helpless I felt. The derision in his face matched the girl's voice on the telephone. He looked as if he was watching the most ridiculous performance imaginable. As I backed off, he began to writhe in pain, but with a dignity which struck me as rather splendid.

I asked him how he knew who I was.

"I studied jazz at the art school," he said. "You used to bring Miriam sometimes." When I asked him if he ever modelled there, he laughed. "The Brig's a bright guy," he said. I wondered how many more times I would hear myself called that. And when I asked where Didi was, they all started laughing.

"Which Didi? You looking for a screw?"

I approached the hi-fi and lowered the volume while they watched me, amused and frightened. To them, I was the typical monster fitting the slogans at all the demonstrations against the Occupation.* Whereas I was thinking maliciously what excellent soldiers I would make of them. They were like the Chief of Staff's pets whom Miriam had taught how to conjugate *I love, you love, we love*. I had the feeling that it would all come down to that in the end. I figured that even these kids could go into battle with me, accepting the principle of sacrifice and devotion, a sophis-

*The Israeli occupation of the West Bank and Gaza, following the Six Day War in June 1967.

ticated principle of despair through which anybody might snatch victory from the jaws of defeat by sheer will power. Once you win a seemingly lost game, you make the enemy blink and turn tail, while your own select forces become one for all and all for one.

The tall kid said his name was Noam, no Didi was living there, and they hadn't had a telephone for over a year. Then he tensed up, and I wasn't so sure he was telling me the truth. When one of the other kids tried to say something about a girl who wasn't around, whom he called "that Didi", Noam cut him short and looked at his friends strangely, as though he was simultaneously their leader and scapegoat. It was the look I'd seen on my daughter's face when she'd come out of the lift across from the Chief of Staff's office just as I was leaving his office, after retrieving my Army Reserve file from him. It was a moving occasion for the Chief of Staff, my friend since my youth, though every effort was made to minimize the element of ceremony. My old comrades turned up. No great love existed among us, but we'd come a long way together. True, they were sick of my tactlessness, my endless controversies which upset the balance within our narrow circle. I was always stubborn, always sure I was right. Even so, they all wanted me to stay in the army and get promoted. As the candidate chosen by both the Minister of Defence and the Chief of Staff, I was offered a command, but I no longer felt I was capable of making a contribution. The army was too enormous for me, with no backbone, preoccupied with things of little value instead of long-range strategy. Here and there some giants stuck out, otherwise everything was mediocre. *He loves, she loves, they love.*

All my comrades there were bold tough veterans, tired by the petty struggles and jealousies and silences following battles of attrition over principles. From the original group of the fifties, we few were all that were left. We probably hated each other more than we loved one another, but even at our worst moments of anger we were always close enough to drink one another's health. We raised our glasses as sadness hung in the air. Now, in the end, everything was a mess. I was resigning, dejected and

30

weary, and everybody knew both how wrong I was and how right I was, leaving no room for compromise. An organism so big and so mighty was by nature incapable of painful self-scrutiny. No bureaucracy can correct itself, it merely preserves the *status quo*. We needed a Minister of Defence with "vision".

After the ceremony, as I was heading for the lift, I saw my daughter in uniform, her captain's insignia decorating her shoulders, *en route* to the Chief of Staff's office. I was now a civilian. Downstairs was the Mustang I'd purchased with my soldier's compensation from a diamond dealer whose husband had died in the middle of what she termed their "union". She wanted the car to belong to a "brave soldier" like me. Diamonds are the army's best friend nowadays. I could have asked my daughter when she'd enlisted again and why she hadn't told me, but that would have violated our agreement. As long as she came home on time, I wouldn't ask her where she'd been. Her smile of victory was like a scowl; she had rejoined the army without my knowledge but would still be home on time! She stood there, her face matching Noam's, asking for both a fight and a reconciliation. She too was trapped by the need to belong within a framework, to do something fundamental out of loyalty – I'd say out of idealism if that word hadn't become such a cliché. Perhaps my hang-up on loyalty, even my faithfulness to Nina which so provoked Miriam, was something she had inherited from me. When I had asked her once why she stuck with me if she was so disgusted by how I spoiled her with all my cooking and housework, she answered, "Oh, I could have my own life, my own flat, my army salary is good enough for that. But maybe I need to be with you to witness your shame, your atonement – no, not your atonement, that's impossible, you know, just to be the other half of your conscience." Actually, we were a twosome, enmeshed like twins, each knowing what the other would say, two sides of the same coin.

But our meeting outside the Chief of Staff's door had not been her doing. It was the Chief of Staff himself, I realized, who, trying to block my resignation and keep me in the army at all costs, had timed her arrival perfectly so that all the clerks peeking through keyholes would see my disgrace; that my own daughter had returned to the army as a welfare officer to teach the grammar of love. I told her, "Okay, go in, he's waiting for you." She said, "Joseph, what are you angry about? I came because he told me to. I didn't know you'd be here today."

"Maybe you did know, Miriam," I said.

And she answered, "Yes, maybe I did."

After all, when they asked her to participate in the documentary, she said she had a cold and practically sneezed into the phone. Yet later I'd found her, or rather surprised her, speaking enthusiastically on the telephone with the director.

Last night's repeat of the documentary still bothered me. What was wrong about it? I couldn't figure out why I thought it shouldn't have been shown. The Jaffa kids were at ease now, passing their joints around. To everyone except Noam I was a joke. Only he knew that I was looking for someone real – the rest of them thought I was a ghost buster. I explored the rooms and found all kinds of stage props, racks, old dresses, everything in chaotic piles. As I held up a dress, one of the guys called out, "You can have it, maybe it'll do you some good." I put it down. Miriam didn't have many dresses. Then again, I wasn't really familiar with Miriam's regular jeans, skirts, or shirts, I merely inspected her army clothes once a week. In the back room hung a hammock, with a girl of about fifteen or sixteen asleep in it. I approached her. She smelled of hashish, vomit, and toothpaste. She slept with her hands outflung like some crucified Jesus but smiling. Perhaps she was praying in her sleep. She was holding an army beret in one hand. I took the beret away from her. It was slightly wet, with no identifying tag on it, and smelled of the sea. The girl opened her eyes, looked at me half-asleep, then she laughed, "Daddy, you've come to see your little girl!"

"Go back to sleep," I said, and she started to cry, turning over. Noam said, "Take the beret, maybe it's Didi's." He was still making fun of me. I was disgusted and kept prowling through the flat. Another kid said, "A fisherman,

Jahash, brought the beret over, he had a customer last night who wanted to fly balloons from his boat. He said she was in uniform, wore a golden coat, and her hair was blue." I asked where I could find this fisherman, and he said, "Down at the piers," adding, "She sounds weird."

"Weird?" I said. Noam, looking very jumpy, tried to stop him, but the kid paid no attention. "Yuh," he said. "All night long the girl told him that Shakespeare wasn't so great a genius, and the fisherman told her, 'Look, miss, it doesn't interest me that much who's a big person and who isn't, for me there's just big fish and little fish.' She told him her theories on light, and that all balloons were comparable to spirits from another . . ." At that point Noam punched him. The boy shuddered, looking at Noam in utter amazement, and stopped dead in mid-sentence. It was almost like slapstick, but it enraged me. Anyway, the kid was so high on alcohol or hashish, that he couldn't stop talking even after Noam had halted him. "Jahash said he got an earful of cuckoo stuff about Freud, disembodied voices (what's that?), balloons connected directly to God or death." Then Noam shouted, "Enough!" Noam was furious, and when the kid tried to add some more, Noam sat on him and almost choked him, but I heard the kid say something like, "She said she had to swim to her mother in America."

I knocked Noam off the terrified kid, who jumped up and fled in a panic. "Remember," I told Noam, "I'll be back." Noam answered, "Can't wait, Brig. You don't scare me. I wouldn't whimper if you set me on fire. I'm immune to pain. I once sat in a crate full of nails for three weeks until I was bent out of shape, just so the army would reject me later as a psycho. I'm the antidote to the dead heroes you produce." His sad eyes were smiling. "Go build up your mini-empire, Mr Krieger. In the end, a hundred million Arabs will finish you off. Your little army of four hundred cabalists which you want to set up won't help you, neither will all the finesse and guile your Jewish mind can come up with." Suddenly, as I looked at him, I realized that he and I shared a certain vision, we both understood the same thing. That startled me. But whatever was between

33

Noam and me was not the issue now. My daughter was. She was in serious trouble. But I had to find Didi first, and she didn't live here. No girl had lived here for a year. Noam and I definitely had something to discuss, but that could wait.

Outside the custom-house, a pleasant winter sun warmed the concrete plaza that for the past three days had been drenched in rain. The fishermen sat at their ease, looking proud of themselves. Somehow they disgusted me – I hadn't felt such loathing even for Noam, whom I suspected of concealing something. I saw them as bums who had no right to exist, if only because of the simple-minded arrogant way in which they spoke among themselves, amid laughter and smoke. I approached, they looked up at me happily, like men who must spend entire nights in isolation, facing the vast sadness of the sea while waiting for fish, learning all aspects not only of the wind but of loneliness. The rage burning in me upset the image of myself which I'd nurtured all my life, the image of a man of restraint. Miriam always said that I only understood power, which was the opposite of violence, as the sublime desert was the opposite of beauty. Or as my father once said, watching the sun sink into the Judaean desert, lamenting the loss of his precious Germany, "Death is God."

The moment I'd entered the port area I'd felt spooked and profoundly ashamed. Miriam was everywhere but nowhere. Then I saw the man I knew was Jahash. He was drinking his coffee, basking in the good sun and the safety of this concrete plaza, surrounded by the lovely houses of Old Jaffa with their round windows and balconies, with potted geraniums blooming along the sills. Jahash's eyes were weary but boyish in their joy as he looked towards me and laughed. I stood there for a moment, looking back at him and his friends, then suddenly I lifted him up on his feet and began punching him. The other fishermen sat where they were, watching in horror and silence, as though everything was fated. I was professional and savage, the blows came so fast and furious that it was as if I were just standing there. The fishermen couldn't see where a single blow was coming from, but they saw their friend's contorted face and were baffled. When they finally rose to defend their friend, they did so as a matter of form and it looked ridiculous. So far, not a word had been spoken. Jahash himself hadn't even asked why I was hitting him, as though he wasn't offended or angry. They acted as if this were a movie and I were Chuck Norris, even though Jahash was actually getting beaten up and I obviously was no Chuck Norris. They acted as if it would take forever for their amazement to give way to anger. Finally Jahash dropped in limp submission like a small dog lying on its back, humiliated, to announce that he could no longer fight back against a bigger dog.

The others looked defeated too, after having taken only a few blows here and there. I was the wrong actor for this film, and a lousy one at that. The film was more theirs than mine, I thought, while recognizing how perverted and disgraceful, never mind élitist, that notion was. I didn't care any more. All I could think of was what might have happened to my daughter, and that turned my stomach. They had fought as if they'd just wanted to feel scared. Once Jahash gave up they all sat and gazed at me with their exhausted eyes which grew smaller and smaller until they almost disappeared. I fired some questions at them, now and again giving Jahash a shove. When Jahash answered, he hardly moved his lips – that's how depleted he was. The fire had gone out and the coffee already smelled burnt.

Jahash explained that he'd taken a girl out to sea with two junkies. The girl had flown silver balloons while the junkies smoked and slept. "A beauty," said Jahash, "not too young, not too old, she couldn't stop talking. Too bad I gave her beret to Mr Noam," he added, "then you wouldn't have come after me. She didn't have the look of a soldier, but wore a uniform under two coats, a raincoat and an army coat. Mister, I never touched her, I don't know why myself. A mysterious girl, she flew balloons and talked about everything, Shakespeare, antennae, voices, you name it. The sea was rough, there weren't many fish, neither of us slept a wink, balloons were flying and her mouth kept moving. You know what, she acted like a younger sister does, as if she were two people, a girl and a woman, but not the kind you screw even at sea with two zonked junkies around. The whole thing looked like an act to me. She was trying to be somebody she wasn't. Understand? I couldn't believe she was even a soldier. So I said to myself, 'Jahash, this can't end well. She wants constant attention but puts up a high wall around her. Look how she wants you to remember her, she talks to you, acts nice, she brings you a drink of water when you can't leave the wheel for hours because the sea is rocking the boat. But there's that wall, and she acts younger than she is . . .' Mister, I don't know why I keep saying she was young, I don't. Then, at the end, her hat. I was scared she left it behind on purpose – don't ask me why – I yelled to her, 'Miss, your hat!' But she was already far away and shouted back, 'You can give it to Noam,' and she was gone. So I went to Mr Noam's and gave him the hat, which he took, and he and his friends there all laughed."

The silver balloons in the moonlight, which Jahash had created with his words, now sailed into the silence around us. I was totally unaware of the fire burning again, or the coffee percolating, but now the coffee was being served in cups all around, and I was sitting among them drinking, overtaken by admiration for them and anger against myself, or perhaps remorse. The coffee tasted wonderful. Jahash bore me no resentment, as though he'd actually waited for this nightmare and was glad it was over. They said, "Come again, but no Chuck Norris!" And they laughed, not even asking me who the woman in the boat was, or why I had kept the beret, or why I had hit Jahash. Some people know what to ask – and when.

Walking along the concrete sea wall, I found a deflated silver balloon. I took it with me to my Mustang. The fishermen got up to leave, then stood there admiring my car from the distance. Noam was at his window, he'd seen everything and wasn't smiling. I hailed a passing police van, collected the IDs of all the fishermen, presented them to the sergeant, identifying myself, and said, "I don't know exactly what's happened, but my daughter will be a missing person in a few hours and I'd like you to investigate around here." The fishermen were laughing. The whole thing struck them as pointless but inevitable. Noam yelled down something which the wind garbled – "Theatre . . . go beat up someone else." Ashamed but determined, blocking out my grief over my daughter's disappearance, as if there were some explanation for everything, I stepped hard on the accelerator of my Mustang and drove off in a flash, in the way the car had been designed to perform. In my rear view mirror I could see the police sergeant's mouth drop as I shot out of the port. I must have looked like a menace. The beret flew against the steering wheel and I realized that the strangest moment in Jahash's tale was when Noam laughed after the fisherman brought him that beret. His laughter somehow brought me even closer to him, as if by now he was a part of my pain.

3

CAPTAIN Gideon was waiting for me at the entrance to my house. I'd never met him before, but immediately recognized who he was. We went upstairs. He sat facing me, drank the coffee I gave him, and said, "Nothing new for now, but I'm following a few leads. A soldier named Yossi has turned up. He's sure he rode with Miriam on a hitch from Hadera, I've got to talk to him again. Yossi's home now, but he'll be back at his base in two hours. I didn't want you to worry," he added with a quiet, measured tenderness which I appreciated. I looked pretty miserable, drenched in sweat, my hands smelling of Noam's hashish and Jahash's fish. Suddenly it dawned on me that I should never have left the port, I'd followed the wrong lead, Jahash was a mistake, though a logical one.

Then Sergeant Rose phoned to say she'd spoken with her commander who had told her, "Ah, Brigadier Krieger, if he says he's looking for his daughter it's serious," which to her meant that a missing officer's daughter would get special treatment. "I wanted you to know," she said, "that we're starting our search now. More I can't say. Somebody will be in touch with you." After a pause she added, "She'll be back, Sir. I understand what you're going through. Eight years ago my brother was killed, but my father is still in mourning for him. With God's help may it all end well," and she hung up.

Gideon stood, he looked strained, and I wondered why he'd chosen to come in person rather that just phone. Then a call came from down-town police headquarters as Gideon was on his way out. While I spoke, he wrote something on a piece of paper, handed it to me, and left. The note said, "I'll either phone later or come by." The investigating officer kept me on the line for more than an hour, going over every detail. He said he interrogated the fishermen, but hadn't got anything more out of them than what they'd already told me. "As a veteran interrogator," he said, "I can see they really don't know much, but we'll hang on to Jahash for another day."

He spoke, I spoke, we spoke. Then hunger hit me and I ended the conversation.

Although the sun had warmed the window, the room itself was cold. I reheated the soup and schnitzels which I'd prepared for Miriam the day before, but as I ate I felt like a cannibal consuming his daughter. I went to the bathroom and vomited. I looked pale and weak. For half an hour I dozed in the armchair. When the phone rang I didn't answer it at once, and by the time I got up, it had stopped ringing. I rushed downstairs and drove like the wind to the port. The fishermen weren't around any more. Their boats, looking freshly washed, lined the shore. A procession of prostitutes crossed over to a house with a low door. Seemingly miserable under their flashy make-up, they peered at me with what I took to be amusement. I climbed up the stairs of the custom-house. The flat was deserted. One of the fishermen noticed me and approached, saying, "Jahash is down at the police station; Noam left by taxi with a suitcase, his pals went with him too, but they never lived here, only Noam. Noam what's-his-name has lived here a long while and people were always coming over, one big party. You know, they smoked and did their thing. Out at sea or right in front of the windows. The smell! He told me he was going, didn't say where."

"You know where! Tell me!" I shouted like an idiot, while he smiled. "Look, Sir," he said, "you're an officer, aren't you? That's what Noam said, a soldier and all. I just know he must have had some reason to split for good, because anybody who leaves home with a suitcase and coats and hats and a taxi isn't heading for the movies. Am I right?"

39

If this were the official log-book of my service in the army, it would now read, "Took unnecessary losses, adopted an original but irrational battle mode, not recommended for promotion." I stood there and imagined myself removing the insignia from my epaulettes. Never before had some fifty-one-year-old general stood alone in an abandoned port, with a gaping hole in his heart, demoting himself to the rank of private and then trampling himself in a rage. How had I allowed Noam, whoever or whatever he was, to slip away from me? And was Didi his psychological slave?

I got into my car and drove off. Something else was troubling me, not just my imaginary demotion or my thoughts on Noam, something vague, almost forgotten, shoved to the back of my mind. Only when I saw that I was nearing Ben Shemen forest on the road to Jerusalem did I realize that what was bothering me was the airing of the documentary last night, but I was on my way to clarify the matter now. The case was still open, perhaps full of grief, but also full of hope. Others were working on it, there had to be some explanation, people didn't disappear for no reason. But the timing of the documentary was uncanny. For over a year now it had been sitting on the shelf, yet on the night my daughter, the star actress, disappears and at the exact hour she is supposed to arrive home, the programme is shown. That was what had been rattling around in my head all this time. I'd almost caught on to it during my talk with Didi, through her secretive mocking tone and rapid-fire speech, but it had eluded me. My mind went haywire at the image of my daughter flying balloons in a boat, especially after meeting Noam, but now I'd found a connection, some thread running through it all. So, at a speed even the most lenient judge couldn't condone, I headed for the television studio in Romema, Jerusalem.

Recognizing me, the security guard at the gate let me in, took my ID, and asked what he could do for me, while cameramen entered carrying their equipment, and editors and anchormen passed by. I remembered the guard from Suez. He'd been a brave soldier, now he was supporting himself as a security man. I was too embarrassed to tell him my story. "I'm here to speak with the person in charge of last night's broadcasts."

Immediately he tensed, as if I'd touched a sore spot. He closed his eyes for a moment, trying to think of something. Cautiously, fearfully, he asked if it concerned the documentary. I waited, not wanting to answer. "Look, we screwed up," he said, "and have already got hell for it. What do you care about the documentary? You're just in reserves." I wondered why he was so agitated. "It's a complicated matter," I said, "I must talk to whoever was editor last night. He has nothing to be afraid of, I'm not here in any official capacity."

Two other guards, sitting behind the reception counter, looked at me with dry curiosity, saturated with boredom, as if they'd heard it all before and were now telling themselves, "What harm can one more complaint do? Anyway, what's it got to do with us?" When they signalled for me to go on up, the security guard said, "Last night's duty clerk is still here. Poor kid, once every two weeks she's on night duty and she catches all the shit." He spoke to me as if everything I'd told him had gone in one ear and out the other. Suspicious bastard. From what he said, I figured that the night clerk was still around this morning because of last night's mistake. I could expect her to be exhausted, and I'd had enough of weary people today. I myself was so exhausted that I had actually dozed off in my armchair. But my daughter was missing, that was already acknowledged by Sergeant Rose and I had a right to be anxious. The anxiety here was just semantic, technical, connected to authority, perhaps to work schedules, negligence, dirty tricks. I guess that's what goes through the head of somebody who has demoted himself from Brigadier to private.

There was quite a frenzy on the top floor. People were shouting and scurrying, typewriters were clicking all over the place in open rooms, everything was done on the double. I was rushed into the duty clerk's office by a secretary whose eyes said, "Another pain in the neck has arrived."

I should have been surprised to see Joy sitting at the desk, but there really wasn't much surprise left in me.

"Joseph," she said and laughed. "Well I'll be damned, it's actually you in the flesh, should I close the door? What about tonight – my place or yours?" She always had that nervous laugh. Yet I had the vague feeling that my arrival wasn't such a big surprise to her. Somehow she sounded as though she were reciting a well-rehearsed piece.

"Don't, Joy," I said. "With us, it's never been my place or yours. You've had your troubles, Joy. If there's anybody who understands trouble, it's you. So you must have noticed that the star of the broadcast that has raised hell around here was Miriam Krieger."

Joy didn't reply. She just looked me straight in the eye, shoving aside the paper she'd been writing on. After I acknowledged her tentative challenge with a nod, she made a telephone call which lasted a long while. She was stalling for time. She seemed exhausted. Her eyes were bloodshot like Jahash's, but she looked as beautiful as when she had been one of my officers. She'd served under me for five years, and then stayed on for another two. We had spent, after all, some rough years together; even in those days her eyes were bloodshot. Whenever she demanded explanations, I refused to give her any. She dropped hints about Nina's unfaithfulness, but never openly accused her the way Miriam did. Perhaps she'd been my best friend, someone who understood and loved and loathed me as much as Nina had. My Joy, I'd forgotten she worked in television now. Thin Joy, she almost had no flesh on her, and her handsome chiselled face lacked warmth and mystery. She had a doll's symmetry instead of a woman's beauty. Her lips were carved as if by a knife, her eyes flashed with a taut, taunting desire which could suddenly turn off in moments of despair and defeat, but she never lost her polish. She always observed the proper dress code. Even in the desert, after two weeks of battle and unbearable living conditions, she had always looked spick-and-span.

She was smiling at me now, but hadn't yet answered me. Even after a woman came in with coffee, she still waited. We both knew by now – perhaps she had wanted me to know it – that my coming here had been no surprise to her. But she looked expectant with that same cheeky lasciviousness I used to like, though I never responded to it. She ignored the constant ringing of the phone, instructing her secretary not to transfer any calls. Behind her hung a bulletin board, inscribed with names and numbers. Beside it was a photograph of the two of us standing next to a tank, with my signature across it. Immediately I could conjure up her sexy voice from the past when she used to say that they didn't make men like me any more, except that she had intended it as a reproach, referring to my ridiculously obstinate loyalty to my wife. She deluded herself into thinking that I'd be hers forever, loving her always, if not for those rigid moral laws I'd forged for myself. She had never accepted my profound dependence on my loyalty to Nina, on monogamy as a faith without ritual or fuss. Mine was a domestic love. To Joy that was incomprehensible. Like a child, she gawked in wonder at any campaigns I planned or participated in, and loved to hoodwink herself about the nobility of my war medals and decorations, as though they were signs of my love for her over Nina, who wasn't a native of the Land of Israel as she was.

She took everything personally. She was married to the State. Her favourite words, the words she worshipped, were *yearning* and *mastery*. She loved tough heroic songs about the homeland and Zionism. I wasn't her type. Never one of the boys, never using foul language. A lover of obedience, but gifted at improvisation and at finding weak spots, I was known in the army for "original ideas". Actually, precisely because I tried to be like the others, I wasn't like any of them. Precisely because I believed in routine, in ceremony, in correct order, I was what my comrades called "surprising, devious, and dirty". Miriam understood me. She once said that my stubborn determination to be ordinary and conformist was the source of all my doubts in any situation, which led to my finding some original solution. She realized what Joy never did, that I was bourgeois and square, that my strength came from my weakness. The legend of my originality, for which I paid dearly, was the outcome of my inability to be like the Chief of Staff or my friend Reuben.

Joy thought I didn't deserve to be betrayed by Nina, and was furious over my indifference to whatever Nina did. She bugged me. She felt she was my true friend, and not Nina who called all our campaigns in which many young soldiers had died "Children's Crusades". The smell and aura of death that I brought home with me had turned my wife into my enemy. For Joy, war was intoxicating. She was willing to pay its price and not ask existential questions. Not Nina. The only battle she fought was with God. Nina was a leftover from another world.

As I sipped my coffee, Joy eyed me, flushed, still not uttering a word, then she said, "If the coffee isn't good, you can go and make your own." I told her that it didn't make any difference to me. Our game was so old and skilful that I could wait it out, even though it annoyed me. My worry was my daughter, my missing part, my great love (along with Nina), the only love I had left, the only one permitted me. Weighing her every word, yet speaking in her usual rapid-fire manner, Joy explained, "It was aired, Joseph, because of a slip-up. I didn't even notice that Miriam was the star of the film, because of the uproar it caused. The Chief of Staff himself phoned, our television director was livid, the General Manager bawled me out. But what could I have done, when the whole system was in a state of chaos?"

Her tension was obvious. We knew each other too well for either of us to hide our uneasiness. Suddenly I wondered why Didi hadn't seen the broadcast, if she was Miriam's close friend. And again my blood boiled because of Noam. How could I have let him slip through my fingers without even finding out his last name?

Joy said, "Total pandemonium broke out here last night. Only forty minutes before the news bulletin, footage from Beersheba got lost after editing – important stuff, one of our lead stories – and everyone was running around like crazy looking for it. How could it have vanished from the building? Then some soldier arrived at the gate. The storm was over, it had stopped raining, but it was still cold and some of the crews were late. Apparently the soldier said she was a sergeant from the Military Spokesman's office, she gave her army number, showed documents, and everything was in order. The security guard called me. I was a bundle of nerves. I hurried down. I was so agitated I could barely talk to the soldier. She'd come at the tail end of the storm. She was still standing there at the entrance and hadn't come inside yet –"

"Joy," I said, "was it Miriam? You must tell me!"

"Joseph," she said, and I was stunned that so much bitterness could be contained in one word, as if it had been hanging about her lips for years. "Joseph, I don't know what Miriam looks like! Have you forgotten? I saw her only once when she was six. And she's despised me ever since. She said I was trying to take you away from her – even back then. She refused to come and see you if I was at the base. Before she'd come, you would have to send me home. Nina I saw, but not Miriam. How could I know whether that was Miriam? She stood there in a huge army overcoat, I didn't even notice if she had insignia on her epaulettes. There was a question later on whether she was a sergeant or an officer, but I simply hadn't paid attention."

Joy's voice had suddenly lost all trace of bitterness. There was just passion in it. The old intensity. I recalled how once, after a fatiguing military manoeuvre, I had arrived in a jeep to greet the weary soldiers who were returning, as a bus-load of girls from the pre-military cadet corps pulled up to welcome all their friends with hugs and flowers and kisses. The entire company was embracing while I stood there with Joy off to one side. Unable to contain my pain, I told her, "Miriam has never kissed me, I have never in my whole life had a kiss from her." And she stood there and said, "Joseph, I have a million for you, each one of them is worth a thousand Miriams, let me give you some." Her mouth was full of kisses, but my lips turned away from hers, insulting her so deeply that her tears hung in mid-air as if frozen by the night frost and afraid to melt. They looked blood-red.

"Joseph, you make me laugh. What are you after? Miriam? You've lived like a nation unto yourself, and what are you left with? You sleep alone in a bed you make yourself – a man like you? Ah, you amaze me. After Nina, after everything, after living with Miriam in the same house what do you know about her? What sort of life does she lead? All you care about is that she arrive on time and say goodnight to you nicely?" Joy had read my mind, she knew I was grieving over the kiss which Miriam had never given me, and now she wanted her pound of flesh and she wanted it raw.

"Do you know how often she used to phone me and ask about you, as though she didn't realize that I knew nothing? Yet she refused to meet me in person. She said that she'd been forbidden to do so. I know it wasn't forbidden to do so. I know it wasn't you who'd forbidden it, so who had? You're looking for her? Then go find whoever it was that forbade her!"

"I didn't say I was looking for her, Joy!" I screamed, and I was so furious that, if I hadn't needed her help, I think I might have strangled her.

"Didn't you say so?" she asked. "You mean you've come here just because we mistakenly aired a year-old pro-gramme? If our anchorman had suffered a kidney attack in the middle of his broadcast, would you have come by with your Mustang to follow up on what happened?"

"You must have known what Miriam looked like, be-cause you saw the programme!"

"I told you I didn't, I wasn't interested."

"When was the last time you spoke to her?"

"About a week ago."

"What did she want?"

"To talk about her life. Nothing specific. She knew I was on duty, so she phoned."

In other words, Joy wanted me to believe that Miriam knew who was on duty at the studio. But even so, Miriam couldn't have arrived here in Jerusalem while she'd been seen by some Yossi at the Hadera crossroads, or while she was in Jaffa flying balloons. I couldn't figure out what Joy was trying to conceal from me. As always I didn't trust her, or perhaps it was the other way around. Anyway, I was still dependent on her. Something in me did belong to her, and she wanted back the blood that had flowed from her eyes.

46

"I once told Miriam," she said, closing her eyes for a moment, " 'Yes, love, I'm crazy about your Dad, but I'm not on his list,' and Miriam laughed right into the telephone and said, 'Poor Joseph, he could have lived with a real woman and not with a thick, black butterfly like Nina.' "

Until now, I'd always felt that Joy at least understood that my loyalty was not the only reason for my helplessness where she was concerned. The other reason was my naïve need to be a husband and a father without knowing how one did it. Suddenly I felt that her despairing love-dance was no longer intended for me. It was a solo – or a dance without a dancer.

"I was downstairs with the soldier or officer, who was handing me all her papers," she continued, sounding like Didi with her antagonism. "The studio was in a panic and here was a soldier saying that the Office of the Chief of Staff had requested that we air the documentary before the news."

Obviously, Joy had jumped at the opportunity. I knew how her mind and her passions worked. She was always a computer Cupid, a machine on heat. By showing it, she knew she'd get me in her office, face to face, and have a laugh. In fact, she tried to laugh now, but I knew that deep down she had lost her love for me – rather her vengeance which she called love in order to defeat me.

"The soldier came in a Renault 4," she said, "by way of the West Bank. Someone had seen her on the road. I'm telling you everything I know. We tried locating the General Manager but couldn't get hold of him, he was *en route* to some meeting and his bleeper was apparently disconnected. The television director was unavailable too, and the night editor had panicked over the missing footage. So I had to make the decision to air it right after the fruit ad. After I went back up, Hanoch Levi spoke with the soldier, Hanoch's an announcer, he's *divine*," she emphasized in her sexiest voice. "I waited for Hanoch, but he apparently kept talking to her. Then all the calls began coming in, with everybody yelling at me, including you now. It's pretty scary for me, Joseph, not just for you."

"I never said I was scared, Joy. Are you sure it wasn't Miriam? You know her voice at least. If you'd wanted to, you would have been able to tell if it was Miriam or not."

"Maybe, Joseph, but the fact is, I just don't know. When I asked you to show me a photograph of her, you took a piece of paper and drew a head – with eyes, nose, ears – that looked like a retarded child, and you said, 'That's Miriam, my little girl!' Now it turns out she's not a little girl any more. Hanoch claims the girl he spoke to was a knockout."

"You always had sex or God on the brain. I wish I could believe you."

"You once told me," she said smiling, "how much you admired Shakespeare, though Miriam says he's not the genius her father thinks he is (not that anybody really knows who he was!). But didn't you say that if God – whom you acknowledge when it suits you but can't stand when *I* mention Him – if He really did have a son it wouldn't be Jesus but Shakespeare? Your Shakespeare who wrote,

'Men's evil manners live in brass; their virtues
We write in water.' "

"Henry the Eighth," I said like a fool, and she laughed and said, "Henry 8 or Renault 4?"

I crossed over to her and hugged her, not knowing why. She fluttered under my hands, but it was obvious from her eyes, her voice, her rigid body, that she was no longer mine. She snuggled against me for a moment, as if we had a chance of becoming a twosome without betrayal, then pulled away, her eyes full of pain but not panic. I saw that she would no longer mother me, instead she'd only toy with me. After all, she'd never had any shame or modesty. In her crazy yearning for humiliation she'd transformed her cruelty into a delicate perfume which she now used on herself quite liberally.

I left and drove home defeated, not knowing what I was going back to and not even wanting to go back. Just as I was leaving, Joy had said, "This should interest you. A soldier from the Military Spokesman's film unit said he

48

tried to get a lift from a soldier in a Renault 4 but she stuck her face out of the car window and shouted, 'I haven't any more room, I've got the corpse of a girl here, I can't stop, my father's enlisting Japanese in the army.' "

4

BY the time I came home, it was evening. I found
myself thinking of a high school composition Miriam
had written, which I knew almost by heart because it was
really about Nina and me. She wrote: "In a marriage
between an Israeli and a holocaust survivor, the holocaust
survivor dominates. [The Israeli is dwarfed; his life-giving
Israeli seas recede. Camels are only an ephemeral substi-
tute for the verdant landscapes of his parents' childhood.
After all, his parents' parents had lived and wailed in cel-
lars, and if he'd learned survival at all, he'd learned it from
the ghetto dormant in his blood, and from his wife. Here,
in this country, he has learned to express joy and anger,
but he has lost historical depth. Wiliness and evasiveness
come from over there, not from the Jezreel Valley. The
native Israeli, the Sabra, married to a holocaust survivor,
lives with the secret of his wife's sadness, which infuses
him like a poison. The army is his solution, betrayal is
hers. But before there can be betrayal, there must be love.
Her revenge is to live without remorse. That's something
you don't learn in a new country which hasn't the stench
of smoke from over there.]"

I was pondering those words as I saw Mr Haim in
the entrance hall, searching for his wife in the fuse box.
Captain Gideon and a sergeant who introduced herself as
Naomi were sitting on the steps by the door of my apartment. They looked as if they'd been sitting there for hours.
The sergeant's eyes were greenish-brown. She had a kind
of powerful, bridled femininity. A muted sadness seemed
to glow from her. She stood up and put out her hand and

50

it was the sweetest gesture I could have hoped for all day. Gideon did not look so sure of himself this evening. He sagged a little. I was tired. I wanted to answer the phone which might ring, maybe Didi again, maybe Noam, maybe Miriam, but Gideon took command.

Naomi at once went into the kitchen. I protested. Since Nina had left, I'd turned the kitchen into my territory. Miriam had made fun of me, everyone sniggered, but it was important to me. All of a sudden this youngster comes in and finds out that I've catalogued everything in a precise, close-knit order. Naomi made coffee, she put a level teaspoon of sugar in mine, and a quarter of a cup of milk. Amazingly exact measurements. Nina and Miriam never managed to make my coffee the way I liked it. Joy had tried for years, finally giving up and shouting, even at staff meetings, "If you like, come and put the sugar and milk in yourself." When Naomi gave me the coffee, I sipped it and asked, "How did you know?" And she laughed and said, "Men can be divided into five types of coffee drinkers, and you belong to the sixth." Gideon said, "She knows everything, that girl." Naomi said, "A few things anyway. Ask Gideon, he chose me from among fifty sergeants. By the way, who's that woman who was peering at me from next door?" I told her it was Madame Frau Birnbaum whose father used to hunt lions for Germany's zoos before the war, and she was afraid the beasts would come and take revenge on her. Naomi smiled, fixed me with a warm, shrewd look, sat in Miriam's chair, crossed her legs, and examined the photograph of the dead soldier. The thought fleetingly crossed my mind that she had expected the photograph would be hanging there.

Gideon was sitting with his eyes on his coffee cup. He said, "Sir, I came to give you a preliminary report. I've been checking all morning, I also phoned the police and the Military Police Investigation Department. There are some inconsistencies, but nothing's certain yet, and if I were you I wouldn't think the worst, because maybe there's an explanation. She went out through the gate of the base at about –"

"The reservists' gate?"

51

"No, the main gate. Why the reservists' gate?"

"Because there's some malicious speculation," I said, "that Miriam drove a Renault 4 to the West Bank and from there to Jerusalem, that she went to the television studio and caused an uproar there after handing them the documentary she starred in, and managed to get it screened last night for the first time in a year."

"I was told about it," said Gideon. "However, not one soldier or officer left our base in a Renault 4, neither from the reservists' gate nor from any other. Miriam left through Gate A, you know the one, don't you? It was about the time when the storm let up, there was still a wind blowing, and she left exactly as the tanks were returning from manoeuvres. The guard said he'd seen her but he didn't manage to get the number of the car's licence plate. You have to remember that he's very fond of Miriam; Miriam helped his family a lot, both in the line of duty and privately. He'd also done some time, and they wanted to throw him out of the army, but Miriam intervened and he stayed in. When his mother had to be hospitalized, Miriam helped her. He's nuts about her and maybe that's why he didn't think it important to note the car's licence plate. It was a civilian car. A brown Citroën GS, a '79 model, Jahash said."

"Jahash?"

"The guard, his name's Shimon, but they call him Jahash. Miriam shouted that everything was okay and he let her through. He only remembers that she said to him, 'Jahash, I'm on my way home!' and it seemed strange that she should tell him personal details, as though she owed him an explanation. He yelled at her, 'Obviously, Captain, so what are you telling me for, all of a sudden?' And she said to him, so he claimed, 'I have an agreement with my father, I do as I please as long as he knows what time I'm coming home.' This made Jahash laugh and he said to her, 'You're pulling my leg, but I'm still crazy about you!' " Gideon paused and then added, "You know, Miriam also told me once that she does what she wants, but if she ever were late because a lion attacked her, her father would bring the animal in on charges of sabotaging the established order."

I thought to myself, "Since when all this intimacy?" Gideon looked pained, Naomi sat withdrawn. I looked up and met the eyes of the dead soldier, whom she was staring at, too, until Gideon interrupted, saying, "I'm sorry for what I said . . ." And Naomi gave me a look, as if she also felt that he had overstepped the line. I thanked her with my eyes. "Yes," continued Gideon, "Miriam introduced the driver to Jahash as Major Avinoam, Reserves. Apparently that had bothered Jahash, because this morning he said to me, 'Hey, have we got a Major Avinoam here?' I didn't know. Then after about an hour he came back and said to me, 'I checked, there's no such person, and there isn't a Citroën GS '79 on the base, not even in the reserves.' I told him, 'Okay, Jahash, we also have no Ferrari and no Captain King Kongs,' but he didn't think that was funny. I didn't either, half an hour later, after you called and things got hairy. I questioned him further, but he had nothing more to add, except that he insisted that, because of the lousy weather and the tanks splattering everything with mud, he couldn't possibly have caught the licence number anyway, and a transport officer confirmed what Jahash told me. When I asked Jahash if he was absolutely certain it was a '79 Citroën GS, he said, 'I can recognize any car, Sir, but a licence number is mathematics and I'm weak at that!' Jahash is no fool, Sir, if he's afraid for Miriam, he won't say a word that might harm her," said Captain Gideon and suddenly, perhaps because of the slight smile I saw on Naomi's face, I understood that he was referring to himself as well, that he'd go by foot to Metullah on the northern border just to get her some chewing gum if she wanted it. I wondered what everybody was doing in my life, Joy, Nina, Miriam, these two Jahashes, Captain Gideon with his mysterious intimacies, dead Delilah if dead she was. Where was Miriam, gone to Metullah to get me chewing gum?

Naomi was looking at me, her look was encouraging, warm, she implanted in me a feeling of trust and an overwhelming sense of ease, but it annoyed me how dear and decent Captain Gideon was, how strong, straight, handsome, and young!

"Look, Sir, I've already told you that one of our soldiers, Yossi, a religious fellow, saw Miriam at the Hadera crossroads. I've had a pretty hard day, yours has been worse of course, but it isn't easy to join the loose ends." It sounded almost as though he was asking me to participate in his sorrow. Maybe that wasn't so ridiculous. We were all one family, and any missing member was missing to all of us. Gideon continued, "This Yossi was waiting for a lift at about seven-thirty or eight, I think closer to eight, even a bit after. It was already dark when a blue Peugeot stopped at the soldiers' hitching point. A colonel got out. And after him, Miriam. You'll soon see why it must have been Miriam. This colonel then said to Yossi, 'I'm dropping off this captain, and you're going to keep an eye on her until she gets to Tel-Aviv.' Yossi was exhausted. He'd been called from the Lebanese border and had been on the road for hours. The officer said, 'You look after the captain like she's your own sister, understand?' Then, according to Yossi, the colonel made a U-turn, against the one-way traffic, and roared off in the direction of Givat Olga. Yossi couldn't figure out why he hadn't dropped the captain off at the crossroads which were only a few yards away from the hitching point, but the colonel had given her, as Yossi said in English, *door-to-door service*. Yossi's cigarettes had got wet in the storm, and he asked Miriam, who had introduced herself, for a cigarette. She had dug around in her bag and given him one."

"That can't be," I told Gideon, "she doesn't smoke." Gideon smiled suddenly, he'd scored a point, as though everything that had happened was nothing but a struggle over a girl, for some sort of easy victory. He said, "Sir, she keeps cigarettes in her bag, and you take it so lightly that you've forgotten. She doesn't smoke, she loathes cigarettes, but you do, and when you forget to buy cigarettes you go haywire and start hunting for butts. She says that's your only sin." Gideon smiled for a moment, then was serious again; I looked at Naomi, not a muscle of her face moved. "Apparently she likes to see you ask for cigarettes."

"Beg, not ask," I corrected. "I'd be ashamed to see myself squirming the way I do, like an idiot, sucking pencils. Oh, she keeps them for me all right, she holds on to them. Yes, but she'd never give them to anyone else, she would never have offered that soldier a cigarette."

Gideon said, "Maybe. Once, at an officers' meeting she wouldn't even give one to a colonel who had suddenly run out of cigarettes. But she keeps cigarettes in her bag and Yossi swore to me that she offered him one. That's a fact. A *Time* cigarette. In the light from a passing car he saw the chaos in her bag. I know that bag, she keeps everything in it, even books she read a year ago, it isn't a bag, it's a gigantic file. The girl must have been Miriam, you'll see. It's not easy, Sir, I just want us to reach some kind of understanding, something must be done and perhaps there's some clue in all these things, the Peugeot, the Citroën, the officer, Yossi, that'll lead us somewhere. Look, a lot of time has gone by, hours, you know what's going on these days, kidnappings, soldiers disappearing. I don't have to lie to you, an old soldier like you. Just listen carefully, maybe I've missed something that will be clear to you. The Chief of Staff phoned earlier and asked me to take over; I told him okay and he said, 'Don't let up. Joseph is like a brother, Miriam's like a daughter to me.' "

I kept quiet. An inexplicable sadness out of nowhere, cut off from every other sadness, filled me. The sadness of purposelessness, of bewilderment, of acquiescence. Maybe the Chief of Staff was the reason. We were back at the beginning, vying for love again, tugging at each other's heart strings. Miriam had returned to the army after a year and a half at art school, on his advice. What could Gideon do? He'd come at the end of a long, full game; suddenly we were again the Holy Trinity, the Three Musketeers of our childhood, the Chief of Staff, Reuben and me. And another Miriam was involved, a different one this time.

"We've got a sergeant-major," said Gideon, "not from your time, who used to be a member of the Rabbinical Burial Society in his town down in the south, I forget the town's name. On Thursdays, he would work at his stall in the market and everyone knew they'd better not die on a

Thursday – until the mayor died on a Thursday. There was hell to pay. The mayor had seven brothers; some bones got broken and he came back to the army where he now breaks soldiers' bones. Miriam rules him as though he were a puppy – I don't know how – but he does whatever she asks, he and Jahash and a few others," he said with a smile. "She's got influence, your daughter." His enthusiasm was so annoying that I said nothing. Naomi was calm. Nina was too far away and suddenly not far enough.

"The sergeant-major is the soldier Yossi's uncle," said Gideon. "Miriam happened to mention him to Yossi. This made me think," continued Gideon, "maybe Yossi's recall from the border had a meaning I didn't catch at first. Look, why did he get recalled to the base when his leave was due a week later, and the base is on his way home? There's tension up north, katyushas, the whole border's saturated with explosives, you know. But the sergeant-major won't talk, plays dumb."

"He looks at us as if we're decomposing corpses," Naomi suddenly said, and I didn't know what she was talking about. "Isaac, how beautiful that Isaac was." Gideon, like me, jerked his face in her direction. She was sitting there, strong in her serenity, with tears flowing down her face. I asked her, "Who?" I was boiling. She said, "That soldier, in the photograph, the one who died. Isaac."

"Do you know him?" I was smoking the fifth cigarette since we'd come in. She sensed how thirsty I was and went to the kitchen where she started preparing something. She brought me a glass of water. Gideon had some more coffee. Naomi said, "How could I know him? After all, he died before I was born. But he was as beautiful as a god, as an angel at the back door of paradise, so lovely that other angels must now caress him with languishing eyes." I asked her, "But how do you know him?" It irritated me, I'd forgotten his name till now, the name Isaac took me back. Those eyes. Miriam was suddenly part of a gigantic conspiracy, her disappearance, Jahashes, Didi, sergeant-majors that worked in the Burial Society. Naomi said, "I don't know. What will you have to drink?" It struck me as strange that she was refusing to speak, as though she'd broken a closeness that had grown between us, or maybe she needed time. Having let Noam slip through my fingers this morning, I could allow her to delay her answer. I felt helpless. Everything was closing in on me.

Miriam at a hitching point in Hadera. Mother used to say, "Let's go to the Hadera forest," and my father would laugh, looking at her with eyes full of the same horror as Madame Frau's, and he'd say, "What they call a forest here! The Hadera forest is a miserable woods!" He had spoken on behalf of the insulted Black Forest and the Harz Mountains, as though he himself had created them.

Gideon kept on talking. "She played rather a lot on the fact that Yossi would be going to the base, or maybe it just seems so to me. She'd said to him, and this appears in the transcript of the conversation between me and Yossi, 'Tomorrow is the anniversary of the death of a good friend of mine, maybe the best friend I ever had, her name was Delilah, and you're religious, aren't you? So pray for her soul tomorrow,' and Yossi had said, 'What kind of a name's that? I won't pray for the soul of a woman called Delilah or Vashti or Madame Pompadour.' "

Gideon sounded amused and panicky at one and the same time; Naomi didn't smile, she looked at Gideon, a trace of disdain or maybe criticism in her gaze. She brought me something to eat; I ate and drank and Gideon asked, "Who's Delilah?"

"Miriam's dog, she died years ago. Her picture's on the wall of Miriam's room. She hung it there the night before she disappeared." Gideon rose and went to the room. Naomi stayed where she was and watched him go. She didn't turn towards me. We just sat there waiting until Gideon returned. He sat down and asked for a little brandy. I gave him some, and he drank it down as if it were the first drink in his life. He grimaced; I almost hugged him.

Then I realized that I'd made a stupid mistake. The anniversary of Delilah's death had to be in the summer. I remembered the sun-baked, hardened clods of earth. Naomi got up to do the dishes. I wasn't fighting her any more and didn't protest.

Gideon didn't respond to my words. He said, "Naomi's

staying with you till . . . and that's an order. The Chief of Staff said I was to leave a sergeant here, she's got time off, she's free until further notice." Naomi smiled at me. I was indifferent, inarticulate, I was waiting for some signal, a way out. Gideon hadn't finished what he had to say. Meanwhile I was thinking that maybe Delilah was only a cruel diversionary tactic. I don't know why I thought this.

"Finally, a white Ford Cortina arrived," Gideon said, virtually talking into his coffee cup. "Yossi said the Cortina came to a halt right in front of them. The driver looked familiar. Only after they had been talking in the car for a little while did he realize it was Hanoch Levi, the television announcer. They didn't really know each other. 'I was sitting in the back,' Yossi said to me, 'I was tired, fell asleep a few times as they were talking, as the announcer was trying to make a pass at her. They spoke as if they were strangers, and yet he called her Miriam; she answered him curtly, but as though she knew him.' Hanoch Levi had sounded startled to Yossi, and Miriam mocking, but afterwards, she became serious and moved his hand off her once. There was tension in the air, as if something was at stake, some communication."

"But Joy said that this Hanoch Levi had spoken to the girl, the soldier, at the studio."

"I don't know," said Gideon. "Miriam never said she knew him. I knew her well, we were close, not in the way you perhaps think, but we were close." He was blushing.

It was late, around ten. There had been some phone calls from police officers and the Chief of Staff. I'd answered curtly; I'd wanted to hear what Gideon was saying. Now I drew the phone near to me, called the television studio, asked for the night editor and was put through to an irritable girl. I said this was the Chief of Staff's office speaking and that I wanted Joy's private phone number. She asked for my name and some other details. I concocted some good answers, won her trust, and was given the number. I dialled; a man's voice answered. I kept quiet, he kept quiet. I waited until I heard somebody taking the receiver away from him and I said, "Joy, this is Joseph. When did Hanoch Levi speak to the soldier or officer, and where were they standing when they spoke?"

She didn't answer. She said, "Just a minute, just a minute. What do you want?" Her voice was hard, distant, hostile. I said to her, "Joy, you lied to me." And she said, "I don't know what you're talking about," and then I asked her if I could speak with Hanoch Levi. She answered that this wasn't Hanoch Levi's number. Then she added, "What's happened to you, Sir? After all these years you've decided to get jealous?" I said to her, "Let me speak to him." A silence fell. She knew me; she knew by my tone that she'd gone far enough. Hanoch took the receiver and asked what I wanted. I told him, "I have a daughter, her name's Miriam Krieger, you are supposed to have spoken to her at the television studio, or to have driven with her from the Hadera crossroads to Tel-Aviv, or where was it?"

He paused for a long moment, then said, "I didn't see any girl at the studio because I was on the road. I picked up two hitchers at night. Actually, I picked up more. I don't know any Miriam Krieger," and he hung up.

When I reported this to Gideon, he sounded surprised. He gave me a long look and suddenly said, "Yesterday I was watching television all night and I didn't see any film with Miriam in it. How come I didn't catch the broadcast? Are you sure it really was aired?"

"It was aired," Naomi said, getting up to go to the kitchen again, "but it's ages since they last showed it." And I thought to myself, "Gideon's strange, he looks and doesn't see."

"Anyway," said Gideon, "we haven't finished with the hitch-hiking story. Hanoch Levi's lying. We're finally getting somewhere. We only have to tie up a few loose ends." Naomi came back into the room for a moment to take the cups and glasses. She was more than just smiling now. The gentle devoted expression on her face seemed to say that she would stand by me. I had the feeling that my own look went straight to her heart. I wasn't flirting, I wouldn't know how. Miriam used to mock me, saying, "Why don't you let any woman get close to you?" I thought she said it out of jealousy as well as pity, for a while anyway. Then

I wasn't sure. That dead soldier came into our midst. But I was still the only man in her life, and our enmeshment, father and daughter, troubled me and scared me. She also was afraid. We found ourselves quarrelling and angry and devastated. Nina would weep that she was sick of the whole story. Miriam said to Nina in my presence, "Why did you marry him instead of one of the others? There were three of them, weren't there?" And Nina had answered, "Because he seemed unattainable, uninterested in women, he didn't flirt, he was hard to reach, trapped in his love of the army, yet still brimming with his pathetic need to be taken care of by a woman." And Miriam said, "Women have no place in his life, he has a daughter and a wife at home, what does he need women for? Still women want him, though he's no Robert Redford. Look how Joy's dying for him, such a beautiful woman; she wants the man who's turned off by her, who humiliates her. She feels she can train him, get him to toe the line. She wants to latch on to his tendency to eternal devotion."

Naomi, I realized, was only a year older than my daughter. Had she blushed now, as I stared at her, the whole thing would have ended right there and then. Instead she went pale. Her link with the dead soldier, Isaac, had depressed and angered me, but her blanching had given me the reality I needed. Naomi wasn't Miriam. Miriam was off in some secret zone. All the stories about her conduct and whereabouts struck me as distractions from the truth that had been all over Sergeant Rose's alarmed face with that lipstick of hers which celebrated nothingness.

Gideon seized the moment and began talking again. He needed my help, but he also knew that I needed his. He said, "Yossi was dozing most of the time, but he heard Hanoch Levi and Miriam talking. The announcer was tense, Yossi said, he seemed to be trying to suggest something to Miriam. Yossi didn't know what. She was cold, polite, not at all as she'd been at the hitching point; she'd been full of life then. The announcer was pressuring her. Near Netanya she suddenly said she wanted to get off, since she had a friend there. Hanoch Levi became angry and said, 'You're going to Tel-Aviv.' Miriam told him, 'Let me off at the crossing.' Yossi also joined in and said, 'I promised the colonel in the Peugeot to see that you got to Tel-Aviv.' But Miriam said mockingly that she already had someone to take care of her, she didn't exactly need another father. Yossi was offended, but he was too tired to put up a fight. Hanoch Levi, who'd stopped the car, was speaking in a venomous whisper, and she laughed in his face and got out. He tried to hold her back, and she pushed him roughly. Yossi attempted to say something, but Hanoch Levi cut him short with 'You shut up,' and when he tried to get out of the car, Levi wouldn't let him. Some hitchers crowded around the car, clutching their rifles and kitbags; Hanoch had no alternative, he had to fill the car with soldiers. It took them a while to get in with their huge backpacks and M16s. Yossi said he looked outside and to his confusion saw that she wasn't going in the direction of Netanya. She'd gone through the crash barrier where there was a narrow opening few knew about; she'd headed straight for it, as though she'd known she was going to get out of the car there, as though it was planned, and Hanoch had said, 'How does she know about it? She's not a Netanya girl! What does she know about crossing points?' The soldiers were yelling and it was hard to hear; it annoyed Hanoch that he was helpless. He was afraid they'd recognize him and tell tales about the radio and television announcer who was looking for a roadside screw and picked up only female soldiers! Yossi was a seasoned hitcher, he knew soldiers and how they thought, but Hanoch must have understood them too, as though his status was the most important thing he had. Meanwhile," said Gideon, "Miriam had reached the other side and the road to Bet-Lid."

"Isaac was killed in the Bet-Lid area," Naomi said quietly and waited, glancing at me. I didn't say a thing; the name Bet-Lid gave me goose bumps. After a hundred battles and who knows how many wars and half-wars, that incident remained like a deep wound. The photograph bore cutting testimony. Why, of all the sergeants in the army, did Gideon have to bring along Naomi, who would sit before that photograph with serene sadness. I stole a

61

glance at her, but she didn't return my look. I said to her, "Isaac died before you or Miriam were born," and she replied, "That's right, he's had a very long death, sometimes death lasts much longer than life and also casts a heavier shadow. But that's not what's important, nor why I know him. It has nothing to do with your daughter, Sir. I know because I know. Before everything, before his death, he had a girlfriend, and I knew her. She's older than me, I've seen this photograph in her house. Anyway, Miriam simply stood at the crossing. Nobody said she went to Bet-Lid. You're going too far afield, seduced by easy landmarks. Maybe she wanted to get out of that car, to get to the other road, and go to Kfar Saba which is in the same direction as Bet-Lid."

"The Military Police," said Gideon confidently, "looked for and found a taxi driver who took Miriam from the crossing to the Bet-Lid junction! When they came to Bet-Lid, Miriam told the driver, 'I want to get off at Bet-Lid.' But since they were already at Bet-Lid, he'd asked her why she didn't just say 'let me off here.' To which she'd replied – and her words made such an impression on him he repeated them verbatim to field security – 'Maybe we all have to die at the Bet-Lid junction.' He didn't like that one bit, and tried to tell her that the junction wasn't safe at night, it was too close to the old border. But when he saw her heading that way, he figured she must be one of the communists from Kibbutz Yad-Hannah out there.

"Anyway, he gave a clear picture of the officer. Confused, red-eyed from weeping, talking non-stop, off her head. And heading for the communist kibbutz along the old border, the site of recent terrorist activity, obviously with the help of informers. Remember, Yossi told us she acted cold and strange in the car. And now, according to this man, she was an hysterical wreck. A lunatic. He said she talked about foreign agents, and pointed at the desolate landscape, saying somebody was living there. And he suddenly felt sorry for any officers like her who had to live among communists at Yad-Hannah in order to report to the Chief of Staff on military movements in the area while her fellow commies were reporting directly to Moscow, and Moscow to Arafat or the Syrians. He called field security and they sent out a search party. At Yad-Hannah nobody knew anything. Nobody had seen a female soldier around there. And that's all we know," concluded Gideon. "She walked down the road towards Yad-Hannah and she hasn't been seen since." Then he added, "According to the driver she didn't start crying until she got out of the taxi."

Naomi looked at me with a bitter smile of victory, the kind I was intimately familiar with. I asked her if she might have loved me thirty years ago when I was twenty and she wasn't born yet. Gideon almost cried out but stopped himself. And Naomi said, "I've been in love with you from before I was born. What have you got to say to that, Sir?" Suddenly tears came streaming down my cheeks. They both stared at me; Gideon in amazement, Naomi in sympathy. I said to her, "What's happened to my daughter?" And Naomi said, "It all fits too neatly, Sir."

"Call me Joseph," I said.

"Joseph," she said with unexpected pleasure, as though the word had been ready at the tip of her tongue for a long time. "The broadcast," she said, "Bet-Lid, Yossi, the sergeant-major, it's all too neat. But thank God that finally you can cry."

"Why finally?"

"Because you've never cried before."

"How do you know?"

"I know," she said, heading for the kitchen. Gideon, who looked so alert before, was now asleep, his head lolling back against the headrest of the armchair he sat in.

I let Gideon sleep. Naomi sat in silence. The room was perfectly still. I knew how late it was (my biological clock was working), and I could hear the muted surge of the sea, like a sweet whisper. I opened a window. It was cold. There was no more kerosene and the electric oven barely gave any warmth. Naomi sat huddled; I threw a blanket over Gideon. Apparently we all slept for a while.

5

WHEN I awoke Naomi's bright eyes were looking down on me. Gideon was still sleeping like a baby. "Wait here," I said, and after seeing the inquisitive look in her eyes, added, "Don't ask any questions."

"Sir . . . Joseph," she said, "you're wasting your time. The more you chase after a mystery, the more it eludes you. Wait it out, or set a trap." I smiled; she sounded so warm, I wanted to hug her.

I went downstairs, started my Mustang, and raced through the empty streets. There, in Bet-Lid, I parked on a dirt road, cocked the revolver I always carried with me, and set out. I searched through the old orchard which hadn't changed much in all these years. For hours I criss-crossed fields and orchards. It was a clear cold night; the stars were so bright that they turned the darkness blue. Finally a gauze of reddish white, gloomy and harsh, stretched across the horizon. I returned to the car, drove closer to the old border, then trekked some more. In the distance I saw the lights of Tulkarem. I was walking half-asleep, depressed, my eyes watering from fatigue; the revolver weighed heavy in my hand. Three hours later, I was back where I started, covered with dust, my clothes soaked with rain and ripped by thorny branches. Another car was parked on the road, its headlights on. When I approached I saw the Chief of Staff and his driver inside, looking out at me.

I leaned against his car. The Chief of Staff smiled, extending his hand. We hadn't seen each other for ages; he looked good. On a signal, he and his driver got out of the car. As he hugged me, the driver sat down again behind the wheel and drove off. The Chief of Staff then gently led me to my Mustang, placed me in the passenger's seat, sat at the wheel, and drove me home, where his car and driver were waiting for him.

At six in the morning we parted and I went upstairs. Naomi was sitting in the same spot. She stared at me; I don't think she had slept a wink. I patted her head, unsure what else to do. The grief inside me had left me numb. The unshed tears from years past were now ready to fall. A man like myself doesn't break, he conserves his strength; but now I didn't know if I had enough strength even to sleep, which was all I wanted to do.

For a few hours I dozed and dreamed that I was looking for my daughter. In my dream my daughter was a little girl with shiny hair, scrawny, serious. I was looking for her in my dream exactly where I had searched for her earlier in Bet-Lid. I awoke and realized that it wasn't just a dream; on the other hand, it was in fact a dream and I was lying in my bed. I looked around for Naomi; she wasn't sleeping beside me, but in the other room. I dropped back to sleep again, woke at nine, rushed to the balcony, and called out.

Madame Frau emerged, studied me, and said, "What a night I had, awful, my eyes didn't close once. First I heard your Mustang, then other cars, then I saw soldiers, but why bring all that up now? Who needs insults today!" When I blew her a kiss, she added, "Like father, like son. Sweet and sour!" And she went back inside.

Naomi was no longer around. I showered, and by the time I was dressed, the coffee was ready. She had bought fresh rolls and was now spreading butter and jam on them. Gideon arrived, together with the Military Police and regular police officers. For over an hour we discussed the case. I told them everything I knew, my conversation with Didi, my trip to Jerusalem, the photograph of the dog Delilah, the skirt, the whole business. Gideon had already told them about the hitch-hiking and Bet-Lid. I said, "Bet-Lid was a code word between me and my daughter; I'm sure she wouldn't have said what she did if she didn't think that it would get back to me."

After the officers had left, Gideon drank another cup

of coffee, as though he were just waiting there for Miriam. She was hovering everywhere in the house. My own dependence on Miriam was overwhelming. Naomi was there to cauterize my wound. I felt like a frightened child. My skin was peeling off, my wrinkles were laughing at me. My daughter's absence turned everything into a senseless riddle.

My experience with women was limited. In my youth there was just Miriam Hurwitz. Everybody was having affairs but me; I was known as a blockhead. While I had told the officers my story, Naomi had listened carefully, with a kind of craving and total trust; she looked as though she was praying. She said, "My soldiers are gossips, they know and reveal every secret. Hanoch Levi's fair game to them. His affair with Joy is longstanding. What I heard this week was that after all his romances – and not an iota of information on them is missing – he always returns to his wife. Yet for some reason he promised Joy he'd leave his wife for her. That was big news at the television studio, and the story made the rounds in Jerusalem." I pondered over what Hanoch had told me. The military investigations officer was on his way to question him. If Hanoch Levi had lied, he would pay dearly for it. But I didn't consider Hanoch that important; Gideon also thought he wasn't involved, except perhaps indirectly. What interested us was where Miriam could possibly be now. For some reason, Miriam's disappearance did not seem this morning to be connected to the horror of homicide or kidnapping, perhaps because she had left behind her so many scattered traces.

I sat in thought. One night, years ago, after Isaac had died in the dynamited house, an old tailor was murdered near Tel-Mund. I was immediately sent out on a retaliatory strike with my unit. We didn't have time to plan it properly. The Chief of Staff, a captain then, was one of our group. He was wounded at the outset and taken back on a stretcher. A short battle had erupted. The enemy had been waiting for us and had set a trap. But in the end our goal was accomplished, though our group had run out of ammunition.

The manner of Isaac's death in the earlier raid had left unpleasant repercussions. Not that any charges were ever officially made against me, but the soldiers had to find some scapegoat, since Isaac's fate had been so brutally unfair. I became the target of their secret campaign which attacked me not as a soldier but as a man. Not one of the veterans who'd been through the mill ever knew Isaac. But his unexpected death, his startling dash into the buckling house, and my own explanation of his panic, that he had wanted to die for a cause, an explanation which I myself hadn't completely thought out and which was probably nothing but an effort on my part to assuage my conscience, however accustomed I was to soldiers dying – every aspect of that gloriously brave campaign was the talk of the day. People said, "Just because you're not afraid of death doesn't give you the right to play with the lives of others or gain fame at their expense." That's how, gradually, I came to be held responsible for what happened, as if their own problems would go away if they saw me bleed. They still followed me into battle with their eyes closed, but they had no feelings for me. Some sadistic compulsion in them made them hate and blame me, since I was the one who had taught them how to control their fears upon entering the perpetual dance of death, how to deny their simple human emotions. But what bothered them the most was not my stubbornness or arrogance or self-righteousness; they were offended by my apparent lack of sexual desire, as if I were not a man but a stone.

Right after the Chief of Staff had been hit in the ambush, an incident occurred involving an Arab boy. I can still remember that Arab clearly: tall, scrawny, with wild hair, huge brown eyes, flat cheeks, thin lips. As he tried to escape, he stabbed one of our men. The wounded soldier fell and started to crawl away as we came under heavy fire and others got wounded. The Arab almost got away, but I shot at him from a short distance and hit him right in the head, killing him instantly. It took only a few days for the rumour to spread that I'd executed a prisoner. The source of that rumour was my own lieutenant D., who despised me as much then as now, though I still don't know why. The hints which he so cleverly dropped soon went beyond our division, resulting in a regimental hearing. D. testified against me, lying shamelessly but expertly, always hinting at the worst. Others who testified did so in such a way that the truth would come out but only, of course, alongside their previous affidavits that an atrocity had occurred because everybody had been burning with the desire for revenge. They were looking out for their own skins and wanted to cover themselves. All I needed was to testify on my own behalf and expose them, but I refused. The judge, a senior officer and considerably older than all of us, a veteran of only "justifiable" wars, a product of the British army and the War of Independence, a decent cultured man, had despised me long before he had ever heard the testimony at this hearing. He considered the current standards of the military unsavoury, and perhaps had wished to teach the new recruits a lesson through me. Because of his hatred of me, he tended to believe D.'s testimony, even though it was as full of holes as a piece of Swiss cheese. In those days, to be sure, military ethics were hardly spotless. Perhaps he thought he could use this incident to raise our moral consciousness. In our determination to retaliate the moment we were attacked, it was impossible to maintain what that senior officer was always talking about, the integrity of warfare, as if war could ever be pure. People could sanctify themselves, but war would always be ugly and brutal, especially wars that weren't as justified or as critical as his. Back then, following the War of Independence, during that relatively quiet period when the army was reconstructing itself, there was a need for small savage units that could retaliate in cold blood, inflicting damage out of proportion to our own losses. Not only was it hard for us to place our military acts in an ordinary ethical context, but deep down we felt that it was forbidden to do so. We were few in number and had to train an army of new immigrants. Opposite us was a routed, vanquished, frustrated army hungering for our blood, for revenge. So we became bloodhounds too.

We were a small, exhausted band of heroes without

camouflage, without encampments, without rich and famous ladies waiting to serenade us. We obeyed just one law, self-preservation, nothing else. We couldn't allow ourselves the luxury of philosophy, and those categorical imperatives which used to occupy my father while he sat reading Kant, Hegel and Spinoza in the safety of his modest home, across from Madame Frau, the woman he loved but never enjoyed. As our blood was flowing, the blood of our young soldiers, the blood of our peaceful citizens butchered in their homes, we had no time for such speculations.

The judge insisted that I say something; I said that it would be self-serving for me to speak on my own behalf, that I neither executed prisoners myself nor gave orders for their execution; if my lieutenant testified against me, that was something he would have to live with. My record was good, even the officer who examined me acknowledged it. But the judge called me a "killer" (using the English word), trigger-happy, which I never was. He seemed eager to restore the old codes of military conduct; but perhaps he was just a cynic who knew how to put together a case against anybody, whether guilty or innocent, as long as he would go down in history as a man of courage who did justice against evil. In the end he acquitted me, except that he indicated that the matter was doubtful, complicated. His innuendoes never became part of my military file, but they entered my psychological file, my conscience. Despite his hostility to me, he had understood that my lieutenant had all along been fabricating his testimony in order to make his perjury stick, and that those other witnesses had tried to save their necks even while they essentially confirmed my version of the facts. None the less, he still left the matter open to interpretation, if not further inquiry.

Miriam knew the whole story. I'm sure that my friend Reuben told it to her. For a long while she preferred to believe the darker version. Whenever she brought up the subject in one of our arguments, and we had thousands of them which usually ended in wild accusations against me, I told her exactly what had happened.

"If you'd really had any defence," she answered, "you would have used it in court."

"It wasn't a trial, just a departmental investigation."

Her words had taken me by surprise. Miriam had always understood me with a telepathy that was almost painful. She should have realized that at such an inquiry I would keep quiet precisely because I was innocent; but she wanted to believe the worst.

The lieutenant became my enemy for life. Everybody knew that he lied; yet today he is a cabinet minister. He has learned to look me straight in the eye. Nowadays a liar like him is the norm; back then he was the exception, and the norm was the alleged murder. Like the Chief of Staff, he rose to power by playing the game by the crooked rules. I was already a man with considerable power, but he saw my weakness and crushed me like a grape. He realized that in a few years nobody would remember what had really occurred, and if he was ever discovered to have lied in court, what was perjury compared to murdering an unarmed, defenceless prisoner? Twenty-five years later, when I was forty-five and being considered for promotion to the rank of Brigadier, out came the skeleton from the cupboard. The Chief of Staff argued that it had been exposed as pure slander. Yet the old incident had left a bad taste in everybody's mouth; others had by now used it to their own personal advantage. So the Chief of Staff shelved the whole matter, not wanting to jeopardize his future with somebody else's misfortune; he was only Deputy Chief of Staff then and on his way to fulfilling his life's dream. I had emerged a "killer", and from the same battle he'd come out a national hero. After only a few minutes of combat, he'd sustained a superficial wound (I had dozens of such wounds), but today everyone recalls this battle as "the engagement in which the Chief of Staff was wounded during heavy, desperate fighting as he led his men deep into enemy territory, got ambushed, but broke out and stuck to his objective like a lion over its prey." I'm quoting from a newspaper article which appeared not too long ago, written in purple prose by one of the Chief of Staff's war correspondents.

In a moment of weakness, the Chief of Staff once told me that at the time when my promotion had been shelved, the tales about the canteen of blood and the prisoner's execution were necessary. Subconsciously the nation needed a myth like that. We were in nappies then, the army was full of recent immigrants without motivation. Our senior officers had retired, the Palmach* was disbanded. Apathy was everywhere. People queued up to buy clothes with rations. They wanted a roof over their heads. They needed a symbol. I was the one. A young man from Tel-Aviv and from a good home, his father a doctor in philosophy, the owner of a prestigious book store. A brilliant pianist. It made an interesting story. From the good Germany you had learned about Heine, Schiller, the lot, and you were a killer too! A decent role model and a gunslinger! A fanatical fan of Shakespeare and Plato, and a lover of the desert with its aromatic cactus. Your devotion to the nation, Joseph, only added to the myth. Our conscience wanted the legend of a courageous, cultured soldier, a Prussian Jew! It worked. You had a wife and daughter. You never messed around. But that canteen of blood! Not bad, huh?

I could have got some journalists on my side and waged an all-out war in the papers. But I never allowed a single interview nor invited any bootlicking newspaper man into my home. What they said about me hurt, but I clenched my teeth and wouldn't answer back. Nobody knew. Except maybe Nina. However, she thought it suited me to be known as the man who executed prisoners, and had practically convinced herself it was true. Later, that helped her in her battle with me over Miriam.

*The striking force of the Jewish underground military organization, formed during the years of the British Mandate in Palestine.

6

THE telephone rang. A woman said, "This is Dahlia Gazit from the newspaper *Yediot*." I answered, "This is Hanoch Levi from *Maariv*," and hung up. Gideon said, "They can smell the story already."

The Chief of Staff arrived, together with a veteran police officer named Czeszek, several officers from the Investigations Department of the Military Police, and an Intelligence officer. Despite Miriam's disappearance, the Chief of Staff and I couldn't warm to each other; the score between us was too old to settle even now. He examined the photograph of Delilah in Miriam's room and said, "I remember how she used to jump into my arms and pull the buttons off my uniform." He acknowledged there had been some terrorist incidents in the vicinity of the old border near Tulkarem, but didn't mention Bet-Lid. "If the government will authorize it, we can dynamite or board up a few houses in the Tulkarem district where I was wounded," he said without cracking a smile, as if he himself now believed that he was indeed the hero of our retaliatory raid there.

Czeszek said he'd questioned Hanoch Levi. "Not in depth," he said, "that's for later." He spoke drily like a professional scorched by many years of dirty work. His nickname was "Lie Detector", and people said he could get the truth out of a stone, or a murder confession from a blind, crippled orphan who'd spent his whole life locked in a closet and didn't even know what other people smelled like. "Hanoch Levi's a clever one," said Czeszek. "His story is that he was returning from some seminar he'd conducted for the Military Police up north in Netanya, but for some reason (which I'll get out of him) he decided to go further north to check out some archaeological dig in Nve-Yam, which he'd heard about. Some Danes, he said, were digging under the sea. 'In winter?' I asked him, and he said, 'Why not? For Danes this isn't winter.' I called and found out that there actually were Danes digging up there. They didn't remember meeting anybody named Hanoch Levi, but they don't watch Israeli television. Afterwards he drove south, picked up two soldiers, a man and a woman, at the hitching point in Hadera. The girl looked familiar but he couldn't remember her name. Yes, he admits he tried flirting with her, but says that's just his nature. At the girl's request, he dropped her off at Netanya, where he picked up some more hitch-hiking soldiers who filled the car, together with the first soldier, whose name he had no difficulty remembering; Yossi."

I wanted to interrogate him myself, but Czeszek said it would be better to wait. "We'll give him enough rope to hang himself. If he knows anything, we'll catch him out. I don't believe him, but we can't consider him a suspect because no crime has been committed yet. He's hiding something; that I can smell for sure."

When everyone had left, including Gideon, Naomi said, "You must contact your wife in America. She's bound to pick up some Israeli newspaper – the story will leak out, it's a small country – and she'll be shocked. It's just not fair."

The next morning she was waiting for me with coffee and rolls again. "I have a routine, young lady," I told her. "If I break it, I won't last." Then I went to the balcony where Madame Frau was waiting. "Blowing kisses," she said, "is a sure sign of problems, Joseph. I see you have police and soldiers with you. Miriam was always a difficult child. Come and talk to me, I have contacts with people from other worlds. I have spoken to your father in séances and he sounds wonderful, he's waiting for me there. Let me find Miriam, then you come over to me." She started crying her sweet, silken tears, adding, "The girl in your place now is lovely, I've known her since 1942." She went back inside, only to re-emerge at once. Seeing me still standing there, she said, "His excellency, my Father, could find a needle in a jungle. But as Miriam would say, always quietly so I shouldn't hear, I must go back now to another day's death."

I ran to the pool, avoiding my friend Sokolowicz, who looked annoyed and betrayed. After a quick swim, I gobbled a sandwich while Rebecca tried to pump me. The rumours had already spread. She got insulted when I wouldn't answer her, but I rushed back home.

Naomi was still sitting there with her rolls. When I told her I'd already eaten, she looked not only furious but devastated. She began eating all the rolls herself with perversely exaggerated pleasure, and said, "The old lady next door told me to look after you with respect. So here goes. Your obedient servant!"

The police had questioned Hanoch Levi a second time, and had begun to circulate Miriam's photograph. Apparently, Jahash the fisherman had reacted strangely when he was shown her photograph. I hurried to the port and found Jahash by his boat. He seemed startled, as if he'd just seen a ghost. We sat down and had some coffee. "Look," he said, "I've seen a lot in my life, but this beats everything. When you were knocking me about I said to myself, 'This guy's in real trouble; his daughter's gone, he's going crazy looking for her; I'm a man, I know what a son or daughter means!' But when I saw the photograph the police brought over, something wasn't right. My blood pressure zoomed. I knew what I thought but I couldn't say it. The words wouldn't come out. You remember what I told you about her, that she was acting all the time like somebody else? Well, she was trying to look like that girl in the photograph. But the girl in the photograph was not the girl on my boat. What killed me was that you almost couldn't tell the difference – she was such a good actress. Tell me, is there anybody who looks exactly like your daughter?"

"Little Nina," I said, "her nickname was Didi. She died over ten years ago."

I went back home. Naomi had cooked something for me. It depressed me to be losing my grip on my own home, but I didn't have anybody to look after any more. The word had spread further. My old paratroopers began visiting, drinking coffee, planning actions, and I couldn't get rid of them. Only after I'd agreed to make a two-day, fruitless sweep of the entire Bet-Lid area with them, together with a group of soldiers the Chief of Staff had personally authorized, was I able to disband the command post in my house. Czeszek said, "Get those parasites out of here! They've come to fight their old battles all over again." When it came to the army, he was a professional cynic. He had never been to Beirut or Entebbe; his battleground was in dark rooms. He wasn't about to revive past glories just because some girl named Miriam had disappeared. No matter how old he was, he had always lived in the present or the future, never the past. According to him, we were all, in the end, buried and eaten by maggots. But there was no such thing as history, that was for children. The only wars we had to wage and be ready for were those to come.

The laboratory tests showed that the beret which I'd found in Jaffa was indeed Miriam's. A few strands of her hair had got caught in a fold which miraculously remained waterproof. A hairdresser on Dizengoff Street, who was shown Miriam's photograph, claimed that on the night of her disappearance Miriam had come into what he termed his "exclusive hair salon" at about eight, asking for a haircut; but when she heard the price she backed off, saying she had only two thousand shekels, and left. He said he remembered her very well. She seemed angry, tough, desperate. "The kind of woman I like," he'd said, in a voice which the officer described as whining and effeminate.

I was furious at that barber because I suspected that all he wanted was publicity. But, on the other hand, how did he know about the two thousand shekels?

Afterwards the papers blasted him for fabricating his story. Initially, of course, they'd been glad to carry it, including his picture. They circumvented censorship and increased their circulation. Competition among newspapers was so stiff that they all resorted to scandals. In actual fact what had happened was that a woman had called his shop asking how much a haircut cost; she had given her name as Miriam, and said she had only two thousand shekels. When the barber said, "That's not enough, baby," she said, "Too bad," and hung up.

When I'd gone to confront him, he begged me not to get even with him. I told him he was too small a fish for frying and that he'd seen too many gangster movies. But the newspaper story had brought him a considerable clientele. Naomi said to me, "You know little about such matters, Joseph. How could you have lived all these years in so narrow a world?"

"I was married to death and had no time for anything else," I answered. She looked at me with one question on her face. "Death? Do you mean war, or Nina?"

After I roughed up the barber a bit anyway, Czeszek said, "Look, Sir, if you smash every witness, there'll be nobody left for me to interrogate. Stay at home, swim in the pool, and remember your daughter. Let me and the police conduct the investigation. You're getting too involved. I don't want you littering the road to the solution with broken bones!"

Slowly but surely the true story, or rather the apparent facts of the case, began to pop up in the press. Both the army and the police didn't think it was wise for the papers to be writing about the disappearance of a Brigadier's daughter. If she had actually been taken hostage by terrorists, it would have been better if her identity remained unknown. Otherwise her life wouldn't be worth a damn. But the first to sacrifice Miriam's safety for a scoop were the very newsmen who over the years had condemned all our campaigns for unnecessarily risking so many lives.

After one paper had asked its readers the disturbing question, "Has another female soldier been raped and kidnapped?", I visited the editor and asked him, "Since when do newspapers publish only questions? And why raped first and then kidnapped? Maybe she was kidnapped and then raped. And if she was both kidnapped and raped, what was the exact source of the allegation? If they have none, why did they print a lie? And why was a newspaper article more important than protecting the life of a young girl who might be in danger?" The editor, a Peace

Now* man, an enlightened liberal who had participated in many demonstrations, started lecturing me about the freedom of the press, about the right of the public to have access to information. I lifted him up by his collar and said, "Go to the police and complain if you wish, but if your life means anything to you, watch your step!"

A few days later the paper printed an article on the Yom Kippur war, apparently in connection with the anniversary of the death of some famous General. The article contained an interview with Brigadier General (Res.) D., who mentioned me. "From an officer who executes a prisoner one cannot expect military ethics, true courage, leadership or any commitment to solidarity among soldiers. The legend of Krieger was pure farce," said D., obviously protected by his ministerial immunity. "Today soldiers may study the blitzing tactics of Joseph Krieger, the way he encircled that village where he had a prisoner shot, but the real, alas forgotten, hero of that entire period of retaliatory raids was the Chief of Staff, who had planned the attack together with me; whereas Krieger, with his typical megalomania or paranoia, had almost turned that fierce encounter into a total disaster. Like the idiot that he was, Krieger, thinking only of himself, had sought the halo of a hero by executing a prisoner, a tactic he employed subsequently in other battles."

The editor called me for my reaction. In his flat monotone he asked me if I had anything to say about it. "I don't have anything to say to scum like you," I said, and hung up.

Then the stakeouts began. In search of any morsel of information, journalists monitored my every move. They saw Czeszek and all his officers, then printed their malicious speculations. Finally forced to issue some statement to the press, the police acknowledged laconically that "an investigation was underway concerning a female soldier." Naturally, Miriam's picture appeared in the papers, over the innocent caption: "The show that shouldn't have

*The Israeli pressure group demanding peace between Jews and Arabs.

been aired." In just a few lines the papers noted that a government-sponsored documentary on the military's Remedial Education Project, starring the daughter of Brigadier Joseph Krieger (Res.), was aired by mistake this past 21 January, which must have shocked Miriam Krieger, a captain in the army, to see herself on television again after the show had been shelved for over a year. "Who had authorized the screening?" asked the magazines with raised eyebrows, in the best tradition of investigative journalism. Two inches above Miriam's picture, they ran a supposedly unrelated story about the current inquiry into the disappearance of a female soldier. Only an idiot could miss the connection.

Joy called, sounding scared. "We're not mixed up in this," she said. "We never released any photos to them."

"Joy," I said, "it was a shot of her from the documentary, your exclusive pictures."

"I don't know," she answered. "Maybe someone in the building was trying to play a trick or get even with me. You must believe me."

"You've lied to me before. You're just protecting your lover."

Her voice suddenly went cold and metallic. "When I said earlier that I thought I'd seen Hanoch Levi in the building, I was wrong; it was just somebody who looked like him. He was on the road at the time, giving Miriam a hitch."

"You're a real joy," I said. "A honeybunch! Since when are you ever interested in anybody who has a lookalike? I thought you only went for originals!"

"You ought to know, Joseph," she said.

Then Czeszek subjected Hanoch to another round of questioning. This time he put him through the ringer, but ultimately not much came out. Hanoch admitted recognizing Miriam's face from her army gigs. With a father that famous and a face that lovely, claimed Hanoch, how could he not recognize her? But she hadn't recognized him. He had tried to take her all the way to Tel-Aviv. She insisted, though, on being dropped off at Netanya.

Then Joy called back, sounding like a wounded animal,

accusing me of turning the police loose on innocent people just to even the score with her.

"What do you expect, Joy?" I said. "Miriam is missing and your friend lies about giving her a lift. Maybe he was the second to last person to see her."

"What do you know!" she shrieked. "You think you know everything? Wait until you find out the truth, then you'll fall on your face and break your nose. I can promise you one thing; Hanoch you won't screw. You already screwed up ten years of my life stringing me along. Now it's your turn to suffer, Joseph. You'll soon discover that Miriam isn't the girl you thought she was. Meanwhile, take my word for it, your Czeszek's a joker. I've been in this business a long time, sweetheart, and I can pull all the strings I want. If anybody so much as lays a finger on Hanoch again, you will regret it. I solemnly swear to you, Joseph, that should a certain ex-lieutenant of yours, now cabinet minister, visit me one evening and ask for information about you, I will tell him whatever he wants. Look what that man has achieved, and look at yourself. He has a string of women, including some of my friends, from here to New York, but his wife hasn't left him, because he's a real man not useless like you! His daughter's not missing. Nobody has taken her out to sea so she can fly balloons. Watch out, Joseph Krieger!" she said, her voice rising to a shriek. Then she waited for my response. "Joy," I said, "some day Hanoch Levi will come crawling to me on all fours begging to learn how to escape from your arms. Till then, goodbye and good luck!"

My neighbours organized an action committee, sending their representative, Mr Haim, to inform me that I should seek their experienced counsel in searching for missing persons. They also sent me a huge bouquet of flowers and bitter-sweet chocolate. Finally Naomi told me, "Look, Sir, you have no other choice. Before it's too late, you must locate Nina. I realize you've tried and failed, and you don't know what else to do, but I understand that Reuben could help you. The Chief of Staff called and wanted me to give you this message. I quote: 'Phone that shithead, he's been expecting your call for a week now, swallow your pride, brother, and give him what he deserves. Nina must be located, otherwise you'll bitterly regret it.' "

7

LONG before articles of Miriam's clothing had turned up on Mount Carmel, before all the frame-ups and conflicting reports, before the case had got out of hand and started to look like an unsolvable mystery, Reuben should have found Nina but didn't. He just waited. The Chief of Staff could appreciate Reuben's dark intentions as well as I could. After I'd told Naomi some of our history as the three Musketeers, she said, "You owe it to him. If she was that dear and special to him, he might jump at the chance to help her out."

The Chief of Staff, Reuben and I were friends since first grade. I remember how, back in 1941, by the seashore, we used to pretend we were defending the fortress of Massada. We were just children, Rommel was already at the gates of Egypt, and everybody was talking about our having to make our last stand. For us Jews, it's always either total destruction or redemption, nothing in between. We played "Massada" among the caves of a limestone hill facing the sea, by an old Moslem cemetery, near the spot now occupied by the Hilton Hotel. Reuben wasn't anything like the Chief of Staff or me, except when it came to his fantasies. He was always bored and lazy. I'll never forget how he once stood all night with a retarded orphan girl, waiting for the chance to feel her small breasts which were just beginning to grow despite her young age. Supposedly, he brought the girl there to watch the sun rise, but he was facing the wrong direction, looking out to sea.

We'd made a blood pact, as in the books. We'd smeared each other's faces with blood, except that I could tell that

Reuben had used tomato juice. Of course, out of love for him I didn't betray him to the Chief of Staff. Reuben was always squeamish and couldn't handle even his own blood. To this day he prefers to conduct warfare from a distance, as if he were just holding up cue cards, and if he *must* kill somebody, to do it with gloves, preferably white ones. But he was always brilliant, and I was always jealous of his sly retorts, of his razor-sharp mind. The Chief of Staff, on the other hand, was a somewhat confused, though flexible and lively boy.

We used to sit in the old Turkish fortress on Ben Yehuda Street, where the Army Canteen building now stands, and dream about our futures as soldiers in a new nation, fighting nobly to rescue our people. What infuriated us was that we had all missed out on the War of Independence by three years.

Each one of us loved the same girl, Miriam Hurwitz, who was three years our senior and who, therefore, hadn't missed that truly justifiable war. She enchanted us with her looks, her femininity, her biting humour, and her perpetual melancholy. She was the group leader in our youth movement, and on her account we came twice a week instead of once. She adored us, but we didn't always understand her, since she seemed to carry a gloomy secret inside her. She was like a silent princess, the kind I would soon meet – though in a debased, more tormented version – in Nina.

We agreed once on a plan to determine who would be Miriam's boy friend. "If she looks at either of you two first, she's yours," said the Chief of Staff, who had thought up the idea. "If she looks at me, she's mine." Reuben refused to have anything to do with games of chance; even then, he wanted only a finished product in his hands. The Chief of Staff and I waited for her in the Turkish fortress which we knew she had to pass on her way to work. She wore a Mexican poncho, and her hair was loose. I anticipated that warm look of hers which she'd bestowed on me when she had visited my home. Together we'd worked on preparations for the youth movement's tenth anniversary celebration. I'd painted while she made placards and posters. Instead of the piano, which was my instrument then, I was scheduled to play the recorder (I don't think I've ever played it since). Miriam had always treated me as though I were much older than I was, and my own lyrical love for her knew no bounds.

Now, waiting in trepidation, I wanted everything to be conducted according to the codes of chivalry. As Miriam approached, she spotted us and seemed to give the Chief of Staff the longer and more fixed look. "Wow!" he said. "She looked more at me!" When I agreed that he had won, he became furious, claiming I'd ruined the whole game. Unlike him or Reuben, I didn't love a new girl every day. I was always loyal to my one true love. The Chief of Staff was already what Reuben calls a "professional risk taker". He insisted that I should have argued that she had looked more at me, so we could have fought to see who was right.

"What's important is what actually happened," I said. "All that counts is the truth. You just want an excuse to fight, but the truth is she was looking right at you." We came to blows. I was stronger and more agile than he, but he could slip a punch and counter-punch better than anybody. He positioned himself in the narrow passage to the roof, so I couldn't get back at him for all his punches. Finally I went home, and he headed for our bunk to tell Miriam that I no longer loved her and had handed her over to him.

She laughed, and then gave him hell. "What are you talking about, boy? I could be your mother!" He was so stunned that he didn't make the obvious point that even Miriam Hurwitz couldn't have given birth at the age of three. That night she came to my house and told me in an agitated voice, full of humiliation, "You think you can take me to market in a wagon drawn by a donkey and sell me like an orange?" She smelled sweetly of perfumed soap and flowers, her voice drenched in a restrained passion which a few years later I would have recognized as sexual desire. "You cannot give me to anybody," she said, "because I only belong to myself. Don't play childish games which don't suit you."

The following morning I told the Chief of Staff that I'd lost her forever, and that if I ever had a daughter I would name her Miriam. Years later he himself married a woman named Miriam, and had two children by her. But when I'd reminded him in my congratulations that we had once both loved a woman of that same name, he said, "Who was that? We loved a Miriam? I don't remember, I loved so many girls then!" After they had their children, his wife was killed by an old rifle which went off accidentally in their guest room.

Miriam Hurwitz found a boyfriend, a soldier in the Palmach who was killed in the Galilee trying to save a fellow soldier by falling on a grenade. During the siege of Jerusalem, Miriam worked in a makeshift hospital which had been set up in an orphanage, or a monastery. She became strangely attached to a man who'd suffered horrifying multiple injuries. She was always hovering over him, as if chained to his mouth. That was all he was, a mouth. They say it practically drove her crazy. But after she had administered a fatal dose out of mercy, she finally understood what he was trying to say to her, not that he wanted to die but to live. She was appalled. Profoundly ashamed and disgusted with herself, she pulled the bell rope and vigorously shook him.

I remember her shutting herself up in her parents' home for a whole year, after she came back from the war. Throughout the day she studied something, and at night she walked along the shore. When I tried to engage her in conversation, she acted as though she didn't know me. But she answered once, "Pick me, I'm an orange."

"Miriam, you look awful," I said.

She laughed in my face and said, "What remarkable insight you have!"

Then I was drafted into the army, and didn't see her for years. She moved out of the neighbourhood, but came back to live in a worker's residence with her husband, whom she'd met years earlier in Jerusalem when he had been wounded and taken to the hospital she'd worked in. His name was Asa. He was an eccentric genius, full of phobias. But the person he feared and hated most was himself. He became the talk of the neighbourhood. He was always writing books for himself, never for publication. He and Miriam remained childless.

When my daughter Miriam was older, I wanted her to meet the other Miriam, but my daughter refused. Finally, I don't remember exactly when, she consented. But she came back from her visit saying that Miriam and Asa acted in a hostile way not only towards others but towards themselves. However, when Miriam became hooked on the photograph of the dead soldier, she also got attached to Miriam Hurwitz. Nina complained that I was trying to hurt her through the child, getting back at her by forcing Miriam into the arms of death, which Miriam Hurwitz sanctified and worshipped. "Nonsense," I said, "You're just a victim of all the rumours about her." Naturally, Nina continued to despise me.

The two Miriams became almost like one. "I found your broken heart," my Miriam told me, and I answered, "Precious, what good is that to me now? I don't want it back. I'd rather have no heart than a broken one." As usual, Miriam suddenly lost her sense of humour at the wrong moment, and thought I was making fun of her.

While Miriam Hurwitz was leading a group of her students on their annual field trip, they were attacked by terrorists. Miriam was seriously wounded and died a few days later. Nina quietened down, even though Asa started visiting us. Miriam didn't like him; after Nina ran away to America, Asa stopped coming by. Sometimes I still wonder about him. He's probably sitting and writing some story that will never see the light of day. A tale about a famous soldier whose daughter has disappeared. About three childhood friends, the Musketeers.

Yes, Reuben was the one person who could find Nina.

Meanwhile, a number of terrorist organizations claimed to have taken three Zionist hostages after fierce hand-to-hand combat, among them one female officer. Each organization had its own version which contradicted the others. We knew that no battle had occurred, and no Israeli soldiers had been taken prisoner. But Miriam was, after all, missing, even by the strict standards of Sergeant Rose. Although we didn't believe the terrorist announcement, we couldn't dismiss it completely. Again I tried to locate Nina, to no avail, while Reuben sat in his office waiting for my call and enjoying my failure. Naomi couldn't understand my game of honour and said, "It's unnecessary and childish!"

"You're making my gorge rise," I said.

She stood in the kitchen preparing a cold drink and burst out laughing. "I'm crazy about the way your generation talks! Nobody of my generation would dare say 'My gorge is rising' or 'It is I' instead of 'It's me.' " She gave me a toying look and said, "My father spoke that way and dropped dead at fifty-one. You must contact Reuben. Czeszek says that Hanoch Levi has now admitted he did more than just try to flirt with Miriam, and that one of the hitch-hikers damaged the rug in his car. Czeszek told me to tell you that Hanoch says he now knows why you don't want animals like that in the army being taught the syntax of love by female officers. Czeszek has tried his best to squeeze out of Levi the information he has on Miriam, and how he recognized her, but according to Czeszek, Levi is receiving expert legal advice."

"Legal advice? Joy's his adviser. She's the expert on Joseph Krieger, and she could sell anybody the hole in a bagel."

"Czeszek claims he'll break him yet, and get from him whatever he needs but . . ."

"But what?" I asked.

She handed me the drink. And her gesture was full of tranquil charm, like part of an Oriental ceremony. She sat opposite me, her eyes fixed on the vial of tears as though avoiding the photograph of the dead soldier, and said, "But Czeszek may be wrong. Joy has a strong hold on Levi. Hanoch is a typical married man. He likes to play the field, but he always comes home. The women in my office are familiar with the sex lives of every citizen in this country, and they say he always returns to his wife. Joy must have something on him if he's promised to marry her. That's why she's protecting him. She must know something that Czeszek doesn't, and whatever she knows is what is keeping Hanoch under her thumb."

"You're right, Naomi. That's just like her. But I'll get what she knows out of her."

Naomi smiled. "It's worth a try, Joseph." It was the first time that she called me Joseph on her own, without hesitation or any prompting from me. Till now, she backed away from all my requests. She slept only where she wanted, not in Miriam's room as I'd asked, but on the living-room sofa.

"But, Joseph," she said. "Be careful. The most dangerous animal is a wounded one."

As the sun suddenly burned brightly in the room, I looked at her and wanted to touch her, but the phone rang.

It didn't suit me to rely on bogus defence measures. I had a reputation for maintaining my guard in the midst of contradictory facts, for not getting caught in the trap of wishful thinking and permitting any notion to lead me by the nose. But in the end we all fall into the pit we have dug for someone else in the name of our highest ideals.

The terrorist organizations continued to bombard us with their glorious bulletins, claiming responsibility for even the slightest fire in Tel-Aviv. What scared me was that it took only one terrorist, one maniac, to harm my daughter whom I longed for. I could imagine her pain and how abandoned she must feel. Now that the newspapers were openly debating the identity of the female soldier and dropping hints, the terrorists could cash in on their hostage, a Brigadier's daughter and an officer herself. I saw signs of genuine worry on the Chief of Staff's brow. He loved Miriam, but he didn't look forward to exchanging hundreds of convicted terrorists for her release, especially in the face of public fury and grief and all the protests from the extremist groups. I began to fear that Reuben knew more than just the whereabouts of Nina. Didi's tale of the balloons wouldn't leave me and somehow urged me to follow its clear lead in another direction.

Reuben was hard, brutal, but fastidious. Always looking

out for himself, always covering up his animosity. He had an immediate grasp of any military situation, but reacted too slowly on the field. He lacked the abandon and resourcefulness necessary for the brief savage battles which we fought in the fifties. He was transferred to inter-rogation, and then to Intelligence, excelling in both areas. He rose up the ranks, from Intelligence to Internal Security to Foreign Intelligence. Towards the Chief of Staff and me Reuben was always mannered, guarded, mild-ly envious, arrogant, but nothing could break the bond between us. We had spent too many years together, from school to the army, from basic training to retaliatory strike units, from there to officers' training. In order for Reuben to outstrip us, it was simply a matter of his maintaining a reasonable distance from us. But our love for each other remained as genuine as it had been in childhood. Reuben had a knack for profound anger; he was practically born with it, a gloomy theatrical rage. He lusted after every-thing, women, food, power, like a hopeless outcast. A man with no clear centre but many dark corners.

The Chief of Staff was his opposite. Innately cheerful, centred, without a single dark corner. He wanted others to identify with him and love him. He always showed up at the right battle and at the right moment, radiating trust and authority, so he would stand out and people would talk about him afterwards. His basic tactic was to befriend the right sort, not to use them to achieve his own ambitions (that came later), but to become a stepping stone to help others. Except for his fairness and tenderness he had no real talents, apart from his ability to turn his disadvantage into an advantage. That was how he always found a good spot for himself in the middle, wherever he was. All he did was compromise. Since he took so much time to make any decision, people thought he had worked everything out logically and carefully. But actually he was simply so confused that he would just compromise as a safe way out of any dilemma. When he was only a captain, Nina predicted that he would some day be Prime Minister, and he probably believed her. Gradu-ally he learned not to strive for greatness but just to extend his hand to those in power and accept rather than take.

It was really Reuben who turned our friendship into a race for revenge. But perhaps even as kids we were caught in a three-way friendship which had no hope of success. What glued us together was a false sentimentality. Unlike other kids, we didn't have the foresight to explore our natural gifts in either art or science. Instead we romanticized war and were always fighting against or hurting each other. We fought even over an ice-cream cone.

In the Yom Kippur War, when the battalion I'd been sent to rescue had been wiped out, I was left with just two tanks; one had no chains, the other had a defective machine gun and a cannon whose barrel had been damaged but still worked. Over the radio, the Chief of Staff – who was then second in command to the General – told me, "Before you, stands the whole Arab nation; behind you, the Land of Israel." Reuben somehow managed to get on the line from some cellar he was in, and said, "The fate of our nation is in your hands." I admit, it was scary to be confronting a powerful enemy by myself, assisted only by a wounded sergeant. Naomi told me that at her N.C.O. training course it was a well-known story. I'm sure that Reuben was already composing my eulogy in his jesting gloomy mind. But I also knew deep down that I couldn't have accomplished what I did if it hadn't been for what they had told me. Despite my inevitable scepticism, I believed that I was truly alone, the privileged remnant of two thousand years of history.

Even at primary school we taught ourselves how to fight. The Chief of Staff's father was the treasurer of the synagogue on Ben Yehuda Street. He looked after his son's welfare. A short Jew from Lithuania with red hair and freckles, a long nose and a tight mouth, he always put his eggs in several baskets. While the other members sent their children to a religious school, he gave his son a secular education, though he kept a kosher home and observed the Sabbath. The new nation looked like a better bet than God Himself, and the synagogue's treasurer understood who would be calling the shots during its early years. He was also willing to pay the price. Namely his own son. He didn't imagine then how wary his son would turn out. And he never knew quite what to make of me. As for my father and his friends, the treasurer considered them all bums with forged IDs. My playing the piano made him even more suspicious, though he wanted his son to appreciate Beethoven. He both despised and exploited me, the son of an arrogant played-out man whose life circled around everything that was dead, either dated music, or ancient Greek, German, and Latin literature, or Madame Frau, the survivor of Germany's zoos. But he found a good use for me long before his son had learned to climb on my back to get somewhere. He understood that I would help his darling son to get ahead.

Reuben he hated, too. Reuben was talented in everything, from painting to mathematics, and he spoke Arabic fluently, not to mention English as well as Hebrew. For a brief period of our boyhood, Reuben considered himself a Canaanite* and wrote all his letters to me in ancient script. He always knew how to hurt us with his cruel silent treatment, until the Chief of Staff would give in and compromise. Reuben worked on our conscience as a way to advance his own position, always attacking our weak spots with his scathing wit.

We hung together, the three of us, eagerly following the political struggles of the adult world around us. We knew that it was up to us, the new generation, to make the critical difference on the battlefield. The military option was our nation's only way to survive.

While everybody else cursed basic training, for us it was a picnic. When we were just ten years old we used to go on long forced marches with our backpacks, we knew how to shoot a rifle, and we would swim for at least three miles in the sea every morning, winter or summer. Our officers belonged to the generation – to us somewhat ridiculous – trained by the British with their energetic

*The name given to a group of poets and artists in the 1940s and 1950s in Israel, whose aim was to evolve a new "Hebrew" nation, as opposed to a "Jewish" one.

observation of protocol, salutes, and all the melodrama of the British army of the Empire days. Together with a large group of other soldiers at our officers' training course after basic training, we secretly worked out a new military strategy along the lines of the Palmach but without its socialist ideology; we opposed the obstinately conservative approach of our commanding officers who, in their few engagements with the enemy, had suffered nothing but smashing defeats. What had enchanted us about the Partisan generation of Palmachniks was their solidarity as soldiers, their individual bravery which taught by example, their ingenious tactics, endurance and surprise. There were not many left now like this. They had been sacrificed to the new nation. They had done their job, now it was our turn.

The three of us fell in love with Nina on the same day. Lieutenants then, we'd been sent out to help set up transit camps for recent immigrants in Beer Yaakov. In the middle of a winter rain storm, three young men from north Tel-Aviv struggled with defective tents that wouldn't stand up, as streams of foul water rushed through our legs and a freezing wind bit into us under a black sky.

In one of the tents we saw Nina. She was living with a woman much older than herself, whose eyes were laden with fear. The older woman stood by their nearly demolished shack which stank horribly, trying to strike the dark sky with a long twisted branch which she had obviously broken off a tree in a nearby orchard. When Reuben spoke to her in Yiddish, she answered him in German, which Reuben didn't understand. But I did. She said she was attempting to persuade the sky to clear up. She looked like a farmer's wife with a simple German face made of solid brass.

Then Nina stepped out to see what was going on. She had heard us talking. She was utterly pale. The gloom surrounding her was overwhelming. None the less, she was rather well-dressed considering the primitive conditions of the transit camp. Her eyes displayed both glory and beauty as she examined us in her melancholy pride, as though she were our slave and our master. With her sunken cheeks and strong chin, she was a capricious woman and a sturdy rock, at once a sovereign princess and a hypochondriac. With her grey eyes and her long brown hair, well-groomed as if to challenge the driving wind and rain, and that mocking weary expression of hers, she already fitted Miriam's description of her as a "lioness poised but poisoned".

Of Nina's past I knew very little. Reuben knew more. He investigated; I didn't. She claimed that the old woman she lived with was her aunt. But later, even I found out that she wasn't her aunt. Once Nina and I had married, Reuben tried to sell me information on the so-called aunt whom Nina visited occasionally in Haifa, where she'd moved to. Naturally, I'd refused, foolishly considering it beneath my honour.

Suddenly the love we had all dreamed of had appeared in the form of Nina. We danced attendance on her. We danced to her tune. She was so unusual, from another climate, not of our world. She was from our darkest past, from what we called in our flowery phrase "The Jewish People". Thousands of other Ninas came to our shores on ships overflowing with passengers, filling the new Jewish State with their practically burnt-out souls and bodies. We were drawn to the mystery which blazed in her burning eyes, to the scent of death which she carried on her like perfume, and to her utter humiliation and rage. She said she was just waiting for the chance to emigrate to America. The woman who had come to us directly from the eye of the hurricane, on whose account we had fought at night along mosquito-infested borders, among cactus shrubs, and howling, desperate, starving dogs, could make even the smallest act look magical, whether she were brewing tea or just raising her hand to her face, turning that miserable tent into a palace and her despair into something exalted far above whatever we represented. Our struggle was no concern of hers; she had never chosen to come here and had no faith in any Jewish State. As far as she was concerned, Jews were something to light a fire with. She wanted a real *terra firma* under her feet. She wanted to walk on earth where it was safe. She said she would never give birth to a Jewish child, which made the old woman, her aunt, laugh through her closed mouth while she continued to strike the sky with her stick, shouting, "Whore! Whore!" And Nina laughed back at her. The aunt was the only person for whom she seemed to have pity.

I didn't know then that this old woman, her "aunt", was a Christian German, a friend of Nina's father's family, who had concealed her in her home after Nina had escaped from a concentration camp where she'd slept in a dog kennel. I didn't know anything about such things then. But I was captivated by her enchanting harshness and her delicate femininity. That strange laugh of hers reminded us of those jackals we'd heard as kids while we roamed the seashore or played by the Moslem cemetery.

After refusing to learn Hebrew for years, speaking instead the fluent English she had learned in Germany, she suddenly started studying Hebrew. I didn't realize that it was just to gain ammunition; she planned to escape from here once she'd picked up enough Hebrew. First she let us fall in love with her, then she figured out a way to exploit us without our knowing what she was up to, except perhaps for Reuben. She checked us out like horses, to see what each of us was worth to her, and selected me, most probably because she'd sensed that my love for her was the only one with absolutely no strings attached. She simply needed me, but I didn't know her game then. I was hopelessly in love. Reuben and the Chief of Staff were, too, they with all their previous experience and many affairs, and I with only my single, childish adoration of Miriam Hurwitz to my name.

From the outset she understood that our friendship was based on competition. Each of us had kept his love for her a secret, but she knew that sooner or later we would have to come into conflict with each other over her, since she could work on our instinct as soldiers used to going it alone in battle. She loved how we came to her from the battlefield smelling of blood. She wished that her body could reflect death the way ours did, though even then she'd already begun to despise us for fighting wars. To her, power meant rising above our miserable game of war with its rifles and machine-guns. Of course, Reuben had already switched to Intelligence and, after only a few months away from us, he was a changed man, radiating that graceful, arrogant dryness typical of his secret work and inimical to our close-knit friendship. But the Chief of Staff and I would still come to her after having defended the border where it had been breached or having crossed it on retaliatory missions.

In our unit, solidarity was everything, forced as we were into the valley of death relying on fanatic courage, incited by team spirit, individual daring and the smell of the enemy around us. I fought for my friend, the Chief of Staff, protecting him like a younger brother. Nina made fun of me for that, claiming that the Chief of Staff, by riding on my back, would go farther than I ever would. Likewise Reuben. I didn't answer her. I wouldn't let love come between me and my friends. I was sure that the Chief of Staff would be the first to win her, next Reuben who after a while would get bored and drop her, then I would have my turn. Although I didn't trust women or my power over them, I was too much in love with Nina to give her up for any reason. Except, of course, in a game played strictly by the rules. But she didn't allow us to play games with her. She knew that we all wanted the same thing. She needed us to struggle against one another over her. She was the unthinkable danger which the three of us had secretly longed for, and we were inescapably attracted to her the way the soldier Isaac had been drawn into that house in Bet-Lid, compelled to join the old Arab woman in death.

It was Nina, who had come from what we then called "the garbage depot of our history" – a subject we discussed in our gatherings and raised like a rallying flag to justify our national struggle – who actually killed our friendship. Perhaps Reuben realized the exact nature of the garbage she came from; he saw her naked and exposed before his eyes. To me Nina was the future mother of my child, the family I had looked forward to, the sweet smell of victory, something to last forever.

Nina would let us take her into town for a good time,

but then instigate an argument among us. She ate ravenously, wolfing down her food as if she had been starving for years. That always shocked us. We dished out large sums of money to satisfy her hunger in restaurants with dark blinds where the black market blossomed.

From the age of seven I had stopped crying, and even Nina couldn't get a tear out of me. Reuben played right into her hands. Whenever she asked for a present, Reuben knew where to get anything she wanted, even in those years of austerity. We were always in debt on account of her, and she kept demanding more and more. Always gorgeous and capricious, she created an aura around her, as though whatever she once had given others for a penny she wouldn't give us for anything. We had to become her slaves before we could become her lovers. Her beauty was ascetic and gloomy, yet wanton.

Wealthy society ladies would bring clothes to the transit camps while their husbands were attempting to build a cardboard Hollywood in the new nation under their command. They speculated in railway tracks that didn't exist and trains that had never run; they wasted fortunes in their games of prestige. Still, their wives continued to purchase meat and clothes on the black market, taking these rags to the "unfortunates" in the shanty towns, who had put diamonds up their rectums in the hope that their day would soon come. Nina lived in two worlds. When we married she had twice as much money as I did. Her ability to survive, which got her here, far exceeded the combined strengths of the Israeli Palmach and the British army. But we didn't know that then.

At night we protected our idiotic leaders whose social engineering made as much sense as selling refrigerators to Eskimos. All the machinery which they had imported from abroad lay idle, falling apart and succumbing to rust.

Nina turned into a true alley cat. Making a good living for herself off her three sweet soldiers who kept bringing her everything they had, she accumulated an impressive, secret cache of money, gold, and jewellery. While were fighting at night, her agents were out on the streets selling cards, watches, condoms and contraband English cigarettes. Suddenly the historical gap caused by two thousand years of the Diaspora between ancient Bar-Kochba and modern Zionism, which had been erased from our minds both at school and in the youth movement, was now an awesome reality, which included Nina and the transit camps. We were learning from the streets – which were full of misery and affliction.

Nina sensed that Reuben would be the first to sign up on her ship but never to set sail with her. Of the three of us, he was the trickiest. His treachery both excited and frightened her. Ultimately, Miriam was my daughter, not his.

Now Miriam's gone, for him and for me, yet the bastard sits and waits. The Chief of Staff may weep in pain over Miriam, but in his heart he's glad she isn't his daughter. I ought to give Reuben what he deserves. He loved Miriam as he had once loved Nina, even after Nina had married me, long after, even while I remained as faithful to her as her own shadow, like Miriam's shoes that were always at her door waiting all night for her to wake up, until the morning she disappeared, when they challenged each other like slanting tombstones.

If somebody were to come to me today saying that Reuben was behind Miriam's disappearance, I would be shocked, but deep down I would believe him, and even forgive Reuben. That was what bugged Reuben about me. After all, he had lent considerable credibility to the rumour that he was Miriam's real father by refusing to either confirm or deny it. During one battle deep in enemy territory, when I was the commanding officer, Reuben had submitted information to me about mine fields and the enemy's whereabouts which I sensed was inaccurate. I didn't have to tell him, we both knew it. Reuben hadn't deliberately misinformed me, he had been the victim of his subconscious. To his credit, he wanted to turn himself in and confess. Although we were not talking to each other then, except on military matters, for three days I begged him on the phone not to make a confession. He wept like a child and said, "How could I have sent you out to certain death?" Finally he agreed not to give himself in, to remain silent. During the battle, miraculously, one of my soldiers had said he could smell the army, I had sensed a trap, retreated, regrouped, and improvised a new attack at some other point. To this day Reuben is waiting for me to bring up the subject again, but I don't intend to, ever. Even in these pages I haven't divulged either the time or the place of that incident. And even now I haven't yet picked up the telephone to call him.

When Nina announced her decision to marry Reuben, she expected us to fall apart as friends. Neither I nor the Chief of Staff will ever forget Reuben's smile of victory in Nusbaum's seaside café. Once it had become clear that all three of us loved her, there seemed to be no way out of the mess. Still, we wanted to face the problem like men. I don't remember who came up with the idiotic idea, but we all consented to draw lots at the restaurant and take turns accompanying Nina along the promenade to help her make "the irrevocable decision". We were fairly decent about the allotment of time, stipulating "approximately ten minutes each". In our eyes, the plan was testimony of our great friendship. Each of us would have his chance to present Nina with his declaration of love, and then Nina's decree would be final.

Reuben went first, taking her to the London Garden nearby. I went second and immediately asked her to marry me. She gave me a lofty, quizzical look and said, "You're a babe in the woods, Joseph; too honest, too innocent; that's why you accepted the verdict on Miriam Hurwitz. You'd only get lost in my dark alleys and eat your own words. Don't pin any hopes on me. I couldn't accept you even if I wanted to." The Chief of Staff came back from his turn looking like a zombie. Then Reuben, who'd kept us both waiting for half an hour while he had gone to the bathroom, invited us to his wedding. He'd offered Nina a deal he was sure that she couldn't refuse. He never even mentioned that he loved her, he told me later. All he said was that he was better and smarter than we were, and she needed somebody she could rely on. "I'll build you a highway to Paradise. When the moment comes, you can choose either Israel or America." She was confused. In the end, the woman of our dreams wasn't the pillar of strength we had imagined. Only Reuben knew what a lonely, lost, shaking leaf she was. So for now she was his.

When Nina scolded me and the Chief of Staff for reducing life to such a childish game of taking turns, we insisted that it hadn't been our idea, that Reuben had probably suggested it first, but it was too late. She had already given Reuben her hand in marriage and we had to follow the noble codes of chivalry established long ago at the court of King Arthur, since we were noble knights. Nina must have figured that Reuben was her only chance to win in this crooked life where everything was fixed in advance. While the phonograph played Beethoven's Seventh in the background, as it did every day at Nusbaum's seaside café, we sat defeated and depressed, beers in hand, watching Reuben offer us his worrisome signs of solidarity. He raised his mug to our happiness, and we answered with congratulations to him and Nina, hiding our grief, faking our gaiety, until we got stinking drunk. Nina was laughing as the Chief of Staff and I declared our undying love for her, but Reuben, loaded as he was, kept his sentimentality under wraps.

On the way home, the Chief of Staff said he intended to kill himself. I told him that I hoped he would reconsider. But I wasn't really worried about him, I was worried for myself. Then, along the border in the barren wastes of the Negev, where we were stationed for a few days on some manoeuvre, a female soldier took a liking to me on my second day there. She saw me pining away, realized she had a dreamy knight on her hands, and gave me a smile sweeter than honey. And I didn't know for a while what happened to Nina and Reuben. Later on, Nina filled me in. But only when the crisis over Miriam's disappearance reached a climax, would I ever discover what Nina had omitted, because I hadn't bothered to investigate anything for twenty-five years. That would have violated my sense of honour and propriety.

After returning from the Negev, I stayed a few days at my parents' place on Ben Yehuda Street. The phone rang. It was Nina. Her voice trembled. She said that she regretted her decision and wanted to talk to me about it. I tried to calm her down, telling her that Reuben was my friend. I wouldn't betray a friend. She laughed, said something bitter and mocking, and sounded confused and gloomy. Her laugh was short and gruesome. Then she hung up. She must have phoned the Chief of Staff immediately afterwards, because when I spoke to him a few minutes later, he said she'd called and had told him the same story. He had refused, too, though not as quickly as I had. Later, when Reuben informed us that Nina had been delighted by the way we'd rejected her pleas, he was smiling like a Cheshire cat.

Then came the full-blown tussle between Nina and Reuben in their apartment on Yad Elijah Street, Nina with knife in hand. From what I heard, I couldn't tell why she went for a knife. It was a hot summer's day, an argument erupted, blood was flowing. I really don't recall the details, or perhaps I refuse to. For the first time in his life Reuben lost his temper. He struck her, maybe out of jealousy but I don't know, he battered her, discovered who the aunt was, and was ashamed of himself. A trial was held. Nina, who felt betrayed, didn't exactly defend her lover, or her fiancé as he was called by her aunt, who by now had moved out of the transit camp and had settled in Haifa with a woman whom she claimed was her daughter. The knife had punctured Reuben's hand but hadn't caused much bleeding. None the less, it had been, ironically enough, the worst hand-to-hand combat that Reuben had seen for a long while, blood or no blood.

The knife was Reuben's, an odd toy for a man who preferred to kill with white gloves or over the telephone. He denied that she had wounded him and refused to file any charges against her. Nina insisted she had stabbed him with his own knife, but didn't claim that he had provoked it by beating her. Each tried to protect the other for some strange reason, perhaps out of anger or as a way to disengage from each other without altogether relinquishing their profound, fierce desire for one another. Reuben for once had acted like a man, though he lost his love anyway. For once he was routed by his own not so dishonourable choice.

When Reuben learned, though, that I had rushed to Nina's side at her request, he was hurt. I couldn't help myself, she was like magic to me, her love outweighed his anger. Reuben was now the traitor betrayed and he never forgave me for that. Only a man like Reuben could imagine that the acts of love and revenge were interchangeable. All these years he has kept me in the sights of his rifle.

All because the trial turned out to be more than just an investigation of a stabbing. A man had shown up in court claiming that Nina had informed against him over there, far away, but he couldn't document it. Nina's "aunt" had now disappeared, as if swallowed up by the earth. Also, the question was raised whether Nina's ID was forged, whether she was in fact Jewish. A certain rabbi testified against Nina in a blind panic. Then poor Reuben, with his hand all bandaged, tried to defend Nina, who only shortly afterwards would become Joseph's fiancée. That's what killed him, her not waiting for them to come together again. He presented a letter, which the judge read in chambers, and which moved him to tears. Subsequently, the judge spoke to Nina the way one might address a child who'd been run over by a locomotive and was still hanging on to life. What compassion poured out of him! He wept at the mere sight of the document which none of us had seen or read before, but which had transformed the judge into a bawling advocate for Nina. Reuben never said what was in that document, or who had given it to him, but the judge ripped it to pieces, saying that Nina was the soul of our Jewish history and deserved our everlasting gratitude and respect, never mind an ID. As for the agitated, furious rabbi who had vilified her in his juicy Yiddish, the judge told him to get lost. What gladdened the judge was that Nina had somebody like me to rely on, whom he recognized because of his own army connections.

Reuben screamed out, "You can marry and enjoy her, but remember that I was the one who gave her to you. If not for me, she would be sitting pretty in jail now!" I was sure that he knew what he was talking about, though I didn't know enough details nor did I want to, or maybe I already knew but refused to admit it even to myself. I certainly didn't know then that Reuben had decided not to marry her, but instead to keep her as his mistress for life, or that Nina would always consider him the real hero not me, precisely because he had despised her, because he had rescued her from a jail sentence with the intention of throwing her to the wolves when it suited him. He still had her on a leash. If he had whistled she would have come to him. Poor Nina. She never learned that she had a right to live as freely as any of us. She was a cut-out princess, a fake beauty. Life frightened her because she thought she had desecrated it.

Reuben exploited her fear; he knew what he was dealing with. Because he had investigated the scum of her past, that's all he saw. He never acknowledged – unless to himself, but certainly not to me – that Nina was a noble woman after all, and behind the filth and treachery hid a tender creature who had wasted her life for lack of pride which, as Miriam always said, is the opposite of arrogance.

The Chief of Staff dropped out of the game. He saw that Nina spelled trouble and would only be an obstacle to his dream of a career. He gave her up without a fight, but not without emotion. Thereafter our friendship cooled. Reuben advised me to carry a whip, but he was the one who continued to do so. "With a whore you don't play the intellectual, you play the terrorist. Bring whisky and a stick," he said, and his eyes looked almost blank.

So that's how it happened that Nina and I married, and she bore me a daughter, and my friends distanced themselves from me – except for an occasional glance through the breaches at our old amity, while Nina sought to detach herself from our homeland. She wanted the privileges but not the responsibilities of citizenship. Perhaps she relinquished her dream of emigrating to America, not her mixed feelings about life itself. She was still contemptuous of my notions of chivalry, which were utterly absurd to her. My loyalty to her, though, became a reliable if partial solution, as did what I offered her in our bedroom, an amazingly gentle love which I never knew I was capable of.

I had longed for a wife of my own, a mother to my

child. But my pure love only puzzled her, she couldn't interpret it to her satisfaction. When she finally realized that she actually loved me and Miriam, it was too late, she was caught in a labyrinth of her own making. She left me for Miriam's Talmud teacher, and together they went to America where she wrote fervent letters to Miriam and me which neither of us answered.

The wedding ceremony had been a disaster. My mother, who never acknowledged Nina, had refused to attend. My father came almost incognito, accompanied by Madame Frau and Mr Haim. Mr Haim was the hit of the evening. Wearing a frock and cylinder top hat, he handed me over to the rabbi as if I were a rare rooster. We forgot about Reuben's animosity towards us, whereas he never did. As he climbed up the murky ladder of success at the Mossad, he often placed my life in danger, counting on me to beg him never to confess it. His sense of justice was contingent on whether or not he could get away without it. At night I would be off on manoeuvres or actually fighting ferocious battles, no thanks to that charming general from previous justifiable wars. Our task was to demonstrate to the enemy our ability to strike back wherever it would hurt them the most.

The Chief of Staff was preoccupied with his own promotions and was no more aware than I was of Reuben's lethal contest with me over Nina – I with blood forever on my sleeves, and Reuben with secrets up his.

While her belly grew big with Miriam, Nina started to talk strangely. We were living then in Herzliya in a small, old, isolated house I'd bought, which faced the sea and the faded limestone pathways along the scarred shore. Denying that she was pregnant, Nina said she'd been overeating, that foreign agents had taken measures against her to empty her brain and fill her belly. I had to travel home from manoeuvres late at night to watch over her; to keep people away from her so they wouldn't become frightened. She wouldn't stop talking about her missing mind, about the poems she'd written under several assumed names for newspapers, about the love she was constantly asking somebody to deliver to her, and about

102

the homicidal man of unjustifiable homicide, Joseph, who had stuffed her belly with heavy stones.

She said she was embroiled with foreign agents who meant to harm her and she asked me to contact her aunt in Haifa, who came, sat down beside her, cursing me with her cold eyes, and immediately put her on a diet to lose weight. "Don't tell her she's pregnant," she told me. "You're not a woman and wouldn't understand. Your food has poisoned her, your nation has poisoned her, everything here has poisoned her. You will have to pay a high price for taking in so many refugees all at once. The poison we came with shall swell like Nina's belly!" Then Nina and her aunt argued, about what I don't know, and the aunt left. I took a holiday and cared for Nina all day. But while I always spoke sweetly to her, she answered me with curses. So when our daughter was born, I didn't even bother to ask Nina what to call her.

8

IN her ninth month, when even Nina had to admit she was about to give birth, she began to cry non-stop, millions of tears pouring from somebody who barely drank any liquid whatsoever. Despite her hostile, estranged look, I knew that she was still my wife; even if she were the tip of the iceberg in my territory, I had to protect her. No matter how much she insulted me and mocked me, I never stopped loving her. She tried to miscarry by weeping over the embryo inside her. She danced in the rain, howled at the full moon, stuck herself with knitting needles, accused me of scheming against her, said that a sanitation department whore like her should never give birth to a Jewish child, said that I was exploiting her, robbing her of all her money and jewellery. Again I took time off, and Nina refused to get out of her bed. Our house was in a kind of no-man's land; dry flattened grass covered the desolate pathways to the sea. Nina, unable to rise, lay in bed and wept. At the front door the jeep was parked. When Nina went into a difficult labour, I brought a doctor who insisted I take her immediately to the hospital. Through her tears Nina laughed like a wounded hyena.

At the hospital she froze in fear, except for the tears which kept flowing. Her pain was apparently unbearable. She turned away, her mouth stretched open in a silent scream; I went around to the other side and saw blood: she was haemorrhaging. Suddenly she looked so delicate, dear, cold, that even the doctor's hands trembled. A vase full of flowers, all irises, stood at her bedside. She grabbed the irises, threw them to the floor, and right after she'd delivered the child, she slowly sipped the murky water from the vase, once more turned her face away, and wouldn't look at her daughter.

The next morning I told Nina, "You have a daughter now, you must pull yourself together." Nina asked me "What's the bastard's name?"

"Her name's Miriam and she's not a bastard," I said.

She answered, "Don't get me mixed up with your bastard Miriam. I had nothing to do with it!"

I took Nina and Miriam home, and I hired a nurse. My mother came by once to tell Nina what not to do, but refused to help, claiming that Nina could take care of the child by herself. I told my mother that I had enough troubles without her. So she returned to the Clinic, resuming her slow death for a few more years. A recent immigrant from Morocco, who had recently lost her child at birth, came to nurse Miriam.

Nina lay in her room staring at the wall. I went to the Chief of Staff, who was by then a captain, and told him I needed to take a long leave. He answered, somewhat vindictively, "I don't think that'll be possible." I went to the commanding officer, the man who had conducted those justifiable wars, and sat opposite him. He said, "The army can get along without you, nobody is indispensable. Maybe you'd like permanent leave." I told him, "Sir, that's a luxury you can't afford yet, we both know that. As disgusting as I am to you, you need me. Building a new nation takes some dirty work, though I wasn't the one who stuffed an Arab's head in some beehive during your justifiable war, that was somebody else who was promoted to major. On the day that the lamb and the wolf lie down together and everything is hunkydory, I would still rather be the wolf, but for your sake I'll babysit for the lamb. I'm requesting a few months' leave because my daughter needs me as her mother." He laughed. The idea of me playing mother amused him. But unlike the Chief of Staff, he figured that it was worth granting me extended time off, on the chance that the raging bull might return a poodle. When he himself finally retired and everybody at the big celebration was joking about the "commander of the plumbing system", I defended him. Although he despised me, calling me a "trigger-happy savage", he knew that I was the only one who was genuinely grateful to him. As a child I had memorized all his battles, which are now forgotten, in order to train myself to be a model soldier later. He hadn't been an outstanding military man, but he had at least conducted two or three important battles. Whatever I knew then came from him, regardless of whether he'd actually accomplished anything.

Over the next few months, after Miriam had been weaned from the Moroccan's breast, I took care of her, feeding her, wheeling her in the carriage which Madame Frau Birnbaum had bought for us, and played with her in her playpen. By the time she was one I'd taught her to walk along the limestone paths to the sea, as I talked to her. She was full of life. Nina watched us from the windows. When Miriam saw her she cried. Nina yelled that I was wasting my time playing with a kitten instead of being a man. My army salary wasn't enough now, so I worked as a guard. Finally my father, hearing that my life was practically in limbo, gave me sufficient money to enable me to care for Miriam without taking on an additional job. My mother complained that he was robbing her of her security, that she would die forsaken in an old people's home. To my father's credit, he wouldn't give in, saying, "Ethel, you should be ashamed of yourself. He is your own son, your flesh and blood, and she is his honoured wife." He loved Miriam, and would come by bus to play with her in her pen while I took a brief nap to regain my strength.

At night, Nina and I had bitter fights. When my friends, former comrades-in-arms, would come by with their medicinal cognac and their bloodshot eyes, to sit, drink, and sing old Russian songs, Nina became frightened; she smoked one cigarette after another and started rambling again, claiming that enemies were plotting against her, emptying her brain while she slept and inserting stones instead, as well as instruments to measure her femininity. She weighed herself and said, "You see, I was never pregnant, I just ate too many stones." Her hair was dishevelled, she wore rumpled multi-coloured clothes which she'd kept in a suitcase smelling of kerosene. She looked gorgeous in her fragility, dressed in a costume from some play which I couldn't remember. And she always excited in me a desire which I could never quench. Every night I had to promise her that I wouldn't desert her, that I would look after her; she insisted that I prove to her how much I loved her. She wanted me to speak ill of our daughter, which I couldn't do. But she kept insisting on it, over and over again, in German, Polish, Russian, Ukrainian, as if she were rolling in the imaginary vomit of her own self-hatred.

None the less, when I held her in my arms I would forget everything, even the infinite sweetness of my growing daughter. I pitied Nina, pitied the beauty she was losing. Yet she continued to mock me, saying, "Only a cat can bear kittens, but who knows who fathered them? Besides, she's yours and Miriam Hurwitz's, your one and only love." Whenever I mentioned our daughter, she plugged up her ears. In the secrecy of her bedroom she improved her Hebrew, perhaps as a future tactic, and spoke about the sweetness of revenge, but I didn't know what she meant because so many strange things were pouring out of her mouth then.

Sometimes when Nina would peer out at us from the lattice, the child would look back at her in silent terror, then a malicious, almost violent smile would stretch across Nina's lips as she stood there proclaiming her contempt until Miriam began to cry. I pushed Nina away from us, Nina backed off and locked herself in her room. By accident, I bumped into Miriam Hurwitz again, who wasn't yet married, and accompanied her to her apartment in the workers' residency. I wanted to be with her, someone who understood me. Her feelings for me weren't the same, but her body was burning with desire. I lay next to the woman, hugging her, but I couldn't make love. She lay there and looked at me without mockery or compassion, and said, "You're a decent man, Joseph, a killer but decent, and also faithful. You couldn't make love to me now, even though I was once your so-called great passion. Now you have Nina. Even if it makes no difference to her what you do, it does to you. You don't even understand what a romantic you are, Joseph," said Miriam Hurwitz. A nursery rhyme which Nina usually sang at night was humming in my head. This was the first time I had ever been impotent. "Just as I expected, crime and punishment," I told Miriam. She said, "Justice prevails only in technicolour, but the films and wars we die in are black and white." Right afterwards, she married Asa, a frustrated writer even then. When I came home, Nina was holed up in her room. I told her, "I tried to be unfaithful to you but couldn't." She laughed. "For that, sweetheart, you deserve to be called an exceptionally good man, but if you think I will now move one inch closer to that embryo you claim came out of me, you are mistaken."

One moonlit night, I left Miriam in charge of a baby-sitter, a girl who lived in a house not far from us, and I drove into town to do some necessary shopping. I found powdered milk and eggs, but I didn't have enough rations because Nina had refused to accept what was due to her as Miriam's mother, and the Rations Department wouldn't acknowledge a child who had no mother. When I came back, the babysitter was waiting for me outside. She looked utterly terrified; her eyes gaped in panic and pain. She emerged from the purple bougainvillaea which climbed up the wall of the house, and she trembled in my arms, breathing deeply for a few minutes until she said barely audibly, "I couldn't help it, Mr Krieger, I couldn't. It was awful." And she burst out crying again, and almost choked on her tears. I put the groceries on the ground, peeked inside, didn't hear a sound, but as soon as I entered I heard footsteps and the door to Nina's room closing. Miriam was asleep and breathing as quickly and quietly as ever.

When I came back to the babysitter she hugged me again, shivering, and said, "Earlier, I don't remember exactly when, Miriam suddenly shut her eyes in the middle of our game. She was in bed, and I swear to you, she stopped breathing and looked dead. Her eyes were open but I don't think she could see anything. I panicked, screamed for that woman who lives with you, the lady who goes around in fancy rags and is always telling peculiar jokes, but she wouldn't come; she made believe she didn't hear me. I was sure Miriam was dead, as pale as she was. She wasn't breathing, I tell you. I have never been so scared in all my life. Then I saw some man in the window. I had seen him a few times before, passing by when you were away, looking out of his car window, a huge cab with all kinds of antennae on top. He stood by the window, I recognized his eyes and yelled for him to come in.

"By now Miriam's eyes had gone white, her pupils had disappeared. The man came inside, listened to her heart, glowered at me, you should have seen that face! Then he went to the room where the woman was, screamed at her until she came out wearing an evening gown, but looking miserable, her eyes red from crying. I was petrified. Look, I'm still shaking. She walked like a queen. The man stepped aside, as if he were scared too. The woman seemed terrified herself. The moment she began to crouch in front of Miriam, I saw a vindictive smile cover the man's face and I wanted to kill him, but the woman started to weep over Miriam's face. It looked just like a ceremony I once saw in a church in Greece. I remember, I'd seen things like that before they took us to the camp. We're here now, but I still remember what went on in those white churches in the mountains. It was like witchcraft. The woman spoke some words which I didn't understand, in a language I didn't recognize. And the way she swivelled her body made me shiver like a duck. She didn't even notice me, though; she looked right through me as she kept on with her kind of dance.

"Her tears and the man's mean smile scared me even more. Then, as her face hovered over Miriam's, her earrings fell on the child's face, along with her tears, face powder, and rouge. She was in a trance. I've seen trances like that on the boat we came on. There was one man from India who said he could revive any wretch from the dead for a fee of sardines and a bowl of soup. With everyone almost fainting in steerage in that stifling ship, a witch like him came in handy. As the woman kept dancing, the man started to cry, which made me stop hating him. But Miriam was still not breathing. I have never been scared like that before.

"Remember the photograph on the wall, you know the one, near the closet, the young man by the sea, a faded photo, I once saw you cleaning the glass, a lovely boy with gorgeous eyes. Miriam began to choke, the man panicked, he even got more scared than I was, because suddenly Miriam looked like she wasn't from our planet, as if she were an alien from outer space. Her eyes were bulging. Only a year and a few months old, but she already looked grown up. Maybe she'd been transported to where that woman was from, because they both looked alike, as if they both understood where Miriam had been to. I'm telling you now what I was thinking then, when I was frightened out of my wits. Then Miriam crawled towards the photograph and stood up, while the woman watched, as though everything had been planned ahead of time. Miriam took down the photograph, put it on her belly, and started to shimmy and sway, she and the photograph, her eyes wild and wicked like the woman's. It scared me as I watched from the next room.

"The woman had almost no make-up on her now. She shoved the man away. He backed up, went outside, then tried to come near her again, but she shoved him away once more. Boy was he furious – at all of us! 'Look what you got me into, little girl,' he said to me, as though I'd tried to harm him. He just happened to be around, hiding in the bougainvillaea, when I'd got scared. Then, the two of them, your daughter and that woman, started laughing. I mean crying and laughing in a disgusting way, and hugging each other. Your daughter was hugging that woman as though she was the one who had saved her instead of me. The man started up his cab. I watched from the window as the car moved slowly at first, then zoomed away.

"The woman yelled at me to get out, she didn't need me any more. I told her, 'Look, I'm babysitting for Mr Krieger's daughter.' But Miriam looked at me without as much as a smile of recognition, even though she'd always been glad to see me. So I came outside. I'm telling you, Miriam isn't the same child!"

From that day on Nina took care of Miriam, as though

she'd given birth to her right there in that room on that carpet. But she never either denied or confirmed that the man in the cab was Reuben. I resumed my army duties, while Nina and my daughter became incredibly devoted to each other. When my father died during a heatwave, my mother refused to remain in the apartment any longer; she wanted to live in the Clinic, near the Magen David Adom. Seeing the tragedies of others allowed her to imagine that her own turn had been postponed for the time being. Although she had taken her husband's death as a sign that she herself would be spared for a while, she still didn't want to take any chances.

I put up the money for the apartment on Ben Yehuda Street and we all moved in. Miriam was three years old when we settled into the home I had known in my youth. The day we arrived, Miriam met little Nina in the lot opposite us, which was vacant then. And they were inseparable until the day little Nina died. Meanwhile Madame Frau grieved over my father. I started to take his place every morning on the balcony, and like him would insult her. In one of our morning conversations, Madame Frau once said, "I was in a séance yesterday; somebody you don't know, Mr Haim's neighbour from Berlin, told me he bumped into Miriam there, where he lives, among the dead, but she returned somehow to life." Like the innocent I was, I laughed.

I didn't know that Nina had resumed her great romance with Reuben or that she had renewed her friendship with the Chief of Staff when she had turned into a mother and a loving devoted wife. She did the housekeeping, and coped with living with a man whose time was spent mostly on sofas, at the front, on retaliatory raids, in Gaza, the Six Day War, border skirmishes and the Yom Kippur War. She had to fill a tremendous void, and she did it with Miriam. Suddenly, despite my love for her, I was stricken by what she had decided to call "emotional sterility", an unexpected need to disengage myself from her and follow my own concerns and consider my own work the most important thing in my life; to do without her or Miriam and to become a robot, somewhat dry, incapable of maintaining any deep, human connections, only capable of becoming involved with myself and the army, cutting everything else out of my life, not even noticing that she existed.

Nina was as strong as she was fragile. When I came home at night to her, she was good to me. I loved being with her then, protected and protecting. She no longer talked about going to America, about Christian children. She had completed three years of a university correspondence course; then, after a branch school was established in Abu Kabir, she travelled there by bus and studied with uncharacteristic discipline. Since I felt that I could always turn the switch on and she would be mine again, I missed what she really saw in me and didn't see that together with Miriam, she was spinning a web for me all the time. Unlike Reuben, who had dropped out of my life, Nina and Miriam, I now know, never once did that. Nina and I were an amazing couple. Reuben may have known what Nasser had for breakfast and what his bowel movement was like, or what colour underwear the ruler of Iraq wore, but he never understood the peace which Nina found in my warm idiotic loyalty.

Nina apparently saw in me the kind of enemy she needed. Her suffering, which gave her joy, wasn't dressed up or adorned, but bitter. Her love was full of dark corners and desires which she had brought with her from places I couldn't recognize. Her devotion to me was like a translation that always leaves out something crucial, making the text indecipherable. I was born by the sea in a luminous town full of balconies, sour cream and bananas, water-melon, ice-cream and falafel, lacking any profound investigation into mysteries or the secrets of forests, Nazi soldiers, and two thousand years of Jewish history constituting the longest volume of tears.

Perhaps our game scared me, but I was sold on it; it gave me strength, turning me into what I once dreamed of becoming as a child, a Hebrew soldier, a Hebrew knight, all on account of Nina. Perhaps *only* on account of her. Daring and bold in lost battles, trained for survival and deceit by a woman with a battered soul instead of by the heroes of our indigenous Israeli past, our underground movement for self-defence and the rebuilding of our nation, or even back to Bar Kochba's revolt against the Romans. Rabbi Yohanan Ben Zakkai, who had fled besieged Jerusalem in a coffin, was more like her, and therefore more like Joseph Krieger too, a bold champion in the midst of defeat, rather than Bar Kochba who, in one sweeping Wagnerian act, had brought disaster, however glorious, on the Jewish nation. From Nina I learned a sad lesson, full of unimaginable entanglements; I was the raw flesh behind the lovely skin on whose behalf all those friends of Noam would regularly demonstrate for peace in Kings of Israel square. I once told Nina that the Americans killed the Indians like John Wayne and then, three hundred years later, were as remorseful as Marlon Brando, whereas we Israelis have tried to play both roles, Wayne and Brando, at the same time and on one field of battle. She said I was just using fancy words to cover the fact that my work was dirty, but history would ultimately judge whether what I had accomplished was a breakthrough or a waste of time. "Let's wait then," I said, "but in the meantime I must provide Miriam with a safe place in which to grow up."

Nina's insanity looked more like a ritual, part of a rigid game, though occasionally carefree and festive. It was years before she complained about the way Miriam would sit before the photograph of the dead soldier and recite her words of love to it. It pained her. And she tried to get me to put a stop to what I considered the fruits of her own mental illness. But Miriam's conduct also calmed Nina; perhaps she saw it as a playful sign of her victory over me. Yet another victory and example of her control.

Miriam was a gifted child. Other children were drawn to her. She had a natural talent for leadership and a deep grasp of morality, as if her conscience had absolute pitch. After Little Nina had died, Delilah the dog replaced Little Nina as her love. They slept in the same bed. When I returned at night from work, I would look at her and think to myself, "It's hopeless, she has learned from Nina how to torment and oppose me." But I myself didn't know how to approach her and say the right words, how to initiate something and really get close to her. Nina had robbed me of her love and I behaved like a spanked child retreating into his own shell. Miriam made fun of me, saying, "Don't beg so much for love, Joseph, it's either there or it isn't. That's why I can't kiss you."

The Chief of Staff came by one evening. I'd just returned from an exercise in the Galilee with the vial of tears from the cave I'd discovered. The two of us were still friends then, even though we were starting to go our separate ways because of our endless arguments over what the army should become or look like. The Chief of Staff was not yet in any critical position of authority and couldn't withhold something from me which was in his power to give. Now he brought along a bottle of vodka which we both drained. He embraced little Miriam, giggled with Nina. A complicated man now middle-aged, self-involved, rising up the ranks without actually fighting in the field, a fear of settling down still deep inside him as in our youth. Drunk on vodka, he said to me, "Reuben is a prince of traitors, and you are excessively loyal. Don't you understand that Miriam loves you and is proud of you but needs Nina more, or that Nina by her nature will always oppose you despite her love? No matter how great your love for each other is, Miriam has to decide between you two, and that's too difficult for her. You keep giving her a tough choice. You must leave her out of your struggles. You were her mother for a year and two months. But when she needed a father, you weren't there. The freedom you give her works against you. It scares her. You cannot be the hero who rescues her from yourself. She needs rules, limits, a strong hand, which you don't give her. To each and every soldier under you, you impart the feeling that you are somebody important, but not to her." For some reason I couldn't bear to hear what he was saying. I was afraid for my daughter's future. I couldn't forget the fury with which she'd buried the dog Delilah, the coffin she herself had made, her eulogy at night, as if it had been directed at me for holding on to God too closely.

So I went to see Madame Frau.

Madame Frau advised me to have a full-blown wedding ceremony with my daughter. She said she'd had such a

114

ceremony with her father once which lasted all her life, until my father came along. "But he didn't invalidate my marriage to my father," she said, "just as I didn't invalidate his marriage to your mother who, in the meantime, has passed away," she added with a smile that looked forced. "You must have a rabbi, perhaps a Reform one, they're liberal, in order to tie Miriam down and hit her hard as though you were hitting an enemy, then marry her. Maybe you should use a dog as rabbi instead, or a lion," and she giggled.

I told her she sounded like Nina, whereas I was from Tel-Aviv, rough, pieced together from the sand, the shore, from the aroma of lemon and sweet basil, all the intoxicating citruses, that I didn't understand magic, witchcraft, abracadabra. Madame Frau answered, "That's your generation's problem, you're not Jews any more and you're not anything else either. Just new, something cheap, without backbone, people of wood, sand, rock, without manners, screams, greenness, without genuine magic, fear, despair or pride in your eyes."

She herself looked like Nina's double. I was flabbergasted. Now I understood why my father remained with his wife whom he didn't love, whom he actually despised; he too had something to be frightened of in Madame Frau. She looked like Miriam when I couldn't understand her. Without warning, Miriam would turn into a total stranger, her mother's daughter. I feared for myself and for her, and looked into her eyes which she'd inherited from her mother, and saw two thousand years of suffering; while her face, excluding her eyes, showed no pain. I saw a tremendous abyss in her, meaningless and merciless, a politeness to the point of stubborn indifference. I also saw, well-hidden, her wantonness. Was she out to break me? Why? What for? I didn't know. I never understood any of the women in my life; when I gawked at them like a fool, they laughed, giggling in confusion and pain. In their eyes I was both an ogre and a darling, their contempt for me was drawn from the depths of their womanhood. Miriam seemed more and more connected to Nina's world, to her mystery, her calmly grinding craziness.

115

I didn't want to think about all this, or about Miriam's apparent romance with the soldier who'd died two years before she was born. To me, it all smacked of dangerous idolatry. "I won't marry my own daughter," I told Madame Frau, and she answered, "You are a coward. You are brave only in war, not in life. Nina and Miriam can make mincemeat of you. I once asked your father why he didn't leave your mother and marry me if she was such an idiot, and he said, 'About life, Fräulein, I know almost nothing. But about marriage I know enough for the two of us.'"

Nina, hearing the end of our conversation, asked, "Why did you go to her? To hear again that Reuben is Miriam's father?" I said that I was trying to understand hatred. Nina replied, "It offers more than love does! I don't rely on your love, Joseph. I rely on your inability to be unfaithful to me. My whole childhood was one long betrayal. I'm an expert in it. On the other side of your war is not the Arabs but what I brought with me. Your rifle, Joseph, is pointing at me." I slapped her. She wept. Suddenly I realized, with profound grief, that she and Miriam were all I had. "Yes," she said, "you and Reuben think strength is sexy, just like the soldiers over there with their image of themselves as noble savages. Your mothers created here a model Hebrew soldier, a Jewish Aryan! That's your magic, you aren't afraid of death. To you death is a turn-on. From whom do you think Miriam learned to love death? It's not death you're scared of but life, me. Miriam is really your mirror image, she learned the awful enchantment of death from you. Your devotion to death was born out of your many battles, out of your abstinence! You are death's true poet, Daddy."

Then Madame Frau came out with a judgment which I don't think I'll ever forget. In her flowery German, she said, "Joseph Krieger, you were always like the day to Miriam, you have what the day has, a smile, courage, good heart, cheer, pristine innocence, integrity. Nina has what the night has, the dark side of the moon. When night comes, Miriam marries death. During day, she's the daughter of an officer, Brigadier Joseph, the good man of authority. At night she burns at the stake, as I did when a Turkish eunuch took me to Sweden, and from there to Palestine. In the day, Miriam is married to you. But when I told you to marry her at night, you were scared, you didn't understand that Miriam, come night, is death's bride. You think that Nina is the source of your solidarity as a soldier, your fantastic loyalty to the truth. But your truth is only a small part of the whole. Nina, Miriam and I can see another truth, or perhaps we are forced to see it. Here you are Sabras, you have falafel with pitta, heatwaves. You don't grasp the nightmares we brought here with us. Miriam is grafted on two trees. One branch is old and rotten, but beautiful; the other is young and healthy, but ugly, utterly unappealing. You may be clever or special, even deep, but all you really know is battles and bullets, though on the sly, in the Beirut operation, I'm told, you once pretended you were a woman, or maybe you're not the one and some other man was. But you were there once, back then, I know all about it. So what can happen to Miriam? It's all your fault, and you don't even know it."

9

REUBEN'S secretary left me hanging on the telephone for almost an hour. All I heard was whispers as I smoked one cigarette after another, and I finally hung up. I sat fuming, and waited. Naomi looked at me as if she couldn't believe what she saw, as if she had no appreciation for the way my throat had dried up on me like toast. At last Reuben called back, perhaps to show me who was the adult between us and who the child. In his coldest voice he said, "So what exactly do you want, Joseph?"

"You know what I want. Nina's bound to come across the story in some newspaper and that won't be so nice. I'm asking you to find her."

"My secretary was following the computer's old instructions," he said. "At the name Joseph Krieger a red blotch shows up. I'll have to update the computer. You're no idiot," he added, "you must realize that even if I think you're a bastard, I won't sit still and let Miriam get hurt. But you probably called because the nitwit Chief of Staff suggested it; he checked first with my deputy. He himself wants to know where Nina is. So do I, Joseph. But if you think that we're going to be friends again just because Miriam's in trouble, you're deluding yourself."

"Rube," I said, and it was the first time in more than twenty-five years that I'd called him Rube, "I must know where Nina is. Find her for me. You're the only one who can, and you know it."

It was a try-on, and I must have come off foolishly, but it led to his sounding a bit human. "I'm everybody's last resort," he laughed.

118

"That's right," I said, handing myself over to him on a silver platter, or rather on a meat hook.

Once, on a mission to Paris under an assumed name, dressed like a Bohemian, as I was leaving the hotel with three Parisians who thought I was an Israeli leftist, the Frenchmen began openly condemning Israel while I even defended Moshe Dayan, with whom I was in bitter disagreement at that time. A few months later the Chief of Staff called to say, "Rube informs me that you were sitting in a taxi in Paris at two in the morning defending Moshe Dayan against three bastards."

"You have the upper hand on all of us," I told Reuben. "Do something. If you know when Hussein masturbates, you can also find Nina." He shouted back, "Who told you he masturbates?"

That broke the ice between us, but we were both too proud to admit it. I thought back to the days years ago when Reuben acknowledged that he'd learned something from me when I'd told him that everything we were doing went back to the myth of the stranger; every foreigner had to carry some secret, and every secret had to involve some stranger. I knew that Reuben wouldn't disappoint me now, even if I was afraid of what he might find out.

When my house was finally empty of all those guests who were always streaming in, I took a quick shower and emerged naked as Naomi was sweeping the floor outside Miriam's room. She blushed, burst into a short laugh, and said, "Sir, you look great barefoot but others might not agree." I covered myself with the towel and approached her; her smile froze, her eyes opened wide, and she suddenly began to cry huge silent tears which stretched across her face like strands of gleaming silk. In the dim light of the corridor, her eyes glowed with unexpected sweetness and feeling, as if she understood and accepted me without any reservations. I took her in my arms. Perhaps my thinking of Nina had made me feel even lonelier. Naomi let me hug her but didn't respond, as if an invisible barrier separated us. I felt foolish, ashamed, and backed off from her. "It'll be okay, Joseph," she said, in a voice I almost couldn't recognize. "I'll take care of you." She looked as though she were light years away, and I felt slighted far more than I had a right to be. "Everything's going to be fine," she repeated, closing her eyes for a moment, and stroking that portion of her body I had embraced, like a blind person feeling for something lost.

I screamed, as if I'd been caught in a net, "I need my daughter! It's not fair, she couldn't just vanish into thin air and leave a thousand question marks but not a single landmark!"

Naomi reached out and massaged the back of my neck; I rested my head in her hands, but I was still tense, bewildered by the way she had pulled back from me. She looked at me tenderly, in fearful pain. She seemed familiar to me again. And I said, in panic, "You can't count on me, Naomi. I am a broken reed." She laughed, "You come from a lost generation, but at least you sound great." She looked as though she had just walked out of a nightmare. "What words, what confessions, they just kill me," and she went back to sweeping with her broom with redoubled fervour.

I left for Blumenfeld's Pharmacy, where the last of the Germans from my street stood around and looked at me. Naturally, I was obliged to step on to the old scale, play with the weights until the beam was perfectly still, then announce, "Sixty-six kilos." Old Mr Goldman, who had cut my hair from the time I was six until about a year and a half ago when he'd gone out of business – and since then I hadn't found anybody to replace him – now inspected me with those penetrating, watery eyes of his, with that concentrated expert glance he used when he would back away from the chair, one eye shut, and study my head from a distance as if he were Leonardo da Vinci and I Mona Lisa, and then with one decisive but creative action, beautiful to behold, give me the typical Israeli haircut which he had given me for forty-two consecutive years. Goldman, who knew only four haircuts but played the artist with a charming seriousness, now said softly, "You must be going to some hair-stylist, there are no more barbers anywhere, only hair-stylists." He sounded bitter. "Goldman," I said, "since you retired I have nowhere else to go." He looked pleased. Then everybody felt free to talk all at once. They had simply waited for my usual conversation with Goldman and my traditional weighing-in. They all said how sorry they were, acknowledging how difficult it was to find a missing person, and they offered to help me. Miriam was their child too, their "little daughter", they said, their eyes filled with love and torment. After all, I had grown up on their knees.

Mr Blumenfeld asked me now in his soft voice if I needed any pain-killers, and he smiled his shy smile. "Gustav," I said, "I need perfume, the best you have," and they all laughed. The earlier moment of embarrassment was gone. Nobody could believe that in Israel people could just vanish, certainly not a Brigadier's daughter. As I blushed, they smiled even more, their crooked gold-filled teeth gleaming for a moment in the flashes of light from the street. Blumenfeld looked in his glass cabinet, picked out a perfume, and refused to take any money. When I insisted, he said loudly to that group of old-timers who regularly, except for Madame Frau, congregated every day here towards evening, "With the money your mother sank into this pharmacy for over forty years, you could build Buckingham Palace in the desert, that's just for medicine she needed; but from the money she spent on medicines for diseases she didn't have, I could build even more." Everybody laughed, with the exception of ancient Mrs Brime who protested, maybe out of her fundamental distrust in life, or out of friendship to my dead mother. "But she died in the end," she said. "And nobody dies healthy. She died from a sickness she had, so how do you know which pills she didn't need, maybe she needed all of them?"

Nobody bothered to answer her. Not one of them really liked my mother and secretly believed that she would live forever. After all, who could die while living in a Clinic next to a Magen David Adom, where a doctor would come for her slightest ache? As my thoughts turned to Miriam, their faces clouded again and they looked the way they had when I'd first arrived unexpectedly. They, the last of the downtrodden, were still amazed at the slapdash, rapid resettlement of Israel. The white Berlin which they had built in their youth here was already played out, but they still yearned for it. They were lodgers for the night in a hostile land now full of Turks and Persians. "Everywhere you go you see Turks and Persians," said Goldman, as if he had read my mind. "You used to walk down Huberman Street and smell German cakes and whipped cream on every corner."

It started to rain. I rushed home. For the first time Naomi was wearing a dress. When I handed her the perfume she paled. "No, no," she whispered, but in the end accepted. She dabbed some on the back of her hand, which she then offered me with a touch of coquetry. It smelled sweet and delicate.

"At my age I have to buy women with French perfume."

She looked as if she wanted to throw the bottle at me, but she didn't. I was happy to see again some of the old domestic drama which Miriam's disappearance had put a stop to. She said, "You know, this is my first perfume."

The next morning, Reuben called just as I was on my way to the pool. I hadn't swum for several days and wanted to return to my old routine. "You realize, of course, he said, "that we don't ordinarily get involved in personal problems like which French perfume a retired army officer in reserves should buy for a girl young enough to be his daughter." I didn't answer, just waited, letting his cruelty pass over me no matter how much it hurt. "Listen," he continued, "if you ever tell Nina who gave you her telephone number, you're *history*," and he laughed at the force of his own word, but didn't take it back. As he gave me the number, his voice sounded almost friendly, and then he hung up.

Naomi left the house. Now that the rain, which poured all night long, had stopped, Czeszek came by to give me the latest information on his investigation. He sat down, passing his hairy hand over his nearly bald head, saying, "We have something new on how well Hanoch Levi knew Miriam. Basically he has an excellent alibi. I can't take any drastic measures against him. Miriam could be in hiding; maybe she's lost her way or her memory.

We can't pin any crime on Hanoch because as far as we know nothing has happened yet. But anyway I'm on his trail. The religious soldier Yossi got sudden orders from his sergeant-major to go home. That sergeant-major was a close friend of Miriam's and she says Miriam knew that Yossi would return because she needed him for some gig she was putting on in Yeroham, but the sergeant-major didn't know what the hell it was. One of the soldiers under Miriam's command didn't know what the gig was all about either, but she found Yossi's name on Miriam's bulletin board. I drove down there and checked. What she'd written was, 'Yossi, soldier, sergeant-major Yeroham, re *I love, you love, we love, they love*.' According to the testimony of female soldiers in her office," said Czeszek, "Miriam had many conversations with Joy. Joy has definitely been hiding something." When I explained to Czeszek the meaning of the grammar of love, he shrugged his shoulders, thought for a moment, and said, "Somebody has taken a lot of trouble to give us a lot of false leads. But don't worry, it'll be okay, we'll get to the bottom of it. Be patient. They always make one small slip-up."

After the newspapers had begun publishing articles on the incident, a senior officer from the Military Police Investigation Department protested against these disclosures at a newspaper party. But the Chief of Staff didn't make any response to them. That afternoon, I telephoned Nina.

For two years we hadn't spoken to each other, yet Nina didn't act surprised at the sound of my voice. All her answers seemed prepared in advance. I told her I'd promised Reuben not to say who gave me her number. She laughed so loudly that I had to pull the phone from my ear, but her laughter vibrated all the way up my hand.

"That's very nice of him," she said. "He also found me a suite in this hotel. If he didn't have such a high position, I'd say that he probably gets a commission from every customer he brings in here." From her tone I recognized that she felt frightened and caught. Whenever she was insecure, her laughter fumbled, as if she'd swallowed it. Miriam hated that laugh, it made her scream and argue and look for weak points to attack, only to end up crying in sheer guilt and pain. I told her about Miriam's disappearance, suspecting that I was wasting words on her. I tried to speak in a calm even voice, which was something I was used to. After the Yom Kippur War Joy and I had to lie to grieving parents, telling them it was forbidden to release any details, it was too early, but we were stalling for time until the telex would inform them. I spoke like a hollow man, and Joy was as tough as nails. For a long while Nina was totally silent, then she said in a cold voice which sounded forced yet sprightly, "I got a letter from Miriam in which she says she dreamed that she disappeared and you were looking for her at the crossroads. She wrote she'd gone to the port of Jaffa, bought balloons, sailed on a fisherman's boat and set all the balloons free. Her letters were never so orderly as this one; usually the pages come mixed up. When did you say she disappeared?"

"On the twenty-first of January," I said, not sure that I could still speak.

"That's interesting," she said. "I just got another letter from her. Let me go and get it . . . Here, it's dated the twenty-first of January. She talks about some family in Ekron whose son is a security guard at her base . . . whom she visits a lot, tells them crazy stories . . . the Chief of Staff helped her place the mother in a hospital for treatment."

"What letters are you talking about?" I asked, trying to maintain some self-control while feeling that I was about to collapse. I had never shaken like this in my whole life. A cold sweat poured down my neck.

Nina said, "Didn't you know that she and I have been corresponding regularly?"

"I thought she had cut off all contact with you. She used to make fun of me for wearing the Mexican sweater you sent me. I myself saw her burn your letters."

In a tranquil, beautiful voice filled with vindictiveness, as if she had waited a long while for this moment, Nina answered, "We've been corresponding for almost a year, in addition to talking on the phone. From your hysterical response, I assume you didn't know that. She's some bastard, that daughter of yours."

"She's missing," I said.

"Like hell she's missing!" screamed Nina, the mother of my daughter, who the moment she raised her voice, her defences dropped and she became as vulnerable as a butterfly's wing.

"She's missing, Nina."

She kept quiet, and I felt that her silence was her way of being considerate since every word she spoke was full of contempt for me. "Reuben found her for me," she said. "He arranged a telephone conversation between us. Ask him. She did burn my letters at first, but Reuben didn't want that to continue and, you know, he usually gets his way. For example, we two are talking on the phone on account of him. Who do you think is paying my hotel bill? It's amazing how little you still understand. Perhaps you've worked too hard. All that laundering, house-cleaning, sweeping, and cooking schnitzels has fried that wild, noble brain of yours. The great soldier has turned into a subservient slave."

I didn't pick up her challenge. Instead I questioned her about Miriam's boat ride, but she evaded me skilfully. When I asked her for any news whatsoever that she might have, Nina said, "Maybe Reuben just wanted to make you suspicious, Joseph. Precisely because he knows that until you and I learn to live together, Miriam will remain a lost soul. Out of Reuben's hatred, good things may yet come." I insisted she tell me something. She said, "If you weren't so puffed up with pride, you would have acted like any normal father, Joseph. You would already have searched her room, gone through all the drawers, cupboards, opened her letters, all of which you consider beneath you, but you would have found my letters to her and my address and telephone number in San Francisco, the phone number and address of this hotel in New York, Joseph. If you thought your daughter was missing, why haven't you turned into a wounded animal and hunted for every scrap of paper that might lead you to her? Is it because you yourself know she's not a missing person even if you don't know her exact whereabouts? It's time to stop acting like a knight in armour and behave like a

125

normal, despicable human being, like your best friends, the other two Musketeers, eh?"

"I don't know, Nina," I said. "But didn't she write anything else about the boat ride, or Didi, Noam, the fisherman? I didn't want to worry you when it happened, but Miriam's gone. She disappeared not far from the Bet-Lid Junction. It looks like she was heading for the old border. I'm alone now. What do I have left? I once had you, but not any more. I had Miriam once, but no more. I don't even have the army any more. You're gone, Miriam's missing, the army's over. And I'm without friends. As you used to say, all I have is my illusions. Miriam has vanished without a trace. Come back, Nina. I think you're involved in this. But you're a big girl now and will do what you think is right."

"What about the female soldier in your bed?" said Nina with a sneer that told me I had got to her somehow, and even scared her. "And what about all of your old comrades? Your home has become their command post again. Joseph, you beat up the wrong people in Jaffa, people who might have been able to help you. When the right moment comes, I'll show up." Suddenly switching to a cordial tone, she added, "Look, I'm sure she's fine. She tells me everything in her letters, all there is to tell, and Reuben keeps me informed too, so why look for trouble? Cool it!"

"Nina," I said. "Somebody's lying to you. Somebody's doing a job on both of us. I have no idea how you knew about the fight at Jaffa or the balloons, and I know you won't tell, but believe me, one thing is clear. Whoever planned all this botched it. There are too many loose ends. It didn't happen the way it was supposed to. Miriam's definitely missing; I'm very worried about her. My intuition is better than Reuben's. That female soldier is not my bedmate, she's my homemaker. But if she ever comes into my bed it'll be because I have it coming to me. You clever fool, your heart knows what your head and your Reuben won't let you admit. Listen, don't be so cocky. Come and see for yourself. It'll make things easier for both of us. If Miriam is still alive."

126

"She's alive," she screamed. "Don't push me, Joseph, you're history!" Then my wife Nina started crying, not so sure of herself after all, and hung up.

It was already dark outside, and a misty rain was falling. I raced towards Jaffa, crazily weaving in and out of traffic. I questioned the fishermen again, showed Jahash Reuben's photograph and Jahash remembered seeing him at the port with somebody, but couldn't say when; they were talking to Noam. I went to the fish restaurant, to see Shabtai, who remembered seeing the man in the photograph eating a fish steak with a beautiful woman who drank her tea with a lot of mint leaves. Nina said she had learned about the boat ride from Miriam, but how could Miriam have described the incident a week before it happened? Maybe it never happened? But Jahash was there, and I found the beret which the lab said was hers.

I went back home, drank a quarter of a bottle of brandy; Naomi wasn't around, I sat in total darkness, except for a spider's web of light coming from the heater. I called Reuben, who answered the phone immediately before the first ring had ended. He always sounded as if he had been waiting for your call; sitting by the phone and waiting to pick it up, to hear that one of his hundred agents had been wasted, some of them on his own orders.

"Hello, rat," I said.

"You're funny," he answered, "very funny. But didn't I warn you not to tell Nina how you got her number?" His mockery practically poured out of the receiver.

"You slippery eel," I said. "You knew the whole time, you knew everything but wanted me to twist in the wind. Never mind, have your fun, watch me fall apart. That's all you want from me anyway."

"You're absolutely right," he said coldly, as if our forty years of friendship only meant that if he decided to have me hung by the neck, he'd use a silken rope.

"If you could look into the receiver," I said, "you'd see a broken man. What more do you want, a canteen of blood? You were the one who started that slander. Now you've got a million contacts, you make and break governments, waste agents, dance on the graves of your enemies like a

127

prima ballerina, and you're just waiting to turn Naomi into another sexual conquest of yours like Nina. How many thousands of legs have you spread apart just to prove that you haven't lost your touch? You're rotten through and through, Reuben. I don't know why you still bother to keep me on such a short leash even when I'm loaded with brandy. And I can't figure out why, even now, after you sent me out to die on a mine field, after all your sadistic conduct from then until now, I still care about you?"

That upset him. I hadn't said what he had expected me to; I hadn't cursed him after all these years. My affection for him, like his for me, now made it difficult for him to pursue his cruel scheme against me.

He didn't say a word, which was very unusual for Reuben, as I finished another cigarette and watched the flames of the heater sputter for no reason and then resume their steady, tranquil state. Finally, after several minutes, he said in his lonely voice that hadn't lost any of its aggression, "Don't tell me you still think that chivalry is alive and well and worth something nowadays? You're breaking my heart, Joseph."

He tried to sound cruel and arrogant, but I knew him well enough to realize that what hurt him was that he actually longed to embrace his Joseph.

I could sense his suppressed decency as he said, "You think I'm not worried too? But why get Nina all hysterical?" Then he growled coarsely, to camouflage his anger at himself, "Today you're nothing, Joseph, a nonentity, nobody, zero, on reserves, inactive, *passé*, a toy soldier. Don't get smart with me, you're not in my league. Your brawn is no match against my brain. In any war it's wits that count. Nina was the love of my life and still is. So what if you gave her a daughter? When she was in trouble, even when she wanted to re-enlist in the army, did she go to you? You were too busy. You considered a daughter a doll you wind up once in a while for her to tell you her name and serial number. Your main concern was your own struggle of conscience, for which you thought the nation would salute you. But I kept Miriam in the palm of my hand, while you carried your medals on your masculine chest. Down in the sewer where I've been living all these years, a daughter is the most important thing in the world, worth more than the daily question, 'What happened to you today, Miriam?' You were the military lead in a film for children, Joseph, but the wars were really won in the sewer, my sewer, between a thousand pairs of legs, as you put it. While you were subjecting yourself to a dose of conscience, sweetheart, Miriam came to me when that viper, the Chief of Staff, advised her to re-enlist. She wanted to escape her empty life, her always being up in the air, without a mother, without a father, or in between the two of you. She also wanted to escape the art school you thought was so good for her. What did you ever know about her? Nothing! I don't think anything bad has happened to her, everything can be explained, but if there's been some foul-up in her plans and she's really in trouble, I'll be the one to find her, not you and your Investigating Military Police. Just me as always. If not for the possibility of harm to her, I'd tell you a few things about your daughter's life which you have no sense of whatsoever. Your only concern was that she come home on time, have a good night's sleep, and eat the schnitzels you fry for her in oil which is probably giving her cancer. And do you suppose that Nina came to me because she had it so easy with her loyal man of conscience? You're ridiculous. But, damn you, Joseph, I've been sinking in the same boat with you and the Chief of Staff ever since you took me along with you to the transit camps, to Nina, to all that garbage. Three Musketeers marching towards Nina to ask her whom she'd like to spend the rest of her life with. She picked all three of us. Understand? She had three husbands and a year later one daughter, who was yours not hers. For the moment you possessed what we two didn't, a daughter – she's definitely yours, Joseph, it's written all over her face – and a certified marriage. But as for the rest, you're still learning about that. The rest is history, it hasn't taught you anything, and it's getting late. Maybe too late. It's certainly too late for you to change, Joseph, into another person. All you can do is vanish, put a bullet in your thick skull, which is probably what all your women would like you to do, even Naomi. Ask her about Isaac Raphaeli, and why she hasn't told you how she knows him."

Instead of answering, I poured some more brandy. Reuben had time on his hands, and I time to kill. We were like two halves of one empty world. Maybe he was sitting in total darkness too, except for the flames coming from a small solitary heater.

"What about Jaffa, and Noam?" I asked.

"He knew something, but when you attacked him, he fled. He'd been waiting for you to show up, but you came Hollywood style; instead of using common sense with him you used special effects."

"Reuben, where is he now? You must know where Noam is. And what's the last name of the security guard at Miriam's base? When I called, they said he wasn't working there any more. Somebody is pulling strings."

"Jahash?" laughed Reuben. "From Ekron? You're going round in circles and won't accomplish anything. His name is Simontov. Noam's last name is Raphaeli. Noam Raphaeli, Ramat-Gan, Street of the Seven, number ten."

I remembered the soldier in the photograph, Isaac Raphaeli, whose parents I'd visited at that address. Noam was his brother. Their mother was an English teacher. I felt as if I was choking. If Naomi had been around, I would have strangled her to save myself. I hung up and sat in darkness, waiting for the chance to tell Naomi off. I wanted to visit Noam's parents again, but I couldn't move or think straight. Czeszek came in all of a sudden without knocking, and sat beside me in the dark, putting his heavy, hairy arm around me and looking at me with a pain on his face which I'd never seen there before. Then the lights went on as Naomi and Gideon entered. I stared aghast at them, the brandy and cigarettes burning my throat. They looked like two sad orphans.

"Something's happened, Sir," said Czeszek. "Get hold of yourself. Try to take it calmly. We found some articles of Miriam's clothing on Mount Carmel, and also –"

"Her body?"

"No, not yet," said Czeszek, with total authority but

without feeling.

"Newsmen are snooping around downstairs," said Naomi.

Then for the first time in my life I was carried out like a stone, my feet no longer touching the ground. The mystery was finally solved.

"We'll probably find her body by morning," said Czeszek while driving. "At least she's been found, we know where she is, on Mount Carmel."

Naomi sat beside me in the car, and as we travelled my head sank to my knees.

10

IT was a muddy trek from the car to the thicket on Mount Carmel. Naomi stayed a short distance behind us as Czeszek and Gideon cleared sharp branches from the swampy path we took. I felt as if I were heading for my own sacrifice. Now that the brandy had evaporated, my insides were empty. Soldiers were there, border police, officers. We came to a cave which opened on to the dry bed of a small wadi red with anemones. All around us stood low pines and some oak trees; the mud was thick and black, the wind blew from the sea, the hour was late, we had climbed for quite a while to reach this spot. Now, as dawn broke, I finally saw Miriam's blouse. In one pocket was a bus ticket with an indecipherable phone number on it in her handwriting. The Bedouin scout found the tracks of two bare feet and one shoe. There was no indication of a struggle, just crushed leaves and flattened grass – signs of something having been dragged – all of which added up to what the scout called "an unidentifiable but not violent occurrence". Then some drops of blood were spotted on the blouse, but not enough to draw any definite conclusions. The tracks made by the solitary shoe were Miriam's. The scout claimed that she'd been dragged by the person who was barefoot; where to he couldn't tell.

Not far off, among some shrubs, was a military jacket. When a Military Police officer said that it was hard to distinguish one army jacket from another, I said that I knew enough about army clothes to be able to tell that this was Miriam's. It had to be hers because of a few small signs, the pocket with two tiny ink stains which had faded in laundering and the loose button I'd got angry about. "It's got to be hers," I said, and I was swamped again by a cold empty feeling, a lingering suspicion that somehow forced me to become energetic all of a sudden. The Bedouin, one of the best scouts, was somebody I knew from my years of border patrols. He squatted some distance away, his back to me, and smoked, occasionally peering at me with anguish in his eyes. I had been to his village and visited his home and met his children. Ordinarily he could figure out the mother's name of the suspect from his footprints, or tell you what the suspect's stepfather smelled like just by the way a leaf was bent, and how many pockets his trousers had; whereas now he sat dumbfounded, not even knowing why he was so stumped. "I'm very sorry, Sir," he said, "I could give you the book on every infiltrator who crosses the Jordan, but about your daughter nothing. I'm not worth the dirt on your shoe."

Nevertheless, they decided to continue searching for Miriam. The nights were freezing cold. They had brought tents and sleeping bags. The army combed the area inch by inch, cave by cave, grove by grove, until the soldiers were red-eyed from exhaustion. Naomi gathered some twigs, made a fire, and prepared some coffee. Gideon walked around by himself like a depressed self-accusing introvert, and I too started walking by myself. Each one of us had ploughed a few kilometres through that thick grove, the mud up to our knees. The sea sparkled in the moonlight; then soft rain came down and the skies grew dark. But at least the frost slackened. The Chief of Staff arrived, already aware of my conversation with Reuben. He was afraid that we might have set a trap for ourselves, and maybe in the wrong spot, too. Miriam's blouse and jacket, he said, just about put an end to all speculation, but not entirely.

Others came to help us out, farmers and ordinary citizens dressed in wind-breakers, who spent three days with us searching the woods, breaking off sharp branches, dragging themselves through the heavy mud. It became like one huge multi-faceted picnic, with them drinking, smoking, eating, talking, occasionally even laughing. By the second or third day they seemed to forget the reason for their being there in the first place.

I was surprised to find old Sokolowicz in the crowd, dressed in khaki pants and a tattered sweater. He almost wouldn't talk to me, most probably angry over my not having drafted Japanese into the army. No doubt he felt that if I had listened to him, those Japanese would have found Miriam by now. Yet, he gave me a look of pity and patriotic fury for relying upon a Bedouin scout. He climbed up the mountain like a young goat, astonishing everybody. Finally he hugged me, saying, "You'll see, Joseph, we'll find her alive yet and make up for lost time."

On the final day Madame Frau Birnbaum herself showed up, as if the lion she always feared had at last routed her out of her quarters. Dressed in her old but lovely safari suit, she climbed uphill as though her whole life hadn't been spent indoors. Her energy was contagious; everybody started searching all over again with renewed vigour. She and Naomi took to each other in a way that reminded me of what Miriam used to say, that understanding between women, like violence, was a form of courtship.

Then, after Sokolowicz had thrilled at the sight of this spectacular, rare bird in a safari suit which made him long for bygone days, and after the rain had stopped and the soldiers stood around with their eyes half shut from fatigue, Naomi told the whole team of the command post under Czeszek, "As an officer in charge of a platoon, Miriam must have had the keys to the code cabinet which contained everything, particularly the passwords for the reserve forces, and she must have kept her keys on her at all times. If she was taken here by force, she would have got rid of the keys before they stripped her. Miriam must have tossed them somewhere to avoid their capture. Responsibility was second nature to her. Those keys must be around here. Let's find them."

"Miriam didn't have access to top secret documents," said Gideon, "but she certainly had other papers in her cabinet. Naomi's right, Miriam was a disciplined soldier."

It took just one additional day of searching for Madame Frau to find the keys buried deep inside a bush about five hundred metres from where Miriam's jacket had been found. By then some parents of children already missing for a year had also shown up. Our search had received considerable publicity; they'd heard about it on the radio. In their grief, they wanted to instil in me both a certain solidarity, with which I was uncomfortable, and an anger which I simply didn't have. I was still expecting to find Miriam alive. Because of that jacket, I was convinced that somebody was playing with me, somebody who knew Miriam and me well and understood that I would be the only person who could identify the jacket as Miriam's.

To a career soldier the army is home, a peculiar home which plans and organizes murder with the greatest efficiency imaginable. To do so, the army cultivates and prolongs an atmosphere of childhood quite unlike the world outside it. Nobody grows old in the army, they just die suddenly or live forever at the edge of a cliff. It's one big family in which you obey anybody above you and command anybody below you. An almost mystical hierarchy with a stubborn twisted logic. You don't fight in anger; a good soldier never does. Fighting is a misunderstood profession. Every professional soldier may love warfare and can hardly wait for war to occur, but he is trained and committed to preventing his heart's desire from ever happening. The price the soldier has to pay is living in paradise, a paradise of terror and death but one where somebody else is forever in charge of you, knowing who and where you are, and your only worry is your own small assignment. When you just follow orders your hair seldom turns white. As Nina put it, "The army is the closest thing to God." Or at least the Catholic Church, which recognizes that you cannot find free will either in paradise, the army, or the Church, but you can find happiness and peace of mind under the command of an omniscient power which issues and cancels all orders and controls each and every directive; without which nobody in the army would stand a chance. Instead of the mundane every-day headaches, all you had was either total ecstasy or despair, triumph or doom; gone were the endless worries and agonies over income tax and the meaning of life. You had standards, norms, models, and only as much freedom of choice as the computer had, at certain key moments, been programmed for.

With all those people wandering through the woods, and all the campfires at night and the songs, it looked as if we were having a festival on that mountain. But it was Naomi, not my old army friends, who had the idea to look for the keys, and the one who found them was Madame Frau in her safari outfit who had never sat around a campfire before. I had no sympathy for the parents who'd come to complain against any humane attitude towards terrorists. I told them that there was no proof of any terrorist involvement here, that Jewish killers existed too, that we didn't even know if a murder had been committed, and that vengeance was primitive. "I'm a soldier," I said. "None of you are soldiers, but I am."

Sokolowicz looked wide-eyed at Madame Frau and said, "You found them in a bush? How did you do it?" She answered, "That's my business. Shrubs I understand, they can't fool me." Naomi commented, "Look, he's falling in love in his old age." I almost smiled, remembering that I had once tried to arrange a match between them. But I saw now that Naomi became ashamed of herself for joking while Miriam's life hung in the balance, and she went over to Gideon who looked even more desperate than I did, and said, "How could Miriam have stuck those keys into that bush? If others brought her here by force, she must have tossed them away, but how could they have penetrated the bush so deeply? And she couldn't have dropped them from a car window, because no vehicle could get through this thicket."

To Madame Frau in her safari suit, who after forty-four years in mothballs had managed to get herself tanned and covered with leaves and nettles, this mountain was not only a monument to Miriam, whom she understood better than I did, but also the territory where roamed those leopards and lions from German zoos, animals haunted by despair and dreams of a horrifying revenge against one noble woman abandoned in her solitary world by her only lover who had died in a scorching heatwave, a man whose son had somehow managed to leave the army and allow his wife to abandon him and his daughter to vanish as if swallowed up by the earth.

Contrary to all logic, after all, the keys somehow got lodged exactly where Madame Frau had found them. And as Mr Sokolowicz enthusiastically pointed out, she had made a very startling discovery which deserved praise even in strict army terms. "That's the opinion of a corporal," he said, "with seventy-five years of experience."

Gradually the search petered out. The depressing fact was that whatever little we had come up with was all that we would find. Only a few of us remained now. Madame Frau had rushed back home to protect her apartment from harm. There was just Czeszek, Naomi, Gideon and myself. Except for me, everybody was sure of one thing, that Miriam had been kidnapped. But I thought, in fact firmly believed, otherwise – though it's hard to explain why. The whole thing looked like an elaborate cover-up. Why would anybody go to such trouble if Miriam, or at least some valuable object, wasn't in his hands? If so, Miriam was still a hostage somewhere. The military and civilian police would attempt to piece together all their information – from the boat ride, and the sergeant at the television studio, to Miriam's hitch to the Bet-Lid junction. But I knew that I was obliged to follow my own instinct, exactly as somebody had expected me to, and that if Miriam could talk to me now she'd ask me to rescue her the only way I knew how, the unconventional way.

Czeszek and Naomi were kind enough to agree with me. After all, Czeszek was fond of me and a decent man, even though he was tough as nails, a long-time widower and confirmed sceptic whose hardened heart seemed to pump only cynicism. Now he was open to any suggestion, no matter how bizarre, which might link together Miriam's beret with everything else, the story she wrote to her mother, the fisherman Jahash's reaction to her, as well as the role of Joy and Hanoch Levi.

Because of a shift in the wind it was warm as we headed for home, and even by nightfall the skies were perfectly clear despite the drop in temperature. Upstairs, we found the armchairs piled high with loaves of bread, and the refrigerator bursting with pots of tasty-looking food, courtesy of Mr Feigel and his housemaid Yoni.

Once I had sat down, the telephone rang; I didn't have the strength to get up and answer it. Instead, I studied the photograph. But it wasn't until almost an hour later that I realized what I noticed there for the first time: someone else besides Isaac in the photograph. The young girl in the background, in the blurred right-hand corner, looked familiar to me. Isaac stood in the centre, surrounded by faces that were out of focus. Naomi was talking on the phone; I didn't pay attention to what she was saying. She walked back and forth, telephone in hand, her voice low and soft. I couldn't focus. Something was blocking me as a result of my years with Miriam; I'd been trained to turn a deaf ear to what Miriam was saying on the phone and would end up sitting in my room hearing her voice and not catching a single word. Even after my recent conversation with Nina I didn't go searching in Miriam's room for letters because the sole strength of a man like myself resides in his self-restraint. My whole life was one long gruelling preparation for an event which never really happened. The wars that I had fought were just the minor fulfilment of a dream (something to be placed in parentheses); they were never the war I'd wanted. I had never tapped the secret overwhelming capacity for human endurance that I associated with the Battle of Stalingrad, say, a battle which even a veteran soldier like me had never experienced. I had trained myself to be strong, daring, resourceful even going without food or water, such that one day I might meet the challenge, body and soul, of some hopeless struggle. In the end, perhaps out of excessive preparation, I had soured my life.

The sight of Naomi twisting and turning now, walking up and down the corridor, telephone in hand, talking in a low excited voice, trying to control her emotion, was another challenge to me, but for what purpose I had no idea. I swivelled around and looked again at the photograph, hoping to focus my attention elsewhere, when the pale figures surrounding Isaac caught my eye as if they were watching me more than I was watching them, and would soon float right off the photograph into space along with Naomi's voice, which under Miriam's training I could hear but not understand.

Finally the conversation ended, Naomi entered the living room, and said, "Give me a slug of that stuff," grabbing my glass of brandy and taking a quick swallow; then she lit a cigarette, inhaled deeply, and looked at me and at the photograph.

"I don't know how she found me," she said, "or where she popped up from. I thought she'd gone to America. Do you see the girl in that photograph, on the right, you can barely see her, with the funny nose and long hair? That's my sister, Nira. By the way, Joseph, thanks for not questioning me the other day, when I told you I knew the man in the photograph. You looked like you wanted to choke me. I mean it, Joseph, thank you for waiting until the right moment came. What an incredibly foolish but dear guy you are. You kill me!"

I kept quiet, knowing she would have to go on. Naomi couldn't quite smile as she wanted to, but said finally, "Nira is my personal tragedy, Joseph. She was Isaac Raphaeli's girlfriend. Do you know what she told me on the telephone? She accused me of living with, her phrase was sleeping with, the man whose daughter stole her love away from her, the man who was actually responsible for his death. She's already been back from America for two weeks without getting in touch with me. But when she saw me on television in the news coverage of the Mount Carmel search, she had to call me up. She sounds awful, Joseph. Isaac was killed in '53. He was Nira's boyfriend from the time they were sixteen until the day he died. The'd met on a youth movement hike, she the kibbutznik and he the townie, and they fell for each other, exchanging photographs like typical young lovers."

After staring into space and looking lost in thought, Naomi added, "When Gideon joined the search for Miriam, I heard him talking on the phone and recognized your name. Nira had told me about you years ago. You

were a ghost in our family. We have the identical photograph on the wall in our house. After Nira hung it up,
Daddy wanted to take it down, but Mother wouldn't let
him. Even after Father died, she promised Nira she'd
never remove the photograph. At our kibbutz, Mother
always held the moral position like a firebrand. So that
photograph still hangs where it always did. Gideon needed
a sergeant, so I told him, 'How about me?' That's how I
was assigned here, by sheer chance. But all the while, deep
down, I have felt as if I was fated to meet you. I am much
younger than Nira, and when I was a girl she tried to
teach me, her captive audience, to hate you. She would
visit some man whose name I don't remember, a colonel
or a lieutenant-colonel then, now a cabinet minister, your
bitter enemy, who gave her every piece of dirt about you
he could, and she ran to Isaac's parents to tell them all
the news. She told them that Miriam was controlling their
son and robbing them of him. I don't know much about
the parents; I met them only once in Ramat Gan when I
was six. Anyway, Nira went crazy for a while, but it didn't
last. We were never close even when she tried to pour her
poison into me. Do you remember asking me the first time
I was here if I could love you? I told you that I loved you
from the day I was born. Do you remember?"

"And do you really love me, Naomi?"

"Yes," she said, blushing and she stopped talking. She
peered at me, reached out her hand, and said, "But not
now, we have more important things to figure out." She
looked so dear, so soulful, that I said, "You're a beautiful
creature." That made her confused, but she liked the
compliment and she gazed at me even more tenderly.
I thought to myself, what do I know about love? I have
loved one woman, and that woman is embedded so deeply
inside me that I could never get her out of me.

"Not now, Joseph," she said, "not now; please understand, it's a question of life and death. My sister called
me a killer's whore, that's what she called me. Look," she
went on, "I didn't come here with good intentions. I wasn't
interested in Miriam, I didn't even realize she was missing.
When Gideon and I first came we waited for you, then

140

you showed up by yourself, remember, and stood facing us downstairs? I never saw anybody look so lonely in my whole life. You looked like some commander on a hill surveying his final defeat, the way I picture God, only lonelier, a degraded hero. You lost not just a daughter, but your whole existence. If you couldn't get her back, you were as good as dead. And I knew I hadn't found that murderer my sister had always clamoured about, but the man I could take unto myself as my own lover. I became totally yours, a prisoner of your loneliness, addicted to your mixed messages, your 'Don't come near me, just take care of me,' your 'Give me enough room to be by myself but don't leave me alone.' Your magic drove out Nira's. As far as who's behind Miriam's disappearance, neither of us knows. Noam probably knows something, but after you took him to the cleaners he won't talk. He's as hopeless and dangerous as his brother.

"My sister Nira left Israel a few years ago, after her second divorce. She was a Jack-of-all-trades, an artist, actress, antique dealer, she even ran a nightclub in the Caribbean. But she could never forget Isaac and always came back to him. Then one day, I don't remember exactly when, she found Miriam at the Raphaeli residence and instantly became her enemy, though not entirely, since Miriam was more like Isaac than she herself ever was, and therefore could hold sway over her. Don't think I understand what all this means, Joseph. Look, that conversation with Nira has really upset me, and you probably know exactly why, from what you overheard me say to her."

"I didn't hear a single word, Naomi. She trained me not to listen."

"Who? Miriam? That's so like her, and like you. You deserve each other." Suddenly Naomi looked furious, as if she resented Miriam's power over me, considering it a personal attack on herself. For a few moments she stormed in silence, then she spoke, but in a very soft voice, as if she were talking to herself, whispering in her own ear in a language she herself had forgotten, "My sister said some weird things about Nina, even that Nina wrote to her. I don't see how my sister knew any of the stuff she told me, like your trip to Jerusalem, or about Joy and Hanoch Levi, whom she does know; it all came out just now in our conversation. Her anger doesn't scare me as much as her knowing so much does, as if she's somehow involved in all this. She wouldn't say where she was, but she wasn't at the kibbutz. How come she didn't get in touch with me for two weeks? Before, right after all her marriages and divorces and near re-marriages, after her travels to India, America, Paris, Scandinavia, she always came directly to me, her head heavy with memories of Isaac, to give me another dose of her venom. My sister's very beautiful, very disturbed; her heart's always in the right place, and that's what gets her into trouble. People use her. She believes everybody and everything. But she's not herself now. Something has happened. She's so furious at me, all she did was curse me without mercy. She says that she won't have anything to do with me unless I leave you at once. She wants me to phone her from home or from the station to say I'm no longer 'sleeping' with you. When I told her I wouldn't leave you, she hung up."

Joy called, supposedly to clarify something but really just to bolster her alibi.

I asked her, "What's Hanoch hiding? Flirting with Miriam doesn't make him unfaithful to you; that would take a bulldozer."

"You know nothing, Joseph, you're lucky," she said.

Afterwards I sat there wondering. Naomi was asleep. Her confession, she later told me, was the hardest thing she'd ever done in her life. I sat the whole night watching the electric stove which was on instead of the heating because the kerosene had run out. I stared at the rings glowing in the cold room, and I threw some extra blankets over Naomi. The following morning we prepared a huge breakfast together. Then she needed some time to herself. I noticed that the photograph had been turned around and Isaac now faced the wall, which made me smile. Madame Frau came out on to the balcony, calling, "Send Naomi over. Today I'd like to converse with *her!*" While I got the coffee going, the two women talked. I was anxious to drive over to Isaac's parents, and went out for a newspaper. There was a letter in the letterbox addressed to me in Miriam's hand, postmarked the twenty-second of December, a month before her disappearance. Upstairs, sharing the sofa with Naomi, who kept biting her nails while waiting for me to finish, I took in every word.

Joseph,

While you were making supper yesterday I saw again what a joke you are and what a brilliant career you've made for yourself as cook for your spoiled daughter, and general housemaid (you even do windows). Three cheers, I take my hat off to you, a real man from head to broom. How does Yoni put it, Commander in Chief of Mop-ups? Even in her eyes you're a disgrace. Joseph, it always made me laugh the way you boasted when you reheated in oil Feigel's ready-made schnitzels and they came out just right and the potatoes were crisp. After all you did for me I should have offered to help, at least wash the dishes, but that never occurred to me. You could have hired a maid if you wanted. You were working, and had other job offers. Actually, I didn't have to live at home any more than you had to be my homemaker. The bottom line is that I didn't understand you then and I don't now. Nothing works out; you with or without mother, you with or without me, who came to fill a void perhaps. Mother claims you chose her one day when she was on trial together with Reuben, who was her lover, I think, then. She says you told yourself, "I must have a daughter, named Miriam perhaps, delicate yet brave, intelligent yet kind." You looked at this cracked vessel, my mother, the darling of filth, who thinks only the body can surrender and you decided that she would house your daughter. Then came all the grief, which I remember, the battles over me, each of you trying to steal my love from the other, while I just wanted to keep both of you. In the end, you fell deeply in love with each other, because *you* needed her betrayal and *she* needed your loyalty. But you had the moral upper hand, judging, forgiving, making mother and me feel guilty, Anyway, I finally overcame both of you.

I'm writing from the very base which you once commanded. Maybe you're responsible for those white-washed trees. You appointed the company sergeant-major and the master-sergeant. In a little while I'm going off to visit the Simontov family in Ekron, one of whose sons, Jahash, is a security guard here. When I left base once with a lieutenant colonel named Avinoam, who drove a Citroën '79 (according to him, the sexiest car on the road), the security guard got angry because his brother was in jail. I had to settle the thing and get the brother reinstated in the army. I was an officer in Community Relations. You know the soldiers I had under me, baboons, a hundred times worse than what you described, dear Joseph.

Not so Jahash's family, who couldn't lie if they had to. They live in a house which seems to have grown with them. It began as a one-and-a-half-room flat in a transit camp project, then kept giving birth to one room after another with each new child. You should see the house now! It has a life of its own. The father is a nursery man, an inspector for the Jewish National Fund. The mother first worked as a maid, then she opened a flower shop and fell in love with every plant and seed. She never spent a day in school and can neither read nor write, but her shop has become a booming business. She can identify any flower or plant by its smell – whatever she doesn't know about a plant isn't worth knowing – and tell you how old it is, what it needs to grow, and what it's good for. She grows spices, regularly collecting specimens from various groves and woods, either to be dried or ground up. Some botany professors from the Weizmann Institute drop in occasionally to consult her, thinking they know more than she does; but once she smiles and mentions some nettle they've never come across, they leave stammering. When the father comes home (they live behind the store), everybody sings together. They like Jewish customs, but aren't strictly observant. What a warm bunch, Daddy, very physical, touching each other, eating as a family. One daughter's at the university, one son's in jail, sometimes they get all dressed up even though it isn't a holiday, just because they feel like it; they know how to let go and rejoice, have a good time. As soon as the daughter comes home, she takes off her fancy blouse, puts on an apron, and scrubs the place so clean that you couldn't find a speck with a magnifying glass. The police have files on several of their kids. One's in America, another is an army man who beats up Arabs on the West Bank, he's considered an expert on Arabs, but the daughter is a leftist. They'll never turn into great soldiers, like you. But they didn't have the advantage of growing up in a house with a maid and afternoon tea, or Doctor Spock which you would read to me when I was little. They grew up with warmth and family solidarity but in near poverty. Just so the kids would have something, their father bought them that silly series of encyclopaedias put out by the religious Mizrachi Party; and they decorated their house with shmaltzy patriotic pictures, the central bus station, the Moroccan miracle worker Baba-Salli, Ben Gurion, Prime Minister Begin, anything to be on the safe side. On Friday night they all wear white to greet the Sabbath, and they light Sabbath candles. Never once do they bad-mouth each other. On the wall hangs a photograph of a dead uncle, not a dead soldier. Now, Daddy, I wonder why I bother trying to help you to reach me. If you think you can come close to me through your devotion, through your reversal of roles, who's stopping you; good luck to you! It's not as if I really don't care. Sometimes, when I think about what's happened in your life, Daddy, I weep.

All I ask is that you do not confuse me with your own hollowness. Recognize me for who I am; don't be afraid to admit to yourself what you know about me. Love me for myself, for no other reason, not as a way to fight mother, Reuben, the army, or fate.

Do you only want a daughter who is smart, knowledgeable, funny, clever, a good student and a good soldier? Those are talents, not a person. I realize you've never given this much thought. I'm not saying you can't love me, but that you don't know how to do it. But can a daughter tell her father how to love and raise her? Jahash's family knows to give love the way a flower knows how to be a flower.

How we yelled at one another. You and I, I and mother. But when mother was unfaithful to you (remember how late she'd show up at home?), I became all yours. Later, when you sat all alone in the house at night, almost unable to speak, like a recluse, who taught you to open up? If not for my lessons, you never would have dared to leave the army. With Reuben it was the same story all over again. He controlled you, then he betrayed you. And, you, his puppet, kept on loving him, your bosom friend from childhood; like shit he was! You never had a bosom friend, not in the Chief of Staff, not in Reuben, not in mother. You couldn't catch on to that because you're an army man. You can't accept that something just ends and won't reappear. In the army as soon as one war ends, you prepare for another; you train young soldiers to accept their deaths, and young brides to accept their widowhood; and as you send these young soldiers out to their posthumous glory, you never realize, even for a moment, that except for you and a few others with similarly twisted minds, human beings don't dream of becoming dead heroes, everybody prefers being live cowards.

You were at home while the Talmud teacher wooed mother. What kind of a man was he – a progressive Jew? A professor from a New York college? He came to Israel, a soldier for a new God, without a yarmulkah, a religious man with perfume, an ass-licker, well-grounded of course in Nietszche, Buber, you name it. Suddenly mother had the hots for him, and stayed with him overnight at some hotel. I telephoned her, begging her to come back, saying that *I* was the one who needed her, not you. All you could say was, "I understand, Miriam." But you didn't understand anything. She loved you even while she was in bed with him. She screamed at me, "You're his daughter, the two of you betrayed me, I won't come back, I refuse." You can't imagine how much I pleaded, and how much I needed her back home – partly because I wanted both of you fighting over me, partly because I was afraid that if she were gone, I'd have to take her place and I knew that it wasn't right. It made loving very scary and very difficult. Mother understood me. "I've seen worse things in my life, Miriam," she said. Actually I was well off; somebody adored me, valued me more than the army, more than God perhaps, which was exciting. But poor mother, she was so much more screwed up than I was, but you couldn't see that because you were always blind to anything abnormal, like necrophilia, like falling in love with an SS guard for beating you, or offering God your condolences. What do you know about a woman like Nina, or a girl like me? Nothing!

Yes, I went there and begged some more, right in the lobby of the hotel where that smooth rat was; but despite her tears and mine, she wouldn't come back home. Then you with your Olympian grace said, "It's okay," completely unaware of how deeply involved I was in my mother's business. Not so Reuben. What the hell do you know about anyway? Sure, you can cook, that's because you like to be the best at everything, whether homemaker or soldier; but you didn't make an impression on me, except as a person who enjoyed degrading himself. That was all on account of your power (which always corrupts) which made you think you were an angel whereas you were actually only half a man. If mother were to give birth to me today and go crazy the way she did during my delivery, a little lithium would cure her. But they didn't have that drug in those days. Her depression turned into a power struggle between you two, a battle over my brains, my future, to be waged like any other battle

147

of yours, except that you defended her as well as attacking her. She couldn't stand your pride and your strength; that was unbearable to her. If only you were less mighty and arrogant and more intimate and spontaneous and open. But unlike me and mother you don't know what it's like to feel worthless. You cannot accept that I'm somebody hard to reach, almost opaque; you can't accept that mother suffers in order to feel that she's still alive. She didn't want a soldier for a husband, she wanted a man who would tell her every morning how gorgeous she looked. You never said the right words, Joseph. You let my soldier die, all because you had to follow the order of the day, unlike mother and me for whom anything goes. I didn't re-enlist in the army because I wanted to follow orders like you; I wanted to forget my disgust for the whore's life my mother was leading, and for the glorious Children's Crusade of the marching dead which you were conducting. A healthy man hardly needs the *esprit de corps* of your Zionism, which meant nothing to me anyway, because a Jew always suffers and I hadn't suffered enough yet. My mother had, but she went to America and wouldn't come back to you for all my tears. So I wouldn't forgive her, wouldn't answer her letters. Then everything changed. I became your pupil and death's bride, finally understanding that life was merely the means to an end, an accident, the uneventful bridge to the inevitable. Your teachings prevailed.

Remember when I cut myself in the bathroom with the bottle of after-shave? You poured cognac on my hand, then licked the wound like a real man, except that you turned it into a scene from an opera, as if the end of the world were nigh, as if you were confronting a hundred million Arabs in that tiny space between my cut hand and the wall, within sight of Madame Frau's balcony. Of course, that makes sense. Somebody always has to play the soldier, so why not you? But it also meant that I lost a father and gained a lover – which was more than I could handle.

148

Once Nina left, she had abandoned me to the hero of her dreams, forever out of her reach and therefore out of my reach too. Forgive me, Daddy, you never treated her like a whore the way others did, the way she *wanted* to be treated. Others knew that she was just a hole to be filled, and not with a child either. I came out of a hole of darkness burning bright, the source from which I could never return. That's all Nina saw in herself, the hole from which I emerged, whereas you saw a warm house.

Are you in any fashion a man? Why didn't you at least screw Joy? You could have been unfaithful too, you could easily have screwed her. Are you made of stone? Mother is elastic! But she wanted to have a daughter against her father, a cunt against the world rather than a resting place for the warrior returning from battle reeking of sweat and blood. Mother loved you; still does. But everything you do, you do by the book. That's how you raised me. That's how you held back your anger, afraid of letting out the animal in you. You saved that for war. "He's a tiger in battle but a lamb in bed," said mother. "He treats me with respect like a father." But she didn't want to see honour, she wanted to see stars.

Both mother and I wanted you to be what you couldn't be. That's an awful thing to say. I know how much you think you long for us, but I'm not sure you really do know whom you long for. I must finish up because the mail goes out soon. Joseph, tomorrow morning, after you wake me so sweetly, you'll turn on the shower in order to warm up the water for me, you'll boil water for my coffee; then we'll leave together, the old lady at the number 4 bus stop will give us a nasty look, we'll stand there, you on your way to the pool, I to my base, the world where I now live and where you haven't the faintest notion what I'm like, a world without you in it. You'll stand there sensing some danger awaiting me, you with your premonitions, the way you once explained to the parents of that soldier you were sure would never come back alive from the battle in Bet-Lid. And you'll think of saying to me, "Come on, take a day off, we'll head down to Kishon Street and have lunch at the Olympus." You'll want to call me baby, invite me to a matinée or a café. I know that it would have been lovely, but you'll never say the words. Instead, you'll think to yourself, "Miriam went back to the army against my wishes; she hurt me, she enlisted permanently, and was promoted to Community Relations officer just as I resigned. But now that she's in the army she has to make it on her own, without any pull from a Brigadier in the Reserves." Exactly, Joseph, you would never step out of line, not for anything, certainly not after thirty-one years in the army. How could you ask your daughter to take a day off from the army and spend it in a restaurant or at a cinema if she didn't have a medical excuse? It's always the same devotion, whether to Nina or to the army, which will prevent you from asking me for a date, Joseph, which is such a pity. You'll head for the pool; I'll ride off in that tin can of a bus, at least noticing how you'll still be standing there lost in thought, wondering why you have no guts. Oh for war, yes. But to ask a daughter for her company at a matinée or a luncheon – now that his wife has run away and he's lonely – that's impossible.

So you'll give up, routed, but your honour intact, as in all your battles, remaining the hero who doesn't deal in bullshit! Daddy, that's how you played into their hands. All they wanted was somebody to toe the line, not a bold original officer, not a troublemaker, your sort.

You thought you would make waves by resigning from your command and writing letters to the top brass. But your letter just sat in some mailbox until finally it came back to you unopened. Nothing was accomplished, except business as usual, because you never once went outside the system, you never took your complaints to the newspapers like everybody else. The ass-lickers were waiting for your stuff,

150

but you refused to play their game or make any deals. That would have been beneath you, the lonely loyal soldier. The last gunfighter. Sound sublime? Ridiculous!

Do I hear you ask me any question? Like where I've been? Like hell! That would violate our sacred agreement! As long as I come home on time, no questions asked. So how will you ever know where I am if you can't ask? Only when I'm dead? At my grave will you look at your watch to see if I've come on time? If I have, you won't ask me where I've been. You'll just examine your vial of tears to check the level, and discover finally that I was a big girl, huh?

When I buried Delilah I also buried myself. Yes, you did come, but I expected more from you, just as I expected you to take your wife Nina back home by force; I thought you would read the order of the day, like in the army, over Delilah's grave, and you would give one of your spectacular eulogies. For a dog? Why not! She was my queen. Poor thing. And you were the King of eulogizers. Mother says that when you die, she'll finally feel the way she has always wanted to feel but life has not permitted her to. I know that's cruel, Daddy, for you have always loved us. But what has your love been like? A labour of conscience. Yet conscience, Joseph, is love's opposite, don't you see? I expected you to mourn Delilah; that wasn't for you. You're comfortable only in the army, your real home. You belong to a lost generation which grew up with power for a father and despair for a mother. So go look for me now, your little daughter who apparently loves you too much.

Miriam

11

I let Naomi read the letter and watched her as she attempted to fathom it from her perspective. Finally she said, "One thing is clear, Joseph. Whatever she has done or cooked up, whatever has happened to her, your daughter loves you. Deeply, painfully, she loves you."

What puzzled me was the postmark from Rehovot a month prior to her disappearance. I phoned Reuben, expecting him to help me out the way he did when we were children and I would always turn to him to extricate me from some problem I had with my father, or Madame Frau, or my mother and all her ailments, or with my teacher Mr Bloch. And Reuben would sit me down and say, "Brother, every problem has a solution, you just have to find it. If no solution existed, you'd never find one, no matter what you did. But since one does exist, we'll find it somehow."

He was cold and perhaps somewhat scared too, if I could trust my senses. He said, "Go find your women by yourself. You've surrounded yourself with Bedouin scouts and come up with a military jacket, a blouse and trampled grass. You've even come up with a lovely green-eyed girl to keep you company at home." He sounded lonely, caught in a web of sadness, and I didn't understand why. When I asked him if anything had happened, he said, "Maybe Nina was here for a visit, or maybe I'm not the one to ask, Joseph. After all, I'm not going to tell you what you want to know. Like who Nira is and how she fits into the picture. You've got troubles. Miriam is your daughter not mine. Nina loves her. Just because she left you doesn't mean she doesn't love her daughter. You can cross out that Talmud teacher. After she dumped him on a street corner, he's still looking for her and thinks she belongs to him because he screwed her in some hotel, but he doesn't count. Nina declared her independence many years before you woke up and started looking for Miriam on Mount Carmel."

The day passed. I wanted to visit Isaac's parents but something was still preventing me from going. Naomi understood, and went out shopping. She said she needed a toothbrush or "whatever". I asked her what she meant by "whatever". She pondered and repeated, "A toothbrush." With night came a heavy downpour. Reuben's words came back to me; every solution was just waiting to be discovered. By now I knew Miriam's letter by heart. Naomi returned. We were alone together, frightened. Suddenly I realized that it couldn't have taken her an hour just to purchase a toothbrush. I asked her if she'd made her purchase, and she said, looking confused, "What was I supposed to get, Joseph?"

I could feel Nina's presence, as far away as she was. Her laughter reverberated in my gut. I headed for bed, and I could hear Naomi taking a shower. I lay there and stared at the window. It was shut but the blinds were open. A faint light penetrated the room, but what got to me was the sound of the sea stirring in its perpetual loneliness. The sky pulsed with the flickering lights of a passing plane. The rain faltered and then picked up again, slapping the window. The tree groaned and shook as if in pain. Naomi left the light on in the bathroom and entered the bedroom. Barely visible in the gloomy light coming from outside and from the bathroom, her face looked expressionless, almost not human. Standing by the bureau, she began to undress and did it so dryly it looked routine. She placed her garments neatly folded on a chair, as if nothing was disturbing her. If we had already been married for sixty years, she couldn't have undressed and folded her clothes on a chair with any more apathy. But she didn't take her eyes off me. It was all done as if she were going through the motions of a very familiar act. She sat down naked at the edge of the bed and shivered in the cold. Suddenly her eyes showed that same innocent joy in life which I so much loved about her.

She was the first woman, after Nina and Miriam Hurwitz, that I had seen totally naked. To me, though I was fifty (and therefore it may sound ridiculous), the moment Naomi would enter my bed, she would disinherit Nina. I was a man who could only have one woman, and my feelings for Nina ran deep. But once Naomi came into the picture, she would replace Nina forever. As Reuben said, all you had to do was find the solution, because knowing that it existed precluded all regret, guilt and helplessness.

Naomi got into bed and wrapped herself in the blanket. She was still cold and shivering. On the wall facing the bed hung an old electric heater which I hadn't used since Nina's departure. I took off my pyjamas and turned on the switch of the heater which was next to the bed. Slowly, from the reddening glow spread a wonderful warmth. Naomi jumped out of bed, put out the light in the bathroom, locked the door of the bedroom, came back into bed, wrapped herself up again; so the two of us lay isolated and apart in the red light which warmed the room and lent a bewitching hue to a bed no longer as barren as it had been for two years. When I checked, she was actually there, present and accounted for, uncontesting, peaceful. She reached under the blanket and took my hand in hers. Then she didn't move. Neither did I. She said, "It's all so sad." I didn't reply. My heart was heavy with joy. Our intimacy had grown so gradually, without any games, as if not of our doing but the magical work of our bodies; we were together like two children. My body forgot how old it was. The electric heater forgot that it belonged to Nina. And Nina's side of the bed no longer remembered how she breathed or what her name was. Uninhibited, released from all bonds, it was a rare moment of death and resurrection, an inner dream but an open secret.

So naturally I had to spoil it. "I could be your father, Naomi," I said. She was smart enough, though, to answer, "But you're not!" As she paused, her breathing sounded like a distant bell ringing without bitterness or anger but drenched in melancholy. Then she said, "You're here, I'm here. I've never slept with a man who only had one woman."

"I almost had two," I said. "But Miriam Hurwitz was too righteous." Naomi smiled, and her smile turned red in the light of the heater. The rain struck the window, there was thunder, the antennae rattled on the roof. We were close together, there was no going back. I was afraid of what would come next, but soon it did happen, the inevitable. From Madame Frau's apartment, despite the superb acoustics of the house which my father never stopped boasting about, with an obstinacy born of his anguished yearning to believe in something, however incidental or insignificant, after he had lost his faith in the truly important things of his life; from her apartment came now the thunder of Beethoven's drums. With the profound intuition of someone who had come very close to being my step-mother, Madame Frau turned on her phonograph to its maximum volume. The Fifth was perhaps too heroic for the occasion, but a woman as forlorn and lost as Madame Frau, who could present herself in a safari suit to honour her would-be son, felt obliged to soften somewhat her Napoleon's fall and celebrate his victory, too. After all, she knew exactly when Naomi and I were making love with a passion neither of us could escape from; a wily old virgin like Madame Frau could figure such things out to the minute. She often told me, "What creates great passion is tragedy. My father was destined to be my avenging lion, but I knew nothing, I was swept off my feet." I pondered about her, about Naomi, about Nina who in one instant had practically lost her right to exist. I didn't know if Naomi realized what our moment together meant to me, but she understood. Perhaps she was even able to visualize Nina, two years after her departure, now making her final exit from her room never to return again. Perhaps Naomi was the first woman in my life to appreciate, and not just exploit it the way Nina did, my cursed characteristic need to be monogamous. Our bodies responded to each other, we formed a labyrinth together, a tangle of deep pleasure and gratitude. Maybe that was the key to it all, my gratitude and her hopes. We made love like persons released from a long jail sentence, but without panic, unrushed, exquisitely aware of our senses, as if – as she had said on our first meeting – we had long ago been fated for one another, from the moment she had come into the world. It was foolish to think such thoughts, but they were the only thoughts I had.

I also began to compose a letter in my head to my daughter, should she still be alive. Maybe I felt guilty for having it too good. Somehow I remembered a line from Stendhal in which he wrote that the Italians "had been bored for a century" and then awakened only after Napoleon's invasion. Naomi had roused my soul from a deep slumber where there was room just for that vicious circle involving me and my daughter, the dizzying game of policeman and officer. I may have finally grasped what had occurred, why Miriam had left behind her a trail of so many clues. But the following morning I no longer recalled what I'd figured out in bed with Naomi. Temporarily, at the first soul-bearing instant, I saw in a flash what had happened to my daughter, but my guilty conscience had dictated everything to me out of my concern and my love, each suggesting the other, each different from the other, though born from the same source – a barren man in possession of love only three times. Myself; the only kid in my neighbourhood who had to look up the word masturbation in a dictionary. The other kids joked, Reuben explained it to me, the Chief of Staff blushed and laughed. Should I tell Naomi how uninformed I'd been? The music struck the window. Poor Madame Frau was certainly guarding us now with her old toy rifle.

I was enjoying my stolen pleasure; then the music ended, the rain too for a few minutes. The window showed a dark sky and a distant horizon cut by lightning. Naomi lay on her back, looking up at the ceiling, and she let her head rest alongside me. She stirred a bit, trying to get more comfortable. I lit up a cigarette, drew the ashtray closer to me, studied Naomi's profile. Naomi asked me why I had wanted to live in the house I'd grown up in since I was six. "It's never made any difference to me where I live," she said. "Why is it so important to you?"

I said, "I never knew anybody who lived in the home they'd grown up in or were born in. That always bothered me. In France I met people still living in the house in which they and their parents and grandparents had been born. I was delighted. The idea of constantly migrating from one place to another troubled me. Your back was always to the wall, ready to make another exit. It offends me how rootless we are. Look how easily Israelis adapt to living in America or anywhere else. Every house here was built from scratch, there's no tradition, no real settling down, it's all temporary, just for the time being. To me a house is a declaration of loyalty, commitment, life. It's important to me," I told Naomi, who obviously wasn't expecting such a long sermon, but I was in quite a state; we were together and she, the second woman I'd ever been intimate with, so young, would she understand me? "It's important that I stay in touch, at every stage of my life, with who I once was. I always come back to the same bed in the same room. That gives me respite from all the battles and wars, from everything," and I added, "I'm falling in love with you, and that's dangerous. Today was a break-through for me."

She smiled, as if she were thinking to herself, "We slept together, big deal!" I was sure she wasn't thinking anything of the kind, but maybe I gave her too much credit. I said, "I don't know how to bend, so I'm in danger of breaking. Nina continued living here while she was occupying other beds too. I needed to live among those old Germans who'd been seeking, for over forty years now, the absurdity of their loss. At night they dream that they're swimming to Berlin, to Vienna, to Prague, to Leipzig. I was born on 3 Mendeleh Street, today it's a post office. Back then the house was by the sea, now what divides the sea and the house that no longer exists is the Dan Hotel. We moved here when I was six, and I've lived by the sea since then, excluding the three years in Herzliya, but even then we were not far from the sea. I love what's familiar; this area is what I have known all my life.

"Notwithstanding a few visits abroad on missions, I've

grown accustomed to the sixty-four steps of my house, and the scent of the lemon tree downstairs. I don't know why I'm telling you all this. I'm virtually a widower, practically a bereaved parent. I'm afraid for you, Naomi; I'm afraid for myself, for Miriam, and even Nina. But all of you shift around, whereas I believe in the magic of remaining in the same place, loyal as a link in a chain. As the world turns, I stay put. Pure stubbornness. I know that there are more beautiful spots in the world, but I prefer it here. As far as I'm concerned, once you entered my bed you cannot leave it, even if you betray me the way all those dearest to me have. You're here to stay, or at least that's how I'll always think of you. If we hadn't made love, Nina would still be in this room as the woman of the house. When I look out of the window I know exactly when the moon will rise, how the tree will stoop. It used to be that people would remain in the houses they were born in, which gave them a clear sense of who they were. Nowadays does anybody know who he is? We lack that fundamental nobility attached to the earth, to climate, to order. I am a lover of order, Naomi.

"Not order imposed by man, but inevitable absolute order. When you know there are no easy answers and life is complicated and without panaceas and you have to choose your life from a shelf full of inflexible givens, all you can do is try to be strong. I love continuity, which is the other side, perhaps the completely opposite side, of what Miriam's friends would call 'progress'. All the Josephs who ever lived converge here in my room. To overcome depression I count up all the doors and windows that I can remember. When I lie down at night in summer, and hear that special sea outside my window, and feel the scorching breeze, I know on which side of life I am, and I can calculate when the wind will enter my window.

"Listen, you're the strangest thing that has happened to me. If I saw you in the street I wouldn't stop. I wouldn't notice how beautiful you are, I'd see but not notice. Yet, when you prepared coffee for me the way I love it, something clicked. You're in bed now with a man who, when he was a child, slept in this very room dreaming while his parents were away, fashioning in his mind the sort of man he would be in thirty years. On the identical spot where you are now, I was once a young boy and then a man, all before you were even born. Doesn't that lend support to the idea of continuity, as if we were all just running a relay race? You know what, I think this is the longest speech I've ever given in my life."

She began to laugh now, but her laughter was frightening, like the screech of a seagull blended with the scrape of a toothbrush. She grabbed me, almost dug her nails into me, and kept on laughing until she wept. The rain and the music were over, but she kept crying and laughing until again we made love, this time without any courtesies, just the abandon of despair to the last scream, and then she held me tight, not wanting me to fall asleep. She forced open my eyes with her fingers, and talked on and on for hours to keep my weary eyes from closing and leaving her alone. She clung to me with a passion that was gentle yet desperate, and I too held her as tightly as I could, but finally we fell asleep together in each other's exhausted arms, for she somehow forgot to keep talking and touching my eyes. My head sunk into the pillow and I was gone.

12

W HEN the newspapers started fabricating reports link-
ing Miriam's name with Noam and a secret gang
of drug dealers, some of the veteran fighters, who still
frequented my house to plan actions to rescue Miriam,
suggested that I liquidate a few members of the press.
I almost came round to their way of thinking. Those
journalists tormented me. They knew how to build a case
out of nothing, handing over the intimate details of our
lives to the public in the form of lies or innuendoes. But
I continued to bite the bullet.

Several telegrams arrived from Madame Frau. She stopped appearing at the balcony in the morning; instead her
telegrams requested private work sessions with me, what
she termed "advisory sessions concerning Miriam Krieger".
Fatigued from all my non-stop analysis and conferences, I
postponed my visit to Isaac's parents. Maybe I simply was
scared of what I might have to face there, some startling
or final news. That was ridiculous. Even at the most
critical moments of battle I was known always to keep
my cool, taking one step at a time, never boxing myself
into any fixed position, and attacking at the spot least
expected.

Miriam's second letter came three days later. I was
finally setting out to visit the Raphaeli family – after
having lost my nerve each night with Naomi and each day
as soon as I began to imagine what might be waiting for me
there in that house in Ramat Gan. Determined this time, I
went downstairs with Naomi at my side, and saw the letter
in the box.

The letter had been mailed from a post office in Beer-sheba a week before the first letter. In her tight compact hand, Miriam wrote:

Joseph,

Maybe you already know why I returned to mother. Anyway, what's left for us now? You, she, me, and the shadow on the wall. I dream that you are in a burning house but in the end you are somehow rescued. It's the same dream, with a few changes, every morning on the bus on the way to the central station; and the tall driver who almost always takes me there, says he can tell when I'm dreaming by the lines on my face, which he sees in his mirror; so on my account he turns on the music. This morning it was Bach, one of the Brandenburg concertos, elegant, cold, special. I remember, in one of my mother's outbursts, the kind you didn't even acknowledge as you didn't for that matter mine, how mother said or screamed that she met Bach in the camps when he came to visit in brown uniform and played on the organ, and from the pipes rose smoke, together with the stench of charred children. Afterwards Mahler wove his songs on the death of children – those sublime hymns which, she said, expressed her own emotions; and you should have seen the look which she gave me then . . .

I'm writing to you because it's hard for me to talk to you face to face, at least about myself and what's really hurting me. Once, after you and I had yelled and argued, you wrote me a letter, remember? I had told you then, in a voice so calm it grated on your nerves, that you'd ruined my life, and you wrote me a frightened, pathetic letter, as if my sorrow had really hurt you and not me, as if my pain had simply been a way to get back at you; yet, after all, I was the one who was suffering and not you, not that you don't suffer, but you can keep your mouth closed when you scream. Look, Joseph, the truth is that you didn't destroy my life, the truth is that Nina didn't have

161

to run away – don't think I haven't taken everything into account. On the other hand, what kind of a life did you offer her, after everything that she had gone through? Just because you felt that you didn't need a fancy refrigerator, you thought she'd be satisfied her whole life with the old refrigerator that she'd bought in the days when she had money. In the transit camp she had more cash than you did, so she said. But in your pride you told her to hand over her money to you; you bought her some things, then became tight-fisted. Your salary would have to do, period.

But, Joseph, mother and I aren't at all as you've painted us. I'm the Miriam that I am, plus whatever you and Nina have invented. You're an intelligent man, how come you made such a mess of things? I remember travelling with mother to Herzliya when I was six and passing by the house we'd lived in before moving to Ben Yehuda Street; it was so gorgeous there, though my recollection of the place was shaky, and I said to mother, weeping, "Why can't we live here along the beach, by the sea, among the vineyards and the trees and the sand and the breeze and the clear air? Why must we live in the middle of the city on an ugly street?" I told her I didn't like Mr Haim and Mr Klaupfer and all those old folk who smelled of kerosene and looked at me as if I were their lost child whom they'd left behind in Germany; and mother said that you'd decided to die by the sea. That's what she told me, that when you were twenty-six you had already chosen the death you wanted – by the sea where you were born! And I thought to myself then, "Did he ever ask how I felt about it? Or mother? He just decided it would be good for us." I heard you say that we all loved living in the old house you grew up in, but that was all wrong, all a lie, we didn't love it, neither mother nor me, we didn't like Mr Haim who hoarded loaves of bread and wrapped cigars and looked for his wife in the fuse box. But you never asked us, you simply determined what was good for us and announced that we were all in agreement.

162

Yet, in that letter of yours you wrote that as far as you knew, you had been a fit parent, and that's true. You never hit or punished or shamed me; you gave me everything. But maybe that was your way to avoid offering me something deeper, which comes with beatings and insults and kisses. I never understood your code language or what you really wanted. You always confused me. I got the message that all you cared about was order, not explanations. You were a man with a closed mind, a monogamist without loopholes. But any monogamist who tells his wife just five times in their life together that he loves her, needs to go back to school and learn all over again. It was more convenient for you not to know anything about mother, about her childhood – like my letters, whether hidden in my room or out in the open in our mailbox, which you refused to read because it was easier for you to be a decent father than a real one, a father who cared enough to degrade himself and search through papers. You loved your image of us.

Long before I was born, you concocted a daughter for yourself. According to mother (and I believe her) her madness had a method to it, as nuts as she was. And you wished to arrange my life so that I would duplicate in my subconscious whatever Nina had experienced in real life. That way, I would never know exactly any of my motives. Actually you would have been even happier if you had fashioned me from scratch with your own hands, since you never wanted to share my existence with anybody else, not even Nina, who supplied you of course with a ready-made pretext for excluding her by reason of her illness, her overwhelming anxiety after delivering me. For over a year you raised me by yourself. You would have sent Nina to a labour camp and afterwards to a doghouse owned by some cowardly, hostile friend of the family's, allowing her to get crushed but rescued to be sure, and to set sail for Palestine on an illegal ship – all for your benefit! Not for hers. In order to make

163

your daughter in accordance with your recipe. Ten milligrammes of Jewish suffering, ten milligrammes of Israeli pain, ten milligrammes of fire, a pinch of Mandate police units and Palmach, a heap of Hannah and her seven sons, a teaspoon of youth movements, as much of the Warsaw Ghetto as possible, at least a whole kilo; and the goal of course was to come up with a set of genes full of fury which, when restrained by an emotionless sense of law, would result in a fighter like you, who always took on the nightmares of others, never your own, since you had none; you were too perfect for that, too gallant, forever without anger, unaggrieved, a mutation of the historic Jew, ideology's mercenary, always fighting wars that left you no other alternative, as well as wars that did, but always with some convenient enemy sitting at the end of your rifle, making it all justifiable, always justifiable.

Why didn't you go off to fight the Germans? They were far away, and had turned Nina's mother into soap. But you played war games and purchased gas masks from them, and got into shape to fight Arabs. You never grasped how deeply justified the Arabs felt. I may not accept their sense of justice – I'm incapable of that and must agree with you – but I can at least understand it; they opposed Jewish immigration not out of animosity to mother. They said, "It's our land, in ruins, desolate, but ours; let the enlightened world find another place for the refugees." In the end, yes, only a few refugees were left, and they had lost their own lands. Up to this point everything makes sense, but once you go beyond it towards your extreme self-justification, you become if not fanatic, colour-blind. How did Isaac Raphaeli put it? You'll never have enough bullets to kill off a hundred million Arabs, and since his death you must add on another hundred million.

Why do you think they were obliged to understand the intense suffering of all the Ninas? Who gave you permission to speak on behalf of all those Ninas? Now with bitter sorrow I laugh at everything you told me, yet I still do as you do and follow in your footsteps, perhaps towards whoever is after me.

After me?

Ah!

There is no justice, Joseph, only a lousy flowery self-justification on both sides. It's a joke how much I think like you yet act the opposite; I join mother against you, but join Joseph against mother.

Then what? A Reuben you weren't, so mother in the end chose all three of you; and it took me a long while to figure out why you with your twenty laps, your powerful monogamist's body, your principles, intelligence, height, and so on, weren't enough, not for Nina. You were a desert hiker, ascetic, heroic, ruthless, but that wasn't enough for her; even the cosmic nurturing of our sacred earth wasn't enough. Sacrifices at the altars of Wotan in the holy land? Reading Shakespeare at night? Not enough. A canteen of blood? Not enough. A knight of blood? No, still not enough. If you had investigated her past you would have acted otherwise. How could you have not seen how shattered she was? You told yourself that Nina was cruel, but that was your own invention; you investigated death instead of her. For how long could you play with death? Meanwhile other parents less noble than you, perhaps not even monogamous, were taking their children on picnics to Galilee, to Eilat, abroad, and had steaks and played the radio. Shit, they spent the whole afternoon together over lunch, and afterwards probably went to some hotel with their lovers; they had a family, they screwed on the side, but they told their wives once a week how much they loved them! What did we have? A phenomenal victory over our enemy and an absent father; and if we made a trip, it was into the desert to climb on to tanks, to examine the barrel of a new cannon. We had a kind of cool, impassive hatred of the enemy; and naturally also patience, given your enlightenment. You taught me everything in an abstract way; always the Destruction of the Second Temple and the Jewish tank with the face of a man who would never have even the slightest, ugly, yet damn it, human paunch!

I remember, as a child, the summer after the Six Day War, our travelling to the old border where all the children were bathing in the sea; by the palm tree landscape in Dekalia and Akziv they splashed in the water, ate ice-creams, while Nina and I, as nervous as hell, in no-man's-land, sat in a torrid car; the dust and the sand and you all excited to point out to us the old border line, conjuring up the breakthrough on the fifth of June, the bloody sheet, the exact locations of each and every general. I was crying, mother was crying; the heat was awful, but you had to be the teacher of the new generation, a lone wolf, tortured, full of plans, handsomely tanned, confronting the desert. What could you do about our tears? We just wanted a little sea water, some ice-creams, not all those heroes you named for us, just somebody like Isaac Raphaeli whose name you forgot, though you made a hero out of him while he pissed in his pants. You let him die and then turned him into a hero. It was just a story, Joseph, like everything else, me, mother, Isaac, all of us.

Yes, we had some good times. You have a few amazing traits, like your profound sense of fairness; in a strange convoluted way, you are the most ethical person I have ever known. You always seem to know what's proper and what isn't, but not when it comes to your own family. Your speciality is abstract justice or the nation or the moment, but the road was laid with traps. Occasionally, you almost caught on, but then fell back on what you wanted to hear, so it all went to hell, and in the end mother was forlorn, I was what I always was, and you remained by yourself, always the loner. Maybe you're not a monogamist but a castrated god. At night we were terrified, Nina and I; planes shrieked across the sky; we didn't know what to expect, war? We waited and worried. But who calls to reassure us? Reuben, not you. And she weeps, makes a scene, waits for you to phone to say you love her, that there's a war but we'll win. She waits for you to tell us what to do, whether to go down to a shelter. However, you maintain a silence at your command, knowing what's what. So Reuben has to inform us that everything is as it should be; but what about you, don't you have to be as you should be?

Do you think I enjoyed meeting her lovers? How I begged her at the hotel to come home and forget about that disgusting Talmud teacher! But I understood her a little, in the end I always did, even after I fussed and cursed at her. Nina thought that you had sent me, at long last, out of jealousy; but how could the likes of you ever be jealous? Your overblown pride, along with your arrogant modesty, don't allow you to be, not you. It always devastated her when she saw again and again how you were not jealous, but it took years for her to admit that you'd never be and that's what finally crushed her.

Last year I went with friends to Carmel. Gideon joined us, a captain at our base and a friend of mine. We found a bunch of keys in a shrub, deep inside; go figure out how those keys got there. And there was also a blouse – a young woman's – with a few blood stains on it, and an army jacket with a slightly loose button and a few faded inkblots on one pocket, like mine. Also, some footprints and trampled grass leading to a cave, and we wondered what had happened inside to the woman. Weird! Gideon wanted to run to field security but we told him to wait. I said, "Look, the girl must have a father. If she's late, he'll take his Mustang and race to Carmel and find her. She's probably waiting for him in the woods." You remember, you once quoted to me a line from a poem by Nellie Sachs, "We returned without footsteps." So we must have found her non-footsteps there.

Little Nina's mother once sat with me – it was after Didi's death – and told me about mother's non-footsteps and hers, about that ship they came on, about the camp near Hamburg where they'd met, about Didi's deceased father. During one war here,

167

mother actually fled, you never even knew it; Reuben composed a sentimental poem about it, the kind that you would use for toilet paper, but he published it in some New Year's supplement under an alias. I'm sure you never got to that section of the paper, but if you had, you wouldn't have identified it. The poem was about a German officer, exquisitely dressed, pointing a revolver at the women who had fled with mother. They held children in their arms; Nina held a small boy whose mother had been killed. She had good reasons, Joseph, why she didn't want Jewish children! And that officer, a handsome guy, in his immaculate uniform, caught up with them at the edge of the forest, shot one child after another, and soon it was the turn of the child that mother was holding. He wore a uniform you could never forget, high pighide boots, and the symbol of the oak on his shoulder flaps. But then suddenly Nina saw a wedding ring on his finger, and she said like a wounded animal, "One day my son (but it turned out to be her daughter and not her son, since she couldn't really predict the sex of her child), one day my son will take revenge on your son!" And the officer made the connection. He had children; the boy in Nina's arms was a child, a human being not a bedbug. And his hands trembled; he couldn't shoot any more.

Mother once had a friend, who now lives in Israel in the south, a dentist – dentists had a lot of work to do when the others were dead; an S.S. officer came up to him once and said, "You're the best here, so you'll have to fix the teeth of an S.S. officer. There's not much in the way of apparatus here, or sleeping gas, but the moment any S.S. officer utters a cry of pain, you're off to the ovens." And this dentist pulled teeth for a year and a half without sleeping gas, and not one out of a hundred S.S. officers ever cried out in pain. Who, then, was the survivor? You? With your cannons and tanks, or mother who learned from a dentist how to pull teeth so gently that not a single S.S. guard felt any pain.

But mother adores life and needs a lot of it. She had no freezer or magazines because you denied her. You Puritan, you sufferer! We had to get by on your salary alone. She had a bunch of lovers then, since your monogamy left her cold. If only you'd known how to buy her with flattery like Reuben. You fell in love with death on account of what you'd imagined she'd gone through, without knowing the facts, and she fell in love with life on account of what she saw in you. You were a cold barren rationalist, busy at war as if you weren't actually fighting, just using a machine-gun to write your *War and Peace*, an Einstein on reconnaissance duty. Tell me, how could anybody toss an ordinary bunch of keys into a shrub without passing by in a car? Yet no car could have got through there. It's interesting what can occur in that area after the rains, when the whole place is mud.

You think I wanted to hurt you by re-enlisting in the army permanently. Maybe the Chief of Staff wished to punish you, in his power game with you; all I did was discover how easily he and Reuben played into my hands. They understood me better than you did because they had to rely on manipulative tricks to force me to oppose you. It was convenient, Joseph, but not that pleasant. Perhaps what explains it all is that I wanted to be like you, and that your loyalty finally infected me. Do you suppose it's just a coincidence that I'm still a virgin? I'm twenty-six, almost twenty-seven, and look what a disaster both of you have made of me! Being faithful unto death only established it as my proper territory. Mother comes from it, you live in it, and I seek it out. That's why Isaac's photograph was the appropriate means of revenge against myself and perhaps against you too. But the source of all my grief was my love for you and mother, a love meant to have two opposing faces. I'm pretty sick and tired of all my corpses, Joseph. You wanted a house and family, so I stayed around; it was an easy life for me, but perhaps after all I'm still your daughter, two sides to one catastrophe. You'll

soon see it, soon know the whole calamity and why I
cannot live with the one person I love other than you
and mother. You allowed me just the smallest area for
any game of love, so today I'm for and against you.
I also belong to your enemies – Reuben, the Chief
of Staff, the Arabs, Jewish history, "their" claims of
justice. Finally what have I got? Not myself, not you,
not Nina. What a book of lamentations I've ended
up with!

His Daughter and Her Father

not a bad title, eh?
Yours.

Gideon was stunned after I let him read the letter.
Beforehand, Naomi had said, "I know Gideon, he was my
first love, nothing great. He then met Miriam and fell for
her hard. Gideon and I had nobody else then. I wanted
somebody tender yet distant for my 'first'. After what my
sister went through, I was afraid of men. He isn't the type
to harm you or Miriam. This letter is weird."

Czeszek came by and read the letter. He said, "The
blouse and jacket were planted on Carmel after she wrote
the letter. Somebody is trying to drive you nuts, commander."

Again I put away my pride and telephoned. Reuben was
suddenly friendly. I read him the letter and he sounded
perplexed. He even cursed out loud, in his anger, and said
he'd call me right back. The next day he called to say that
Gideon couldn't have planted anything on Carmel because
he hadn't travelled anywhere for the past few weeks. The
footprints weren't his, and he was a straight guy, with an
excellent record, and not a liar. Also, Miriam couldn't have
been the soldier who showed up at the television studio.

Meanwhile another letter from Miriam arrived. Each
letter had a postmark from a different city or town in the
south. All the postmarks were clear, without any smudges,
as though somebody had taken pains that the date of each
postmark would be unmistakably legible. And each letter
was dated earlier than the previous one, apparently to

place me in a receding nightmare. None of the letters mentioned anything which came up in the other ones – which arrived later but were dated earlier. The final letter was written (or dated) three months prior to Miriam's disappearance. The postmark said Rishon Le-Zion. She wrote:

Joseph,

Greetings. When I was a girl, I used to write you short letters and conclude with "Greetings", instead of commencing them that way. On Yom Kippur, in that war, I sent you postcards with a bunch of "Greetings", but by then I placed them at the beginning. This morning I went down our sixty-four steps and realized that you have lived in this house – not counting the three years in Herzliya and, say, three more years of absences from home on army duty (Sabbaths and holidays, of course, don't count) – all told you've lived here a net total of forty years. If that's the case, you have listened to Madame Frau Birnbaum 14,400 times; and assuming that you climb up and down those steps twice a day – that's a minimum – it adds up to 1,840,200 steps, all in the same house. Now that's exhausting, like going to the moon. Listen, maybe you do really want to die by the sea.

This morning they finally started painting the staircase, and the fumes from the paint were overwhelming. How strange, I thought, more than a million steps, all your life in this run-down house that looks anaemic, on its last legs, when suddenly it's revitalized and getting a coat of paint! Who's paying the bill? The tenants can't even afford their own apartments and have to be subsidized. Except for you and maybe one other tenant, everybody pays just one hundred shekels a month, which amounts to five dollars or even less. Anyway, today I was thinking about all the craziness in my life. Perhaps the sight of those painters painting the house made me miss you, so that I suddenly wanted to call you Daddy. The way I did that morning at the bus stop.

When I was a small girl, Daddy, I realized that

171

we were cursed. You were my cancer; I was yours. Of course, cancer of the mind. But if we are each other's cancers, who are our bodies?

In our first year at school, Didi and I once got silly in class. Eve was our teacher. Maybe you recall that she taught all the parents, including you and mother, how to play with our rods by the Gattegno system so you could help us at home. Do you? They were like olives, brown, yellow. You sat in class and built towers with the rods, and you looked like children. It was in the evening. You were barely able to fit in our chairs. And our teacher Eve instructed you, and you called her "teacher" or "my teacher", and both of you had a great time being kids again, building towers and houses from rods; and Didi and I sneaked out to school, and peeked through the window (you didn't notice us). Later, in class, we remembered how funny it looked and burst out laughing, and Didi said, "Your Daddy's big bottom couldn't fit in the chair!" Our teacher Eve, always the pedagogue, made us stand in front of the whole class and explain what was so funny and why we had behaved so anti-socially. And I told the class that my father didn't allow me to laugh at home, but the teacher Eve, unlike my classmates, didn't think it was a joke. During recess she took me aside for a private conversation and she asked me in all seriousness, with that pedagogue's face of hers, if I had any problems at home; and she stroked my hair and added, "It's okay to tell me!"

I told her she was right, that I did have problems. I just wanted to instigate trouble, I didn't know why. The teacher then hinted about it to Nina during a parent-teacher conference. When Nina went to you – I'm not sure that you even remember it – you told her, "How can some teacher know so much about our child?" You made light of her. I listened to the two of you from behind the door. Nina was serious; she knew that a problem existed, but was still a frightened woman then and couldn't pinpoint exactly what the trouble was.

172

Actually, as I think about all of this now, I come to the conclusion that you yearned to be a father but just didn't know how. Our symbiosis, though, is something separate. Whatever you feel, I feel; I know in advance what you're going to say. My relationship with mother is healthier. I may have long-standing grievances against her, a massive anger, but despite her strangeness she always made sense to me; that's why I couldn't anticipate what she'd say or do. With you it's different. I always know what you'll say, but I really have no idea who you are. To understand mother, all I need is to be alive, I can let go of all my tensions with her and just feel, because loving her is simply a matter of being and living as I am, with all my emotions up front, including anger. But to understand you I must delve into my hidden depths, which scares me; I must bare myself and practically shed my own existence, whereas I want to be who I am and not just your shadow. I may be dependent on both of you, but my dependence on mother is more like a crutch than a disability, while my dependence on you is like an addiction which I hate and want to break. I desperately want to withdraw from you, but just as desperately want to hold on to you.

When I'm with you I feel played out instead of playful. You are what I'm trying to escape from but cannot – perhaps because I don't really want to. Running away saddens me; not running devastates me. You inhibit my life, yet I feel I must always measure myself against you. If I'm happy, I want you to know it, not as if you were my husband but as if I were your widow and you my dead man. I never did manage to love you as Didi said one should, the way it was in films. We were just children then, and love was something we knew about only through movies. But from the beginning I remember feeling as though I were your widow, and big Nina realized it and was worried. Your wife was amazingly perceptive; she saw me from the outside but could fathom things in me simply through her feminine intuition. You fathomed me from the inside, from your own gut, the way I understood you, but you must realize, Joseph, that I am your greatest failure as well as your widow.

You had no idea what my private life was like, outside the house, in my own time. How I, like you, played with death, since I was born the widow to a father who had lost a daughter. How I challenged death. How, like you, I tried to stretch my limits of human endurance to the edge, beyond pain, and then parachute – not with a real parachute like yours, made of silk or nylon. I remember that when I was a kid, you took us to the Negev to watch a parachute drop; and I stood there down below with mother and whispered a prayer: "Let the parachute rip. Let him fall. I must mourn for him." Then, at Didi's funeral, I spoke about you, not just her. When you had landed safely with your parachute, I felt so lousy and guilty that I wept, but you didn't notice because of the dust and the heat. I'd already begun to mourn for you, but you were too busy extricating yourself from the parachute.
You'll see . . .

The letter broke off unsigned, in mid-sentence, but it came in an envelope, and the address on the envelope was clearly in Miriam's hand.

The following morning, at seven, I went downstairs. I wanted to mull things over at the pool. In the entrance hall of the house stood some painters; on the floor were buckets and cans of paint, brushes, ladders, and huge sheets of tarpaulin. They asked if I had any special requests for my door. They were having a great time, and called me Brigadier. I became angry. When I asked who had hired them, they said that my neighbours hadn't talked to me about it because they didn't want to give me any unnecessary headaches.

In Miriam's letter she spoke of the house getting painted, but she wrote that letter four months ago; the postmark said October. Miriam had disappeared on 21 January. I stood outside; a pleasant winter sun hung in the sky, the street was humming, I looked back at the painters, from an open window I could hear the voice of a newscaster reciting the day's doings. Czeszek emerged from a car and approached me. He seemed downcast and didn't try to hide it. He took my hand and squeezed it. Without saying a word, he climbed upstairs and I followed him. He warmed his hands over the electric stove which Naomi had left on, and he said, "The news isn't so good Commander, but take it with a grain of salt. Nothing is settled yet. Some more of Miriam's clothes were found, her ID, the contents of a purse, a lot of blood, but no body. Up in some cave in the Galilee, which the Office of Antiquities had camouflaged. The blood was tested that night. It's hers. There's no doubt about Miriam's having been there."

I put on my uniform, I don't know why, maybe I felt as though I were doing reserve duty. I wore a jacket. Naomi got into her uniform too. And we drove with Czeszek. Czeszek said that some Arabs – he called them "minority folk" – were being held for questioning, and that the Chief of the Investigating Military Police believed that a confession would soon follow. "After the confession, maybe we'll get to the bottom of this, but maybe," said Czeszek, "it's all just a wild-goose chase. In this case, as I told you, anything is possible."

Czeszek was cautious. Naturally, he couldn't have known why my face fell the moment I heard that all these items had been found in the cave where the vial of tears came from. Only after we'd arrived there did he show me the "murder blade", as he called it, which was stained in blood. I shut my eyes. In the recesses of my mind I saw Miriam's disappearing face stuck against the window of the bus as the red light changed and the bus moved on. The rain came down like bullets. I opened my eyes, and for the first time I felt that my daughter Miriam was my child who had died.

13

It surprised me how well I remembered the cave. The sharp, mysterious odour, the look of the walls, the murkiness. We found most of Miriam's remaining articles of clothing. I already had the beret from Jaffa, the jacket and blouse from Carmel; now we'd located the rest. There were signs of someone having been dragged, as well as clear signs of a struggle. Few knew of the cave. The Department of Antiquities had closed it up, concealing it even from archaeological eyes. For lack of money for basic research and digs, the cave had to be kept a secret, especially since there were so many other caves in the area. It was situated close by a well-travelled road which went to Peki'in, to Carmiel.

When Miriam was fourteen, I couldn't help but take her there for her birthday. We went inside at dusk; I made sure that nobody noticed us. She was very excited. We sat, it was chilly, we drank from a water flask, and Miriam said she felt as though we had penetrated into the domain of the dead. Unlike my officer friends, I don't have a collection of ancient artefacts. I never cared for them or looted any the way most of my army pals did. I have that one vial which was presented to me as a gift by the archaeologist who came to close off the place – a meagre recompense, as he said, for my having discovered the cave and kept it a secret even from Moshe Dayan, who was Chief of Staff then. Dayan suspected something, nosed around, put pressure on me, but I told him nothing. To the credit of the guy from the Antiquities Department, he never panicked like his colleagues or revealed anything.

He didn't buckle under to Moshe Dayan or his numerous lackeys. The source of my military inspiration was not the heroes of ancient Israel, whom everybody sought through artefacts of antiquity, but Nina's eyes of sorrow.

The secret of the cave was safe with Miriam. She never divulged it to anybody; in all her trips to the Galilee with her friends, she never revisited the cave. I said to Czeszek, "You saw how hard it is to get into the cave? And you saw that not a single item on the list which the district appointee brought with him has been taken – absolutely nothing is missing? The sarcophagus hasn't been broken open; everything is exactly the way it was before. Look, whoever dragged Miriam here or wanted us to think that he had, must have known about my connection to this place and Miriam's indirect link to it, but who could that be?"

This time the search party was even bigger. Soldiers and police combed the area. They dusted for fingerprints. I never worshipped the dead, never drank whisky at the graves of my deceased comrades, never sang old sentimental songs by their tombstones, never edited books and anthologies in their memory. The unit which I commanded didn't have idols or statues. *Yes*, I linked my fate with that cave, in a way which I cannot quite fathom. *Yes*, I hung Isaac Raphaeli's photograph on the wall of my apartment (next to the vial of tears). I should think hard about this, because somewhere in the cave and its vicinity, among all the things I'd seen there, was a clue. Czeszek seemed locked inside himself, as though he'd lost his earlier guarded optimism. Even Naomi looked perplexed by what I'd said. There was the feeling that everything had come full circle, we were at a dead end, it was just a matter of time before the corpse would turn up.

The Arab suspects in custody were interrogated. Soldiers combed every square metre, but didn't find Miriam's body. Czeszek looked terrible now, exhausted and disappointed. He tried to listen to me with his eyes shut; I saw horror in his face. Somebody had toyed with him too. "It's all there in that cave," he said. "The signs of dragging, blood, fingerprints. Somebody came and took the body and hid it. Where? In some house? Over a hundred thousand people live in the area, in tens of thousands of houses. Where should we look? In every house? She has to be around here someplace! Doesn't she?"

A few days later we went back. No more letters had come from Miriam and I was practically the only one who believed that Miriam was still alive, though I myself began to have doubts. I knew we were looking in the wrong direction, but I didn't know what the right direction was. Occasionally I would envision my daughter dead, and then ask myself where she was dead, or how she could possibly be dead if there wasn't a corpse. I thought about Nina, who had witnessed death in the shape of smoke; she would have understood all this better than I, but she wasn't around.

What pained me even more, perhaps, than the articles of clothing that we'd found was seeing my staircase painted when I got back. The door of my apartment was grey, the walls white, the house actually looked better than it had for many years.

But somehow the house made me think of a funeral; newly painted on the inside, while still ramshackle on the outside, it reeked of death.

Meanwhile the press dropped the story. Syrian jets had been shot down, a soldier had disappeared in the vicinity of Hadera, a female soldier had vanished not far from Carmel, along the seashore, pretty close to the spot where Miriam's jacket and blouse had been found. I tried to question the tenants in my house. The landlord, who'd lost a fortune on the house and had neglected it because of rent control, came by one day to ask the opinion of every tenant on which colour was preferable; he had smiled mysteriously – that's what Mr Feigel told me – and explained that the money to paint the house had come from some secret source. When Naomi consented to Madame Frau's entreaties and telegrams and attended a séance at her place, Madame Frau had told her that a widower had sent the landlord a letter (with American stamps on the envelope). Inside was a fat cheque made out to the landlord, a gift to what Madame Frau called, quoting from the letter, "my old residence and heart's joy". "Pretty fancy Hebrew," said Madame Frau, who had never been an expert on the language. She said that the donor claimed to have lived in the house years ago, then emigrated to America, but loved Mr Haim and Mr Feigel, and all the other old-timers whom he knew so well (whereas nobody could or would remember him!); and therefore he decided not only to give the landlord a present for suffering under the rent control law which had turned many houses in Tel-Aviv into a disaster area as bad as any pogrom, but to let the tenants themselves select the colour used to paint the indoor premises. The letter even stipulated, the landlord told me after I'd phoned and he'd acquiesced to my demands for information (except that he wouldn't agree to tell me the amount he'd received for himself), the letter specified that Mr Krieger, being a veteran army man and contributer to national security, should be relieved of any inconvenience attached to the house's being painted, and therefore be allowed a free trip – at the landlord's expense – during the days allotted for painting; Mr Krieger could stay at a spa until the job was completed. "I called you before," said the landlord, "to suggest that you take a trip, but you weren't around. Mr Haim said you'd gone away, and I read in the papers about the cave in the Galilee. I understood and didn't want to disturb you. I hope that your daughter will be found safe and sound."

At the séance it was established that Miriam was journeying along the byways of the earth, alive, looking for her father. "Heaven says she hasn't arrived there," Naomi informed me without cracking a smile, when she returned from Madame Frau's apartment.

I went to the city archives. A clerk, whose husband had once served under me, sneaked me inside; she'd read about Miriam and felt sorry for me. I looked for the name of anybody who had once lived in the house and was now perhaps residing in New York, but I couldn't find any. Naomi said out of the blue, "Nina wouldn't have sent money to paint the house, and if she did, how would Miriam have known about it unless they'd planned it together? But what for? Why would they want you away from the house for two days? How did they know you'd actually go away? Anyway why did they choose that cave in the Galilee?"

While I was busy seeking out the widowed donor and postponing my intended visit to the Raphaeli family, four Arabs confessed to committing murder in the Galilee. Czeszek seemed encouraged. I asked him if a body had been found, and he said, "Not yet, but we do have murder confessions."

In the dim depths of my consciousness, I knew what had in fact occurred; something I'd heard or thought and forgotten about as Naomi and I talked during our first love-making, a solitary detail in the mishmash of conflicting facts, some critical clue had flashed for a moment, but like a fishing boat at night turning off all its lights, my mind swallowed its knowledge without a trace. I tried to let it guide me. I concentrated again on Hanoch Levi and on the Bet-Lid junction. I travelled to Jerusalem and surprised Joy. She lived in a small old house surrounded by thick olive trees, with a lovely red roof, large rooms, impressive windows, and sweet basil in flower pots. Joy was more involved in my life than I'd ever suspected.

She was wearing a purple Bedouin dress, embroidered with hundreds of tiny patches of colour, and she invited me for coffee. Her face was tense. I knew she was thinking about Hanoch. I wanted to snare her with her own lasso. The moment I sat down, I sensed how she was already building a protective wall around her man. Out of a certain instinct which Naomi, perhaps, had rekindled in me, the instinct of a hunter who knows every manoeuvre of a woman, whether offensive or defensive, I locked eyes with her and spoke about Hanoch for a minute. She anticipated that and went along with it. I made her sweat and pretended I knew something; she tried to anticipate my thoughts, but I wouldn't let her. I followed the steps which she would have taken: I buttered her up and yet wouldn't let her off the hook. She was actually scared that I had something up my sleeve. I made a point of belittling the arrest of the suspects in the Galilee. And without her realizing it – since she was so busy trying to defend her

Hanoch – I got her to fall back on her old seductive ways, until she had almost resuscitated her bewitching charms. That's when I managed to eke out of her what I'd come for; I got her to say that she and Reuben knew that Nina had recently visited Israel for a short while and then gone back. That was all I really wanted from her. She told me about it because she thought I was close to uncovering some fact concerning Hanoch. Her effort to conceal that information allowed me to manipulate her. When she told me how Hanoch Levi had returned late at night from Tel-Aviv, after dropping off the religious soldier Yossi, she said that he didn't drive home but went directly to her, and naturally I knew she was lying.

The disclosure that Nina had paid a whore's visit to Israel and hadn't got in touch with me because I was, in her words, "living with a young woman", Joy threw at me with a passionate eagerness that was simultaneously cruel and polite. She was just trying to create a diversion, given her suspicions about me, but I kept my cards in my hand. Only a few days ago I'd already seen how an experienced investigator like Czeszek had fallen victim to mental exhaustion, how his mind had simply gone on holiday in the wake of a sudden, brutal defeat which forced him into a premature finding of facts in the wrong place.

She spoke about Hanoch, and said that she'd sat waiting for me here for years, but I hadn't come; and now that I'd arrived she was away, and it was too late anyway. As she looked towards her enormous bed, I asked her, "How did you trap him?" She was insulted. "I am a beautiful, intelligent woman, Joseph, and he's crazy about me."

I told her, "But he always returns to his wife, he needs her. That's a fact. He fell into your hands because you know something which keeps him on a short leash." She got angry, threw a cushion at me, screamed, but I calmed her down. She was fighting for Hanoch Levi's life, and he did apparently have something to hide. It was the only way to milk out of her a real betrayal. I felt like Reuben, but without his sense of victory. That was the province of a shit like him, who could wind anybody around his finger and press at one spot to get water to come out of

181

another spot somewhere else. He knew in advance what he was after, but if he got anything extra, so much the better. So I played Reuben, and she didn't catch on. I was disgusted with myself, but I was the only one who could have pulled this off, nobody could have helped me out. I was forced to put the squeeze on Joy so she would endanger her Hanoch. It worked like magic. How easily a woman betrays.

In the end I became submissive, letting her think that she had won. I told her, "Hanoch Levi doesn't interest me that much, I'm looking for the link between Nina, Reuben and Miriam, and the fact that she visited Israel explains a lot." Joy was still suspicious. Her face showed that natural, primitive caution which never leaves her. Behind this conversation were ten years of unrequited love. Through the window were the Judaean hills, veiled in the day's last light. Joy looked sad, as if she had no fight left in her. I had somehow aroused her latent longings for what had died in her long ago, and she was genuinely aching over it, as though now that her man were before her again, she might wish to turn the clock back, but not to the humiliation she had once felt.

At last the mask was down, and she looked utterly frail. She didn't turn on any lights. We remained in near darkness. The only light which reached us came from a street lamp which stood by a window whose blinds were still open. Joy said, "He'll leave his wife and marry me, Joseph, and that's all that counts. A few months ago I was invited to a party. Some of the television crowd gave me a dress as a gift. It was my birthday. The zipper on the dress was at the back. It got late. A girlfriend was supposed to come by to pick me up; we agreed she'd hoot and I'd come down. I stood in front of the mirror and saw that I didn't look so bad; the years had passed but hadn't taken that much away from me." She was smiling now as she spoke, taunting me again, full of that rough, abandoned charm which was typically Israeli yet foreign to me, and I almost felt as if I were sitting opposite an obituary in the form of a woman. "Look," she said, "I stood before that mirror and couldn't zip up that dress. I tried, bending over, turning every which way, but I was stuck there with my dress still opened at the back. My girlfriend was already downstairs honking, I wanted to call out to her to come upstairs and help me, but I felt like a fool and told myself so. Do you know what else I told myself then? I said that I needed a man around the house to zip up my dresses for me. Hanoch Levi was already my lover, only it wasn't serious. We were together a lot, but he had others, some beauties too; after all, he knew Miriam and she's prettier than I am."

"How would you know? If you claim you never saw her?"

"He told me," she said quickly and gave me a playful look, as though she felt sorry for me for having spoiled her sad joke. "And he knows what he's talking about. But he was never involved with her! That's something I do know! Look, he's an admirer of yours, a fanatic when it comes to heroes, Hanoch is. I know my goods. He worships heroes, but is afraid of his own shadow. To sit in the evening in some general's house, to talk about battles, to milk information so as to be in the thick of things, to know secrets which others don't, to hear any dirt about generals, that's what he's crazy about. You were his hero from way back. When he heard who I once was, and what had or hadn't gone on between us, he refused (to this day) to believe that we weren't lovers. It turned him on. In the beginning it actually amused him that you of all people had been my man. He looked for you inside me, never understanding that you hadn't once entered me, you bastard you, making me wait for so many years in vain! With no love scene! But what do you have left finally? A girl of no substance, a lost daughter and a wife in America . . . Listen, he began to question me about you, to smell you on me, trying to fathom what made you into such a glorious officer, your principles, your devotion, your loyalty, hell, he never realized what a square you are; perhaps he could never understand that basic fact about you, but I never disclosed it . . . He has a wicked beauty which I adore; he's like a boy who never grew up, but in his own area he's a wise old man. He takes pride, though, in what he isn't, instead of what he's really good at. He's as curious, intelligent, and evasive as a child, that's what makes him successful, but that's not what he's proud of. He's proud of his two lousy days of fighting in the Six Day War or of his ties to headquarters, or of some manoeuvre he was once invited to observe in the Jordan valley from a helicopter ... and you ought to remember that, because didn't you complain about it to the Chief of Staff? You said that inviting entertainers and politicians on helicopter excursions to watch a man-hunt and slaughter was prostitution, that war was not entertainment, and murder not theatre. What were you then? A major? The Chief of Staff in those days told you, 'Don't be such a nincompoop, the commanding officer is just a wiseguy!' And that's all he had to say on the subject. But Hanoch Levi, who was just a young radio announcer then and crazy about those heroes, actually refused the invitation, even though he was ridiculed for it. He'd been psyched by the invitation but refused to witness the awful hunt because you had complained about it, without of course knowing Hanoch Levi, and had almost taken the matter to the military court. You the man of principles and justice, Joseph Krieger, where are you today and where is your friend D., eh?"

After a brief pause Joy added, "I finally told him something, I had no other choice, he wanted it, you were larger than life for him, dangerous, drenched in greatness. Things which to me were just plain memories – the teleprinter, the Sinai nights, the ambushes – it all suddenly acquired a new meaning; as far as he was concerned, I was your widow –"

"My widow?"

"Your widow, Joseph. What's wrong? Are you startled?"

"No, but Miriam wrote to me that during all these years she felt like my widow."

"Interesting." Joy almost doubled up; something was hurting her, she seemed apprehensive again, perhaps I had unwittingly got under her skin. She returned to her former guarded tone. I gazed at her. It amused me how easily everything looked simple and just as easily looked not so simple. She waited a bit, perhaps evaluating in her mind our last exchange, and then deciding that it was all right. Apparently, it was important for her to tell me; she'd waited years for it. I guess her small revenge had greater significance to her than her precaution did. Poor Joy, how disappointed she was to hear that I knew what Miriam had said.

She began talking again. "Hanoch also tried his luck with Nina. That was long ago. I think he was one of the few who didn't make it with her. I don't know exactly how he met Miriam, but he flirted with her. Maybe his experience with her mother had stung him. Look, I didn't get an angel for a present. I got what I really needed perhaps, a darling little devil who hangs on to me like a mummy's boy, and I need somebody to zip up my dress – not a stranger who comes and goes but someone who will stay at home. He's a scaredy-cat, that's why he's so afraid of any investigation, but he has nothing at all to hide. So what if he made a pass at Miriam? He's always ready for that. He's a mechanical Don Juan. A Don Quixote of words. You turn him on because you're a hero, but what he really loves is a woman in bed. It's what he knows best. He's just a great lover, not simply screwing by the manual, but real, true love! He's always matching himself against others, who's the better lover, who's more handsome, more intelligent, always competing, always measuring, and always losing or thinking that he's losing, so he has to run quickly and prove himself. That was his way of demonstrating his intelligence and power, through women, whereas others like you had alternative ways. He can be mean, but he can also be tender. Look, you may be a dangerous man but you don't know anything about women; he does. He's gallant and cruel; you are not. Miriam really liked him, I think; he frightened Nina. Women are something you nurture, Brigadier, not shoot down with missiles. But hurt somebody? He couldn't hurt a fly. You're excellent material for betrayal, Brigadier, because you're too straight and, in the end, despite all your heroism which Hanoch so adulates, you're as easy to manipulate as a spoon."

I sat quietly, caught up in a kind of compassion for her, for Hanoch, for Miriam, even for Nina. I said to her, "Joy, as I sat and listened to you, suddenly you seemed sweet, not a wounded lioness, just an ordinary woman alone and unfortunate who wanted somebody to zip up her dress for her. That was fine. But you're a liar, a shameless liar. You told me about Nina's visit to Israel because you thought I was on her trail anyway. And it was to your advantage, too, since any attention given to Nina takes the spotlight off Hanoch Levi, who may be a charming man and know about women, but he also knows something else and is involved in something that you're quite aware of; that's your ace, you keep him on a short leash so he'll drop his wife who always accepts him as he is, waiting for him to come home after all his exploits; home, to her. You thought one step ahead, you figured it all out – Reuben, Nina, I don't know what else. But whatever information you have is what scares him. I don't understand scaredy-cats, but I do understand Joys and I can snare any Hanoch of yours. In the end I'll catch him. Tell him he's in my sights, whether or not he admires me. Heroes abound like shit, it's a nation of heroes. A state under siege, and all that. You know! Zionism! A Ministry of Defence with a Philharmonic Orchestra. Israel. But heroes aren't such a serious matter, the Germans had their heroes too, and the Japanese, with their kamikaze pilots. The Americans may have been less heroic but they won the war. So I'm the shameful product of the national situation, a mutation of my father, his violin and his books. Madame Frau Birnbaum who is afraid of lions is a hundred times wiser than I, Nina too, and also little Naomi whom I finally found in order to understand what I'd lost even with you."

She wept. I rose and, without looking at her, left. I got into my car. In the mirror I saw her face at the window. She called out, but I didn't hear anything.

14

WHEN I got back home I told Naomi that I'd slept with Joy, but Joy's love for me had died. I told her that I'd gone to bed with Joy in order to ascertain what I really knew. "You must despise me," I said. She smiled, sat cross-legged, looked at me, rose, prepared coffee, and said, "You're a fucked-up generation, Brigadier, you think sleeping with a woman is a big deal. Looking at one another the way we do is more than bedding down, and a whore may get in bed with you but she won't kiss you. Besides, you didn't sleep with Joy," and she laughed. I wanted to hug her, but I suddenly thought about Nina and her visit here. Gideon came in; he seemed crushed. He'd heard about the testimony which had been taken from the suspects, and was certain that the body would be found. I said to him, "Gideon, you're wrong," and all of a sudden I was a joke; I knew how ridiculous I sounded.

I started to travel all over the country, searching randomly. In Ekron I saw the house of the Simontov family, but I didn't go inside. I didn't know what to ask them; I realized that they knew Miriam but I didn't want to fall into any trap that was prepared for me. Somebody was pulling my leg. The Simontov family was, after all, just another stumbling block. I returned to my routine of swimming at the pool in the morning. But first I went out on the balcony to insult Madame Frau, though we skipped all the insults and just had short, sad conversations about life. The Chief of Staff enjoyed the idea that Naomi was remaining with me on orders from headquarters. It was good ammunition for his sense of humour. Reuben was overseas somewhere and it was impossible to locate him. I went to Miriam's room and at long last rummaged through her papers, found letters, read them, but they didn't shed any new light on anything, except that they proved Miriam and Nina had corresponded for almost a year. Most of Nina's letters were ripped up; perhaps there were many more of them elsewhere. That's what I told Gideon, who left and then returned, saying that he'd searched Miriam's locker but found nothing. I had all of Nina's telephone numbers in America, enough to track her down. She admitted that she'd come to Israel for a short visit of about three days; she said it made no sense to contact me if I were in love with a girl who could be my daughter. I told her, "Look, Nina, for some reason you're positive nothing bad has happened to Miriam. Maybe; but maybe she's in trouble. Perhaps she concocted something you know about, but it backfired. Take into account human error, traps; come!"

She said that she had returned to America to settle a few matters and would be back in Israel in a few days. "I'm scared too," said Nina, "and I'll get in touch with you when I arrive. But if Naomi answers, I'll hang up." I told her the time had come for an "ending with honour". "Nina," I said, "nobody will accept any moralizing from you, not even the merciful Almighty." And she laughed, a wild transatlantic guffaw. She laughed through her cascade of tears which I could taste even at that distance. "You're a funny man, Joseph. If only you'd said those words years ago, if you only had! If you'd said just once that you were hurting . . ."

"I'm not hurting now, and I didn't then," I told her. "Don't make the same mistake all over again. Don't be perverse. We have, you and I, one daughter. The letters she wrote to me came in reverse order. I'm not sure, but I smell a conspiracy. There are findings, blood, suspects, I'm worried. Maybe she wanted to break me. Come, the sooner the better; together we may understand more."

After she hung up, I felt as if I were choking. I went to the pool. The conversation with Nina was at six in the morning; she hadn't slept the previous night. Sokolowicz tried to pump some information on Miriam, as my partner in sorrow, but I shook him off; I was boiling and full of resentment, and he was offended. I let Rebecca feed me, I was dripping wet, it was cold and windy, and I went home. Talking to Naomi I called her Miriam. Even to myself I sounded as though something had gone wrong inside me. I drove to a few crossroads, parked the car and waited. Suddenly I realized I was just hunting for Miriam at chance junctions whereas I should be learning something from my daughter's logic. I set up a small tent in the triangle of sand at the Country Club junction. I'd brought along a cordless phone which would keep me in touch with home, with Naomi; and for two weeks I waited for Miriam at a crossroad, because by the inverted logic of her letters, if she were alive and wandering around the country, what was the point of my going from crossroad to crossroad? I could sit down at any junction and at some time or other she would have to pass by. Two months ago if somebody had told me that I would be sitting for two weeks in a tent at a busy intersection like the Country Club junction in order to locate my daughter, I would have sent him to a psychiatrist. But I sat there now, death's baby face, someone who at nineteen had crossed over into enemy territory to visit Jordanian Jericho and returned alive.

Eight hours a day I sat and watched the cars. Next to the wizards and astrologers of Madame Frau, it was the most ridiculous thing I'd ever done in my life. The world of fantasy which I had entered had worked on me; I already believed that Miriam was sitting in some house, pulling strings, while all of us, including God, acted accordingly. I saw people I hadn't seen for years. In my binoculars they looked exhausted and stressed. Five times I saw the Chief of Staff in his car. Reuben I saw, too, and understood that he was back. Familiar faces kept streaming by, and they all looked so much older now. I sat and watched. I'd brought along a thermos and some sandwiches, and now and again I would have a conversation with Naomi who maintained the command post at home. She didn't ridicule me, she tried to understand, though it was hard for her. Miriam's disappearance had implanted in me a new point of view, a sort of shock of recognition which I had denied myself until now. I became a mere citizen, as bursts of sorrow and pain and jealousy erupted from me like lava from a volcano. I realized all of a sudden that I too could feel pain.

It was perhaps a childish craving to outwit my daughter, to break the secret code surrounding her disappearance as well as her life, which I now realized I knew nothing about. She wasn't just missing, she was missing in Miriam's own way.

By the night before the last, I was already limp; the moon was full, a scorching wind blew, the lights of cars crossed and momentarily extinguished the deep caverns of darkness. Then Reuben and the Chief of Staff showed up. As they approached the tent from their car, I sensed how alone I was. They walked in silence; our childhood connection rekindled, in an instant all suspicion vanished. We were no longer the miniatures of the heroes we had wanted to be. Their approach was so solemn it was almost like a death sentence. Reuben was gracious, offered me some American cigarettes. They sat down next to me; and it was the way we were then, on the hills facing the sea, secluded from the world and its standards (which we didn't even know), the founders of a secret homeland by a mystic cave. Meanwhile the nation went past us in their cars, they saw a dot of light and had no idea what we were up to. We reminisced about the old days, about our teachers who exchanged blows among themselves over the new state, about the supposed gallantry of the Jewish government which suddenly became, instead of a culmination, a joke in top hats, with Ben-Gurion standing by the master of ceremonies and getting instructions from him when to smile and what to salute at; there was already a flag, with shopkeepers rallying round it trying to look ministerial – a British dog, a mongrel, would have done a better job of it. They stood to attention in front of flags which had sprung up all over the place and which fluttered in the presence of the buyers and sellers on the black market, and they sang the national anthem half-asleep. We were a transitional generation. After us came the professionals, but we were the middle generation, between the disbanding Palmach together with the few who remained with us, and those who followed afterwards, who were born into the new nation, measured, rough, not always exerting themselves. We had to learn how to be vicious. Officers who had been nonentities in the British army attempted to make a fighting force out of us. It was a joke. The Chief of Staff was already in charge of a whole army, Reuben was already devising his fantastic schemes, but we still had to keep an eye on the younger generation who were forcing their way up, better trained than us but devoid of that dark feeling of the gunslinger at the edge of doom. They were familiar with victory, not defeat.

Reuben had perhaps come to tell me that his struggle against me had also been against himself. We watched the cars, the criss-crossing beams of light, the gigantic moon, as the Chief of Staff pulled out a bottle and we drank. We ate sandwiches and got drunk. Reuben said, "It all began with Nina. She wanted all three of us, one who was innocent, one who knew how to ask questions, and one who could answer them, and she ended up alone, by herself, the only question nobody could answer."

Reuben went on. "I brought her from the airport into town. I introduced her to Noam, and later she told me that she met him again. She came here at Miriam's request. She also spoke to Joy. I helped her, Joseph, but I didn't know what she was up to exactly, in other words she left me in the dark, too, about her battle. Finally she asked me to take her back to the airport. In the car she told me that she had failed at love, that she had a deep blemish, that she had given up, she was a traitor who hated herself. 'They robbed me of my childhood,' she said, 'and they made a cripple out of me. You were the only one who understood how lonely I was.' I told her, 'Nina, I'm getting sick of the game too. I'm suddenly involved again with Joseph, which gets at the deepest layers of my history, at who I really am. You know how much it pains me always to be Joseph's enemy in your bed. The children are already taking over command from us, we're at the end of the road; you too.' "

"We were always dependent on her," said the Chief of Staff, "on her elegant charm, her wild whims. I sit in my office and think about my wife who died and about

Miriam who's missing now. Nina toyed with me too. We were three bosom pals, what remains of it? Bitterness? I hurt you, Joseph, and I enjoyed it, but in the end I just hurt myself because Nina vanished like a whirlwind and I was left alone in my office, trying to reach out to the phone and call you to say how much I cared about your agony, but my hand wouldn't budge. In my imagination I could see your face as you stood opposite Miriam in the corridor watching her jump into my arms while I, for some reason I don't understand, tried to give you pain."

Reuben, who had drunk more than either of us, said, "Not long ago I was sitting in an aeroplane. A lovely stewardess came up to me and said, 'You look good,' and I thought to myself, 'Oh, she's Miriam Krieger's age, what do I know about losing a daughter? Joseph knows, my brother, and the Chief of Staff, my two brothers . . . It's in our blood, one tribe, family, flesh, and Nina after all came much later. It was natural for me to be a bastard, that's my character and also my profession. It's very convenient when work and personality match. I made a career out of being a bastard. But finally I heard that you were sitting at the Country Club junction, and it completely shattered me. When I called, Naomi told me, 'He's sitting there alone and looking for Miriam.' It just snapped me in two. In my dry heart, along the veins through which blood had long since ceased to flow, I sensed something stir from the past, and I called the Chief of Staff who had been waiting for that call like the scorched summer earth in need of rain, and we came, in refuge from ourselves, for nothing . . ."

We all hit the bottle. I'd already stopped looking through my binoculars. Something had died in me too. A warmth developed in that tent, the reunion of friends. I agreed with the Chief of Staff that our arguments now seemed in retrospect perverse, silly, petty. The tent filled with cigarette smoke as Reuben said, "Miriam was the daughter of all three of us, our poor child," and the place reeked of brandy, of things gone sour, of dead youth.

Reuben kept on talking. "Nina loved one of us but I don't know who, maybe it was you, Joseph. Miriam didn't understand her and co-opted her into some lousy plan of hers. Miriam and Nira, Naomi's sister, are rivals over the dead soldier. Nina shows up, with Noam! The fucked-up brother of that dead soldier, who was always his shadow, suddenly took on new life. What really happened? What about the confessions of the Arabs? You believe them?"

I said I didn't.

The Chief of Staff said, "There's something murky here, as though we all know it but won't admit it." And I said to him, "That's exactly what disturbs me. Maybe it explains why I fell on my face and sat here for two weeks. I was trying to escape from the bitter truth which I realize I know but cannot put my finger on."

"Me too," said Reuben.

Finally we tottered, drunk, to the two cars. The earth stank from brandy. We all embraced. Or tried to. And after we botched the embrace, we fell down. Once down, we sat on the ground and began to cry. Three hippopotamuses, battered by war and conspiracies, we sat and wept like children. Cars whizzed past us. The hour was late and the moon had set. There was nothing more to be said. We tried to get up but couldn't. In the end, all three of us rose at the same time, and drove off.

I got home exhausted, drunk, and full of sand. Naomi cleaned me up, and I told her what had happened. She lay next to me, her eyes peering through the edge of the blanket the way Miriam used to in the morning on the way to the bathroom. I got out of bed and started to dance before her. I was tipsy. She laughed at first, then after a few moments stopped. It was the first time in my life that I had ever danced in my house. I didn't know exactly what I was doing, but I wasn't so drunk that I wouldn't remember it afterwards. I was a silly hulk but I danced like a Greek peasant in the movies. A kind of Arab *debka* mixed with a tango. I'm not a dancer. In the youth movement I danced very little, and never since. Suddenly, at the age of fifty, in my underwear, in the bedroom, I'm dancing before a girl who could be my daughter, who looks at me with such trust, devoid of any criticism or puzzlement, as though all her life she has been sleeping in bed while middle-aged men with physiques that are in good shape, if somewhat rusty, dance in front of her and tell her about Reuben and the Chief of Staff and the Three Musketeers and the boyhood blood pact and the coming war with Rommel's men, and the establishment of a Jewish State. Finally we both wept and I climbed into bed. My head was spinning and, like Madame Frau, I had another night's death. A year is three hundred and sixty-five dead dogs.

15

HER rotting body was discovered by scouts in a pile of rubble, in a wadi. Among pillars, at the back of an abandoned olive grove about a kilometre away from the cave.

The press, feeding on the corpse with sickening cannibalism, quoted one of the suspects as saying they had plucked the soldier the way Jews pluck a chicken on the eve of Yom Kippur. After a lawyer from Nazareth protested in a letter to the editor, claiming that not a single suspect had uttered those words, a disclaimer appeared at the bottom of a page. The nation accepted the blood, the photographers milked it. The sight of the corpse was truly horrifying, "one of the most debased instances of murder in the history of our nation", in the words of the newsmen and politicians who came to be photographed alongside the body. It was cut up, charred, and unidentifiable. I stood a whole day by the remains. As Naomi drew near, I tried to stop her. She stood wide-eyed and slowly approached; I supported her and she said she was sorry, that she didn't want to burden me any further, and she held back her tears. Gideon vomited. Czeszek looked solid; the mere sight of him infuriated me, as if the burning, the tearing out of her eyes, the pulling apart of her limbs, had all been done so that he might feel he was in the right and his struggle with evil could end in his favour. In a daze I heard that Nina had arrived in Israel and was staying at the Astor Hotel.

It was warm, soldiers roamed the area, police abounded. Some semen was found, and cloth remnants which the crime lab couldn't link with Miriam. But the three suspects were dragged to the place. They stood with eyes downcast, somebody shoved them towards the corpse, an officer screamed, a policeman was seen hauling one of the suspects by the neck, and the case was closed, the mystery over. The suspects murmured something, I didn't hear what they had said, I just stood there, unable to move from the spot, knowing that I would have to interrogate the suspects on my own.

There was opposition to my being granted permission to question them, on humanitarian grounds. They said I would try to take revenge on them, but the Chief of Staff and the general commander of the police intervened on my behalf. Nina called to say, "Drop it, Joseph. What good is it?" She sounded weary and worried. "She's dead. What will you get out of this business? We have things to go over, I'm grieving in this shitty hotel. Even Reuben won't visit. Stop it!" I told her I didn't believe it was Miriam's body, that Czeszek was too confident, all of them were. "They just want to close the file. They have a confession, a motive, a place. They have it all and are afraid of anything which might upset their lovely order." And she answered, "Don't muck it up, Josie, you always have to be the only one who's right! Enough! Let our dead daughter rest in peace, out of the hands of the newspapers and those vultures ..." When a security officer ridiculed me saying, "Aren't you the guy who went looking for his daughter at the Country Club junction?" I realized how frightened they were, but I also knew that Reuben wasn't the one who was blocking me. By the next day I had already understood that the article in *Ha-Olam Hazeh* about my sitting at the Country Club junction had its source in television circles. There was no need to go any further than that. Meanwhile, the general climate of the community had become hostile; my willingness to question the validity of the investigation and my wish to interrogate the suspects myself had aroused a furore. The Arab press and radio had already turned the murderers into national heroes.

The murder was separated from its painful human context. I didn't pity the suspects, as the newspapers hinted. As far as I was concerned, they could very well have been mixed up in a murder; a corpse existed. Somebody had murdered her, but it was some other woman, not Miriam, whom they may have butchered. I simply couldn't give these Arabs the right to kill Miriam. It was my arrogance which played the key role here. The suspects – and I was the only one who still called them that – sounded to me as though they were trying to take upon themselves a significance greater than they deserved. The Arab press from Tunis to Iraq lauded their courage, calling them "our heroic brothers". A known woman terrorist who had recently been released from an Israeli prison, said on the radio, "All honour to my brothers and heroes, I love you and embrace you and kiss your magnificent hands which have fought bravely against Zionist soldiers, killing a murderous officer and wiping out her soldiers." In an Egyptian newspaper they characterized me as a bloodthirsty, old-time officer who had executed a prisoner and whose treachery had been transmitted into the blood of my daughter, an officer who fought without mercy.

In spite of the protests of security officers, I was allowed ultimately to speak to the suspects. As I entered the cell I felt as if the military guards there were waiting for me with a certain restrained pleasure; they were all prepared for my coming. With their short haircuts and faded look in their eyes, they shoved me inside. One of them said with a wink, "Go ahead, it's okay, we understand." They didn't even frisk me or check my garments to see if I had a revolver. There was the unmistakable indication that if I wasted the prisoners, they would back me. I looked at them in amazement. Afterwards they would tell the press that "the guy came to lick the ass of his daughter's killers because he's a Peace-Nownik and thinks the enemy is a sweetheart; he doesn't understand death, not even his daughter's." They described me as a North Tel-Aviv type, with college degrees. One of the soldiers told me, "If they're not killed, a trial will take place, and that'll cost a bundle of money, they'll appoint a doyen, sit around, make a deal, exchange prisoners, and these guys will go to Syria, then come back and kill some more."

On the day I spoke to them, their status had risen to the level of saints in the Arab press. The Israeli press had already milked every drop of blood. The feeling was that other bereaved parents, who had been at loggerheads with me and confronted a stone wall, now poured out their hearts' blood on me. A member of parliament who felt he had to express his horror, who had come out with the demand for the death penalty for terrorists, no longer considered me a friend. He told one journalist, "The man has gone crazy; he sits there and falls in love with his daughter's murderers. Look to what lengths our self-hate will go. That is the true edge of Israeli existence, the ability to enjoy one's own self-loathing."

They sat opposite me. All by themselves. Looking miserable. One of them was almost completely bald. They didn't know the identity of the murdered woman. They knew few details. I questioned them for hours, using every trick I'd once learned from Reuben, but I couldn't get anything out of them. I couldn't hate them. They were in a fog, incapable of clarity, helpless, drenched in ugly defeatism. Fighting isn't anybody's heart's desire, its a profession. Hatred and envy assist the devil, not the fighter. I looked at them, I spoke to them, and realized that they were somewhere between being absolute ciphers and the agents of an historic mission assigned to them by the Arab radio stations. They tried to answer me but couldn't, and I knew they were not lying. Miriam wasn't in any fashion in their eyes, not in the memory of any one of them. They attempted to prattle about some murder which they had already confessed to, but they didn't have any knowledge of the person they had killed, except through the radio.

I went over the case reports and spoke with the chief investigator. Czeszek sat there, his disgust for me was crystal-clear. His former warmth had utterly disappeared. I accepted that the suspects hadn't been tortured. At the outset they were roughed up a bit, but their confession was clean. None the less, the story didn't ring true. Not just because of the sailing trip from the port or the television studio or the hitch in Hanoch Levi's car, but because of the suspects themselves, who were like empty seashells;

they had been sent to heaven to acquire the halo of heroes but had returned with star dust. No legend would emanate from them, they were a bought not an earned story. I was nauseated, not angry. The press and the rumours about me intensified my sense of emptiness, of a void around me; it was my former enemy, D., who cast the rumours which were caught acrobatically by journalists thirsty for slander and blood. I was being court-martialed *in absentia*. My sitting down with the killers and my inability to identify with the spirit of revenge had transformed me into an enemy.

Nina told a journalist who interviewed her that Miriam was killed and she was weeping over her, but she didn't understand what exactly I was up to. Even the Chief of Staff, who appeared on the programme "The Firing Line", when asked about me, described me in brilliant colours but always used the past tense. If he felt obliged to mention my outstanding gifts, what he called my "great accomplishments", he also felt obliged to protect himself. I had sat opposite three killers or suspects or plain weirdoes who had taken upon themselves the task of murder, and I realized how men can play heroes or villains as long as others pull the strings. Later they will recant their confessions, when they realize that a price will be exacted, and what a price! By then it will be too late. At the trial I will be called to testify, and I will stand there and say, "I do not think they killed Miriam, because they lack details and they lack Miriam. Whether they killed another woman I don't know, but if they did they deserve the full punishment." So I'll come out of it a coward and an egoist and a man without a backbone. I was lost from the outset. D. made sure of that, with rumours one after another. There is no lack of enemies when you stand before a wave of fury, a natural and understandable response to a murder so detestable.

When I got home I found a note from Nina. She wrote, "I won't call. You call. Yours, Nina." I sat, the wall before me, and on the wall the photograph and the vial of tears. In came friends from my paratroop unit. The sight of the corpse had heated their blood. They wanted revenge. They too. They wanted to go out together, as in the old days, and show them who we were, so they wouldn't have even one full night of sleep. It took a while to extricate myself from all this hysteria. Naomi prepared a tasty vegetarian meal, and it was a sad affair, God how sad! Reuben phoned to say, "You need some spirit, Joseph, it's healthy to hate a little, revenge isn't such a dirty word." The man who had killed from a distance with cue cards was trying to teach me a lesson in life, perhaps in public relations. It astounded me that he cared whether or not the papers would make mincemeat of me. I told him, "They're too abstract, these Arabs, they have no real basis, do you understand? All they can hold on to is a photograph of murder, not murder itself, they're too small for that, too polite, they have no sense, just misery. They are not wild fanatics, just human debris, picked up from a garbage can." My voice betrayed me, my rage protested against something that abstract. Reuben said, "Take that anger of yours and learn to release it. You sit too close to your pistol. Maybe Miriam's right; she once said, 'There's only one way to shock Daddy, make him feel as if he has utterly lost his honour, beat him on his own terms, inject his revolver into him like an intravenous needle, so when he pulls the trigger and kills himself he'll think he has won!' " I asked him when she said that, and he evaded and stammered. He asked me, "Why not call up Nina?" and he hung up.

A bereaved father phoned, all excited, threatening, forlorn, and I again felt as though I was sitting at a movie, watching lips move but not understanding the language. I thought about the three suspects, about Czeszek who was so sure of himself. The father told me, "Why are you so high and mighty? Pain is no sin. I would sign a statement of gratitude to God if I had some place to go where I could say my son was buried. I don't have a spot to visit and weep over. You have that, but you sit and say they didn't commit murder. Then whose body is it? Not your daughter's? Don't you want to know where she's buried?"

I didn't know what to tell him. I told Naomi and Gideon that I couldn't attend the funeral of a stranger buried with Miriam's name. Naomi didn't say a word, but Gideon went to the other room to make a phone call. Reuben got on the line and said to me, "Nina and I are coming over, make sure you clean up the house first."

I said to Naomi, "When Nina arrives, you stay. Reuben can't tell me to get rid of you." Naomi stroked me and said, "I have to go away for a day anyway, Joseph. Mother expects me. My sister's driving her crazy. She's alone. I'll be gone for two days. No more." I tried to talk her out of it, but her mind was made up; she quickly retrieved some papers from the garbage can, dusted around a bit, and ran out. The Minister of Defence and the Chief of Staff arrived and they pleaded with me. The Chief Rabbi of the army also showed up. We had one hell of a conversation. Full of screaming. The neighbours peered from their windows. It was windy outside and leaves were flying in the street in the biting breeze. The Chief of Staff and the Defence Minister left in anger. Reuben and Nina entered; Gideon stayed outside and sat on the fence at the entrance to the house. I could see him out of the kitchen window.

Nina looked good, America agreed with her. She was restrained, distant, full of a gloomy cynicism. She roamed around throughout the apartment. As though, after not seeing me for two years, all she wanted to do was look for Naomi. Then she sat restlessly, bit her nails, and said, "You'd better come, Joseph," and I told her that I wouldn't and couldn't, and she said, "You're a child, Josie, you think your protest against death will bring back Miriam? Accept it. It's awful. I was naïve. I thought she was safe. I didn't know she'd get caught in such a foul business. I don't know what happened; after all, when I came here, I spoke to her, she sounded sure of herself, she just wanted to hurt you, you already know that, but to end up dying that way? And you sit and celebrate your self-righteousness, as always, everybody else is wrong but you. It's reached the absurd now, there's a corpse, it's Miriam, I wept the whole night, Josie, what do I have left? What do you have left? What's going to happen now? What will become of us? We no longer have one another."

Reuben looked at me, from where he was in a corner and kept quiet. As he smoked I saw that he was wrapped in that insecurity which he knew how to camouflage. Something in him fascinated me at that moment. Reuben was perhaps the only one, other than Naomi, who could grasp what I was talking about, but he was a man who followed the party line, who maintained contact and solidarity, he would never get up to say that I was right. He remained silent, and Nina was furious at him too. I could sense it, she was also turning him against me. She apparently didn't know about the night at the Country Club junction, that magical mournful night.

Finally they all left and I was by myself. I took out the bottle of brandy and drank. Time flew. The funeral was probably already under way. On the radio they announced that I was absent. I waited for the television coverage. On the nine o'clock news the funeral was shown. They milked it to the last drop. Nina was supported on either side by the Chief of Staff and Reuben, I saw all my old friends, Gideon standing on the sidelines, miserable, broken, and Madame Frau in a magnificent black dress, Mr Haim, Mr Feigel, they all were there. On behalf of the government spoke Minister D.; perhaps Reuben had no hand in that betrayal, but the Minister of Defence could surely have spoken instead. He was furious at me, though, for not attending the funeral; I had touched a sore spot in him by refusing to acknowledge something which was perhaps the climax of his consciousness, the ugliest of scenes to deal with, as though I had opposed justice with injustice, as if I had pulled the rug from under him and he'd fallen, as if I, the veteran soldier, the man who went out on daring raids of retaliation, was protesting against his whole way of life and erasing its essential purpose. There was increasing gossip about my absence. The Minister of Defence had a political reason, too, for not speaking; he didn't want to be identified with me more than he had to. The Chief of Staff looked out-of-it while D. spoke, even Reuben turned his face away as if he knew I was watching him on television. Then he caught the eye of the camera, looked directly at me, well knowing that I was now looking back directly at him, at my worst traitor above all others I'd known, who went along with D.'s eulogy, the man who had made his hatred of me his life's work.

D. spoke about the despicable killers, about the long hand which would reach them and whoever had sent them on this mission. About the future. About Miriam. A lovely young officer whom everybody loved and admired. "They called her," he said, "the first daughter of the paratroopers, a loyal daughter to her homeland, a brave soldier who was guided by values. Precisely her they chose to waste, those great heroes, they butchered a woman, they shredded her!" The crowd wailed, the camera trembled, the cameraman was also, apparently, in tears. It was an emotional moment, a terrifying one. I sat and fingered my face; not a tear was there. I was already drunk. D. said, "We shall smash, crush, destroy, demolish . . ." He was the mouthpiece for an extraordinary machismo. I wanted to break the television screen, and I called Naomi. She wept on the phone. She had watched the funeral on television. I said to her, "I need you, child, I love you, come back," and she said, "And Nina? Isn't she there?" I answered, "No, she's not here. I'm alone with the bottle and waiting for you." She said, "It was terrible, Joe. Thanks, I'm leaving now. Nira's here, she wept with me; she'll take me home to you. I no longer know if I'm capable of forgiving her."

At ten that night Nina arrived. Gideon came upstairs, took Miriam's photograph from my room, and left. He didn't say a word. He looked stunned and pale. Nina made another tour of the house, seemed even more shattered, and asked, "What's the dog's photograph doing up on the wall?" And I told her that Miriam had hung it there the day before she disappeared. Nina loked at me and said, "You're a drunken fool, but you could have at least attended your own daughter's funeral." I rose and, with a force that I'd forgotten I had in me, slapped her face and she fell to the floor. She almost smiled as she dropped. She said, "Oh, the wooden hulk has life, blood, before it dies. After watching the show on television he turns into a beauty!"

I told her, "You miserable excuse for a woman. Our

daughter is gone. If you'd come earlier, not by stealth, maybe Miriam would be sitting here now and not Naomi, who's about to arrive soon."

Nina said in a weak voice, "You're a bastard, Josie. Yes, I was here. But I didn't want to disturb you."

I said, "You're mourning nicely, Nina. It's very touching. You came under Reuben's cover and in cahoots with Miriam and Noam. You called me and said you were Didi, told me the tale of the boat ride out to sea. What were you really after, other than your need for revenge which cannot be just yours or Miriam's, because it's too enormous, inhuman, it belongs to a marriage with death. At one time, in Morocco, young Jewish brides whose betrotheds had died, would marry them in the cemetery making them husband and wife on both sides of death. What happened? Did Miriam marry death, so you and she could be its mouthpiece?"

She smiled but her smile was perverse, fragmented. She asked, "Are you jealous, Joseph?"

I told her I was angry but she shouldn't exaggerate. "I'm drunk," I said, "and you're not worthy of any revenge or jealousy. You betrayed me in a way that has never occurred before. Why should I get angry or jealous? You got what you wanted!"

"My daughter's death?"

"I don't know if she's dead," I said, "I just know she wasn't found in the Galilee, and you've made a funeral for somebody who perhaps deserved such a funeral but certainly not the words in D.'s eulogy. Maybe it was your idea to let him play the vulture over Joseph's corpse!"

Nina flushed. She looked splendid in her mourning outfit. She said, "We're sitting *shivah** at the Chief of Staff's house." And then she asked, "What did that bastard Noam tell you?" I told her that he'd said nothing, that he had slipped between my fingers and disappeared. And she said, "Yes, I forgot. Machoman at Jaffa. What a wonderful show!" She was about to laugh when she remembered the clothes she was wearing.

*The seven-day mourning period observed by Jews.

"You always were a great impersonator, Nina. You could impersonate your teachers, Reuben, the Chief of Staff, his deceased wife, little Nina, you were fantastic at it. So you fooled me, huh? But you almost blew it with the fisherman. He suspected something, but I didn't pay attention and went around like a blindman. Not any more. I'll go it alone, and I'll find out what's happening or happened to Miriam. When I do, you won't want to know, because you've already mourned for her and already buried her. At the real funeral which I hope won't ever take place, you won't attend, not you, your miserable pisspot honour won't allow you to come dressed in mourning garments rented for a second time for the same daughter, huh?"

"And you actually think I'm not dying inside?"

"Perhaps. But not enough." I was really furious now. For years I hadn't been that angry, maybe I'd never been. I hated her, and saw on her face the extent of her defeat. Strangely enough, given the extinction of my daughter, at that moment it almost felt sweet; Nina didn't notice, she couldn't recognize such a petty Joseph.

"Your all-encompassing bogusness and falseness is the deepest thing in you," I told her. "But there is in you another depth, a true and genuine one, which unfortunately you gave away to your whoremasters instead of to the one man who really once loved you."

She burst out crying, I embraced her, letting her spill her flood of tears on me, and then I put her to bed. The Chief of Staff's driver waited to take her to the *shivah*. Before climbing into bed, she said, "I want to stay here, Joseph, forever," and her voice was pleading. I told her, "It's too late. I love someone else and I am an incurable monogamist. My beautiful wondrous Nina, our entire terrifying story, twenty-seven long years of it, went down the toilet, *finis*. It hurts me more than it does you, Nina, but you can act better than I can."

As soon as she left I heard the screech of an owl on the balcony. I stepped outside. Madame Frau stood there in her safari outfit and said, "Somebody's waiting for you here. It's important, Joseph. The priest Emil from the

Galilee. He knows everything. And bring along one of Miriam's dresses."

The priest wore a flattened hat. He had good eyes, and was tall and pale. We conversed in German; he knew I could speak Arabic but he preferred German, perhaps out of respect for Madame Frau who sat there like an Indian princess, her legs crossed, under an etching by Hermann Struck, in a house full of cobwebs. He fingered Miriam's dress, shut his eyes, and suddenly began to speak in my daughter's voice. It was weird. I almost got up and ran to my apartment, thinking that Nina was tricking me again. For an instant I was sure I actually heard my daughter. But he was in a trance, and I didn't move. Madame Frau signalled me to stay put.

He spoke about a young woman, the owner of the dress, as both alive and dead. He saw her leaving a car, leaping over a broken barrier in the road, heading towards an orchard; then somebody came and took her in his car, switched to another car, he wasn't sure who that was, but he saw other cars, or maybe the same car but in different places. The woman had a love who was on the other side of life apparently, aware of things we had no knowledge of, a dangerous man, full of fury and noble, if confused, pride. "Now I see mountains," he said, "a chain of them. And a cave with a vial made of glass. She's crying into it, but she's not inside the cave. There are others in the cave. She's in the woods or the orchard. She's walking. There's a village, perhaps an olive grove. I hear an explosion. Her mother is laughing because she's at sea in her daughter's clothes. A storm blows. that's all I know," he said, as if Miriam had gone back to our future.

And he opened his eyes. A warm shy smile spread across his face. He said, "Look, Sir, I don't know what I said and I don't remember it. Whatever came to me I spoke. Is there anything in it? Sometimes it helps, sometimes I'm all wrong. The powers work according to their will. I speak without knowing what will come out of my mouth."

After he left, Madame Frau said, "Come home with me. Mr Haim will come too, we'll sit down as a family. I attended the funeral in order to accompany the neighbours, so they wouldn't say we don't love Miriam. But she wasn't there, I know, I'm not off my mind, your great father knew that; maybe I should say it in German, I'm convinced it's not the way it looks, there's a mystery here, the priest is correct but I don't understand just how."

We got home. It was one in the morning. My neighbours sat there. We drank the whisky which Mr Feigel brought along. Madame Frau prepared coffee, Naomi arrived and we embraced. We all sat until the day broke; it was warm, we were all one family. They cried, and Mr Haim said softly, "I'm always looking, so what? Better to look than to accept life as a celebration – they make a picnic out of every nightmare here. Who knows? My wife isn't in the fuse box? So what? Why not? Maybe she is? Who knows she isn't? And maybe there's hope. Here you're a brigadier and sit with us, but at your daughter's funeral, sweet little Miriam, where are you? At home. By the television. Because she's still alive for you. So why not for me? My wife and two daughters?"

16

CHIEF-INSPECTOR Czeszek, a fairly senior journalist wrote, was 'incensed' over my refusal to appear at the funeral or sit *shivah*. The reporter quoted him as saying, "When a professional soldier goes soft and falls in love with debased killers, I really begin to worry; and his obstinacy is not on principle, but is its own goal." I knew what really angered Czeszek was the fact that he himself wasn't completely satisfied with the identification of the body, that everything was too neat, the confessions of the suspects, the exultation in the Arabic press and radio – even a street in Damascus was named after the heroes – and he suspected something deep down in his heart: he surmised that the story didn't hold together, that all the clues which we had come upon earlier couldn't have ended this way. I wasn't the bleeding liberal which the papers made me, he knew it very well, I was never a frustrated conscience-stricken leftist who thinks that justice exists only on the side of the enemy. But I also was no fanatic, no self-righteous professional patriot. I was a soldier, a father to my daughter, my wife Nina was a refugee; from Nina's mother, as Miriam said, they may have made soap, but I had been a part of the volume woven in blood which tells how we defended this nation, a partial yet necessary response to disaster. I was busy looking for my daughter; her disappearance disrupted my trust in logic, as well as leaving a hole in my gut which I didn't for one moment forget. She was physically gone from inside me. In my dreams it was no longer I who was cut into pieces, but my daughter; and Nina sat *shivah* in the Chief of Staff's house and kept bombarding me with tearful telephone calls, and hanging up whenever Naomi answered. Then I'd call her back and say, "When are you going to grow up, Nina, you're a middle-aged woman," and she'd weep, "Where's Miriam? Why did she end up this way?" And I had no answer.

One night, when *shivah* was over, she showed up. She was wearing an elegantly tailored, lovely suit, and her hair was gathered back. She didn't look for Naomi who was lying in bed reading, she didn't seem cross or distracted, she didn't come to play games, she came to put together the pieces.

The way she entered and walked told me that Miriam's death had only now begun to penetrate her inner being, from which Miriam had once emerged, though Nina for a year and a few months after giving birth had put it out of her mind.

She sat, drank coffee, cuddling the big cup in her hands, and didn't even glance towards the bedroom where Naomi's face appeared at the door for a moment before softly shutting it. How much confusion there must have been in the girl's mind, how much sorrow must have engulfed her in that locked room.

Nina said, "I'm absolutely empty, Josie, as though I've fallen into a deep pit and cannot climb out. Miriam began writing to me in America after Isaac Raphaeli had forced her to do so!"

Nina's voice was calm. I didn't interrupt her. She spoke from some point inside herself where her blinding pain had penetrated and smashed her characteristic irresponsibility to bits; she didn't say "the dead soldier", as though she were presenting a fabulous fact, she said "Isaac Raphaeli", as though his existence were indeed an established fact, and that there was no question that a soldier who had died before Miriam was born could command my daughter to write letters to her mother. As she spoke, tears rolled from her eyes and did not stop until she herself had finished talking. She was sincere. Her grief was genuine. I wanted to wipe away her tears, but even while she was hurting, I sensed that we had already become strangers, as if all those long years in which I had loved only her were years that belonged to somebody else. The break was painful. Maybe she felt it too. Maybe she considered it the cost of facing the death of her daughter, a price which was impossible to hide from now.

"She loved Isaac," she said. "Except for you, Joseph, Isaac was her only love. I was just an anchor," she added, "someone who, after I'd neglected her from day one, had always been there, in spite of everything I did. I was apparently a devoted mother. Perhaps a miserable crutch, but a crutch none the less. Her love was divided between you and him. If Noam told you that there was anything between them, he's a scoundrel, because there never was ... He's an outstanding bastard with charm, from now until further notice ... And I wanted him, I admit, I'd had my lovers, perhaps more than a few, you know already so there's no point in my playing games, I always loved you but I also always hated you. I had lovers. When I met Noam, I thought he was Miriam's friend. At first I thought she was dallying with him, not sleeping with him, in order to get to Isaac. He was just a bridge to Isaac and there was no romantic connection. I was the one who wanted him, but he refused me. That wounded my pride. Especially since Miriam had organized the whole thing. She figured it would work. She cooked it up by herself and then waited for us to comply; she wanted that humiliation, calling me 'the nymphomaniac wife of the monogamist', and laughed. What a wicked laugh your daughter had sometimes. Noam told Miriam, and Miriam relayed it to me – she didn't withhold *that* from me – that he found me disgusting and old, and he didn't under-stand what I was expecting from him since I had a man at home with decorations for bravery and canteens full of blood! Very few men ever rejected me in my life, Joseph, and he humiliated me. I was full of fear and terror for myself, for you too, for all of us, for our fleeting lives, for our approaching old age. Miriam wrote to me once how much she needed me and how much, on account of what she called 'forced obligations', she was compelled to teach you a lesson. Isaac Raphaeli told her that if you suffered, you would find peace of mind.

Look, the idea was that I would come to Israel, hang out with Noam, take that boat ride, bring Noam a few of her belongings, a hat, whatever –"

"What else?"

"A blouse, a jacket. A few other items."

"And one shoe?"

"And one shoe!"

She continued, "Reuben was in on the secret, but all he knew was that Miriam wanted to renew contact with me, that I didn't want to meet you and my visit had to remain secret. Naturally he agreed. But he sensed something, came to the port, to Noam's apartment, to warn me against doing anything to harm you. A riot, no? The man to whom I was a mistress for almost twenty-seven years ... but I was already in love with that boy, Noam; maybe Reuben was jealous, that was practically his speciality, that friend of yours. After I called you and said I was Didi, that night I went back to the States. Reuben took me to the airport, but he was furious with me. In the end we made love in a hotel, and we drank a lot that night; the bastard tried to get me drunk so I'd reveal a few things, but I never told him what I'd done and all he could do was guess.

"This isn't exactly the time to go over everything. We've covered part of the time. It's highly unlikely that Miriam's alive. She planned something, Isaac was behind it, but it was botched, I don't know how. I came to help her, though in the end what happened had nothing to do with me, I simply thought I was scaring you on her account, it was what she said Isaac had told her to do. She always manipulated me against you, she'd speak badly of you, complaining and crying, and say you were an egoist, that you didn't even notice her, or understand her, that you were torpedoeing her life, but when you got home she would lose her words, you'd give her a sweet smile, ask her how she was, tell her something, and she'd be struck dumb until you left and then she would pour out everything held back, in my presence, as if I ought to know what to do and why you are the way you are, and the reason for your being the kind of man that a woman like me would have to betray. She claimed that it was all your fault, and I told her, 'My child, I have something to say on that judgment too, maybe your father's a saint and I'm just a scumbag, and scumbags and saints can't live together, perhaps, in the same basket.' Except just to bring into the world a girl who is part you, part me, but mostly herself, even if our genes are powerful in her, Joseph, opposed to each other, always in conflict. You're a strong man, I'm fucked up, actually you're fucked up too. We don't resemble anyone else. What can such a girl do whose parents are so unlike others and themselves, so far apart from each other? She fell between two stools, my dead daughter . . .

"The truth is that she not only used me against you but basically, and this is what's important for you to understand, she used me to reach you. She was the most dangerously self-destructive child I've ever met in my life. The sky was too far off for her, the earth was too oppressively close, and in the middle was a void which she felt obliged to fill. She sat on the sidelines, waiting for herself like a cruel evil hunter out to kill rather than capture, and in the end she snared herself. It took me years to realize that she was fond of me and needed me, but she never really loved me. She couldn't forgive me for the first year and a half of her life, and she couldn't forget your devotion to her, but she thought you had done it out of opposition to me and concern for yourself not for her. Later on she may have realized that she was wrong, but she still loved to cling to the notion that your motive was pure arrogance and self-righteousness rather than plain love for her.

"Isaac ruled over her through her fear of you, through her suspicions of you, because you were never able to offer what she really wanted, you were just a father to her, I was your woman and I was unfaithful to you, and she was caught in the middle. On the one hand she wondered why not her, but on the other hand she appreciated exactly what I had in me to offer and she knew that she was only your daughter and not your wife; but that led her into a kind of maze. You left mixed messages or, more correctly, confusing ones. One minute tender, the next indifferent, suddenly you closed off with such finality that all the keys to you snapped. For me too.

Certainly for her. I helped her, she thanked me but felt guilty for not loving me enough. And Noam, he fell in love with her like the rest, like that Gideon, like Hanoch Levi. Hanoch Levi is sleeping with the woman who loved you – how I was jealous of her once, how I imagined what went on between the two of you, though deep down I knew it was all fantasy and that you'd never fall into her hands, but I wanted you to, I did and I didn't. I was so proud of you! Even while I was sleeping with so many types of men that I couldn't remember their names in the morning, I was still proud of you, of your awful integrity, and hoped that you'd pay me back. I also hoped that you wouldn't, that you'd nobly forgive me, but you simply paid no attention. I had plans for our later years, how we would live together, you and I. After all the storms I would be yours alone; no other man would want me then, whereas the women would still want you but you would refuse, you would be all mine, and we would drink tea together, in the evening, on the balcony. Miriam and I used to laugh over the Joy affair. Everybody talked about it. But she felt your pain as if it were hers, and she couldn't speak to you about it. She would ridicule me, defend me, but in some strange way my adulteries helped her, on account of them she got you all to herself. My weakness enabled your integrity and hers to meet without interference. She *wanted* you to have a fling with Joy, but she was also afraid of any such romance. Neither of us alerted you to our secret intrigue. Miriam was jealous of her, of Joy, of the possibility of your getting together with her. I have a rotten character, Joseph. Reuben understood how crushed and vicious I am. He could read me the way a good musician reads a score. Not you. Mr Rock. That's how you used to be, but maybe not any more."

I heard Naomi leaving the bedroom and switching to Miriam's room. It was the first time she stayed there, although she had been in there to sweep the room. Nina hadn't realised. She was too busy with her confessions, with the pain which she genuinely felt for herself and me and Miriam. Naomi was crying in there, I could sense how her tears were sweeping across her face but I didn't get up to dry them.

But suddenly I filled with anger, anger over what might be happening now or had already happened to Miriam. I considered all Nina's words a cover-up. I dragged her to the door of Miriam's room, it was an act of physical force, though she went limp as a rag; she was so deeply embedded in her pain that she was in no way prepared to break through my fury.

I stood her up against the door and told her loudly, "Now tell Naomi something." Naomi screamed, "Let her be, Joseph," and Nina turned pale. Suddenly she realized that our whole conversation would serve as ammunition for her rival, as Nina saw her, and she started to scratch me and yell. I told her, "Tell Naomi she can stay here and that you're leaving." And she said in a faint, dull voice, "I'm going, you're staying." She was humiliated and resigned to defeat. With contempt I visualized in my mind's eye all of my friends and acquaintances marching in a row from her legs.

I told her, "Talk to a decent woman, maybe it'll help you in life, Nina. Speak to a young woman who doesn't take to bed every man she meets."

"But she climbed into your bed!"

"No, I took her there, out of love, Nina, a word which you don't understand."

Finally I realized, in a shock of brutal clarity, that all my life I had lived without even knowing what went on under my very nose. Actually, my life had carried on outside me. So that my daughter didn't even know how much I loved her. She measured the merit of love by Nina and the merits of betrayal by her father. The messages messed her up, I could see that now. She was the inevitable outcome of a set of impossible relationships. She was on my side, but perhaps only after she had linked herself to someone whose photo I had hung on the wall as reasonable proof of a lie which I had built around a hero of my own making – a total fabrication to protect myself from what I perhaps once was, before I had decided on what I would become, before I had dedicated my life

214

to self-discipline, to self-instruction in the ways of the eternal soldier, of obstinacy, rather than to the piano – no more poetic utterances, just the cruel explosive prose of a mercenary killer.

Nina said, "Joseph loves you, child." And Naomi wept. I told Naomi, "At long last you've been lucky enough to speak with a real scumbag."

17

AFTER the week of *shivah*, a spring heatwave began. The telephone didn't stop ringing. People threatened me, calling me abusive names, the receiver was drenched in curses. Somebody said in a whisper of hate, "Softie, go kiss the ass of your killers. A dead Arab can't murder a live Jew." I got a new telephone number, and as I called the Astor Hotel to leave my new number with the receptionist, for Nina, Naomi smiled. Later I realized that Naomi hadn't smiled, she'd just yawned. Apparently I was very tense and anticipated her reaction.

In the mornings, Madame Frau started to hand me salted biscuits in a butterfly net which she had brought with her from Germany. And in one telegram that she sent me – ordinarily she conversed with me on the balcony but she sometimes sent telegrams, being particularly fond of them she wrote: TO JOSEPH TWISTED LOGIC BEGETS TWISTED LOGIC STOP MIRIAM'S LETTERS IN REVERSE SEQUENCE BEGOT THE IDEA TO SIT AT THE COUNTRY CLUB JUNCTION STOP I KNOW STOP I'VE BEEN SITTING AT THE WINDOW FOR FORTY-FIVE YEARS STOP NOT STEPPING OUT STOP JUST A FEW TIMES HAIFA MAYBE FOUR TIMES JERUSALEM GALILEE SAFED ALL INCLUSIVE STOP IN FORTY-FIVE YEARS AT MY WINDOW I HAVE SEEN PASSING BY MY HOUSE TOSCANINI HUBERMAN YASCHA HEIFETZ YEHUDI MENUHIN BEN-GURION SHERTOK THE HIGH COMMISSIONER MCMICHAEL FRANK POLLOCK ZARITSKY THE PAINTER KOLBIANSKY HERMANN STRUCK, ONO FROM BURMA GOLDA ESHKOL ALLON RABIN MISCHA ELMAN TCHERNICHOWSKY ISAAC STERN PAUL MUNI DANNY KAYE LUBIANIKER STOP

That morning, from the balcony, she said to me, "Did you read it? There were many more. You must find your daughter's logic, then you can sit and let her come, because in the end everything comes."

I had begun to read the gossip columns. Something which Naomi had said right after we'd met, when she quoted her soldiers' comments on Hanoch Levi, stuck in my head. Since Hanoch Levi was a public figure and a media personality, I was sure to find something about him. I didn't know exactly what I was looking for, but I still had the feeling, after all, that he and Joy were party to some secret information, and that bothered me; I had to find a way to penetrate their armour of defence. Naomi brought me some weeklies, *Ha-Olam Hazeh*, *La'Isha* and others, and I read quite a lot about Hanoch Levi. In an article in an evening newspaper, which was somewhat expanded in one of the weeklies, it was written that Hanoch Levi had appeared in court, was found guilty of exceeding the speed limit, insulting an officer, and later trying to get off the hook through what looked like a bribe.

What troubled me about that story was the fact that a broadcaster as famous as Hanoch Levi would attempt a bribe, if that's what he did, risking public disgrace over such a minor transgression. Speeding and insulting an officer? For that you don't risk going to jail!

An additional factor upset me, something I thought about in the wake of Madame Frau's telegram. If Miriam was behind the scenes, she wouldn't have co-operated with any airing of that documentary on television, and that brought me back again to the connection with Hanoch Levi. Because if Miriam and her mother had thought of the idea of a boat ride, and on that matter I believed Nina, why the broadcast? If Miriam wanted to punish me, to scare me, if that's what Isaac wished, she wouldn't have allowed me to start worrying that very evening. And Nina was the only one who didn't even know about the broadcasting of the documentary. In addition, since Nina had been in America for two years, she certainly didn't know that it had been shelved all this time. Miriam would surely have built her trap piece by piece, in order to snare her father whom she knew so well. Had it not been for that broadcast, I would have been much less worried, at least until morning. At the back of my mind the show had troubled me all along, though I hadn't realised that the first evening, but whoever arranged the broadcast had known that something else was afoot and had decided to stick this in too. In other words, there was a contradiction; if we take into account Miriam's logic together with Isaac's, who was dead and therefore unaccountable but still clearly accessible, and I write these words without a shudder – as if I were making a report on my participation in the battle at Karame, a battle which I shall never forget, the betrayal, the defective planning, the idiocy, as written up in my report then, with hands shaking, so many dead. I write "Isaac" now as though it were obvious that a dead soldier could become involved in my life, and my daughter's life. If we consider their logic, Miriam's and Isaac's, we reach the conclusion that perhaps somebody wanted to frighten not me but Miriam.

What occurred to me was that Miriam was expected to be sitting at home that evening watching television, and then get a shock when she saw the programme. I told Naomi, "I think your sister Nira is more mixed up in this than you realize," and Naomi said, "Perhaps, then do something about it."

Both of us already knew who would devise such a scheme but we remained in a quandary because we couldn't figure out the connection between Joy, Hanoch Levi and Nira.

En route to the Raphaeli family I stopped at the police station. Sergeant Rose exuded warmth. She said that she had attended Miriam's funeral, but she also understood why I hadn't shown up. With the co-operation of a police inspector whom I'd got to know recently, Rose was given permission to assist me in locating Hanoch Levi's file. When I read it, all that I had suspected was validated. Although I didn't come out with a shattering revelation, I now had a reasonable basis for my assumption. According to the file Hanoch Levi had been stopped by a police patrol on 22 January at five in the morning – 21 January being the day of Miriam's disappearance. Hanoch Levi was tipsy, or at least appeared to be, and certainly smelled like someone who'd had a few drinks. He had exceeded the speed limit on the old road between Tel-Aviv and Haifa near the exit to the road to Jerusalem, not far from Lod Airport. He tried to flatter the police, looked scared, then he insulted one of them, using foul language, and afterwards a woman telephoned the patrol sergeant, made an appointment, and when she couldn't get anywhere with him she offered, with extreme caution but great arrogance, to bribe him. The sergeant was aghast and refused. At the trial Hanoch said that he didn't know any woman of the description submitted by the sergeant. The judge, who couldn't imagine that Hanoch Levi would be so foolish as to attempt to bribe a sergeant on account of a traffic violation, dismissed the piqued sergeant's complaint, but gave Hanoch Levi not such a low fine after all.

The sergeant sought to defend his right to another trial, claiming that his honour as a police sergeant had been trampled upon. Not a single word of all of this ever reached the newspapers. The police hadn't submitted a thing. In the file I found evidence of a top senior officer's intervention during the investigation, and that the sergeant had tried to put a stop to that. Rose paled. She realized that the officer who had permitted us to look at the file didn't know what was in it. I promised her to work it out so that her name would never come up. I called the sergeant at his home. His wife gave me his work number. He was shocked to hear how intimately familiar I was with the details of the incident. He realized who I was, I'd had a lot of publicity lately, and he said he was sorry about what had happened to my daughter.

We met at Café Apropos at midday. He came in civilian clothes. I told him that I was investigating my daughter's tragedy, that I knew what everybody thought of me but I was entitled to continue my search. I reminded him that I hadn't been born yesterday and that I didn't need to be fed with a spoon. I had been a soldier for over thirty years. I told him that he possessed significant information. He asked me how I knew, and I said, "You must swear that you'll never repeat what I tell you." He swore. The incident had apparently irked him and caused him great pain. He was amazed that I'd gained access to the report. I explained that the information was restricted and until his name was cleared and an investigation was completed, I wouldn't say a word. But once the investigation was under way I would stand by his side, because I had in my possession something that could conceivably clear his name altogether. Then, once he was attentive and curious, I asked him to describe for me the woman who had attempted to bribe him. After a few seconds I knew that my hunch was absolutely correct. There was no possibility of mistaking Joy's identity. I told him, "You've already waited this long, so just wait a little longer and at the retrial which you want, I'll bring the woman, because I know who she is. But right now I need her for a matter even more urgent than your honour, which is very important on its own, but I'm talking about life and death. After I complete my personal investigation, I'll serve her up to you on a silver platter and she'll admit to everything you ask her, she'll be frightened, utterly transparent, and there won't be any obstacles, she will clear you of the tiniest suspicion of lying."

Naturally, he pressured me to tell him now, but I wouldn't give in. I told him, "In the meantime forget this conversation. I'll contact you as soon as possible." And I drove to the Raphaeli family. I was encouraged. I didn't know how far I would get but I had something to work on; there was logic to the lack of logic. Why would Joy bother to bribe a police sergeant over a minor traffic violation? Because of the hour, five in the morning, on the day of my daughter's disappearance, in which Hanoch was seen driving Miriam towards Netanya around eight o'clock, eight-twenty to be precise. He had definitely been at the Bet-Lid junction. How did he know that Miriam would be there? Did he meet her then? What was the point of his trip there? Did it indicate that Miriam was sweet on him?

When I reached the house of the Raphaeli family in

Ramat-Gan, I felt as though I had gone back in time, some thirty years back. The house was exactly the way it had been then, even the street hadn't altered much. On either side of the house, where there used to be vacant lots, a few new houses had been built, but in such a way that neither they nor the trees which had thickened and grown had disturbed the fundamental character of the road.

The apartment hadn't changed. Some oil paintings, plain old furniture, no refurbished antiques, not a single photograph of Isaac on the wall, no memorial museum, no sanctuary of the dead, what sanctified his name was precisely his absolute absence. The place remained the way it had been on the day he was killed. Perhaps that constituted a certain denial of his death, since if he were to return home now he would find everything as he had left it. Even the window overlooking the ancient hill preserved the past. Later, I found out from Nira that Mr Raphaeli had used up all his savings in order to purchase the field near the big window, he had pruned the tree, and even made sure that no house would be built too close to them. He persuaded the town to plant a garden there. He had contributed the money for the gardening and it was planted and irrigated until it approximated the pattern of the field which had once grown wild there thirty years ago. What created a sort of anxiety in me was precisely this total lack of change. Time had practically frozen, the dead were alive, discomfort was inescapable, death had entered by the back door. The gloom had not been retrieved by artillery shell fragments, field glasses, a rifle full of holes, torn snippets of cloth from a hat or a shirt; it rested on what was missing.

Mrs Raphaeli was still a lovely woman. Her hair was now white, but she was still full of energy, though that had turned bland, and her former cold vengefulness had transformed itself into a melancholy which lacked bite. Her husband looked pale, almost transparent, his eyes still drenched in yearning. After a few moments of confusion we warmed to each other more than I had expected. Miriam's death had shocked them; she had almost been a member of their family and slept there fairly often. She was, as Mr Raphaeli said shyly, "the living bride of their deceased son." I remembered what she had written to me, that she had always considered herself my widow. In this house she was Isaac's widow. But in life they had never met except through me. That's what made my now sitting in this house so necessary, unlike last time, which had been a challenge veiled in mocking fury.

They were open, eager to offer me some peace and let me share in their experience, wishing to teach me what it meant to be bereaved and how to dream about a dead son. I said that perhaps Miriam was not dead, but they did not heed my words, they had read the papers and knew. They too had waited for Isaac a full year after his death, and only when they realized that he would never come back did they build this emptiness to preserve the full status of the past so his shadow might fall on all the familiar paths.

What I gathered from them was that Noam and Miriam were friends, yet intensely hostile to each other. Apparently Noam desired her – the father said "loved", the mother said "desired". Miriam was scared of Noam, but he pursued her. When she studied at art school, he took up jazz and earned a little sitting as a model there. He brought her home. The Raphaelis spoke about their son with a kind of distance; their sympathies were for me, not him. What I heard in their words was that my daughter had been brutally slaughtered on her way home, whereas Isaac had died in battle and belonged to a bereaved family. A certain aura of bravery clung to him, the customary privilege accorded families of army dead. I had given the father something to hold on to, the traditional heroism of Isaac; perhaps they knew, perhaps they didn't; to the mother it made no difference, to the father it apparently did – and that, after all, was their legacy. Miriam hadn't fought against it, hadn't tried to clarify what actually happened. The mother already knew, the father closed his eyes and didn't want to know.

Isaac was embracing an old Arab woman when he was found dead. Over the years the story surrounding his death was something one could live with and give meaning to, particularly in the context of all our political, ethical, national events. Here was a noble act and a death with some purpose, whereas Miriam had been murdered helplessly, cut into pieces, set on fire, her eyes had been plucked out, and vultures had taken her for carrion. They spoke about it as if they had forgotten that I was sitting in front of them. Miriam was obviously a fresh wound, Isaac was not. I had paid a high price. I didn't even know who my daughter was outside her home, and they surely realized that my tragedy was doubled, that I was suffering over her death and, therefore, also denying it, dreaming about her being still alive while all the facts pointed otherwise. I was looking for my daughter now that she was dead because I hadn't managed to know her very well during her life – exactly like the traditional bravery which I had brought into their house along with my notification of Isaac's death, whereby his passing could be interpreted as a unique event which had redeemed their son of all shame. After all, a death like his could never be justified or offer anybody insight; it was a singularity, an exception, which brought him, perhaps, into another sphere, the world of myth, which touches heaven and returns with something eternal.

They had wanted to contact me for some time now, they said. They'd wished to say, "Brigadier, your daughter is playing a dangerous game," but they didn't phone. The reason, they said, was that Noam forbade it. But they admitted that Noam's injunction alone would not have prevented them from calling or contacting me; after all, how far apart were our two houses? Ten minutes' flying time?

Noam, they said, was naïvely corrupt, though not undangerous. They didn't know where he was. He broke off all contact once Miriam had disappeared. On the night of her disappearance they had waited for her. 21 January was the anniversary of Isaac's death.

Mrs Raphaeli served me cold coffee and cake; I drank, asked for some beer, which they gave me. I had the impression that they had been expecting me for days. The chair I was sitting on had received me like an old acquaintance. Their citing the day on which Isaac had died struck me like

223

an electric shock. For a moment I couldn't speak. For the first time in my life I understood the expression "rendered speechless". I tried to say something but not a word came out of my mouth.

They remembered that a few weeks earlier Noam and Miriam had locked themselves in a room, talked for a long while, spoke on the phone for hours with several people, they didn't know who. Miriam, said the mother, sounded sad all of a sudden. Miriam's death had perhaps robbed her not only of a young friend, but also, and forever perhaps, of her only link with her son. Miriam used to call upon his spirit through sorcery. He would speak through her. "It sounds silly," she said with a shy smile, "but it's a fact, we became dependent on her, we needed her," they both said with a grief which broke through the walls, passing on into the garden and climbing into the trees – a voiceless shriek. Nira had been jealous, they said, Noam became furious with Miriam, over what he called her betrayal with Isaac. "It was a disgusting story," they said, "but we needed him," they added bitterly.

Immediately following Isaac's death, Nira's influence persuaded them to hold me responsible for that death. She had collected bits of slander against me, and had woven them into a thick loathsome pattern, including the executed prisoner and the canteen of blood and what she called my "erotic craving for death". She told them about my ornate eulogies at cemeteries, claiming I had betrothed myself to death and even lusted after it. She said I was the bitter poet of death, its lover and rival, and war for me was an appalling way to offer it sacrifices. That's why I sought out children; because my disturbed soul required the death of these children so that I could stare death in the face and make it blink first.

At the outset they really needed these images. It had legitimized their hatred for someone who had perhaps been responsible for their son's death. The word "perhaps" was theirs. But, anyway, it didn't help for long.

What I got out of the trivial details of their story, the laundering of Miriam's clothes, their love for her, Nira's jealousy, was that from some point of view they blamed themselves for Miriam's death, because maybe it was their son who had killed her!

Or caused her death. And that was beyond revenge, it was a matter of guilt, of fate, of transmigration of souls and mysticism, which was far from them but they somehow lived alongside it or in it, unwillingly and without faith, but with the apathy of those who have nothing to lose any more, hopeless cancer victims who turn to quacks.

In Nina's words at my house, when she was stunned and spoke of her love for Miriam, I hadn't heard the despair which came out of Mrs Raphaeli, that cry from the heart, which made me sense Miriam's presence every instant and yearn for her with almost a vengeance, a kind of pain and anger that would still gnaw at me after I was dead and buried and flash like lightning into my consciousness. Nina had come from a place where death was a pair of slippers, where her mother had gone off to her death the way a woman leaves in the morning for work. Death was a constant in her life, and Miriam's tragedy was like another proof of the impossibility of our ever really being alive before we die. Nina was an obsessive sceptic about life; that's why she lived so compulsively. But Mrs Raphaeli truly loved Miriam, purely, cleanly, though Miriam was my daughter and had later brought Isaac back to life, something which had a separate existence from her ordinary tactics for self-preservation. None the less, Miriam was like a daughter to her, and her absence caused her physical pain. She sat opposite me like Madame Frau, like Naomi, with tender femininity in the midst of her suffering and her love and her hostile gentility, her sense of life insulted by the unsolvable enigma of death.

In contrast to her, Nina was the con-artist of survivors. She loved, she yearned, but she was alive because so many others had died, as she had often told me; she was numbered among the living as if she were a hole in the universe, a hole which others would fill. Life itself was a kind of game to her; one fell, another got up, everybody though was both the vulture and the carrion it fed on. It was just a matter of timing, of being in the right place. There was no clear distinction between life and death. Miriam's loss was a disgrace and a pain but acceptable. For me Miriam was a mystery which I was discovering even as I was perhaps averting my eyes from her death. I wasn't sure, I couldn't monitor my mind so closely then. For Mrs Raphaeli, who knew death through her love for her son, Miriam's death was human, touching, and she was able to open me up to myself in a way which I had feared before. If she were younger and I another kind of man, we would have made a good couple, I thought, and looked at her with vague affection and sympathy which she didn't hide from. No woman, be she even a hundred years old, apparently, can ignore a courtship. For a magic moment, my penetrating masculine glance of courtship – and I was a man who had wooed only three women in his life – was unchecked. Miriam was in this house and belonged to it, something which I suddenly found difficult to say about my own house. What she had written to me about my choice of apartment on Ben Yehuda Street was apparently correct, I'd never asked her or Nina where they preferred to live, I'd told them that we were moving to Ben Yehuda and never posed the question, I just took them to my country, to the house of my youth. I'd had a lousy childhood in that house, a harsh mother, a father who refused to live, yet I wanted to live and die there. Here in the Raphaeli house Miriam could choose a place of her own, and the decor suited her. She was at home here.

They also spoke about Nira. A strange girl, they said, who never settled down. She went away and came back, got married and divorced, then remarried and divorced again. "What could my dead son have done to two girls so young and so beautiful?" asked Mrs Raphaeli from the depths of her anguish. "And Noam was jealous of his brother. He was a strong boy, not a coward like Isaac, but he was a failure in the army. We sat here that night, it was the anniversary of Isaac's death long ago, as I said, and we waited for Miriam who was supposed to come and see us at about nine. Suddenly we saw the documentary on remedial education in the army, which we hadn't seen for a year. Miriam was the star of the programme, of course; and then I thought that Noam must have arranged it,

226

Noam must have switched programmes, because he realized we'd all be sitting together with Miriam and talking a bit about Isaac, we would reminisce about him and share a few moments of happiness with her in Isaac's house, and through her regain Isaac, but once the documentary came on television Miriam would panic, she'd remember who really lived in this house feeling like a stranger because of his dead brother who gave him no room of his own, and she would be wounded. Who wanted to scare her? Then suddenly that broadcaster? And who was behind that? Noam! Another sign from Isaac, supposedly, but really Noam's scheme. His way of hinting to her, *Cut it out! We've made a deal, Isaac will return to Nira and Miriam will go to Noam . . ."*

In a faint, betrayed voice, with a sort of dry detachment, Mr Raphaeli said, "In the struggle between Nira and Miriam, we were on Miriam's side, even though Nira had been here first. You had a magnificent daughter, Mr Krieger, conscientious, ethical, intelligent, beautiful; why" – and his voice picked up suddenly, turned hoarse, scorched by years of longing – "why did she have to fall in love with a dead boy? It makes no sense. Nira could remember him, she was his first love and she would always return to that pure and innocent romance. That's why she was jealous, she had every reason to be jealous. But Miriam? A wonderful girl like her. Yet we took her side in the conflict with Nira, and it was hard for us, and sad, why did she have to love him? Didn't he die before she was born . . ."

Their words were full of a unique, despairing grace, as they took turns speaking. The moment he stopped talking, she would commence, as though they had arranged it in advance or knew each other by heart. I didn't have such harmony with Nina, and I no longer wondered why Miriam loved to spend time here.

"You understand," they said, "that Nira is a good girl. Just confused. She's not Miriam. She lacks her noble splendour, her enormous strength and compassion. She's a simple girl, Nira, full of sweetness despite her bitter experiences in life, experiences which she always knows how to forget and not deal with or learn from, as though at every moment she were once again a child and starting from scratch. She did something against you, perhaps against Miriam, too, I don't know, but she had no intention to cause harm! Noam organized the airing of the film, both I and my wife believe that, even if Nira was somehow also involved. Her innocence would redeem her. An innocence which could fall in love with many men but have only one love. She was a perpetual lover who really could love only one man. Then came Miriam and took it away from her. That was incomprehensible, though perhaps magical in a suspicious way. And Miriam didn't see the programme that night! Nira once said that Isaac worked on more than one front."

"Such things frighten me," said Mrs Raphaeli, "but I've been living with them for quite a few years. To live with a dead son with whom two women are in love, has an effect on you. Nira has a certain caprice. Miriam once told me that her mother was a whimsical woman. Perhaps, I never knew her, but Nira was full of contradictions. For years she spoke against you. You were her enemy. She defamed you with such grumbling animosity that you might think that she knew you. Then suddenly she sounded as though she admired you. She said you were full of strength, loyal, brilliant, that you'd learned how to play the piano, you were a cultured man and a good soldier. There's a certain decency in Nira, no matter how poorly she behaves sometimes. She wrote poems about Miriam, using an alias of course, and Miriam told her, 'I have an uncle, Reuben, who once wrote a poem about my mother using a pseudonym.' Nira sent them to periodicals and a few were published. She has talent, but she doesn't know what she wants, whether to weave, paint, write, have children, be a whore, or a saint, she wants it all. She once had a bar in the Caribbean, and I was told that hers was a good bar, not that I know anything about it, to me all wines are alike and I wouldn't know the difference between any one of them. Noam had begun to hate Isaac," said Mr Raphaeli. "His jealousy was over. We had a hard time of it. This morning, before you came, Nira was here. She told us that her sister was living with you. On the telephone we heard her tell her sister that she wanted to confess in front of her, that she had something to say to her, that she understood and pitied you. Naomi called here just before you showed up, she thought you had already arrived, perhaps you stopped on the way; she was a little worried and said, 'Interesting, why isn't he here yet?' So we were expecting you, we knew you were coming." "Naomi sounded alarmed, I could hear her sobbing," said Mrs Raphaeli. "We met once, but that was long ago when she was a girl of six. She told me, 'Tell him about Nira, he doesn't know, and I didn't know until today, it's rough for me, I'm torn both ways, I want him to know that I didn't have any idea about it, but the truth is,' she said, 'I really suspected it.'"

"Once," Mr Raphaeli said, "when Miriam was here, Noam stood outside and called her to come. She didn't want to. I'd sent my son out because I wanted to protect Miriam who was deeply upset over something, terrified, and she didn't want to be near Noam, she said she could smell her mother on him. She was so miserable, and I said to her, 'My Miriam, why don't you tell your father, why don't you ask him to help you? He has seen a lot in his life, perhaps he can really help, why do you pretend in front of him? You know you love him. Why not tell him everything, face to face, and ask, simply ask, for his help, his assistance, his backing. He won't refuse you; if I understand correctly, he loves you.' And Miriam said, 'I can't. I can speak to everybody else, even a stranger in the street, but not to him. Maybe because he knows deep down all the questions, not just the answers, in my disgusting story, since he's the mirror I look into to see myself and him, and maybe he knows whose mirror it is and also whose the mirror is inside his mirror. But perhaps that's what scares me, because if he knows whose mirror it is, when I look into it again I won't see myself or him any more,' and she wept, I never saw such a downpour, the floor was flooded, the blinds shook from her sobbing, the pictures trembled, glass broke, maybe there was a storm and I'm exaggerating, but it was a terrifying scene."

"You know," said Mrs Raphaeli, "Miriam told me then,

'I'm choking from too much love. Noam is splitting me apart. I depend on Isaac, but he wants revenge against my father and I can't do it. Sometimes Noam dresses up like Isaac and scares me. Sometimes I close my eyes and try to imagine exactly how Isaac looked, not in the photograph but in life, and then Noam comes out, and again it's like a betrayal . . .' "

"Noam tried to prevent us from mourning, perhaps he was trying to cancel his privileged status, which certainly caused him great injustice. I know, he had to live in the shadow of a dead brother. That's tough." The mother spoke now in a voice of anger, the clamour of primeval battle erupting from her inner being. "And then, because of all that has happened, I sometimes begin to identify with Isaac and he starts to control me too, and it's always against Noam, and I become furious at Noam and myself and Isaac, and caress Noam out of compassion. Whoever thinks that a mother and father love their children equally is mistaken. There is a basic investment, and there is closeness. The child comes out of you, born of your womb, but each unto his own. No live Noam could ever be a dead Isaac. He can be handsome, smart, brave, good, but he can never be Isaac, who was corrupt, cowardly, elegant; and I'm torn apart, Mr Krieger, no less than your daughter, who was torn between a father like you and a mother like Nina. There's Isaac, and on the side of fury is Noam, and Nira. Noam applies pressure. He casts love at you like stones. What do you think, if Miriam hadn't been so lonely would she have been so terrified? To be with someone dead is not exactly what a woman, and Miriam was very much a woman, dreams about at night. Isaac was a coward, but he was also a bold sceptic in his own special way," she added, and while she spoke, I suddenly thought about Hanoch Levi. The mother's description of Isaac was the image, almost to the point of nightmare, of Hanoch.

"Nira met Isaac on the annual field trip," said Mrs Raphaeli. "She was a kibbutznik then, and used to hang around here from time to time. Isaac was a bit scared, he loved her, it was his first love, but she was mixed up and pushed him too hard, he felt as if she were strangling him, only Miriam perhaps really understood him. She told us things about Isaac which only somebody who knew him well, and deeply, could say, after years of marriage and intimate contact. Through some kind of opaque magic she encountered the real Isaac and took him away from Nira. It was pathetic to watch the battle raging in this house, with Noam on the sidelines scorning, weeping, laughing, mocking, hurting. And us, what could we do? We pitied you, Mr Krieger. Noam knew things about you, your wife, your friends who had behaved disgracefully towards you. What was there for us to do? Warn you? But we needed Miriam! She already held Isaac in her two hands. To reach him we had to go through her. Miriam once said, 'Isaac was Daddy's cross.' She also said she had killed her beloved dog and was responsible for the death of a girl named Didi or Little Nina. Miriam took upon herself the sufferings of others. In all our life we had never seen anyone who could endure so much borrowed pain on her own shoulders. She would care for abandoned dogs, wounded pigeons, any soldier who had a problem went to her for help, she travelled for days, that's why she had to leave art school, she needed to be closer to give service, care; the misery of others had to be placed like a cross on her back."

When I got home Naomi was waiting for me. At my question she answered that Nira had admitted to her face that she had been the one who travelled to Jerusalem and showed up at the television studio dressed as a sergeant, in accordance with Noam's plan. They contacted a major who helped them, Nira got a military vehicle, drove via the West Bank to Jerusalem, and there was Joy who realised what was happening and was already scared by what she suspected was going on between Hanoch Levi and Miriam; he had spoken about Miriam to her with such passion that she went berserk, since she'd already lost enough years in a hopeless love for the father of the girl who was now perhaps about to take her Hanoch from her. It was all organized down to the last detail. Miriam would arrive at the Raphaeli house exactly on the anniversary of Isaac's death and get a shock. You'd be waiting for her at home but she wouldn't show up, Nina would be at sea with the balloons. It would all come back to you like a boomerang; and Miriam, who thought she had caused you pain, would see the documentary and get scared, she'd know that Isaac was expecting something substantial from her and she would perhaps attempt to reach him."

"What did you just say?"

"I said she would try to reach him. I'm quoting Nira!"

"Hanoch Levi was at the Bet-Lid junction that night."

Naomi looked at me, waiting for some explosion of anger which wasn't in me. I loved her and needed her love, and she was capable of giving it without any question, like a fire which could never be consumed.

"Joy and Nira were in on the secret, especially afterwards," said Naomi. "Nira had Miriam's uniform, she had apparently got hold of it at the Raphaelis'. Nira said that Isaac fooled all of them, setting one against the other. In the end she went to the studio on his orders while Miriam, she said, was sent out at the same time to another area. Joy was fighting for Hanoch, Nira sensed it, and now she regrets everything, she doesn't hate you any more, just the opposite, she is full of compassion for you, and she also knows that you aren't responsible for Isaac's death."

"Yes I am," I told her, "don't take away from me what truly belongs to me. I was an idiot, that moment, and I've had many such moments. I've failed in not just a few battles, and my planning has been terrible too sometimes, though it was all forgiven afterwards. But a final judgment always comes, the true and penetrating one, then I'll be innocent and guilty in equal measure; history is all mistakes, but in my area mistakes are fatal. I caused the death of no small number of people, Naomi. Don't give me what I don't deserve. Isaac was no big hero, but he shouldn't have died that way, I could have saved him and I didn't."

"I'm scared," said Naomi. I tried to pay attention to her, but it was already deep into the night, it was blood's turn now, Miriam was already streaming through my veins, and I attempted, as I did every night, to catch whatever Miriam was telling me. I didn't know, I really didn't, whether she was living or dead; all I felt was that when I placed my hand to my body, smack where my pistol would be, I would hear my daughter speak. This time she whispered, "Why are you alive while Isaac is dead?" She had never said that before. But she and Nina sat in some murky spot inside me, demanding that canteen of blood with which I had commenced my real existence, not the one I had as a child prior to my forging for myself the image to which all my life I would be the slave. Naomi sensed something, drew near, kneaded my shoulder, but a frighteningly cold breath of love blew from her as she said, "In the end you'll betray me the way Nira says you betrayed her dear friend. It has the ring of an ancient curse which I don't understand. Don't leave me, Joseph, even if she is dead, don't betray me and go to Miriam!"

I peered at her. Her eyes were shut. "Am I so transparent?"

She answered, "Sometimes I feel as if I'm hugging a skeleton and I stand there weeping for you. I don't want to weep over you, Joseph. You came into my life like a wonderful autumn when everything blends together, warm and cold, in a struggle of the calendar; it's pure, fresh, virginal. Don't let anything take you away from me, don't let Isaac avenge himself against you!"

Then Naomi sat up and leaned against a pillow. A light came brightly through the open window and touched her face. Perhaps the searchlight on the roof opposite us, which had been out for some time, had been fixed. Her eyes were still closed, I turned to face her, she was bending her thumb back with her other hand as forcefully as she could until, suddenly, there was a crack. Her pain reached her eyes which filled with blood. Her face showed no sign of pride, only brave submission. Her pain was apparently unbearable.

She looked at me amazed; I got up, dressed her, she was like a little girl, and she said, "Why am I giving you trouble, as if you didn't already have enough?" I didn't say a word to her. I quickly got dressed and dragged her moaning in pain to the Magen David Adom; the doctor on duty bandaged her and gave her a shot of tranquillizer.

The day began to break, it was cold but without a wind. Because of the injection Naomi didn't feel any more pain. We walked to the beach and sat facing the sea. We saw a fishing boat returning to Jaffa and a boy and a girl flying balloons. From the direction of the boat we could hear singing. An aeroplane came by, its lights darting, as it prepared to land at Dov airport. I started to sing. Naomi joined in. Her pain had returned now, but she tried to withstand it. We sang the songs we used to sing, each of us in a different generation, in the youth movement. In my heart I always called them Miriam's songs, not my daughter's, but Miriam Hurwitz's. I felt empty, my hand was actually flush at my thigh, by my revolver, which was there even though I hadn't meant to take it with me. It was part of me. Never before had I felt so far away from and so close to anybody I loved as I did then, by the sea, as dawn broke and I could see Sokolowicz running with that gaunt figure of his, but also with an exquisite delight and joy and hesitant, pure grace, devoid of all laziness, running towards the pool which he had defended during the Yom Kippur War, a whole week by himself against a wily foe.

18

I couldn't find Noam, his parents also tried but were unsuccessful, so we agreed to meet again. This time I came with Naomi. Mr Raphaeli served her coffee with pensive gallantry, while Mrs Raphaeli touched her with a tenderness which I hadn't seen in her earlier, perhaps as a response to my previous glance the last time I was there, to that flirtatious moment of arousal. Perhaps Naomi commanded a certain order over the old anger woven into the pictures and furniture. We sat, and Mrs Raphaeli said, "Noam has simply gone, he's hurt."

"But you'll surely find him," said Mr Raphaeli, "he's in the area. I have good senses. I can smell him. For years I just sit and wait without knowing what I'm waiting for. I sit by the window and Deborah says to me, 'Get away from the window, you'll catch cold,' but I stay there and tell her, 'I'm waiting.' 'What are you waiting for?' she asks. 'The Messiah? He only comes, as they say, when he's not needed.' But I'm not waiting for the Messiah, I'm just trying to smell something coming. That's all. They say I'm fragile. So I'm fragile. But what's strength? Isn't that what it takes to suffer? And I deserve all my pain. And you? Who doesn't and who does! What a lovely girl you have, Brigadier, the one who is dead or maybe alive, as well as the one on your arm, the sister of my daughter-in-law." And suddenly he burst out laughing in his fragile pain, but the anger on his wife's face flashed for only a split second.

The next day, when I swam in the pool, Sokolowicz and the old men came over to encourage me. They said that the atmosphere was charged, but that they had never once paid any attention to what evil tongues had said about me, since they were always on my side. Sokolowicz suggested that I make an appeal on the radio and request that anybody who thought she was Miriam should call me. He was charming in his enormous bathing suit; this morning was his seventy-seventh birthday. We raised our glasses of orange juice in his honour, and Rebecca sang "How lovely are the nights of Canaan" until we all had tears in our eyes which wouldn't fall, but halted half-way down our faces, unwilling to touch the concrete.

After I ran back home, out of breath but feeling my blood circulating again, Joy was there. She rose and said, "Are you playing macho again? How many laps?" I ignored her challenge and said, "Twenty," and she said, "Oh." I went into Miriam's bedroom. Naomi sat there, her head leaning against the wall and her hand still in a plaster cast. I told her, "Don't worry child. Everything's okay, and you're in the right place."

Joy drank tea, waiting for me to get dressed and return to her. Her expression was distant and mean, and she seemed sapped by a bitter struggle. But hadn't all her battles ended in defeat? She said, "Hanoch and I are getting married soon." Her voice, though, lacked conviction, as though she were saying something she wasn't so sure of any more and, therefore, had to say it, especially to me. "He'll take me as his wife," she said with a perverse smile, "because I'm close to you, and you to Miriam, and that's how he can reach her through me! It's altogether possible," she said, her smile going nasty again and spoiled. "Wasn't I almost the lover of Miriam's father, physically? The smell of the desert still sticks to my body, and he loves that odour – on others." She giggled, a kind of dry mockery in her voice, soaked in self-pity, and regret, to the point of missing her mark, something which she wouldn't have done years ago, because she always had good aim, after all, that was her strength – her power and her seductiveness and her delectable softness, backed by a dull glitter of tinsel. "You know," she said, "he was practically in love with Miriam –"

236

"So what do you need him for? Maybe he'll dump you too in the end."

She didn't answer; she pondered a bit, a cynical smile oozing from her lips, and then said, "He's the best fuck in town, Joseph, the most stunning, the least painful. And he didn't dump Miriam! He made a pass at her, lusted after her, but he lusts after them all; sometimes he bores me, but I want him and he's going to be mine. I hurt you, Joseph, I had no other choice. All those years you told me, 'Nina, Nina.' When you went to the Chief of Staff to get your release and your appointment to the reserves, and everyone peeked through keyholes to watch how you stood there, degraded before Miriam, while the Chief of Staff toyed with you, they were eager to see the stubborn soldier who had fought without logic and always believed that he was right, who never noticed his wife's continuous adulteries or forgave them if he did; but I wanted to rescue you even then, yet you refused, you humiliated me. What wounded me was that Nina was no longer a good enough excuse. In the end I fell into the hands of Nira and Noam. I owed it to Hanoch.

"Look, the investigation is over. Miriam is buried, whether you acknowledge it or not. The trial of the killers will start soon. I lied to you, yes, Hanoch wasn't at the studio then, he didn't talk to the soldier, I had to lie. He came late. I had to protect him. But he didn't touch Miriam or see her, even if he actually did try to look for her. What I know and won't say in any court of law, and you too won't be able to entice out of me – what's more, by the time of the trial, he'll be my husband and I won't be allowed to testify against him even if he did have something to conceal – what I know is that he came out of all this okay because of me . . ."

After I hadn't said a word, she added, "A deeply feminine beauty like mine, Joseph, is always held cheap by men who are colour-blind."

Once she left, I went downstairs; I wanted to buy something, anything. Naomi was already recovering from her injury, the newspapers had dropped all references to my story, though people didn't always look at me pleasantly.

I found a letter from Nina. She had hidden it in the mail-box with her own hands. The scent of her eau-de-Cologne filled the box. She wrote that she was leaving for America to forget what had happened, to settle her affairs and return to Israel. I went to Blumenfeld's Pharmacy and bought some baby food. I returned home, emptied the incredibly refined food into a pot, warmed it up, and ate the tasteless pap which was so smooth and pure. Then I saw two teardrops in the mush and I thought that perhaps they had fallen from me.

In her letter, Nina had written, "Remember, you were my only love and you'll never be able to love another. Miriam was the glue which kept my body together, thanks to love; now I have neither you nor Miriam. So all men become mere hunks of flesh in my eyes. There is no sin and no magic; you are no longer betrayed. Miriam isn't afraid any more about what will happen. I am a barren woman who deserves to be punished, but maybe that's all I will get, and that's less than I deserve."

Naomi was released from the army and was living with me now and not on the Chief of Staff's orders. Her sister Nira would phone, hang up, and call again; she wouldn't say a word, just whisper something incomprehensible and hang up. Finally she summoned the courage to ask if she could come over. Naomi was at the height of her preparations for her used-clothing shop which had been open for only about a week, under the name of "Poor Little Seagull", not far from our house on the corner of Halperin Street. Naomi, I soon discovered, had superb taste, good hands, business sense, and a direct woman-liness and unsanctimonious ability to give with all her heart, a trait which women liked and they flocked to her shop. Naomi managed to transform rags into luxury garments, and she also looked after me and kept the house the way I liked it. I wasn't a housemaid any more, she wouldn't allow it. She didn't smear herself with ointments or play the submissive woman, but she didn't wish me to be by myself, so she would call me and make quick visits during the day, letting her partner take over for a while. At night she would sew, darn, shear, patch together pieces, run to various markets to purchase rags. Her energy impressed me.

I was busy looking for Noam, and his parents were still trying to help me. Mr Raphaeli, at his window, hadn't brought about salvation, but deep in my heart I already knew what Hanoch Levi had done on the night he'd been arrested. Joy didn't know, she only thought she did.

When Nira finally dared to come by and enter the house, Naomi was at the shop. She tried to seduce me; it was so ridiculous that she herself smiled. She had gone to the kitchen and prepared coffee for herself and me. Her mischievous naïveté made me burst out laughing, and that's what subdued her, even perhaps flattered her. She sat facing me, drank her coffee, and asked me how the coffee was, and I said to her that she and Naomi were the only women I knew who could prepare coffee the way I liked it. And she totally relaxed, leaned back in her armchair, and cast one of her lovely sweet glances at me.

Gideon came, and the looks which flew between them after a few minutes of conversation were clear enough to start playing the wedding march. I jested, "In the end we'll all be one family, Isaac's family." Silence prevailed for a few minutes, broken only by Naomi's entrance; she saw my face and went to the other room, then returned and said, "The cartridge is empty of bullets," and afterwards she hugged Nira and the two of them wept.

We sat on the porch, it was already pleasant, not yet hot, the sea roared, and from a distant house came the voice of a newscaster. Nira and Gideon continued to exchange flustered looks, and Czeszek entered, sat with us, said that the trial had been postponed, gave me an opaque smile and he too apparently understood their glances, and if Czeszek, whose mother was the last woman perhaps to love him, could sense it, there was nothing more to be said.

It finally became a romance. "A glorious romance," said Naomi. And Nira, with a straight face, said, "After all my suffering, suddenly true love has been born, without revenges, betrayals," and Naomi said, "and suddenly I have a sister."

But Nira owed me an explanation. It was on the tip of

her tongue when she first came. What was nice about her was her ability to feel sorry without feeling guilty. So she described for me how Noam convinced her to make that trip to Jerusalem, claiming that Miriam would take it badly but it would help her release herself from Isaac. "I was very tense and furious then," she said, "easy prey for that handsome boy who resembled Isaac. Noam sat in the lobby of the Diplomat Hotel, Nina was in a room upstairs, he sat there and depicted for me how Nina was wooing him, how he maltreated her, and it offended me as a woman, but I was without compassion at that moment, empty, spiritually void, and Reuben roamed around the lobby. I recognized him from the funeral and I asked who that man was and they said, 'That's Nina's lover.' He looked so dangerous in that hotel lobby. So I drove via the West Bank. Miriam once told me, 'My father runs every morning to the pool to hear some old man tell him to enlist Japanese into our army,' which made me laugh because I'd been to Japan and I thought to myself, 'It wouldn't hurt.' A soldier called out to me for a hitch but I hurried to the studio. Everything worked like a charm until I heard Miriam was missing, and I was miserable. I called Joy – Noam had introduced her to me once – and she said, 'Get a hold of yourself, girl, nothing you did is connected to this,' but later she telephoned me at the kibbutz, at my mother's house, I don't have a telephone in my room, I'm just a guest, and she told me, 'You really messed it, baby, they'll soon hold you responsible for Miriam's death,' and I yelled at her."

In almost a whisper, Nira added, "I regret the wrong I have done, but that's how it happened, and that's all that I know."

She was so plagued by her role in this gigantic mystery of my daughter's disappearance, that it took her only a few days to locate Noam for us.

We came, Naomi, Nira, and I, to a three-storeyed house on Shabazi Street. The paint was peeling, garbage was strewn on the pavement, a few houses had been nicely renovated but a half-demolished building adjoined the courtyard, there was a pavement café with deafening music and men seated on stools around small tables having a

240

good time and playing backgammon, the mailboxes were broken, every one of them. We climbed to the second floor. The staircase, which stank of urine, would have looked absolutely marvellous with a little effort. The door was shut but not locked. We knocked, there was no answer, so we pushed it open. In the room furthest away sat Noam on an old armchair with tufts of wool sticking out of it. On the floor was a television set, black and white, which was showing a children's programme. Noam looked lost and exhausted, he didn't have the strength even to look at us. He tried to impart to the occasion a certain touch of fun, however feeble; I sensed the same forced, prettified wickedness which I'd seen before, but now it looked like a mask that hadn't been put on properly, the glue hadn't held. The boy was all alone, without any defences, his eyes were yellow and his hands shook. He had noticed us without any interest. Frail as he was, he looked all the more the poseur against the background of his profound disappointment, of his despair which he had planned, brick by brick, only to see it crack and crumble. The door to the tiny bathroom was open. A powerful faecal stench filled the apartment. The shower was dripping, the drain was clogged, the toilet was overflowing with foul water. The kitchen next to the bathroom was piled high with empty cans, the door to the old refrigerator hung open, and a small bulb flickered faintly inside. A sorry kitten with almost no fur was settled on top of a plate filled with some scraps of rotten stinking food. The cat's remaining fur stuck to its bones. It tried to raise its head, eyes shut. Naomi picked the kitten up in her arms and it trembled, and tears streamed from her eyes. Noam muttered, "In Jaffa I was king, eh, Brig? Now who's the king?" He spoke in a languid voice, all that remained of his naïve bravura was a hopeless attempt to lift his head, just like the kitten, and he simply was unable to do it.

He began to foam at the mouth. We took them downstairs. He let us drag him out. The kitten was near death. A man in a checked shirt standing opposite the blaring coffee house said, "C'mon, get that crap out of here, the nut. I saw him eating garbage with the cat, at the back of the café. The town put some rat poison there. I told him, 'Hey, you maniac, there's rat poison in the garbage,' and he just smiled at me like some Hollywood mogul, a real big shot, and then said, 'So what? Poison is food too.' "

19

As Noam's eyes turned glassy, we got into the Mustang and drove off. The woman doctor on duty took one look at Noam, called for a stretcher, and they carried him in. Naomi brought the kitten by taxi to a veterinary surgeon whose wife had purchased some dresses at her shop. When she returned about an hour later, Noam was in the operating theatre. An old lady was sitting and knitting a sweater with her tears. She had no wool, just needles. A man sat and listened to a transistor radio. Towards dawn, after Noam's stomach had been pumped, we brought him back to my apartment. Nira led him into the bathroom and washed him. Gideon, whom Nira had called, helped her. Standing like a child, Noam let Nira and Gideon take care of him. Then Gideon left for the veterinary surgeon and came back an hour later with the kitten. Naomi fed it, gave it some milk, and it started to purr. She made a pot of black coffee, and Noam, who was now dressed, gulped down cup after cup. Afterwards, we fed him biscuits. The purring kitten climbed on to his lap, and Noam gazed at him in amazement. He looked flustered, wrapped in a sweetness which simply didn't suit him, as though he had given up everything he had worked so hard to make of himself. With a fragment of a smile on his face, he reached his hand out to the kitten, petted it, tried to say something to us, and fell asleep in his chair open-mouthed.

He slept for ten hours without once waking. We found a sand-box for the cat, and we bought some food for it. After his sleep, Noam gawked at us, trying to muster up a bogus anger which he himself found pitiable, and at once he stopped it. He drank and ate, watching the kitten play with a pencil; its suppleness was back and the animal's eyes no longer rolled in their sockets. Noam's eyes too were full of lustre and wide awake. He stared at me, Nira, Gideon, Naomi, the kitten, orienting himself, resembling somebody who had just returned from a long, obscure journey. His eyes fixed on the vial of tears, as though he hadn't noticed his brother's photograph; perhaps he was checking the vial for the tears I once requested that Miriam shed for me. He tried to return to himself, but apparently he had nobody to return to. The rat poison had been more than a punishment, it had acted as a spiritual cleanser of the best kind. Through his pose of vile mockery, his soul peered at me enviously, with routed vengeance, with a despair that was no longer glorious. He was already beyond that, beyond himself.

He said, "I don't know if it was so clever to find me, but you apparently saved my life. I remember a black hole, and I was about to hit the bottom. Brig, I don't know where Miriam is. Other than my brother, nobody hated me the way she did.

"Maybe the word hate is too strong. There were many participants in the story which was supposed to get you to put a bullet in your head – Nira, Reuben, Nina, Hanoch Levi, but each one of them knew only a small piece of the plot. In the end she really disappeared, that's what's so silly and sad, more than anything else. She wanted to scare you, and I wanted to scare her. Finally she fell into the trap she dug for you and I dug for her, but not into the intended trap. I brought all that stuff to Carmel, I left the tracks, the shoe, the bare footprints, the jacket, everything, including the bus tickets with my parents' phone number. But you didn't call because the number must have smudged in the rain; it was in her handwriting. If you had thought straight, you might have got to me earlier. I tripped myself up but you didn't let me fall. What a sad joke . . .

"Nobody realized that Miriam had planned to scare the wits out of you. I realised only later. We thought she was just trying to reach you, to shock you not break you. The bullet in the head I figured out afterwards, once you had beaten me up and I'd run.

"The letters which you received were handled by Jahash Simontov, the Military Policeman in Ekron. Why in reverse order? I don't know. Perhaps from death's point of view everything is the opposite, and life is a tale which has already occurred and therefore is always about to happen. From God's angle, sitting at the edge of the galaxies, billions upon billions of light years away, life on this little planet hasn't yet begun, and he sees it all backwards, everything is dead and moving back towards life. Death's logic is God's logic, maybe that's Miriam's insight. She couldn't get any crazier than she was. She knew what Nira couldn't know, she understood what Isaac was like now, so many years after he had been killed. My parents became dependent on her. She was the only one who could tell my mother – who at night, every night, still dreams of Isaac and never once dreams of me – Miriam alone could tell her what Isaac thought of Menachem Begin or Ezer Weizman. She knew. How? Don't ask me. Nina claimed to know, but she said a lot of things. She also said she had to sleep with me in order to love you better. And with Reuben in the lobby, the omnipotent man, what a sorry sight. Miriam used to give my parents, who were very rational people, and never believed in miracles or attended séances or read horoscopes but had become dependent on her, Miriam would give them their son back as he was at any moment in his life after his physical death. In our house we'd already begun to speak about physical death as though there actually was some other kind of death, other than physical, and Miriam was able to sit and speak to Isaac, but that's what all of them finally believed, since they had no alternative. She brought him back, and it was hard to refuse. She cast a spell on my parents, I would tell her things and she would put them in Isaac's mouth, and even I didn't rebel any more.

"I haven't spoken for a week. My mouth can barely move. You won't find much fellowship in me. Miriam was my worst enemy. Yet, I was in love with her, like

245

everybody else, like the dead Isaac who fell in love with her after his death and banished from his presence that martyred saint, Nira, that sweetheart of a saint, eh baby?

"For two days I stayed with Miriam's mother in a hotel. To tell you the truth, Brig, it helped me; she wanted me and I wanted Miriam, and she was Miriam's mother and Miriam had arranged our meeting. Facing me was an amazingly lovely and sexy woman with experience who wanted me to fuck her. I told her, 'Sing to me' and she sang. I told her to crawl on all fours and she said she had experience of that overseas and she got down on all fours. I didn't screw her, she disgusted me; after all, Miriam had come into the world out of her, it was like some archaic tale. Miriam's father kills my brother, his daughter betrays him with me, his wife begs me for casual sex in order to love her husband. I never saw anybody more degraded than her in my life. I'm spoiled but not vicious, my dead brother castrated me too, Brig.

"I had good reasons to kill Miriam but I didn't. I don't think the Arabs killed her, I think Hanoch Levi did it. But I don't know how or why. I imagine it must be hard for you to discover now what has been going on. Where the hell have you been all these years! I have no explanation for the way Miriam behaved. I never understood her, or maybe I understood her so deeply that I was afraid to think it through to the end. I just know that she and Hanoch Levi knew each other, that he wanted her, and would call her at my parents' house, and send her notes to the Jaffa house where she used to come when there was nobody around but me. She would come to torment me. I bet you're flabbergasted, eh? You're telling yourself that you could have saved her if you only knew. You couldn't have! Don't fool yourself. All my life I have been drowning in such muck, I know it from the inside, I saw your wife on all fours, like a dog, I watched my parents, decent people sitting around and asking Miriam in a hush so that I wouldn't hear, about Isaac's opinion on inflation. You couldn't have helped, because you had to be who you were. That's what enchanted them about you. And me too, though I despised you from the bottom of my heart.

246

An even-keeled guy like you with a wife like Nina, that's tragic, like a dead army hero and his younger brother who is always down on himself, knowing that anything he does will be a disappointment, that it's impossible to compete with a dead soldier, nobody can be greater than someone who is already dead.

"The moment love for Isaac was born the goose was cooked. Somebody had to suffer. It's always a question of balancing the accounts. Like life against death, and death against life. As the poem goes, 'Don't say you're made from dust, you're made from the stranger who fell in your stead.' An awesome poem. Like this line from the same poet, 'Maybe once in a millenium our death has a break,' the break of day and the break of luck or sense. It's wrong, no, inhuman, a distortion of reality, a depiction of a truth which is incomprehensible.

"Miriam always had to choose, you or Isaac. Which was impossible. That you haven't shot yourself only shows you're more naïve than I thought. Look, I don't buy the story that you didn't know about your wife. Not that you didn't play the gentleman, maybe you did, but that you didn't investigate her past, which is what she told me. Unless your motive was not to discover who Miriam was? Perhaps you realized that there was something dangerous for Miriam in Nina's past? And you refused to enter the black pit and closed your eyes instead? Your daughter, after all, is deranged, a genuine lunatic. Certifiably so. Not some neurotic, surrounded by the romanticism of madness, not dressed up like a punk, not looking for attention, or writing plaintive poems about suicide. Your daughter is really nuts – she seems sane, talks to the point, always orderly, with a charming smile, full of affection and grace but a psychotic from head to toe. You didn't investigate. At headquarters, when she went up to the Chief of Staff in her uniform, you didn't say to her, 'Sweetheart, stop playing games now and tell me exactly what you're up to and why.' Oh no, not you. You're too decent. For a killer, you misplace your gallantry, Brig. You wanted a compact army, four hundred Gideons with missiles and computers and neutron bombs and brilliant minds which can kill quietly, tranquilly, impassively, not an idiotic system, not an army of Simontovs whose warm family Miriam loved to visit.

"If you'd only seen those plants there and smelled those spices! But you, after all, had told the Chief of Staff, 'You're setting up the best army in the Middle East.' You're an élitist snob, a real decent, honest racist with a flat stomach, doing twenty laps a day. With a father like that Miriam had problems in our house, a house with a dead soldier who wet his pants and was scared shitless at the only battle he fought! In everything I've said so far, have you noticed how much I have been quoting your daughter and your wife? No, you didn't investigate. Others were living inside your soul, crouched in your gut, but you don't notice, Mister Gallantry, you don't hear and don't ask questions. Proper. As it's supposed to be. You're a true fascist, Brig. You don't like disorder. You'd rather shut your eyes if that will bring order. You always follow the chain of command, like Eichmann. A great planner, superb fighter, top-notch commander, but when it comes to the source from which your wife delivered your daughter, a daughter she refused to see for over a year, *that* you don't attack and don't investigate. You're the strongest and most poisoned, the most disappointing there is, perhaps because deep down you didn't give a shit. For the sake of peace and quiet and smooth sailing, in order to have a nice home, a caricature. Your wife could go wherever she wished as long as she came home, and your daughter just had to be on time. That attitude of mind has murdered more than one person, it has wiped out a whole nation, when taken to the extreme. The spirit of the screwed-up dead Palmach, all the sacrifices to the Palmach's passing, the handsome lads born of the sea. You don't open wounds, you don't cull anything, you don't exert yourself much, you just turn your efforts into a dandy sport – look, mummy, I'm blowing them away with an M16 or a missile! You cannibalized yourself so that *another you* could give you orders; then your daughter struggled against you because she wanted you to be a human being not a hero, a person not a boring knight, a fucked-up fascist. That's why you have *his* photograph on the wall, not merely out of guilt – how much room did you have in you for guilt? He was terrified, and you knew very well how terrified he was. He went to his death, but what could you have done? That vile battle I learned about by heart, I questioned old soldiers who'd been there; they all told me what Joseph made of that Isaac, they didn't know I was his brother, and with an amazement which hadn't died after all these years they asked, 'Why did Joseph turn him into a hero? On account of him we hung around there and almost packed it in, because Joseph ran into the house and tried to save him!'

"Joseph Krieger, you never could have got him out of that house, and the fact that you sent him into battle after imagining that he wouldn't return alive, is something so natural that only you could make a big deal out of it, or your daughter. When I told her what had actually happened, she was angry with me, but she knew about it before I did, and no less than me, either. Look, if you kept in the rear everybody that you thought wouldn't survive, you'd have nobody to fight those idiotic battles for which you have so many medals. You hung my brother on your wall so that, like some orthodox Japanese, you'd always have your harakiri sword close by and drawn . . ."

Noam stopped talking for a moment. He seemed in deep thought, a sarcastic smile bobbing at the corners of his mouth, then he snapped his attention on to his brother's photograph, adjusting his hand as though to erase some picture in his mind, and said, "Brig, face it, you wouldn't recognize much of Nina's life, what do you really know? Why am I the one who knows what she went through, and how her father hid his daughter and fled, and how her mother was taken to a camp? Her father wasn't a Jew, but you have no idea what he was . . . You once met that aunt, but did you ever wonder who she was? Why did Nina have to bring to Israel a Christian woman and her daughter under an alias? Did you ever try to find out what was written on that sheet of paper which the judge at Reuben's trial cried over like a child? Nina's life was a volume of tears, yet she's a survivor with an unquenchable thirst for life, while you fell into the doghouse where Nina learned to bark. After all, she was obliged to show her gratitude to those bastards who concealed her and abused her; her form of revenge was not to liquidate them but to rescue them and bring them to Israel.

"Nina was in love with life but didn't want to play the queen over anybody. You didn't give her what she really wanted, Brig. What games she and Miriam used to play with you! After Miriam had *met* Isaac, she and Nina became close. The things that went on when you weren't at home! And Miriam learned to take all the pain on her own shoulders. She was but a teenager after the Yom Kippur war, and yet she went around to the bereaved parents in your unit, from house to house. She said, 'I'm the commander's daughter.' They told you about it then, Joy told you, but you didn't say a word and you let her do it. I'm not sure, maybe she wrote to you about this; she did, you know, work on five letters to you, she wrote them and told me she'd mail them."

"I didn't get five letters, just four, and one wasn't finished."

"So somebody took one," said Noam. "She wrote five. In Jaffa she read the whole series aloud to me. That was two months before she decided to scare you, when she began to plan the entire thing.

"Then 21 January, Isaac's memorial day, and she didn't come by, instead she suddenly showed up on television and my father almost had a fit. I wanted there to be two houses with apoplexy in one night.

"But you obviously went to the pool the next morning, and later on came to Jaffa. Didi called you after I got back. And that's odd, she was supposed to phone you first thing in the morning. Maybe you weren't up.

· "Anyway, Miriam used to treat me like shit," Noam added and said, "the only one who could. That good little girl, that golden-hearted mouthpiece needed somebody to dump all her aggressions on, and that was me. I'm not asking you to be nice to me, I'm just relating the facts. How many tears I shed by her unrecognizable body! How much Isaac despised me! At the outset, for a night or

250

two, when she almost slept with me, Miriam let me love her body so she could be with my brother naturally, and after that, she didn't need my flesh any more. Just facts, Brig. Do you think she didn't egg me on to fuck your wife, Miriam's own mother? But it revolted me. You officers, Brig, are a screwed-up bunch of ego-maniacs. You fuck like dogs. You're always among young women soldiers who worship you. Your private lives are a mess, your old wives have turned you into incurable womanizers – most of you marry young, don't you? You're squares with square spouses who became middle-aged two hours after the wedding. Talented army men like you, female soldiers want between their legs, so you foul up your kids' lives and later give all your love to your grandsons, trying to make them into your sons. You, Brig, discovered love at the end of your life, but you don't remember any more how to get laid, eh? An old fart in bed with fresh flesh."

Afterwards, Noam rented a room on Frug Street and went to his parents to be reconciled with them. Nira moved in with Gideon, and Naomi's store flourished. Time passed, I didn't pay much attention to that, something was slipping between my fingers, Noam's words had burned into my skin, but at night I dreamed about my daughter Miriam, as though everything I'd learned about her hadn't happened. From the courtyard rose the scent of the sea, sweet basil, and lemon. The wizards and fortune tellers sent by Madame Frau continued to see my daughter trekking through grassy lanes, in England, the Negev, the San Francisco area; the Chief Rabbi took the trouble to climb the sixty-four steps of our house, no mean feat for him, and tried to persuade me to participate in the purchase of a memorial stone for my daughter, requesting me to admit my mistake and allow my daughter to rest in peace. I didn't answer him; he wept, but I kept quiet until he was gone.

Madame Frau even called a tenants' conference in my apartment. Mr Feigel came supported by his cane because of the seriousness of the matter, and Mr Haim wore an outfit which he must have pulled out of an old trunk

251

in honour of the moment. Madame Frau saved the day because she, after all, had lived her entire life beyond the pale of ordinary reality, the way I had lived my life, so she said, beyond Miriam's existence. The fact that she had waited all her life for lions had given her an advantage, her insanity having been taken by many to be just a game, or perhaps a trick.

The neighbours analyzed the situation, claiming to speak as experts on missing persons. The charge was made that perhaps Miriam's disappearance was nothing but a military diversionary campaign, that she was in the hands of the army, that I perhaps was concealing facts even from myself. Their seriousness was laughable, I wanted to laugh but there was no laughter in me, just a kind of shame before these old-timers who sat there utterly exhausted from their scores of years of longing, and who couldn't comprehend that a Jewish brigadier's daughter was actually missing.

Madame Frau said, "Miriam has gone to look for Isaac. That's where she is, with him." And Mr Haim said, "Yes, but on which side?" Maybe he meant which side of existence. Then Madame Frau brought up the subject of my mother's relationship with Miriam. Although my mother had tried to back off from anything to do with Nina, for a certain period she wooed her granddaughter; but maybe Madame Frau was correct, and my mother had planted in Miriam the seeds of her own mother's terror and nausea. It was hard for me to accept Madame Frau's words, since she always had a score to settle with my mother. "Your mother's strength," my father told me once in a moment of truth, "was that she didn't have to love anybody, not one of us," he said, "not even you." But perhaps she had a certain vague affection for Miriam, as though along with her loathing for Nina she had to package some tenderness, which fell on my daughter, who was surrounded by love then and didn't recoil from my mother's presents. I attached little significance to these claims, to the house committee's hints about the link between my daughter and my mother; it was a side issue and not particularly important, even if my mother really did come to learn the facts about that "aunt" in Haifa and actually investigated Little Nina's mother and taught Miriam things which she didn't have to know. That was immaterial now. Perhaps Miriam had been touched by my mother's hidden sorrow, whose worst disaster was marrying my father, as she later acknowledged, after she had learned to celebrate his death in such a noble and poignant fashion, mourning him as her lost love rather than as her biggest mistake. Maybe that concealed grief emerged in Miriam who from the time of her birth until she was a year and some months had lived without a mother. That was something which my mother was capable of doing, if she were more courageous and not always fearful of the satanic treachery of death which was out to ambush her.

Mr Feigel, bursting with a nastiness which didn't suit his tranquil, submissive temperament, told us that Miriam Hurwitz, whom my mother apparently knew – she even knew about her association with Miriam – had arranged for a trust fund for Miriam in America, at Chase Manhattan Bank. A certain Marco Perach had set it up, a former taxi driver from Jerusalem, the brother of Himmo Perach, that unfortunate young man whom Miriam Hurwitz had fallen in love with in Jerusalem, who had become just a mouth and victim of her mercy. Marco had emigrated to America and made a fortune. When the pharmacies and Clinic began refusing to supply my mother with medicine, she apparently managed to get it from him. Mr Feigel said that while Nina was in America she tried to break into that trust fund. It was in Miriam Krieger's name, and to this day Marco thinks that Miriam Hurwitz was her aunt.

So I finally found out how the money got here for our house painting. Miriam obviously knew. She was in touch with Marco. Was the money intended to paint the house or paint what Miriam considered, in her own mind, her Daddy's coffin?

20

DALIAH Levi, Hanoch's wife, received us in her lovely home in Talbiye, an old house which once served as the quarters of the South American Consulate. She tried to control her laughter at the sight of Madame Frau's fantastic splendour and at the sound of her announcement that she had accompanied me in her capacity as my "mother by virtue of love", a term which Daliah treated with more than expected good-hearted courtesy, covering perhaps her surprise since clearly there was no rational explanation for what she saw. We sat in a spacious room, into which the strong Jerusalem light penetrated via the not-so-large windows, leaving the centre of the room dusky and cool. We drank coffee. Daliah knew, of course, the purpose of our visit; her children were at school, and she looked like a queen known for her power rather than her beauty or her age, which was above what I had expected. She wore purple pants and a white tricot blouse and an orange scarf which imparted strength to her tanned face, which was lined with cruel wrinkles; there was also perhaps a small suggestion of scorn in the way her lips met tightly, confining a certain alarm, maybe determination, or control of her emotions. Madame Frau was captivated by her at once, Daliah's solid pain was secretive and pure.

After a few words of politeness which were spoken without haste, Daliah, having to readjust her sense of herself as an exploited person, now that she was facing somebody whose daughter had been murdered in ugly circumstances, poured out her heart – once I'd clarified what I knew already and why our meeting was so crucial.

She wasn't the type of woman who [...]
feelings; I could see how difficult it was [...]
about her husband and about herself. But she [...]
to now. And that obligation released her from her [...]
inhibitions. She tried to describe the events as she [...]
them. It was as if she were talking to me at the funer[...]
with calm intimacy and a feeling of shared sorrow. Apparently she found it easy to unburden her pain, a pain
which was linked to that show which she witnessed on television when, so as to inflame the community, an image of
my daughter's corpse had been flashed on the screen for
a second, a vision which few could forget.

Daliah, who did well to place a barrier between assumption and certainty, did not suppress anything concerning
herself or her status in the life of a man who, in her
own characterization of him, was no small philanderer,
though she always loved him and always would. She spoke
with restraint and grace, in pain devoid of pathos, saying
that she had expected me for some time now, correcting
herself immediately to say that she'd been waiting for "us".
Madame Frau thanked her with a smile. Perhaps she also
had a need to unload herself before strangers, and Madame Frau was a good choice. We were all ears, though
she was too proud and it was hard for her to speak, but
somehow we were inferior to her and hence acceptable,
like a chance stranger at a railway station, as the sounding
board to her lament.

She spoke like a machine, the tone of her voice vibrated
smoothly non-stop, a dry slight tremor, as if she were on
auto-pilot, a charming yet ominous version of a challenge
that was also a submission.

According to her, Hanoch had become negligent lately.
He had always been too clever to allow his actions
to interfere with his work or his family life; now his
work was definitely suffering. By her estimate he was a
professional of the highest order, unusually intelligent,
inquisitive, creative, an original thinker. Now he was in
trouble. Suddenly Daliah smiled, and in that flash it was
easy to recognize her love for her husband. Daliah knew
him better than anybody else did, and she said she always

255

re," she said. She let him play
at he needed his pathetic man-
always come back to her, his ties
nd he really loved only her. "Not
said. "And I'm older than he is
days are over, but in my youth
. Hanoch loved me when we were
years ahead of him." The difference
r him; she wanted us to understand
return to her not just because of their
close in... He comes back," she said, without the
slightest blush, cause he can't find more pleasure in any
other bed, and I'm not the only one he's told that to," she
said, "but those young chicks he sleeps with, they used to
phone me, those fools, to tell me so. Our bond is powerful,
and Joy is no exception. She simply trapped him when he
was lost and vulnerable, with his awesome self-love, his
comfort, his honour. Joy realized what his Achilles' heel
was, his fear, that's how she controls him. Me you cannot
scare," she said, "I'm like lead."

"It all began with Isaac Raphaeli," said Daliah, smiling
her sad smile, and all at once hundreds of small crinkles
and lines vanished and her face lit up with an inner femininity, with a beauty which only monogamists like me and
her can recognize, the loveliness of familiar faces at the
moment of love, a kind of renewed contact with a field
known and ploughed to exhaustion when suddenly there is
a shadow, a resonance, something new, a brightness which
wasn't there before, and no stranger's face has that hidden
secret glow.

Even Madame Frau's legs swivelled into a new posture, and she looked sexy, like some ageing actress in
a sentimental Hollywood film embodying Madame Frau.
"Isaac," said Daliah, "poor dead Isaac."

"Hanoch," she said, "*met* Isaac while he was having
a quick affair with Nira, after she had returned from
some exploit of hers in Japan." Daliah depicted Nira as a
nice girl, a perpetual seeker, wearing long Indian dresses
in those days with colourful ear-rings. "She came back
divorced, selling mysticism with a plaintive but brazen

pushiness. She meditated, switched gurus, spoke about kabbalah, spoke in a soft, sexy, agitated voice about her exaltation, and sought spirituality in the gutter. Out of excess other-worldliness she went around barefoot, lived for a while in Rosh Pinah, in an old house, with some hippies who were in fashion then and with some local guru, and smoked marijuana which she called grass, using the American idiom. Hanoch had a quickie with her, and came back stinking with sweat. For a long period she didn't bathe because her guru claimed that water was in the service of egoism. For two months she washed herself with one glass of water a day, while she sipped an ancient Japanese potion, that's what she called it, and Hanoch lusted after her, she turned on that boy.

"Hanoch and your wife Nina," said Daliah after swallowing some of her coffee and looking as if she were trying to wipe away an ugly memory, "met when Hanoch did a television programme in collaboration with the Chief of Staff. You," said Daliah, "were on one of those missions across the border, and he interviewed the Chief of Staff. Nina got there somehow, and Hanoch knew she was your wife. You were a part of everything he admired, that bravery. He took Nina home because the Chief of Staff was called back to headquarters for some emergency, and Hanoch started to flirt with her. He courted her with poems which he copied from the ones he'd written to me twenty years earlier. Poetry was never his strong point, that's why he always had to impress easy lays who didn't know the difference between a lemon and a Cadillac when it came to poems. Nina, apparently, loathed him. He put pressure on her at her weak spot. Precisely through his aggressive sexual drive he may have reminded her that she was a soul as well as a crotch." Daliah sounded furious but amused. Perhaps she had to degrade herself in front of us in order to appear stronger than all her rivals. The outcome was that he'd had all these women except Nina, who didn't want him and rejected him. And that was charming since Nina was my wife and the mother to Miriam whom he later went wild over, according to Daliah, and it all came full circle, a small one, Nira, Nina, Miriam and myself.

"Hanoch was wounded by Nina's arrogant conduct, found Miriam, and through her he wanted to get even with Nina. But Miriam was also the daughter of a hero – something he was incapable of even in his dreams. And," said Daliah, "he was embarrassed by what he truly had in him: his prodigious, brutal intelligence, his eloquence, his knack for engaging the public's interest, not being particularly handsome yet looked forward to with great affection. His endearing indifference and intense, careful curiosity. Like so many Israeli children," said Daliah, "he dreamed of becoming a hero. What he wouldn't give to be a living legend rather than just interview living legends.

"Joy knew about Nina and Nira and Miriam. She was also the one who held all the reins, because the one thing Hanoch couldn't grasp or understand was that you, a brigadier, an Israeli hero, were not a womanizer. It made no sense to him, what with Nina and her tales of betrayal, not to mention what he knew about the army from close up, and about the reserves. He was close to the top officers, and saw them with their young secretaries, with their mistresses, and the whole lot of them said, 'Joseph is a blockhead! Captive to his wife, he pretends that spittle is rain, and doesn't know what his daughter is up to, or that his two best friends have been residing in his beloved's womb!' Hanoch didn't believe them, he sought but couldn't find some dirt on you. More and more Joy was forced to admit her weakness, despite all her efforts, and as much as Hanoch spoke badly of your puritanism, she fought to explain you to him. But as intelligent and clever as he was," said Daliah, "he simply couldn't understand.

"Look, Krieger," said Daliah as she glanced at my step-mother with almost capricious coquetry, "Hanoch was insulted. Nina, everybody's bed-partner, had no use for him. She told Noam Raphaeli that Hanoch knew him through Nira, that he was dangerous and she was afraid of him. When Hanoch came to Miriam, Isaac was already nestled in him like an incubus, and Miriam was a hard nut to crack. He devoted a lot of patience and love to it, but nothing worked, though she didn't reject him out of hand, maybe she needed him for something, an alibi perhaps, since Hanoch was a celebrity. I just waited. After all, I thought it would end the way it always did, and he would come home again. Do I have anywhere to go? He amuses me and he's the father of my children. I don't have, and never did have, any plans for another life. We have been a couple that has watched out for each other so that neither of us would self-destruct. Joy held him on a short leash, she knew something; when I asked, he was evasive, but he wept and explained that even though he loved just me, he had to leave me and marry that vulture of a virgin But I wouldn't buy his explanation or his evasion. I told him, 'Hanoch, you're a big boy now and you must learn that in the end we all sleep in the bed we make for ourselves, and you're about to enter a bed of nails.'

"That got him to tell the truth. He was scared of her, it was something to do with Miriam and her disappearance – by then it was known that she was missing and that you were looking for her; the newspapers had already leaked that she was the daughter of an army reserve officer. Hanoch was in a panic. He told me, 'I was the last person to see her alive, Joy's positive that I'm mixed up in her death. I'm not, but who's going to believe me.' And I said to him, 'You're talking like a baby. The truth will finally come out. You don't owe anybody anything. If you're innocent, and I believe you are,' I told him, 'then you have nothing to fear.' But I'm not sure whether he himself believed he was innocent. In other words, I don't know how much he was really involved. He is a liar, a manipulator, and a cheat; maybe he thought that he was actually guilty of something? Maybe he was scared to acknowledge to himself what had happened? Maybe his relationship with Miriam was something different, unlike all the others?"

Suddenly I got up, looked at Daliah with fondness, there was something in her which instilled trust, something endearing. I understood her devotion to Hanoch. Her last words were said with such intense pain; perhaps we were both from the same mould. I said to Daliah, "If it's not an imposition, I'd like to leave Madame Frau with you and head out. I'll be back by tonight." Daliah smiled and said,

"We'll have a ball," and Madame Frau said, "Fine with me, it's been years since I was in Jerusalem, and I should like to visit the Old City again and purchase a nice Bedouin dress for Naomi." I asked permission to make a phone call, Daliah smiled again, unable to control herself, and said, "In any case Hanoch will pay for it."

I called Naomi, she sounded worried and asked me to take care of myself; I said I would come home late that night. I took leave of the two women who were already deep in conversation and concern with one another; their exaggerated woman-to-woman trust in each other enabled them to enter those dark secret places without waking any demons. In a little over an hour I was already approaching Ekron. I tracked down the Simontov residence, a boy on a bike pointed out the house to me. A pleasant fragrance of spices and flowers greeted me; an older woman was carefully tending to seedlings immersed in piles of dug-up loose soil. She asked me who I was looking for, and I told her. She gave me a bewildered look, almost plaintive, but she didn't play games, there was a touch of shrewdness, however naïve, in her face, which could easily have led me astray, yet she didn't even try to, she just invited me inside. The house was buzzing with people. I understood Miriam now, facing that colourful clamour gushing out everywhere, that chaotic festiveness which literally splashed on to the floors. A girl in wooden clogs and a slightly open dressing gown was attempting to dance to the sound of the radio. Jahash sat and looked at me. I could tell who he was; he may have been expecting me. At least he wasn't slippery, and I appreciated that. The Mustang waited outside like a horse straining after a wild gallop. Jahash sat in the middle of the room, his eyes flashing a strange blur, a cold suspicion. He was a wild cat, alert to the point of terror. Madame Frau would certainly have caught in him the splendour of her father's virtue in one of his big moments. I didn't have a lasso with which to snare him. A girl, younger than her sister in clogs, served me a glass of cold juice, and Jahash waited, his eyes suffused with a pain which had nothing to do with me. I was obliged to point out to him his fundamental mistake, but perhaps there was no need for that now. We were both well-protected for the time being, and he suddenly tried to be festive, though I could sense his inner turmoil. He was a link in my daughter's march of terror, and I was jealous of this house in which Miriam had felt so much warmth, love and understanding, things she never got in my house. Jahash said, "So let's have it, Brigadier. I could have run away, but what was the point?"

I asked him who drove the car that took Miriam from the base, and he said, "I already told them, I don't know. It was a Citroën."

"You're playing games with me, soldier," I said. "I'm already at the end of the road, so it's no problem for me to trample upon somebody like you. The driver was Hanoch Levi, it wasn't a Citroën G.S., you made that up, it was a Cortina. You just repeated what they told you to say. And you know exactly who drove that car."

He looked amused, mournful, evasive. I could smell the wounded animal that he had been all his life, and his addictive loyalty to Miriam who had helped him so much, by granting him a new life in which he could find self-esteem. But she had also disappointed him. His story had been confused because he too, in fact, was betrayed. He understood that after everything he had done, Miriam had never considered him in her league. In the end he had played a small role, helpful but not significant, just another military cop, able to further her scheme but not enter her life. He realized that she had fooled him but it was hard for him to betray her. He waited, ready to counter-attack, but the words died in his mouth.

"You're lying, you saw Hanoch Levi very clearly, you recognized him, Miriam told you to lie!"

"That's wrong."

"I'll have you arrested as an accomplice to a crime; Hanoch killed her!"

"Those Arabs killed her!"

"Hanoch, Hanoch was the killer, he used you, boy, they told you to mail the letters in a certain order and you did it, you followed orders, sweetheart." I could smell his defeat and I added, "You were loyal and in the end got screwed.

261

Nobody valued you; you were, after all, just a tool." He almost wept. "Wrong," he said in a crippled, broken voice. "She was my friend, she cared about me, what a beautiful girl she was, those Arabs . . ."

But his claims began to crumble and fade, and he was forced to admit that *that* was the reason he was waiting for me – to fall apart. It was his own barbaric, excruciating revenge, the inevitable outcome of his guilt over the disaster, his own included. The house was quiet all of a sudden, the radio was off, nobody else was in the room but us, but the walls had ears, full of anticipation and dread. Finally he confessed, Hanoch had really taken Miriam; he had come and asked permission to enter the camp. From the booth he called Miriam's office and she insisted that she didn't want him allowed in, but Hanoch outwitted Jahash and went inside. Then she left with Hanoch, which really upset Jahash; he even felt that they were playing games with him. But he knew Miriam. "At times," he said, "she turned into a different woman, weird, cold, distant, as though she were hearing voices." She had told Jahash, "This is a complicated matter, just say whatever I tell you to say." She exacted a high price from him. "But with us," said Jahash, "it's a question of honour. Miriam gave without ever asking for anything in return. I was imprisoned once, and Miriam went to court, testified on my behalf, and they listened to her. She had an angel's voice. The judge was broken by her and they let me out on probation. I'm indebted to her, and suddenly she asks for something. She hurt me too, but I tell myself that I can play games like anybody else; if somebody like Miriam, a straight and proper woman can come and say that it's important for me not to tell the truth, not even to her father, then she must have good reasons for it. So I did as I was told and I lied even though I didn't want to. And it wasn't just my honour at stake but hers too, that's why it was so hard, because by lying for her I also lost some respect for her, she became like the others, all of a sudden she wanted me to lie, send letters, go to the post office, work it out with my uncles there, I have five uncles and nephews at the post office, in Rehovot, Rishon, Hadera, my whole family is one big post office. So it was my job to make sure that the postmarks were clearly legible, without anybody knowing why. They let me in from the rear, as if they were just going out to get me coffee while I cheated and postmarked all the letters for the only person in my life that I could never believe would lie because she wasn't like me, she was special. She understood my mother, her flowers, spices, plants. I just swallowed it and kept quiet and suffered, and that's how it was ... Then I read the papers and watched television and Miriam was suddenly a big story, and you too, how you wouldn't attend the funeral. I did go, her mother was there, how she cried that poor woman, and I wanted to go over to her, and say something, but she looked right through me as if I were air. Once Miriam was gone, I lost all my honour. What am I? She gave me all the self-respect I ever had. How she loved to come here and sit with my mother, my sisters, my father, to smell the flowers, to get to know my family, but what did it all add up to? She fooled me! I thought she was interested in my relatives. She said she wanted to help, and she really did help them, because it was important for her that they'd all be working at the post office, that's all she wanted in the end, a post office not a family; any way you look at it, she used me and I let her do it."

21

O^N the way back to Jerusalem I figured it out, but
the knowledge gave me no satisfaction. Jahash was
repulsive to me. Weak men depress me. He had confirmed what I should have realized the day Gideon told
me that Miriam had left the base with Lieutenant-Colonel
Avinoam. Hanoch Levi was the last person to see Miriam;
it was unlikely that they were strangers to each other.
Everybody had hinted at some sort of relationship between
them. Yossi was seated in the car as a diversion. After I'd
learned about Hanoch's traffic violation and the court
case, it should have clicked. How Miriam's belongings got
to the cave became a minor issue, perhaps just another
diversionary tactic, amenable to explanation and not in
any way connected to the crux of the matter.

Or so I thought.

I also thought that no military hero, even the stuff of
Hanoch's dream, can be a hero in real life. We are all crippled by life. My daughter is a fluke, an example, a splendid
woman but wrapped in dread before the ordinary human
condition; no child of myth, neither daughter nor son, can
ever be rescued from the need for revenge against whatever life has sold them as a perverse alternative to death,
on whose behalf and honour we are fighting, sanctifying it
as though it were truly worth something, as if it were okay
to use death in order to defend an enterprise as shaky as
life. So the unfortunate Simontov, my second Jahash, was
just a negative, a coarse caricature of my own existence.
Around him, at least, percolated real signs of life, his
mother, the spices, those graceful sisters of his, his brother.

In Jerusalem again. Madame Frau had just returned from a stroll with Daliah through the Old City. She spoke in an innocent, awed excitement about what she called the "Everlasting City". Her eyes sparkled but I knew that she was already homesick for her fortified apartment in Tel-Aviv. "The moment they put a supermarket by the ancient stones of Jeremiah and Jesus," said Daliah, smiling like a Tel-Aviv native exiled in Jerusalem, "you long for the seashore and the crumbling limestone buildings." Then she added in a pensive voice, "After you locate him, I think he'll come back to me," and I told her, "Wait, I'm about to bring your husband to you on a spit." She laughed and said, "Maybe then he'll stick around the house."

"You know," she continued with a smile which didn't manage to erase the growing loss of faith that was nibbling at her confidence, "after twenty years of marriage he still asks me, each time, if it was 'good' for me, if I enjoyed it. So skewer him for me, Mr Krieger; after every escapade of his, and he's had quite a few, he gives a performance full of soul. When he feels guilty he's at his best. But you're not the kind to cut him down to size, Krieger, you're too decent."

I came home a hundred years older, and Naomi, who hadn't aged more than a few hours, was waiting for me seated cross-legged. At long last I was utterly depressed. In my mind clamoured the sentence, "Brig, where were you during your whole life? During the years you were married and had a daughter and considered yourself her father, where were you? Why didn't you look around, why didn't you investigate, why didn't you know what so many others knew?" Perhaps, like my mother, I was barren of feelings, and my monogamy was nothing but a perverted form of emotional impotence.

That evening Gideon and Nira came by, and Noam too, who was coquettishly ingratiating and picked up the phone, spoke to somebody, and then all of a sudden said to me, "My mother wants to talk to you." Mrs Raphaeli said, "If Noam has to stand trial, we'll understand, but don't be too harsh on Miriam, she didn't know exactly what she was doing. She was torn between loyalties; if I could create another world, I would wipe out loyalty from the moral code. I'm referring to the sense of devotion and solidarity, I would leave everything the way it is in nature, the big fish eating the little fish, no tears, no struggle, no desire to have mother against a father."

For a moment she turned off the flow of her words and I waited for her, Noam at my side eavesdropping on his mother through the receiver. She went on. I wanted to say something but didn't, Noam looked at me smiling, Naomi too, who suddenly seemed completely at ease as though a dreadful suspicion had begun to melt. Noam's mother said, "Or whatever."

I asked, "What do you mean by whatever?"

"Nothing," she said, and I went along with her, but Noam took the receiver and said, "Or brother against brother, or mother against –"

And I took the phone back by force.

Mrs Raphaeli let her tears fall freely; her receiver was wet and I could sense it. She said, "Commander, there is nothing crueller than the vengeance of betrayed women, and you have stepped on the toes of such women. No matter how hard you try to be decent towards your children, it's never good enough. To be a mechanic you have to take lessons, in order to operate the most pathetic system you have to go to school and get a diploma; but nobody learns how to be a parent, the most important task in life is not teachable. Watch out, Joseph, you're not the worst father any more than I was the worst mother. Simply, noone taught us what every cat knows until she tells her offspring, 'From now on, you're no longer mine, and I'll fight against you for food, and if you come too close to me when I'm on heat, you're in trouble, and whoever isn't careful dies.'"

After I hung up I told Noam, "Go to her; maybe being 'Miriam-less' is no easier for them than for me, but she needs you now," and he said, "With parents and children, Brig, it makes no difference at what age, it's always too soon or too late."

The strong smell of salt wafted from the sea, mixed with the aroma of superior coffee which our neighbours were now brewing in their houses. Czeszek arrived and told us that the Arabs who had been found guilty of Miriam's murder had recanted. "Their lawyers," he said, "influenced them. They want a retrial to prove that their confessions were forced from them under duress. The lawyers are getting ready to subpoena you for a testimony" he said. "They want to show that even you deny their guilt. After all that has been written against you, you still have the status of a brigadier in reserves. But everything you say will only help them and hurt your daughter."

He sounded exhausted but not particularly disappointed, and I didn't respond to his cruel challenge which he tossed off, as though his anger at me and at the turn of events had become more supple – he didn't like it when any investigation of his went awry, especially after the case had been closed. But maybe he also felt again that something wasn't kosher in his ironclad logic. I said to him, "Czeszek, I'm no tenderfoot. On my belt I have plenty of scalps, it's not what I love to do, but it's a fact. What disturbs me is your convenient mental satisfaction. We looked for her, there were conflicting signposts, then came the cave and the subsequent assumption that her body would have to turn up next, so it did, and at once you had your Arabs to confess their guilt. Things were put together, the nation wanted revenge, the gruesome murder enraged everybody, justifiably, and the public demanded a punishment for the mean killers, but I don't take things at face value. There's a corpse, killers, and a cave, but maybe it's somebody else's body. Find out who else is missing. You're locked into the most likely conclusion. Perhaps those Arabs really are debased murderers who wasted her, but Miriam is too easy a solution. Furthermore, I'm on the verge of understanding what really happened. The Chief of Staff told me something a while back and I didn't quite understand what he was saying. After I'm all done, you may still stand like an idiot and have to apologize for not listening to me. I may be an hysterical father, but you'll be obliged to admit your error. It won't be easy.

"I'm very close to the solution," I said; "look, Czeszek, it's my daughter, alive or dead, it's me and my entire life, not Sherlock Holmes who sits back after solving the murder and smokes his pipe. With me, once the case is done and the mystery solved, that's only the beginning. My grief will eat right through me, because then I'll have no place to go to, nowhere to search, nothing to pin my hopes on. I'm right at the edge of the answer, at least I think I know what occurred, even though not how."

The following morning Noam said to me, "On Friday night Jerusalemites come down to Tel-Aviv. And it's almost summer now. Hanoch will surely be here, he'll sit at an outdoor café and have a watermelon and a beer."

We took off. It was already evening. Noam got out of the car and roamed around. Naomi had stayed at home, Joy had called and sounded restless. Nira had come along for the hunt veiled in her new love for Gideon, all made up, with a brimmed hat, as in the films. Hanoch sat eating a watermelon and joking with a few sharp tongues like him. The sea roared and cars whizzed past the length of the boardwalk. The real summer hadn't begun, a cool breeze was still blowing. Then Noam approached him. He rose, looked around, saw me coming. At the sight of my face Noam laughed derisively.

The car starts up, Hanoch doesn't resist, and I don't have to use force. Nira drives, Gideon is austere. We arrive home. Hanoch looks miserable, but he doesn't lose his temper. Why didn't he run away? He foiled my whole plan. Naomi serves coffee. Nira removes her streaked make-up, and without her hat she looks like a young girl.

Hanoch seemed flustered but not scared. He preserved his secret even inside this ridiculous trap. I was a hunter who had been trained by a huntress after pink panthers. Lately, Madame Frau's ageing eyes had begun to wrap themselves in a harsh, grey glitter. Her adopted son had learned the lonely, noble work of the hunter, like His Excellency her father. He gazed at me, at Naomi, at Noam. It was a long, regretful look, perhaps he was counting the bullets in his cartridge, assessing himself against the accusation which practically sat in my face; he was looking for something in my face, and it wasn't forgiveness which he was after. As he studied me he realized that I knew;

perhaps I pitied him, he was so full of basic guilt and a kind of total distrust of himself. He waited.

And, after all, we both knew what had occurred. Not Naomi, not Noam, not Nira, not Madame Frau at her kitchen window watching the play. We two, he and I, knew. Because a picture flashed in my mind, I saw myself back then, in Bet-Lid, the Chief of Staff was waiting for me late at night to take me home in my car while his driver drove his car right to the entrance to my house. I needed time, but Naomi, who was apparently smarter than I had imagined, now suddenly said, "Maybe Hanoch Levi was the only one who really loved Miriam!"

When she said it, Hanoch's face fell. Noam looked enraged, but Naomi smiled. Hanoch began to wail all of a sudden, not cry but wail, his body shaking; Naomi brought him a glass of water and then a bottle of brandy. He drank, and fixed me with a long weary glance; his eyes were bloodshot.

I looked back at him. Perhaps he did love Miriam with his heart and soul. He stopped wailing, and gave the appearance suddenly of a lover betrayed.

A knock at the door, and Sokolowicz stood there in shorts and a scarf. He entered and sat down on a chair. Sipping some water he asked, "Who is the strange-looking Jew?"

"Hanoch Levi, don't you recognize him from television?"

"I don't watch or listen" he said. "Hey, I came to tell you something, commander. We were all sitting by the pool, the whole bunch of us – who wasn't there! We discussed you and said, 'We must show him we're on his side, no matter how the story turns out or whatever the truth of it is, friendship is more sacred than anything else.' I wanted to tell you that we're waiting for you to come. Why is this Jew wailing?"

Hanoch, who was sunk in a self-examination which had distanced him from us, looked in bewilderment at Sokolowicz, and missed out on the chance to be dumbfounded by the appearance of a strange woman whose hair was dyed a new colour who now entered the apartment and stared at Sokolowicz with eyes brimming with innocent ridicule. Gideon and Nira sat hugging on the sofa. Naomi licked her lips like a cat and giggled, while everybody watched Hanoch intently, expecting something, as though the stage was set now for a confession. Naomi perhaps realized that I was now at Miriam's funeral, that for the first time since her disappearance I was at last sitting *shivah* at home and hence was so indifferent to my visitors; after all, they were coming to sit and mourn together with me, something which was denied them until now. Any minute I would pull out an album and show them photographs of Miriam.

I said to Hanoch, "Maybe you loved her, maybe you truly were the one who had the deepest love for her. When did you find out about the dynamited houses?"

Instantly he shuddered, gave me a look of utter defeat, his mouth gaped in his effort to say something but nothing came out; even Naomi began to pay attention to what was behind anything we might say, and Hanoch said, "You know?"

"I know but don't understand."

"She drove me crazy, Krieger. She was the dearest and most important thing that ever happened in my life; I never knew anything like it before, except with Daliah, and that ended with Miriam. In the end poor Joy is always screwed by the same men. Miriam entered into my very core, too late in life, it cut me to pieces. I would be sitting in the television studio, interviewing somebody, when all of a sudden I'd go blank and think about her, about her pain and anguish, and forget what I was going to ask the one I was interviewing. I would dream about her, send her letters, phone – but not call here, that she wouldn't permit, it was forbidden to call her at home. Here were you and Isaac with his death, and isn't it always you or that death?

"Up to this day," continued Hanoch, "I was sure that you thought the way Joy did, she kept saying that you suspected me. If you were really to believe me when I tell you what I may have done, I'm in trouble, because I have no alibi, Krieger. She disappeared at dawn, and I was the last person to see her alive. But I think I know where she went after we parted.

"I was the first man she loved, other than you or Isaac. That was what turned the story into something impossible and difficult. Maybe that was what finally caused her death, Brigadier, I don't deny it, I couldn't stop loving her just because my love for her complicated her life.

"She did love me. She wrote me a letter in which she said that after all those years of being attached to you and to Isaac and torn between you both, when she was about to punish you by your own hands as well as his, she was at an impasse, because I had penetrated all her defences, those hundreds of thick layers which had protected her. And she, you must understand, didn't welcome loving me. Joy became a wounded lioness once she sensed what was happening to me, and she fought for her life. She said, 'First Joseph and now you! I can't always be a door-mat for desperate men who flee from me.' Miriam was my first breach of loyalty to Daliah. Joy wasn't, even with all her chains around me. And Nina wasn't, who despised me as much as Noam did, who looked upon me as an insect – I'd opposed his brother, and deep in his heart Noam didn't just envy his brother, he loved him. He fashioned for Miriam all that Isaac was. He supplied her with material, told her stories, thinking that he would inherit her once her madness had passed. He was the one who begat for Miriam the Isaac whom she later could hand over to Mr and Mrs Raphaeli. Then I came along and she crumbled. It wasn't easy. Not in one day. First she loathed me. I was everything you weren't – a coward, a chronic chatterbox, a womanizer, my car is stuffed with medicine for heartburn, head-aches, depression, high blood pressure, and anything else you might mention; she was reared in a home of a puritan who never took any medicines, who never had ailments, who swims all winter, stays fit, despises weaklings; she said you were an enlightened, self-righteous fascist, a man of principles, who treks into the desert alone in order to toughen his character, fights like a knight of justice, like an ancient crusader, but she was caught by what was perhaps in me, a severe weakness, an intellectual one, beyond smiles and wit, a kind of thinkaholic's pathology, knowing every single detail, photographic memory, a dilettantish range of information, from soccer to epistemology, amusing, brilliant, like a computer but human, alert, inquisitive, tender, combative, though not following up to the very end, not creative, lazy, spoiled. A person who had a profound need to belong to somebody. An intelligence which she loved. I'm not boasting; this is what she wrote to me. She knew exactly what she was writing, she wasn't writing the way she wrote to you, out of a compulsion for revenge, both loving you and appeasing Isaac; she wrote to me from the depths of her anguish. The moment I became hers, she was lost because now she didn't have to choose between a man like you, who was inaccessible to her, and Isaac who was dead, but between you two and a living man, married, Joy's lover. I wasn't in on her secret plot, her grand scheme, but I am suspicious by nature, an intellectual who always asks questions, and I questioned her. She was evasive, and then came the final night."

22

I told him, "You knew about Bed-Lid, but you also knew about something else."

"Yes," said Hanoch, "I also knew about the cave. On the morning of that day, I woke up and suddenly realized what she was planning to do, and I panicked. It was raining and cold. I had to lecture at a Military Police conference in Netanya. I could smell that she was up to something, but I didn't know exactly what. I had no idea what everybody's task was, Nina's, Nira's, I knew Joy was in on it, but that morning I was the only one who figured out the two places where Miriam might be hiding, the cave in the Galilee or the village near Bet-Lid. She was trapped in her struggle for and against you, and you were the symbol of that struggle. By disappearing, she wanted to shock you, terrify you, and demonstrate the necessity of her presence in your life, your dependence upon her, not just hers on you, because Isaac was a threat to you and she was worried. Isaac wanted something else; he scared me.

"In the middle of my lecture at the conference in Netanya, I stopped, said that I didn't feel well, and then drove to her camp. Jahash wouldn't let me in, he wasn't particularly fond of me, and I spoke to her by phone from his booth. She tried to forestall our meeting and said, 'Hanoch, I'm mixed up, it's hard for me, I love you but you came into my life too late, I've had enough, let me be today, don't spoil it.' I begged her and put everything I had in me into that entreaty, and finally she let me in. But she tried to keep me out of her room, nobody was around at that time, there was a staff meeting in the next

273

room. The secretary had gone out too; I persuaded her to accompany me. She left, and was seen heading for the car park; nobody saw me, I knew they had noticed her and thought to myself, 'She's looking for an alibi, something big is going on, her mind's elsewhere,' but it didn't matter to me. Later, I understood that Yossi, the religious soldier at the Hadera junction, was an alibi which she had arranged with the sergeant-major who was Jahash's uncle. When I went outside, the rain had stopped. She kept talking to Jahash at the gate about all sorts of things, she was flustered, as though she had tossed a snowball and could no longer retrieve it, she wanted me and also wanted me to disappear. I laughed because there was nothing else I could do. Those tears which I shed just now were formed then.

"We quarrelled as I drove along Wadi Ara road. I wanted her to explain herself to me, but she was confused and drained and frightened. Then, all of a sudden, she asked me to stop. When I did, she quickly opened the door and started running. I made a U-turn and drove off. I went back to her camp. I wanted to talk with Captain Gideon. She used to speak fondly of him, and considered him her true friend. Since I was afraid that something had happened – I could smell a rat but was trying to deny it – I thought that together, Gideon and I, we'd phone you, warn you, or whatever. Alone I couldn't have done it, I didn't have the guts. But Jahash greeted me with an angry face, muttering curses under his breath, so I didn't re-enter the base and went back. I was afraid of my own shadow. In the end, I was the one who gave her her last hitch.

"Not far from the base I saw a Peugeot pulled over to the side of the road and an officer standing alongside it. He was the typical professional, a cliché, a miniature reproduction of somebody like you. Quite young, but he tried to act older. In my car I have more than a pharmacy; I'm afraid of getting stuck somewhere, so I have a whole warehouse. I stopped. He needed a jump start, which I gave him. Together we started up his car and I said to him, 'Listen, up ahead a bit there's a woman officer who

274

needs a lift, pick her up,' and he said that was fine with him and thanked me for my help; but he added, 'I'm going as far as Olga and then turning towards Hadera.' 'Take her there,' I said, 'that's good enough, just make sure she gets to the hitching area.' He recognized me, and it flattered him considerably that I had come to his assistance.

"When he picked her up, she didn't notice that I was following them. She was preoccupied with her own plans. I could still smell them, and was scared, but I had nobody to discuss it with. At Hadera, I pulled up for her. As she got in, together with Yossi, she was pretty angry, but on account of Yossi, who was there by prearrangement, she had no choice. If she entered, he would too; he had to come along in order for him to say that she had gone off in the direction of the Bet-Lid junction! Inside, she pretended that we were strangers and that I was just trying to make a pass at her. Didn't you catch on to that from what she wrote to you in her letters? That something new had entered her life, and she was at a crossroad which didn't match anything she had experienced until now? I was the greatest danger Isaac had ever faced, and both he and she knew it. And that fifth letter of hers is all about me. I told her, 'Don't send it, he won't like it,' but she insisted, and we argued, until she wept and handed it to me, saying, 'Show it to Joseph one day.' "

"Where's the letter?"

"I have it, Brigadier. I held on to it. I knew that some day you'd find the real trail and need it. Although it won't explain anything you don't already know, it's full of bewilderment over what you really are in her life. She finally gave me the letter, with deletions, saying Isaac would never forgive her and we would all have to pay for it."

Hanoch searched in his briefcase and came up with a sealed envelope. Sokolowicz saw how agitated I was, my hand trembled. In anger he said, "What is this Jew doing to you, Brigadier?" And Madame Frau said, "Sokolowicz, you're the blindest bat I ever met in my entire life. You ridiculous old man, I'll tell you the truth, Herr Sokolowicz, I will pay your sons all my reparations, all because I want

275

Joseph Krieger to have a view of the sea in his window, so he can know that he'll die by the sea next to which he was born. We came from far off, Sokolowicz, from the diaspora we both came. I with a Turkish eunuch. But this is a sabra here. He's already a native. A mix of rifle and music. Piano, which you've never heard, but I have. So I will inform your sons that I want my stepson, I call him that, to see the sea until he and you are gone, then they can build a ten-storey building if they wish."

I raised my eyes and looked at him. The envelope was open now. Hanoch was hypnotized by the sight of the piece of paper with my daughter's handwriting scrawled on it. Sokolowicz sat humbled, more than I'd ever seen before, then rose to take Madame Frau's hand in his and hold it tenderly, saying, "Sorry."

She looked at him in astonishment. He had said only one word, but that word contained anguish, challenge, grief, innocence, and despair; she kissed the old man on his forehead and he squeezed her hand and sat back down. Suddenly he shouted, "The Jew gave you a letter, who is it from?"

"From Miriam," I said.

"So read it!"

I sat and read the letter. Hanoch asked for a glass of cold water, which Naomi brought him. Miriam wrote:

Daddy,

So let it be. You worked hard for it. Daddy isn't a word I use, but so what – don't you deserve it? After all, I must arrive on time finally, and if that's the case, how can I best be on time? On the split second? No. That won't work. I must break the time barrier, for you to know that I have arrived on time. But then you'll sit and think, not why I did this to you, not why I'm dead to you, but (unlike your mother or anybody else) why you didn't stop me. You couldn't have, Daddy. None the less, it's a nice and noble gesture on your part. Maybe Hanoch could have, but that fool, the man I so love, has come into my life too late.

You know that your mother, that rotten woman, tried to use me as a weapon against Nina. She didn't even realize what she was doing, she had so much hate and pity and love for herself, that she took hold of me to make me into the worst person possible, so that life would always be shitty and we would always fail, inevitably so, and lose our sense of direction, forever defeated, *kaput*. She prepared me for the dark side of life, for what Isaac would later take me to, the black hole, death and its sweet aroma of despair, its power, its magic.

And Hanoch came at the very end. What did I see in him? Your opposite. For him it was worth living, but I was already at the point where life was but a meagre protest against death; maybe I didn't want you as my father any more, throughout all my childhood I felt that I was your widow.

But you know that.

Look, Little Nina and Delilah gave me something important, they let me believe in who I really was, on my own. It's so hard Joseph, to know yourself. They imparted to me some contact with constancy, which is the other side of my flightiness. Death is constant. Only after death is memory accurate. And longing genuine. Death never loses. Hanoch grasped what death meant to me, how all my life I had been its slave. Death is the place and the time we all vanish in, including you and mother and me as well. You brought me into the world to play with me like a toy, you against mother, she against you, as though only that struggle would rescue you. I went along with the game because there was no honest way possible for me to take sides or not take sides in the struggle. Death and my addiction to it released me from the fear I was hooked on. Hanoch understood me and my fear, he understood me as I was. You were incapable of that, you don't grasp the meaning of fear, and Nina was born from it. Alongside death I no longer had the sensation of dread. Isaac admired my fear, but pushed for vengeance, while Hanoch wanted my life in order to give it back to me, though he also knew that he'd come too late.

Look, Joseph, I want to write "Daddy" but the word gets deleted. My anguish has preoccupied me. I feel elated yet burdened. I think about religion, which I consider an astrology of human wisdom, but profundity isn't for everyone; it intimidates because the cosmos is a colossal snake devoid of moral values. All thought demands logic, which arouses sorrow and frustration. I am concerned with astrology because through it I have attained the ultimate of my capacity to understand my life, within limits. I've had a romance with and against a dead man. Now I'm involved with a charming bastard. Suddenly I'm in love, really in love with a man. An ordinary man. Obviously, I must put an end to all that. Isaac wants to be the only one, but I am forced to abuse him too, my lover of so many years. In the end he won't get what he wants, only what I think he wants. Eh? I'm crazy about you, Krieger, you're like crystal, you don't change, you're strong, you can take punishment without bending. But in the end what will come of it? Will you crack? Isn't that what happens when you can't bend?

Well, Joseph, in my whole life I only kissed you once. I can't explain it. You made such a big deal about kisses, back then, when I was a child, and got offended but never said a word. It became an issue. I didn't know how to get out of it. Listen, I kiss you now, for all those years, a plain kiss, what's just a kiss, especially one on paper, but take it, it has been sitting on my lips for twenty years . . .

Hanoch Levi saw that I'd read the whole letter, he saw the wet glaze in my eyes. The letter had cut off in the middle, as though there would always be something remaining which could never get said. Hanoch looked around, still the man playing the role of the trapped figure, except that everybody surrounding him, not just myself, realized that he wasn't acting any more, and that his sense of entrapment was his pathetic protest that everything had been worked out so that at a certain moment all the scraps of information would have to be set like a jewel, thereby releasing him from his anguish and transferring it to me, and from me God knows who was next.

Hanoch said, "I owe you the exact account of that final night. I've already said that I took her from the Hadera junction. Yossi was in the car because in the original plan (in mine, of course, he had no role) he would be the sad Greek chorus shedding light, bogus except for himself, upon the events. She got out. I knew at once where she intended to go. She wanted to slip out of my hands, but she craved for me, as though she were dead and gone and I was like her father, no longer hers, just Isaac was around, on the side of death, yet it was also as if some of Isaac's magic was missing.

"After I dropped off the soldiers and Yossi in Tel-Aviv, I hurried back. I'm a good driver, experienced, they didn't catch me. Miriam said that except for those daily scenes and your swimming, your only sin was speeding. I exceeded the limit and reached the Bet-Lid Junction, looked around for her, and there she was. I don't know if she was waiting for me. But she seemed lost in her confused thoughts, and she started to talk about cosmic rays, about what they had plucked from her brain, then she confessed to my face that she had dreamed a dream, a dream in which she was a young girl, of indeterminate age, Reuben was her father, and he was standing at the window of the house you once lived in; big Nina burst from her room, dressed in a robe and with her hair dyed, and as her make-up floated off her face, she looked like a witch. And Nina said, 'They're picking my brain, they're coming with thongs to tear out my head. They'll insert a new brain.' Miriam dreamed about how she stopped breathing, and then she said, 'Something weird occurred to me in that dream. I remembered dying, really dying, and coming to the other side, and then mother, under the watchful gaze of Reuben at the window and some girl hiding there in the bougainvillaea covered with flowers, placed a photograph on my stomach and the photograph

279

penetrated me somehow, so I started to breathe again. Then mother's tears fell on me, and Reuben ran off, insulted, screaming; and Joseph came, big Nina suckled me from her breast but blood came out, not milk, I don't remember who was in the photograph,' she said finally."

"It was no dream," I said.

Hanoch lifted his head and looked at me. He tried to smile but couldn't. Noam seemed lonely, desperate, wrapped in terror. Only Sokolowicz and Madame Frau rose to the occasion. Sokolowicz said, "This Jew talks a lot." And Madame Frau said, "If Joseph's mother had already died, they wouldn't have been living in Herzliya and the whole thing wouldn't have occurred."

Then Hanoch spoke. He tried to slow down his words, gaining time as he talked, trying to translate correctly what I had said to him about this memory of a photograph, about Miriam's flash into what may have tasted as bitter as the blood which she drank. Hanoch went on, "She was at a loose end, Krieger, I grabbed hold of her and stopped her from talking; there were citrus fruits all around us, and the overwhelming stench of decay. I told her, 'Not yet, not here,' and she said, 'Hanoch, something awful is brewing, people are doing some strange things now, it's all going down, a huge machine at work, my mother and all of them, and I'm running away.' I told her, 'Come, let's hit the road,' and she said, 'I've been on the road a long while, he's expecting me,' and I said, 'So am I.' She answered, 'But he's much stronger.' That's when I forced her into my car and drove off. After a short while she took over and began directing me, I didn't even pay attention, for some reason that trip from Bet-Lid, which at the time struck me as a delusion, was no chance journey, she was directing me and I was at ease; in my characteristic arrogance, I thought I had overcome that look of hers which had been drenched in the desire for death, or maybe her passionate face made me think that she would regain her balance and untangle herself. I knew what was waiting for me at home, with Daliah, with you, with Joy; I was ready, no longer frightened, but she was the one who was really driving and in a few hours we came to the cave.

"The sky was clear, the earth smelled of rain. After all, the storm had raged for three days. The trees looked shattered. A cloven forest. In the distance a jackal howled, and the moon brightened the tops of the olive trees which sparkled like dark silver. She held the flashlight until we entered the cave, then I took it from her, I don't know why, maybe I just wanted to hold on to something which belonged, and didn't belong, to her. The cave was a secret spot, its recesses were clean, she told me about the vial of tears which you had taken from there and which stood at home. She said, 'After I die, it will hold a lot of tears, or you can cremate my body and put the ashes in the empty vial, so then I'll be on my Daddy's table, not just on his wall.'

"Again she spoke about that dream, about her mother, herself, and you, about Noam Raphaeli who persisted in creating Isaac for her, because he thought he'd ultimately win her. She said, 'Nobody really needs me, nobody knows how to love me as I am.' Then we got undressed, it was bitterly cold, the cave was murky and ominous, and I'm pretty squeamish, it's either too hot or too cold for me, but I didn't think about it now, we were together naked, it wasn't cold any more, Krieger, she was a virgin, it stunned her, she cried at the sight of her blood, I couldn't believe that a woman of twenty-six would still be a . . . but she laughed and cried and tore up some of her garments and cut her hand with a knife. She told me how sweet and cruel and painful and beautiful it was, and she was cutting herself with that knife which was just lying there! There was also a blunt hammer. And while she was shivering in the cold and saying how much she loved me, she claimed that some stranger had apparently got inside and discovered the cave, which wasn't fair. All of a sudden that's what bothered her! As though the intrusion into the cave had wounded you! She said she often came here, but you didn't know about it, and this was the first time she had brought along anybody with her. She stood naked and shivering. Her clothes were soiled. I ran to the car. I had a suitcase with clothes there, which I dragged around for my gigs, because I sweat a lot and I like to have a clean outfit to change into. I dressed her in my garments, and she left her own clothes behind, and her purse; I thought she did it on your account, she wanted you to find them there.

"We had a terrible argument which ended up with her admitting that I not only knew how to make love in general, but I knew how to love her, and she agreed to think it over but was so confused, so lovely, a kind of crystal, chipped and fragile. I carried her to the car, through the mire and the biting cold. We drove leisurely, caught up in our emotions and what had occurred in the cave, trying to understand what was really going on between us. I left a part of her in the cave, and I was scared. I don't know what else frightened me then, I had nothing to demand of her, and told her so, but I felt like an excited animal, like a silly young boy, infatuated, and she too was weak and tender. And she spoke about you sadly, how you could never reach each other, how there was always some deception in the middle, how everything remained hidden, secretive, obscure. As though on purpose, so that the whole thing would be peculiar.

"We kept driving. Then we were on Wadi Ara road again; it was late. As we approached the vicinity of the Bet-Lid junction, she wanted to get out. I told her, 'Don't you dare,' but she started to tussle with me, with a crazy abandon which suddenly poured out of her. She began saying it was all too late but it was wonderful us being together, that she was in pain but there was no hope for us and she had to rescue you; that's what she kept saying, that she had to save you. I asked her, 'How? Why? From whom?' And she said it was all an escape. The disappearance was for your benefit, to move and shock you. I asked her, 'What disappearance?' And she said, 'Mine, Hanoch, I'm missing, I didn't go home, they'll search for me. Isaac wants your blood, now I know, now I understand his hollow, twisted hatred, and there's just one way to rescue my father from Isaac,' she said, without specifying the way, and I feared for her, not you, I admit. She spoke about the absolute; her lament was the fatal one of a child who is afraid for herself.

"Krieger, in the end she simply fled from me. As quick as lightning. Or the devil. I wasn't prepared. I was so exhausted that after I'd tried to catch up with her, I fell asleep on my feet. I had a flask of brandy in my pocket and took some slugs from it to wake me a bit. I drove along tracks and got stuck in mud. By four-thirty in the morning I knew I had lost her; I'd spent the whole night chasing her but she had chosen to disappear, and I was so knocked out and miserable and drained that I didn't know what to do. Out of fatigue and depression and despair, I drove until I was caught by the police. It was terrible because by morning I knew she was definitely missing, which made me an accomplice, as the last person who had seen her alive; yet I must say to my credit, here, in this house, I'm putting my arrogance behind me, my slick vanity. Miriam taught me to speak badly of myself and to see myself in a new light as well, as though I was actually worth something, and not for what isn't in me but for what is, no matter how slight that is, yet it is mine.

"We fought there, Krieger, and I begged her, but her mind was made up and her eyes were glassy with love for me and with her first anger and perhaps (I say perhaps guardedly) her first real and deep challenge against Isaac and his need for revenge – and all this, Krieger, to deliver you from his hands."

"She belonged to him alone, you didn't take her away from me," said Noam, and suddenly I realized how much shame and destruction was in him; Hanoch smiled at him, weary and swept by his feelings. He fixed his eye on Noam and understood him; something joined them together. The expression on both their faces showed me how opaque and transparent it all was, and how painful. I was cut to pieces as I had never been before, and bleeding. In the end that was my daughter's vengeance. She realized what Isaac wanted from her, and she decided to spare my life and not grant Isaac his revenge. But she was still attached to him, hence like her mother she had to function both for and against – for Joseph meant against Isaac; she couldn't devote herself to Hanoch or to me with any absolute commitment. She had a responsibility, as a man's beloved, and she was loyal to him even after she had been angered by him. He had led her by the nose for a long while and had aroused her anger as well as her pain, and had undermined her self-confidence. It was Noam, after all, who in search of utter humiliation, had given Isaac over to Miriam so she could realize her love for him alone; that's what he really thought, as the rejected brother seeking all his life for love and always being pushed into a marginal existence. At the threshold of his own abyss he had found her but she scorned and pitied him. He had no identity. And Isaac, via Noam, led my daughter to her encounter with Hanoch, who rescued her from him but came too late, and she got torn apart saving me, or thinking she was saving me. Isaac's whole story was a double plot, through Noam and through her, each separately, two conflicting strategems. Perhaps she understood in the end that at the hour of her disappearance, Miriam was missing in a way over which she had no control; she may have cooked up some ingredients like Port Jaffa and Noam and the trip to the television studio, but Isaac was always one step ahead of her, spinning his poisoned yarn with the patience of the dead, a ubiquitous vampire always attentive to the sweet, cruel cry of vengeance, but after all even in his life he was a trickster. Embittered, disgusted with himself, fearful yet proud as a peacock, he wanted to have the final word, which was the speedy termination of Joseph, me, the fool who almost rescued him from that house and made a hero out of him. Noam knew, Miriam knew, Hanoch realised and struggled with it but what could he do? She was at the end of the road, he was drunk and exhausted, it was late at night, he couldn't find her, he tried again the next day. He saw soldiers scouting, learned about the explosion. Afterwards, he was forced into doing just one thing, becoming Joy's slave and covering his tracks.

23

We have just now returned from Miriam's funeral. It was hard to organize the event because of the complaints and conspiracies, but Reuben acted like a man and handled everything. Perhaps he realized what a trap he had set for me with his love for my wife. The rabbis cowered before his rebukes and threats, and the legal authorities worked overtime. Czeszek was there, and the Minister of Defence too, they had to admit their mistake and they did so. Another investigation was necessary to determine who was the burned woman found in the Galilee, and a new monument had to be erected and the other discarded. I insisted. Naomi told me, "Joseph, you're acting as if you were intoxicated." At night I hugged her tightly and she cried. Nina came, her face gaping with a pain which suddenly, after all these years, erupted from her like molten lava. She looked both very brave and very resigned, she had no forgiveness for any of us. And she said to me, "I broke away from you when you and Miriam had your never-ending quarrel; you would sit together until midnight and I felt left out. She raged at you, shouted that you were crazy and stubborn, but she really understood you and let you baby her like before, when she was a small girl. That's why I grabbed that pathetic Talmud teacher and said, 'Okay, take me to America.' "

Nina knew how it had all worked out – she had been a cheap enough actress in this ugly drama. Hadn't she already poured out her beautiful tears before the television cameras after the cruel killers had been found guilty of her daughter's murder? This time nobody would know how Miriam got to that house in village K, or exactly how she died there; I didn't give out any details, nor were the Chief of Staff or Reuben willing to do so. It was our own private affair. Actually, mine and Nina's. That's how we stood at the grave of my daughter; Naomi didn't hide herself any more, but stood at my side. I said *kaddish*, then they covered her body with dirt. And she was gone, it was over. Naomi tried to be upbeat, to sprinkle a little *joie de vivre* into this heavy sorrow, though like Hanoch Levi she too felt that everything had come to an end and that I was a man in his last flutterings, a man who thought he could never be forced to capitulate, and never did, but marched to the bitter end, insistently consistent, seeking out his beloved daughter until he found her.

After Hanoch Levi had finished his confession, I had called the Chief of Staff, who phoned Reuben. They gave me no trouble. A military caravan came, jeeps, bulldozers, and demolition equipment; at village K, in the Tulkarem district, were two houses which the army had dynamited a day after Miriam's disappearance, on 22 January. From these two houses came a team of terrorists who had murdered two civilians and a hitch-hiking soldier, and placed an explosive device in a supermarket. I chose the house which looked right to me despite its demolished state. But maybe the word right is inappropriate in this context, or ridiculous. The soldiers worked carefully for two solid hours, under the Chief of Staff's supervision. He claimed that he had initially ordered the house's demolition but then countermanded his order. Somebody misunderstood his instructions and followed the first order – immediately.

Miriam had actually been there. Flattened by a concrete wall which turned her into a paper-thin woman, bodiless except for her face, which remained intact. It was a shocking sight. Because of the instantaneous collapse of the concrete wall, her face got stuck in an airless bubble and therefore her flesh was preserved. Her eyes were open, still lovely but alarmed. On the way back, when someone said that she just wasn't normal, I said with all the quiet still left inside me what I had once read – that a lot of normal people murdered a hundred million others in the first half of our enlightened century. She lay crushed, beautiful, so cruel in her pampered arrogance, inside her bubble of death, mysterious to the end, her mission of rescuing her father accomplished. And Noam said, "What a fool you were, Miriam," and he spoke with a warmth and love which all of us felt, Hanoch, me, and Nina. He told her what she would understand best, "Isaac wanted *him* dead, not you; he wanted you to come to him alive. But once Hanoch Levi appeared and robbed you from him, you had to return to him dead, so my brother vanquished you. I'd like to piss him back to life in order to kill him again!"

The inquiry showed that not one of the soldiers involved in the dynamiting of the house remembered seeing Miriam, though she had somehow managed to sneak inside and conceal herself there for a considerable time before the house's demolition at 4:07 in the morning, according to the official report. An Arab villager said he thought he saw a girl enter the house right after its occupants were vacated. But the demolition team came maybe a day later and said they weren't sure of their orders. "Then," he said, "the Bomb Squad received new orders to dynamite," and he figured the girl was a demon. And perhaps she was. Isaac had taken care of that long ago, many years ago, even before she was born.

There was no problem with identification. Czeszek stood in silence, his face full of anger against everybody, especially my daughter; and I think the whole country felt somewhat guilty, and therefore also enraged because I had robbed them of their sweet revenge. She went to her death the way Isaac had, with a blindness which turns an awesome pity into longing, into a refuge, until the soul weeps and aches to the point that the body must interfere and ask for some respite, to calm it down, to quench life in order to merit another life. But that can be done only by the God of your metaphysical astrology, sweetheart. The true God of the distant Milky Way you spoke of is far too brutal and disappointing; He doesn't give a damn, He's bored, He rolls the world like a ball of dung.

We finally got home. The Chief of Staff prepared coffee

287

and told Naomi, "You sit by his side, don't shut your eyes for a moment, he needs you." Nina sat as if reprimanded. I pitied her sense of exclusion. She drank whisky, Reuben was busy with paper work, we took out Miriam's photo album, and we were all dazzled by her beauty. I functioned like somebody bitten by a snake, I was no longer really there with them. I pushed Naomi away from me, Nina too, and remained alone with my agony, frightened for the first time in my life.

I have come to the end of my diary of these events, words upon words upon words. Once evening had fallen, we sat facing the sea, Sokolowicz's small house affording us a sliver of the dull, moonlit waters. We were a bunch of senior citizens of the nation, nothing had any meaning any more. Naomi came to sit by me and I said to her, "Never approach me again. I'm wounded, Naomi, wounded, wounded." And I went to my room. My writing is over now and I sit waiting for Isaac's mercy. I wonder what time it is and know exactly, 8:10. I turn towards my alarm clock, which reads 9:00 p.m. My body has betrayed me again.

My hand trembles as I put down the paper. Another minute, one more minute and . . .

Postscript

WHEN I received the hundreds of pages which Krieger wrote in his elegant handwriting, Naomi asked me to edit them. I changed little. I tried to be faithful to the man who had composed them. Where he doesn't explain himself further, I let it stand. In these pages, I appear as a frustrated writer, the one who was Miriam Hurwitz's husband and enemy. But the sorrow over her death cannot hide the fact that Krieger, in his youth, and I all my life, from the time I was nineteen, both loved the same mysterious macabre woman, a touch of whose character emerges, perhaps, in her namesake, Krieger's daughter, Miriam, who in so tragic a fashion was forcibly driven by the cruel inevitability of death's wheel and died inside a house which the army had destroyed in retaliation against terrorist activity in the area around village K. in the district of Tulkarem.

I am not depicted in a particularly positive light here, but I won't alter anything. Also, my wife's love for Himmo Perach is not explained by the author. In this book, where I am one of the characters in a libellous story which denies me the ability ever to be proud of myself, there is no satisfactory explanation for Miriam's relationship with Himmo, a wounded soldier, without arms, legs, a basket case with a wonderful mouth. Did she really love him? The author doesn't clarify that question of love, he doesn't explore the obscure mystic link, which so annoyed us in the Jerusalem hospital, of Miriam's attachment to Himmo. Can a beautiful woman actually fall in love with a mouth? I think so. Perhaps love is just a dead alley. I'm not talking about casual affairs or the arrangement of sexual partners with joint income tax portfolios, I'm speaking of love, genuine love, which is always impossible and hence inevitable. Like body and soul, like man and God (not God and man). Like Miriam Krieger, Joseph Krieger's daughter and Isaac. Who was Isaac? A phantom? What sort of phantom? How was she able to create such a gloomy penetrating bond? How could a girl whom I knew, a delightful, intelligent, gorgeous, and typically Israeli girl live by such black magic which her sane, rational father depicts in these pages as though it were self-explanatory? But that's how it goes, explanations don't exist, love is always a hopeless flight into space. I loved Miriam Hurwitz all my life because I knew from the outset that it was hopeless, she couldn't love me, but she also couldn't live with anybody else but me.

But I am not here to interpret. Let each have his own interpretation. That final night, Reuben and the Chief of Staff were sitting with Krieger when I came. We hadn't seen each other for quite a while, actually since the time my wife, Miriam Hurwitz, died. Krieger shook my hand with restrained warmth.

He hinted that I should read the pages which he had written. And in Naomi's presence, he told me, "I wrote them as they are now, putting down whatever I knew at the time, and later on I understood more. I didn't have the wisdom of hindsight, I simply documented the facts." They all sat facing the sea, Naomi grew sad and said, "Miriam won against me, too, and against Nina; Isaac won against Miriam and Joseph." She was bitter, but looked charming and feminine, and tried to get close to Joseph whom she loved to protect, but he was already far away from her, from us all.

In the end he sat in his bedroom. When she became nervous and went to him, he kicked her out and the Chief of Staff said, "In one month I complete my command and become a civilian," and Reuben said that he too was about to resign. There was the feeling of closure – quiet intimacy. How does Thoreau put it? "The mass of men lead lives of quiet desperation." A sad, slow, silent finish, no more glorious leaps into the fire, no more prodigious anguish just daily problems, petty and grey, the roads you take but never conquer. The sea skipped in the moonlight, at two in the morning, in that stillness; we drank cognac and ate the tasty snacks which Nira had prepared. Then we heard the shot which we had been waiting for all this time. Naomi sank into her chair. "The bullet which he fired," said Naomi, "has been in the barrel of the gun from the first day. Isaac put it there, Miriam pulled back the safety catch, and all the others, my sister, Nina, Noam, they all slowly pressed the trigger until Krieger finished the job." And the Chief of Staff said, "He had no choice." And Reuben said, "Bullshit, he did, this is a disgusting act, why did he have to leave us now? How does it help him?" Reuben was furious, like a frightening storm, but Naomi said, "You don't understand how he hurt inside, how all the while he was waiting to find her and then knew it was all over. I understood. Miriam understood, too, that without her, even if he loved me, life would have no purpose for him, and the burning would be unbearable. In order to gain real freedom, stillness, an end to his anguish, that's what the bullet was for, already loaded in the barrel, and it would be impossible for a soldier like Joseph to point that pistol to his temple say, next January, with the enemy now smack in his sights, his finger on the trigger and the safety catch pulled back."

The next morning I heard Madame Birnbaum talking on the porch, I stepped outside, she was standing there, in a safari outfit, her eyes yellow from sorrow, looking a hundred years old, dyed, her hair straggly, no longer attending her Health and Beauty sessions, and she said, "Ah, what a family they were. And all dead. Dead in Israel. Here there was supposed to be life for Jews, but Jews die here. Demons from the land of His Excellency. Lions came, but to the wrong house. Yes, they ravaged, but the wrong people. First his father. He was tired of life and died in a heatwave. What a waste. And his mother, a wicked woman but boy did she want to live! Then Miriam, like her Little Nina and her dog Delilah, both deceased, what beauties they were, in the eyes of every family, and they're gone! He's lying in a hospital now, I'm going to him, he won't recognize me, he doesn't understand, can't speak or think, what will happen next? Most likely he'll die, but perhaps not. Maybe Naomi will bring him back to me. I have nobody to come over to me in the morning and insult me. Nobody tells me that some lion has docked in Haifa by the Law of Return, properly circumcised, *en route* to the Elite Coffee factory to be turned into powder, and put in my cup, and my toilet water, where it'll have a drink and become a lion again, to chew me. He invented all that at the end of '48. He was already fifteen, maybe fourteen. The calendar confuses me.

"And how they all perished, as if a kiss could save the hope from destruction! Miriam tried. That Isaac. I was always scared of his picture. And now the house is empty, except for that delightful Naomi. All dead. What a family, those Kriegers. Father, son, Miriam, my grandchild, step-grandchild, every one of them dead because they wanted to fight a windmill, to create love from thin air, to kiss death. It's impossible . . ."

Hanoch Levi came to visit. Gideon and Nira got married. Naomi is a strong, young woman. Life goes on as though Joseph Krieger has not been lying half-dead in hospital for two months, hovering between life and death. Isaac didn't even let him die, only escape, as Miriam surmised, from his intolerable pain. He recognizes nobody and understands nothing, and he could recover or not recover. Naomi sits next to him for six or seven hours a day, talking to him, but he doesn't know who she is, or who anybody else is either; Joseph Krieger, stubborn, daring, ridiculous, somebody who has gone out of fashion, as my wife once told me, made all of a piece, including tenderness and melody and awesome hardness, cruel but not vain, terrifying but honest, unable to recognize real evil but always fighting for bread, homeland, nation, life. I must finish. I inserted some commas and full stops, and here and there made a few tiny corrections. Naomi will sit down tonight and read this book. Perhaps she'll read it aloud to Krieger, maybe he'll regain consciousness, maybe he'll have pity for her, for himself, for Reuben who has become so human and friendly, while Nina calls from America like a lunatic, for himself, for Reuben who has become so human and friendly, while Nina calls from America like a lunatic, travelling from place to place, restlessly; but maybe all this had to happen. The vial of tears is waiting and is still empty. After all these monstrous deaths, not a tear. Again it's winter and raining and windy, and Krieger isn't running to the pool any more. He is locked behind the door which he closed upon himself. In the end he did reach the night-time of his life, which he didn't even know or recognize; he pulled the trigger in order to get as close as possible to his daughter.